JFK
SECRETS OF
CAMELOT REVEALED

By Alexander Malcolm

TABLE OF CONTENTS

BOOK THREE

After the Assassination

BOOK FOUR

Final Justice

PROLOGUE

Codicil One

I, Peter J. Sharkey, affirm that this is Codicil One of my Last Will and Testament. I direct that this amendment supersede any previous instructions. I further direct that the manuscript identified as my memoirs – and consisting of my personal experiences and remembrances, as well as my many years of research (including private revelations from a secret source within the Vatican) related to the people and events therein – shall not be released to the public until the last siblings of President John F. Kennedy shall have passed away.

Signed,
Peter J. Sharkey

CHAPTER ONE

DALLAS ASSASSINATION

It was hot and stuffy in the tiny hiding place surrounded by crates and cartons of school books, but it was not the heat or the stifling air that was making the man holding the rifle so uncomfortable. Indeed, the man had been imprisoned many times and had endured conditions much worse than those he was now experiencing.

He had also killed many times before, both in combat and to protect either his country or his family. But the enormity of his current mission made him sweat profusely.

His country had suffered a great many embarrassments from the United States over the years. He had also personally suffered many affronts and injuries from them. It was now his mission to prevent the United States from causing any further harm to his country. And maybe pay the Americans back for all the injuries they had caused him!

He was convinced there were major clandestine plans underway against his country from the Americans, and that his action would prevent them and thus protect his beloved country. He knew the only way to stop these plots was to kill the American President, John F. Kennedy, and thwart his evil plans.

He continued to sweat profusely as he awaited the arrival of the Presidential Motorcade. Assassinating the President of the United States was a much bigger task than he had ever before undertaken. Plus there was the danger he would be detected by the Secret Service or the Dallas Police Department and be arrested. If that happened, he was prepared to kill himself before he would reveal anything that would implicate his country in his actions. He had an extra cartridge in his rifle just in case. He hoped that wouldn't be necessary. Thus far, his plans had proceeded successfully and he had high hopes this success would continue.

He moved forward from his hiding spot in the shooting perch on the sixth floor of the Texas School Book Depository in Dallas, Texas to take a quick look at the street below. He was confident the men on his team outside had positioned themselves according to their instructions. They would continue to follow the plan exactly as he had ordered them.

His other accomplice, Alek, was here in the hiding place with him. Alek had been instrumental in setting this whole thing up, including pushing the cartons of books together to construct this shooting perch. Following orders, Alek had obtained a job in this warehouse weeks before in order to make this whole thing possible.

But Alek, although he had proven himself a dedicated Communist willing to follow orders and willing to kill for the Cuban cause, had also proven to be less than a marksman. During a previous trial run to test him, Alek had tried to assassinate General Edwin Walker, a virulent right-wing enemy of Cuba, but his shot missed the target. Now Alek believed that he was going to get to fire the shots at the President, but his accuracy could not be relied upon. That was why the man with the rifle needed to get Alek out of the hiding place for a few minutes while he himself fired the deadly shots without interference from Alek.

Alek knew the man with the rifle only as El Coronel. When they first met, the man with the rifle addressed Alek first in Russian and then in Spanish. Alek was fairly fluent in Russian, but knew no Spanish. The man told Alek that he should only call him El Coronel, which is Spanish for Colonel. El Coronel told him there was no need for them to know each other's real names. Although El Coronel certainly knew Alek's real name.

Despite his sweating, El Coronel's senses seemed to be on overdrive. His vision was so accurate that he thought he could almost read the badge numbers on the cops patrolling the street below him. His hearing was so acute that he could hear some of the conversations by the people below him in the crowd. He had never before felt so empowered and vibrantly alive. He felt he was living on a new, higher level of awareness – and he was confident that he would soon be able to complete his mission!

El Coronel learned from the transistor radio plugged into his left ear that the Presidential Motorcade was right on schedule. He'd purchased the radio right after he arrived in Dallas several days ago. He lied, however, and told Alek the Motorcade was delayed and used that as an excuse as he instructed him to go down and bring back a Coke from the lunch room.

It was approximately 12:30 p.m. CST when the Presidential limousine entered Dealey Plaza after a 90-degree right turn from Main Street onto Houston Street. The limousine was slowly moving directly toward the Depository and El Coronel had a clear shot to kill the President.

Since the President was a threat to his country and represented all that he hated about Americans and their arrogance, he felt driven to take a shot now while the President was an easy target. But his years of military training overruled his emotions, and so he waited until the limousine passed beyond him to enter the designated killing zone according to the plan. He had to wipe the sweat from his forehead so it wouldn't obscure his vision.

He had developed the plan, and his team members expected him to follow it. He couldn't react too soon! The killing zone was the position where both he and the other shooter on his team would be able to fire crossfire rounds to guarantee the assassination of the President. El Coronel would shoot him from the rear and his team member would fire from his position atop a small grassy knoll and shoot him from the front. It was a deadly plan almost sure to succeed at this close range.

The Motorcade was quite long and that would require precise timing from El Coronel so that his associate would not mistake one of the other vehicles for the target. He needed to be patient. But he continued to sweat profusely. He tried to mentally command his body to relax and stop sweating, but that proved useless. He then tried to just regulate his breathing to relax his body. That helped.

The lead car in the Motorcade was an unmarked white Ford police vehicle that carried the Dallas police chief and several Secret Service agents. The second car was a Lincoln Continental convertible that included two Secret Service agents in the front seat, one driving. Behind them were Texas Governor John Connally and his wife, Nellie, in the rear jump seats. Behind both of them sat First Lady Jacqueline Kennedy in the left rear seat, and President John F. Kennedy in the right rear seat.

Following them was a convertible that was driven by a Secret Service agent and which had six other agents along. The next car was a Lincoln convertible that was driven by a Texas State Highway Patrol Officer that had Vice President Lyndon B. Johnson on board. The next three cars contained more Secret Service agents, more Texas Police officials and press people.

El Coronel took several deep breaths and finally regained control of his emotions. He was now ready to complete the attack as he had planned it. He was sure that his associate, Carlos, had properly positioned himself in the front of the Motorcade on the grassy knoll. Carlos always followed orders.

El Coronel was holding a model 91/38 Carcano rifle with 6.5mm ammunition. Although it could hold more cartridges, right now it held only four. Three were planned for the attack on the President and the other was to kill anyone who attempted to stop his attack, regardless of whether it was his associate Alek or an outside intruder, or even to shoot himself to prevent arrest. He would not allow anyone to interfere with his plans.

He resisted the impulse to unload and reload the rifle, an action he had already done twice before in the last 30 minutes. He knew it was just a nervous reaction, but he wanted to be sure that the rifle would not fail. But, in fact, he had previous experience with and thus complete confidence in this type of rifle, which was why he had instructed Alek to purchase this specific model months earlier. He was confident in its accuracy and reliable operation. He also knew it had a smooth bolt action that would allow rapid fire. Such a rifle had saved his life years before and he trusted it to do its job now.

El Coronel knew that it would take about five seconds for him to cycle the bolt on his Carcano rifle and fire another shot. So he had instructed Carlos to count off five seconds after he heard the first shot and then fire his own first shot. Five seconds later, Carlos was to fire his second and last shot.

For El Coronel, the wait for the President to enter the killing zone was almost unbearable. Sweat continued to pour down his face.

* * * * * * * * * *

Carlos had indeed arrived at his position on the grassy knoll just beyond a small pergola. He was about 400 feet away from the Depository. He arrived at noon, as most of the other spectators had. They were all expecting to see the President in the next 20 or 30 minutes.

Carlos was dressed in simple workman's garb and was carrying a tool chest. This was the same tool chest he had brought with him all the way from home, and through Mexico City and then into Texas. Inside the tool chest was a heavily modified Dragunov Sniper Rifle. This rifle represented the most advanced technology in a sniper rifle that had as yet been developed by the Soviet Union. It was deployed by the Soviet Union, but was also available to its allied Communist governments in Eastern Europe and Cuba. It was absolutely deadly at ranges from 600 meters up to 1200 meters. It was the pride of both the Soviet and the Cuban Army.

Since this was a very close-range mission, however, the rifle had been extensively modified. The barrel was shortened substantially and the butt had been removed. In its place, the tool chest contained a metal bracket, shaped like a T, which could be inserted into the back of the rifle to act as a substitute butt and support the rifle against the shooter's shoulder. It would be uncomfortable during the discharge of the weapon, but this was going to be a one-time assault with only two shots planned.

The rifle also had a fireproof asbestos pouch tied around it to collect the spent brass after the rifle had been fired. This would eliminate any need for the shooter to have to linger around to collect any spent rifle casings.

The scope originally on the rifle had been removed since it was rather bulky. Because this was to be a close-range encounter, that high-power scope was not necessary. The rifle instead was equipped with a much smaller 4X scope, which had a low profile and which would be more than sufficient for this mission.

The shortened barrel had been machined to accept a custom suppressor, which could be affixed to the rifle with only a one-quarter turn to quickly lock it into place. All of these modifications were made to make the weapon smaller, less detectible and almost silent! In any case, the suppressor would disperse whatever sounds the rifle did make, so that it would be nearly impossible to determine exactly from which direction the sounds came.

The assassination team was part of a supremely capable government intelligence service, which had access to skilled armorers and expert gunsmiths – artisans really, so the modifications to the rifle had been made flawlessly.

But besides the structural modifications to the weapon, it also contained highly secretive and experimental ammunition that had been developed by his government.

There were only two cartridges in the weapon since that was all that the plan allowed. These cartridges contained new experimental bullets which were designated as frangible bullets. They were designed to self-destruct upon impact, thus leaving little or no trace.

In the process of self-destructing, they would also transfer all of their enormous kinetic energy into the target once it was struck. Very lethal, and almost undetectable.

The bullet, which is the projectile at the front of the cartridge and not the entire cartridge itself as it is sometimes mistakenly called, was molded from a carbon amalgam that was not dissimilar to the "lead" in a common lead pencil. His government had developed such frangible projectiles because the technology was simple, well-known and had been in use for years at public shooting galleries at carnivals and amusement parks.

Bullets made of molded graphite disintegrated upon impact, thus preventing any risk of ricochets toward the public. A hit would knock down the target, but the bullet would be pulverized and never ricochet. Just dust would remain.

His government had been experimenting with various degrees of brittleness and frangibility, and had been producing ammunition in various calibers for these experiments. The bullet compositions used in "Gallery Specials" was designed for use in .22-caliber cartridges of relatively low energy. That composition was not suitable for use in larger calibers because of the much higher energy created when the propellant was ignited. A large caliber "Gallery Special" formula bullet would destruct in the barrel and be ejected as fiery dust. But this proved to be an easily solved problem that involved just strengthening the binder-to-graphite ratio to withstand the force of ignition, but still destruct upon impact.

Both cartridges in his rifle were fitted with bullets made from the new formula. They would survive the high energy upon firing and would tear through flesh and penetrate bone matter. But after doing their damage, they would disintegrate into dust.

Because the existence of such bullets was not widely known, no one would be likely to look for the evidence of their use during an autopsy on a victim who had been shot by such a bullet. Particularly if such a victim also had obvious wounds from conventional bullets!

In fact, once the bullets had self-destructed, the gray graphite dust that they left behind would more than likely be washed out of the wound by the blood of the victim. Even the slight residue that might be left behind would be masked by the blood of the victim. Since blood darkened naturally upon exposure to the oxygen in the air, no coroner or medical examiner would be likely to suspect anything suspicious about any very dark, somewhat gray, blood stains.

Following his orders, Carlos had moved into his position on the grassy knoll and waited until the lead car of the Motorcade turned onto the street heading toward him. Then he opened up the tool chest and quickly assembled the butt stock and the suppressor onto the rifle. He felt confident he would not be discovered since virtually everyone was downhill in front of him and they were all looking toward the Motorcade.

Carlos repeated his instructions in his mind, which were to wait until he heard the first shot from El Coronel. Then he was to count off five seconds and fire his own round. Five seconds later he would fire off his final round. He and El Coronel had repeated this drill many times, so neither of them would forget it nor make a mistake. He was told to repeat it to himself just before assembling his weapon, so it would be fresh in his mind. This was what he just did. He was ready to do what he had been ordered to do!

After firing his two shots, he was to immediately dismantle his weapon and stuff the parts back into his tool chest. He was instructed to ignore anyone who might try to obstruct him or question him in any way. Just push by them and head to the rendezvous with his partner to escape from Dallas. They didn't want any confrontation that might lead to their detection.

As the Motorcade moved toward him, Carlos raised the rifle and took aim at the President. He watched with the practiced eye of a well-trained military sniper, which he was, as the limousine moved into the killing zone. Carlos placed his finger lightly on the trigger.

* * * * * * * * * *

Carlos and his partner Eduardo had begun their serpentine journey to Dallas more than a week earlier. Eduardo was now in his vehicle about two blocks away from the main street waiting to escape with Carlos after the assassination.

They had both arrived several days earlier in Mexico City after a short regional flight. Their baggage included not only their clothes and several weapons, but also the toolbox that contained the modified Dragunov rifle.

Their flights, as well as the rest of their travels to Dallas, had been arranged by the government intelligence service that employed them. Their employer was exceptionally well informed about contacts with underworld smugglers and spies throughout the world. So they had a travel plan that would get them all the way to Dallas.

After arriving in Mexico City, Carlos and Eduardo were picked up by their first contact who drove them about 240 miles north to Tampico, Mexico. From there, they boarded a fishing boat that brought them north across the border into Corpus Christi, Texas. The water voyage was about 400 miles and took almost three days.

Although the boat captain had originally thought that he might be able to double-cross his passengers, steal their money and throw them overboard, which he had done with other secretive passengers in the past, he abandoned any such thoughts once he saw the passengers. They were both over six feet tall and well built. One of them had three nasty scars on his cheeks that had probably been inflicted by someone trying to torture him. He was also missing a piece of one ear. Since his passenger was here, he suspected the torturer did not survive the encounter. In any case, the captain knew these were hardened men who would not be easy to overcome.

In addition, they always stayed close to each other; one of them always stayed behind the other to cover his back. Carlos and Eduardo further covered for each other by never sleeping at the same time. The captain suspected they had side arms since they both had a bulge in their chest area, not to mention that one of them was always carrying a toolbox, which might have held an even more formidable weapon.

The captain decided that a double-cross with these passengers was not advisable and delivered them safely to Corpus Christi, Texas.

Once in Corpus Christi, Carlos and Eduardo met up with their contact in Texas. The contact had purchased an old, nondescript, brown delivery van for them and delivered it along with valid Texas registration plates, which had been stolen from another vehicle.

It was about 360 miles from Corpus Christi to Dallas, but Carlos and Eduardo made the trip easily, and cautiously, without ever exceeding the speed limit. Once in Dallas, they went to the garage and office space that El Coronel had rented for them.

El Coronel had arrived in Dallas several days earlier via commercial aircraft from Canada since he had no contraband to smuggle in and had impeccably forged documents. After he arrived, he arranged for the cash rental of the garage and its small office space for Carlos and Eduardo. This was rental space in a run-down section of town. The landlord was more than happy to provide a monthly lease to El Coronel who paid cash in advance for the space. Besides the garage space which would accommodate the van, it had a small office area and included a bathroom, which was essential if his men were to spend several days and nights there.

El Coronel and his team communicated with each other by calling an offshore telephone number that was manned 24 hours a day by another member of their team. This arrangement allowed them to receive important information without having to try to set up a complicated direct telephone call. That was how El Coronel had given Carlos and Eduardo the address of the garage and told them how to get the key to the building, which he had hidden outside.

* * * * * * * * * *

Now, after what seemed like an eternity to El Coronel, the Presidential limousine finally entered the killing zone. When the limousine reached about an equal distance between the Depository and Carlos on the grassy knoll, El Coronel fired his first shot.

The President, in the back of his open limousine, was hit in the right side of his head and the bullet passed out through the front of his throat. The bullet then wounded Governor John Connally who was sitting in front of the President.

As soon as Carlos heard El Coronel's first shot, he waited five seconds to fire his own first shot. He had a perfect shot pattern, with the President fully exposed in the open limousine. Just before he pulled the trigger, he saw the President lurch forward and clutch at his throat, so he assumed that El Coronel's first shot had hit its target.

Then Carlos fired his first shot.

El Coronel recycled the bolt and readied his second shot. As he looked through his rifle scope, he saw the President's head being struck by Carlos' bullet which threw him backwards. El Coronel was sure that this was a lethal shot since it appeared that the back of the President's skull had been blown open, and possibly part of the President's brain was blown out of the limousine.

El Coronel pulled the trigger for his second shot.

The President was pushed backward by the force from Carlos' bullet, but when El Coronel's second bullet struck a further blow to his head, it drove him forward again. This second hit from El Coronel caused the President to fall toward his wife and almost out of sight.

Carlos had already counted off five seconds more and fired his second shot.

But because the President had fallen over and the limousine driver sped up, he was only able to nick the limousine on the top of the windshield. Because of the frangible nature of the bullet, this caused only slight damage to the windshield and just threw flying particles toward the rest of the passengers. Some of the spectators were also hit by the fragments of this bullet as it self-destructed.

El Coronel's third and last shot also missed the President, but went directly into Governor Connally. Connally had already been hit by the first shot that had passed through the President, but now he was grievously injured.

After firing his last shot, El Coronel grabbed his sport coat and turned to head for the door. Just as he reached the door, Alek showed up with the Coke in his hand.

Alek protested, "I thought I was going to shoot the President. Why didn't you come and get me? I went down for the soda like you asked."

El Coronel lied and said, "The Motorcade suddenly sped up and there was no time to get you back up here. Now, Alek, take this rifle and ditch it anywhere you can, maybe way back behind some of these pallets of books. Then come down to meet me behind the building so that we can escape from here."

With that El Coronel handed the rifle to Alek, who took it with one hand. He still had the Coke in his other hand.

El Coronel headed out the door while Alek tried to find a hiding spot for the rifle. Since he was already confused about why he hadn't been able to be the shooter, he was even further confused about what to do with the rifle. He finally decided to stuff it behind several pallets of books far away from the shooting perch. Once he'd done that, he headed downstairs along with the Coke, so as to appear to be acting normally.

El Coronel rushed out of the door on the sixth floor and virtually leaped down the stairs, two or three at a time, toward the ground floor. Although he ran down the stairs as quickly as he could, he had just reached the ground floor when he heard the outside door open. He ducked back behind a small alcove near the stairs and watched as a Dallas police officer ran up the stairs. Once the police officer had run past him, he immediately rushed out the door.

Once outside, El Coronel buttoned the top button of his shirt and donned the tie that he had been storing in the pocket of his sport coat. He now looked like the perfect business executive that he had been representing himself to be. He walked, not to the back of the building, but to the front. There he interacted with the crowd and asked many of them what was happening. He wanted to be remembered only as being an observer in the crowd and not being anywhere else. From there, he walked slowly back to his four-star hotel.

Back upstairs in the Depository, it had taken Alek about a minute to find a suitable hiding place for the rifle, since he hadn't been prepared to do that. Once he'd hidden the rifle, he ran down the stairs. But before he reached the ground floor, he heard the sound of someone rushing up the stairs toward him. So he ducked into the second-floor lunch room, thinking that he would be safe there.

Moments later Dallas Police Officer Marrion L. Baker rushed into the lunch room. He had been outside the Depository when he heard the shots and thought that they came from inside the Depository. He was looking for anyone suspicious in the building. He thought he heard someone running down the stairs and that maybe that person had just run into the lunch room. Officer Baker drew his gun and challenged Alek, who looked suspicious even though he was now doing nothing more than drinking the Coke in the lunch room.

Just then, the building manager, Roy Truly, entered the lunch room. The manager confirmed to the cop that the guy drinking the Coke was a Depository employee named Lee Oswald, who belonged in the building. Hearing that, Officer Baker headed up higher into the building to look for other suspects.

Once the police officer left the lunch room, Lee Oswald bolted from the building and headed to meet El Coronel. But El Coronel was nowhere to be seen, so Oswald knew he needed to proceed on his own. Although he was not sure exactly what to do, he decided to go back to his rooming house and retrieve his pistol before he headed anywhere else.

CHAPTER TWO

ATTACK IN EUROPE

The road to the rural manor house was no more than a double-rutted track that horse-drawn wagons once used. The manor house was located almost a kilometer from the main highway. For centuries, the inhabitants had farmed the surrounding fields and raised animals to support their survival. It was just a typical small farming home, except that it had a very sophisticated radio antenna system threaded between the branches of the trees that surrounded the house. Such a sophisticated antenna system required a substantial amount of space to be properly arrayed, but the trees presented both the proper array and the desired disguise.

Four men had arrived in a Land Rover down the rutted two-lane path that passed for a roadway earlier that day. They pulled the Land Rover into a hiding spot just off the roadway and dispersed around the house according to their orders. They waited for darkness.

The manor house was constructed of stone and its masons had provided sturdy walls. The potential attackers understood this, so they knew they would have to attack the doors or the windows to get into the building. Once it was fully dark, the attackers were in place and awaiting the attack signal from their leader.

Just when the leader gave the order to attack, one of the inhabitants came out the front door and lit a cigarette. He only had about a minute to enjoy his cigarette before he crumpled to the ground with a lethal wound. One of the outside attackers fired a British 4 MK-1-T rifle equipped with a suppressor from about 300 meters away. This was the pre-eminent sniper rifle in the British arsenal and was coveted around the world by knowledgeable military snipers because of its accuracy and reliability.

The man who had been killed never knew what had hit him. His death was sudden and silent.

Moments later, two intruders burst through the front door of the manor house, which the smoker had not latched behind him. They used their automatic weapons to kill two unsuspecting inhabitants who were relaxing in the parlor

Then they ran deeper into the house, where one of the attacking gunmen encountered a man in the kitchen. The man had apparently heard the sounds of gunfire in the front parlor and had grabbed a kitchen cleaver as a weapon. But it was no match for an automatic rifle, so he was easily cut down by the attacker.

The team leader followed his men into the house and moved quickly to find the radio room. That was why he had been ordered here. When he came upon a locked bedroom door, the team leader called for one of his men to shoot the lock open. As soon as the lock shattered, the radio operator sprang through the door firing his own handgun. Using the element of surprise, he was able to hit the intruder that had shot at the door, but the team leader stopped him with a shot to the chest.

Inside the room was the most sophisticated radio equipment the team leader had ever seen. This was undoubtedly the spy operation that his commander had instructed him to find and eliminate.

He ordered his men to strip the equipment from the room and take it with them. One of his men was already attending to his wounded associate. It did not appear that the wound was too serious. He ordered another of his men to attend to the radio operator with the chest wound. Although it appeared serious, maybe fatal, the man was still alive. The team leader decided to take him back to their headquarters so he could be questioned – if he lived that long.

He also ordered them to search the rest of the house.

In another bedroom, they found a frightened woman holding an infant. She was hiding in a closet. He had been told that it was likely there would be a woman and an infant in the house.

But he hadn't been given any specific instructions regarding how he should treat the woman and the child. He didn't want to kill them but he didn't know what else to do.

He considered shooting them, but instead decided to bring them back to the base. Maybe they could be useful as hostages that could be traded in the future.

His team pulled all the dead bodies into the center of the house and set two explosive devices. One was high-explosive and the other was incendiary. As soon as they both detonated, the manor house would not only be blown apart, but also burned to ash and cinders.

BOOK TWO

BEFORE THE ASSASSINATION

CHAPTER THREE

The darkness hung like a black shroud smothering his boat as Lieutenant Jack Kennedy searched the waters around the vessel. It was a night illuminated neither by the moon nor the stars. Compounding the blackness of the night, his visibility was also impaired by the prevalent haze that floated just above the surface of the water. The water temperature in this part of the South Pacific was quite warm, which resulted in a great amount of humidity evaporating off the surface of the water into the air. Then after dark when the temperature dropped, some of this humidity would condense into particles of haze. These particles were not dense enough to be considered fog, but Kennedy still cursed the havoc they wreaked on his vision.

Kennedy was the commander of Motor Torpedo Boat PT-109. His boat was almost 80 feet long and possessed three 1200-horsepower engines, which were capable of propelling the vessel to speeds over 40 knots per hour. Although it didn't have the armaments to compete head-on with a Japanese destroyer, when its three massive engines were pumping out all their power, he had speed and mobility that would allow him to attack a destroyer and afterwards evade any counter-attack from the destroyer. His ship also had smoke generators that could pump out an enormous smoke screen to prevent the enemy from getting an exact fix on the vessel.

But right now, Kennedy, pursuant to his orders, had the vessel lying idle in the middle of some of the most treacherous waters in the South Pacific. These waters were the raceway down which the Japanese sent their vessels, usually high-speed destroyers, to deliver supplies from their major bases at Rabual and Bougainvillea to their outlying occupied islands. The American forces had dubbed these nightly high-speed runs "The Tokyo Express." In fact, his mission normally would have been to try to detect and interdict these vessels to disrupt these resupply missions.

Tonight, however, he was on a mission that was even more dangerous, since he was essentially drifting in hostile waters which made his boat an easy target. The PT-109 was virtually helpless when it was sitting idle.

Once the Americans conquered Guadalcanal and reopened Henderson Airfield, it became much too dangerous for the Japanese to have any slow-moving ships on the waters during the day. The American air superiority made any Japanese vessels vulnerable and subject to attack.

Accordingly, the Japanese commander Admiral Isoroku Yamamoto authorized the use of fast-moving destroyers to make all deliveries at night and immediately return to base, so that they would not be exposed during daylight hours.

Jack could only hope they would be able to complete this mission by locating a swimmer and extracting him as quickly as possible so that they could once again be underway.

In addition to being right in the middle of "The Tokyo Express" raceway, PT-109 was also right in the middle of several Japanese-held islands. The largest island to the north was Kolambangara. Jack learned from his daily briefing that this island had a large garrison of Japanese soldiers.

To the south and east were two smaller Japanese-held islands, Arundel and Vonavona. To the west was a somewhat smaller island, Gizo. Although it was smaller geographically, its position made it more strategically valuable because it was closer to the waterways.

This extraction would be the completion of a mission that began about 36 hours earlier. It had begun yesterday in the late afternoon as Kennedy and the members of his crew were cleaning and inspecting the PT-109 to prepare it for their nightly mission.

Kennedy was doing a final inspection of the vessel when he was surprised to hear, "Permission to come aboard, Captain?"

Kennedy looked toward the dock and saw a young man standing there smiling at him. Although Kennedy wasn't a Captain in rank, he was certainly the captain of the vessel. When Kennedy looked closer at the new arrival, he broke into a wide grin. He knew this guy from when they were both in training back in Rhode Island about a year ago.

Neither of them was properly attired as a naval officer. Jack was shirtless since he had been working in the heat below decks on the vessel, and the new arrival was in just-standard military utilities, without any insignia.

Jack was tall and lean, around six feet tall and about 170 pounds. He usually had a fair complexion, based on his Irish heritage, but now he had a dark tan owing to his several months' service in the South Pacific. He had his light brown hair parted on the left and hanging down on his forehead. He appeared to be in good overall physical condition, but he had a chronic back problem that no one would suspect by looking at him.

In fact, his back condition had almost kept him out of the Service. He had tried to enlist in the Army, but they had rejected him because of his health problems. Jack was devotedly patriotic, however, and refused to sit out the war. He implored his politically connected father, Joseph P. Kennedy, to use his influence to get him into the Armed Forces.

Joseph P. Kennedy had been Ambassador to England before the war and his Naval Attaché had been Admiral Alan G. Kirk, with whom he had a good relationship. Joseph Kennedy had contacted Admiral Kirk on behalf of Jack.

Admiral Kirk, who was now the head of the Office of Naval Intelligence, had received numerous requests from various politicos seeking a safe assignment or deferment for their sons, which he abhorred as cowardly and which he denied by silently burying them. This was the first time he had received a request from a father, who was asking for help in getting his son into the Navy! He was so impressed by this patriotism that he arranged for Jack to enlist in the Navy without the normal physical exam. So, Jack was now here in the South Pacific in command of a Motor Torpedo Boat.

The new arrival bore several similarities to Jack. He was about the same height and weight. But his very light brown hair was several shades lighter than Jack's. He had the same Irish heritage as Jack, but since he had only recently arrived in the South Pacific, he had not yet developed a tan. In fact, his face looked rather sunburned as he stood there on the dock.

Jack responded, "Peter, what the heck are you doing here? Of course, please come on board."

Peter responded, "Hi, Jack. I hope you're doing well. I'm sure you're surprised to see me here."

Jack said, "Nothing you do surprises me, Peter, but I'm sure you're going to come aboard and tell me exactly why you're here."

The PT-109 was tied sideways to the dock, so Peter just had to step up onto the gunwale to board the vessel. Jack and Peter shook hands like the old friends they were and moved to the front of the vessel to be away from the rest of the crew so they could talk privately.

Jack said, "I don't suppose this is a social visit, although I wish it were."

Peter said in response, "Well, I wish the same thing, but Jack, I've got our orders here. Why don't you take a quick look at them and then we can talk about what it means."

"Okay," Jack agreed as he took the papers from Peter's hands.

After reading them, Jack said to Peter, "So we're going to go and drop you off in the middle of nowhere to do something that's not specified on my copy of the orders, and then I'm expected to return to approximately the same spot 24 hours later so that you can be extracted."

Peter said, "Yeah, Jack, that's about it. I can't tell you exactly where I'm going after you drop me off, but I'm sure you know that it's important or they wouldn't have changed your mission from the interdiction of enemy shipping that you usually do."

Jack said, "Yeah, I know. I'm just kind of worried about where you are going and even more about how the hell I'm going to get you back on board tomorrow night."

Peter responded, "Jack, you just get your boat back in the same place where you dropped me off and I'll worry about all the rest."

Jack smiled, but then he said to Peter, "Well, standard operating procedure means that I need to verify your identity and authorization before I accept these orders."

"Of course," Peter said, "Here's my ID card."

Peter flipped out his wallet and displayed an ID card for the Office of Naval Intelligence. Jack looked at it and was surprised. He said to Peter, "What, you're in ONI now? I thought you were in a Construction Battalion."

"Yeah," Peter said, "That's where I started. As you know, back in Rhode Island, I was training to be a member of an underwater demolition team. But when the ONI needed people who could swim and do reconnaissance, they recruited me."

"Okay, Peter," Jack said. "You know I would cooperate any way I could anyway, but even more, I do owe a great debt to the ONI. The Army refused my enlistment, so my father called a friend of his, Admiral Alan Kirk, who got me into the Navy because of his influence as Director of Naval Intelligence. Admiral Kirk and my father became friends when the Admiral served as military attaché when my father was Ambassador to England. Maybe someday I'll tell you more about it."

Peter already had heard during their time back in training in Newport, RI, that Jack came from a wealthy and influential family, but he didn't realize just how powerful Jack's family was until Jack just mentioned that his father had been Ambassador to England. Peter didn't suspect it, because Jack seemed like such a regular guy. Peter didn't want to wait to talk about it "someday."

Instead he questioned Jack, "You mean your father called to help you get into the service, instead of helping you to avoid the draft. I've heard that all the sons of wealthy families have gotten draft deferments or are pulling reserve desk duty in Chicago or somewhere safe in the middle of America. You mean you didn't ask your father to use his influence to help you avoid the service, but instead asked him to get you in?"

"Yeah," Jack responded, "Maybe it sounds nuts. I already had a military rejection from the Army because I've had a bad back for years. It could have kept me out of the fight if I'd wanted to stay safely home. But that's not me, nor my family. I don't fault the Army for keeping me out because my bad back would probably have been a problem on long marches, but it doesn't bother me when I'm swimming. So the Navy is a good fit for me. I don't have to march long distances. And I couldn't have sat at home while my country was being attacked. My father feels the same way I do, so he got me into the Navy."

Peter responded, "Yeah, it does sound like you're nuts, but in a way that I admire. On the other hand, I think your father really just wanted to get you out of Boston so he could avoid having to pay child support for the dozens of bastard children you've probably fathered that might just show up!"

They both laughed and then spread out a map to work on the details of Peter's mission.

* * * * * * * * * *

Jack was starting to get very worried. They had arrived on station for the extraction about ten minutes ago and had been sitting idle in the middle of the "Tokyo Express" shipping lanes without any sight of the swimmer they were expecting. Each minute they sat there idle just increased the danger to the vessel.

Jack's orders included directions for him to signal to help the swimmer locate his boat. Specifically, the PT-109 was equipped with a small, lighted beacon on a three-foot mast installed near the stern of the vessel. Jack's instructions were to flash the beacon three rapid times every other minute. The beacon had an umbrella-like shield to prevent any light from being detected by enemy planes or vessels that might be searching the horizon. The light was red, which made it harder to detect at distance but which assured that it would not destroy the night vision of either the PT-109 sailors or the swimmer in the water.

While drifting idly in the black current awaiting any sighting of the swimmer, Jack allowed his mind to drift back to the time when he had first met Peter Sharkey.

* * * * * * * * * *

Jack had been assigned to the Motor Torpedo Boat Squadron Training Center in Melville, Rhode Island. It was early October, 1942 and the weather in that part of Rhode Island was gorgeous and almost summer-like. The daytime temperature at the base hovered from the high sixties to lower seventies and the nights only dropped to the mid-fifties.

During the war, virtually all of the Rhode Island shoreline was owned or controlled by the Navy. Rhode Island is a small state with most of its land area in a sort of horseshoe around Narragansett Bay which protrudes up into the land from the Atlantic Ocean. The Navy controlled the shoreline on both sides of the bay, as well as most of the islands within the bay. The Army had several shore batteries there to protect the Navy installations. The main base was Naval Base Newport, which was located on the eastern side of Narragansett Bay. The east side of the bay also contained the Naval War College, as well as the PT Boat Training Center at Melville.

The west side of the bay had Naval Air Station, Quonset. This was the main naval air station in the Northeast area. Just north of Quonset on the west side of the bay was the Construction Battalion Base at Davisville, R.I.

The Navy realized they might be confronted with various situations where they would need to construct airfields, demolish enemy fortifications, or construct bases for US forces. So they formed the Construction Battalions. The sailors in the Construction Battalions had been nicknamed Seabees, based on the initials of the unit. They had a logo that was a fearsome looking "Honey Bee" in a Navy cap, holding both a machine gun (to symbolize their fighting ability) and a hammer (to symbolize their construction and demolition mission).

It was to this base where Peter Sharkey had been assigned. As a graduate engineer from the University of Rhode Island, Peter joined the Navy upon graduation and after basic training volunteered to join the Seabees.

Because Peter always loved to swim, having grown up on the Rhode Island shoreline, he next volunteered to train to be an Underwater Demolition Team member. The mission of the UDT members would be to detect and demolish any underwater fortifications that the enemy might have created to impede an amphibious landing. The UDT members were nicknamed "Frogmen." It was known that the Germans had constructed such fortifications along the French coast, called the Atlantic Wall, to prevent an allied landing. Peter volunteered for the mission and expected to be sent to Europe.

While he was undergoing training at Davisville, however, Peter was given orders to report to the PT boat training base at Melville. Peter was told that his mission would be to practice insertion and extraction from PT boats. From this, they hoped to learn how to best utilize the PT boats on reconnaissance missions.

When Peter arrived at the Melville base, the training center commander brought him to Jack Kennedy's boat. Jack had already prepared his vessel to depart, so he was surprised when the commander waved at him to delay. The commander made the necessary introductions and Peter showed Jack their orders. It included dives from various sides of the boat and retrievals from various sides of the boat. They were trying to determine the most efficient way to insert a "Frogman" into the water and later retrieve him. Obviously in these situations, time was of the essence, so determining the best way to do this could be important someday.

The whole exercise was scheduled to take three days to complete, and during that time Jack and Peter became fairly close. It turned out they had a lot in common since they were both Irish, although they had a lot of dissimilarities also. Jack came from a wealthy Irish family in Boston and had graduated from Harvard University. Peter came from a middle-class Irish family in Rhode Island and had graduated from the University of Rhode Island. They both shared an enormous desire to make a difference during the war, plus they both shared a great sense of humor.

On the weekend after the training exercise concluded, Peter and Jack were granted leave. They decided to spend Friday night together on Thames Street in Newport, which was nicknamed Navy Row. It was a collection of cheap bars, plus some middle-class restaurants. Some were frequented by prostitutes, some were frequented by USO volunteers, and some were frequented by local women just looking for some companionship during the war. The Navy Shore Patrol (the Police Force of the Navy) kept a major presence on Thames Street, but they couldn't control all of the drunken rowdiness that sometimes occurred when the sailors were released for the weekend.

Neither Jack nor Peter was a big drinker, so their major objective in going to Thames Street was to check out the women. They went to one of the better night spots frequented by officers and enjoyed a great seafood meal. Being right on the ocean, Rhode Island had some of the best seafood available anywhere and it was very inexpensive. Lobsters were abundant in the coastal Rhode Island waters, so they were both able to have lobsters at a very reasonable price. During dinner they challenged each other to a swimming race across the east passage of Narragansett Bay from the naval base side to Jamestown Island in the middle of Narragansett Bay. They would meet tomorrow morning at dawn for the race. The bet was for one dollar.

After that Jack and Peter split up to meet as many women as possible, hoping that they each might meet one with whom to spend the night.

Neither of them was successful in their quest, so they both arrived on time for the race the next morning. Unfortunately when they showed up at the beach near Melville, the winds had thickened from the south and the waves were choppy and irregular, coming northward up Narragansett Bay. Since both Jack and Peter were very experienced swimmers, the wind and chop did not worry them, but it would make the swim much more difficult than they'd anticipated. Neither of them was willing to back out from the race, however, even though it was going to be worse than they had anticipated.

Arriving on the beach, Jack said to Peter, "Where the heck did this storm come from? I thought we were supposed to have clear skies today."

Peter said, "I don't know either. I guess it's just a quick wind squall or something. Are you still ready to do this?"

Jack responded, "Sure, it's not that far a swim, right? It's about a mile from here to the island, and then a mile back. So what do you think?"

Peter said, "Yeah, let's do it. Are you ready?"

Jack nodded okay and they walked together toward the shore and then they stripped down to their swimsuits. They slapped their hands together and ran to the water, and then dived in and headed for the island.

The waves were coming from their left, south to north, as they swam toward Jamestown Island. Jack was pulling ahead of Peter and was pretty sure that he had the advantage. After they landed on Jamestown Island, Jack was way ahead of Peter. They had decided that they would need to slap a rock on dry land to prove they had been there and then jump back into the water for the return trip. Jack had already slapped his rock as he passed Peter still heading toward a rock.

The return swim was much more difficult than the outgoing swim. They were heading into the chop, which now came from right to left. While it had somewhat aided their swim heading toward the island, it now impeded them.

Jack felt the waves slapping against him each time he raised his arms to drive forward. The wind had kicked up and the chop was about one-to-two feet in height. Jack was making progress, but he knew it was much slower than the swim outbound.

He hadn't seen Peter approaching from behind him, so he was quite sure that he was still in the lead on the race. At one point, however, about halfway across the channel, Jack thought he saw Peter bob up to the surface in front of him and immediately go back under water. Jack knew it made sense that if you could swim underwater you would avoid the restraining force of the wind and waves, but he didn't understand how Peter might be able to swim underwater for so long and for such a distance.

When Jack arrived back on the shore at Melville, Peter was already there waiting for him. Peter was sitting on a rock near where they had previously left their clothes and was using a towel to dry himself down.

When Jack emerged from the water, Peter walked over and threw him the other towel.

"Hey, Jack," Peter taunted, "What did you do, stop out there to enjoy the view? I thought we were in a race."

Jack laughed and then asked, "How the hell did you get by me? You were way behind."

Peter said, "Well, I just ducked under the waves a couple of times. You should have done the same."

Jack replied, "How long can you hold your breath, you bastard? You must have been under there for a minute or two at a time."

Peter said, "I don't know, but I guess for a minute or two."

Jack questioned, "I don't understand how you can hold your breath so long while swimming underwater?"

Peter answered, "Well, I grew up here on Narragansett Bay and my friends and I would dive for clams and I could always stay down the longest. That meant I brought up more clams. I always pushed myself to stay down longer and longer."

"Okay," Jack said, "Well done, buddy. Let's go back to Thames Street tonight and I'll pay up for the bet."

The bet had been for a dollar. Although neither of them was much of a drinker, Jack bought a round of beers that night. They both forgot about the honorary prize of one dollar. They were much more interested in discussing the progress of the war. They also wanted to meet some women!

It was not long afterwards that Peter and Jack finished their training and were sent to other assignments.

* * * * * * * * * *

And now, here they were, in the South Pacific with Jack searching the water for Peter.

"There's a light, Lieutenant, over there," one of his sailors shouted while pointing southeast of the boat. Everyone looked toward where he was pointing and in the sea about 30 feet away from the boat was a small red beacon that had been flashed by a swimmer. They knew it was the extraction that they had been waiting for, but they couldn't move the boat toward him, since there was a danger that the propellers would suck him under. They had to wait a few moments longer for him to arrive at the boat.

The swimmer got close to the vessel and they dropped him a knotted line to assist him in boarding the boat. Peter was almost to the top of the line and into the vessel when another crewman shouted, "Lieutenant, there's something coming over there!"

At that, they all looked toward where the sailor was pointing. Out of the inky darkness appeared a huge pointed hull. It was blacker than the night and was traveling so fast that Kennedy had absolutely no chance to engage the engines and move out of its path.

He and his crew had only spotted the enormous hull of the Japanese ship bearing down on them several seconds before it hit. He knew it had to be a Japanese warship because of its size and speed.

Jack's thoughts raced in the few seconds before the impact. He was concerned about his entire ship, including all of his men and Peter Sharkey. He took a quick glance toward the back and saw that Peter was almost into the vessel as he shoved the throttles into forward. He knew it was a futile gesture, because as he looked upward the massive bow of the Japanese vessel was almost to his ship. He could see that the bow of the destroyer was at least 50- or 60-feet high, dwarfing the size of the PT-109 which was probably only about 20 feet above the water at its highest point.

Just ten seconds after they first sighted the Japanese destroyer, the Japanese vessel struck the PT-109. Everyone on board was battered about and most were flung into the water. The hull of the Japanese ship scythed through the PT-109 like a steel ax through wooden kindling. The wooden hull of the PT-109 was no match for the armored Japanese warship. It was sheared completely in half by the impact. Incredibly, both halves were still afloat.

The wooden hull had been so flimsy compared to the steel hull of the destroyer that the other vessel probably never felt the impact. The destroyer continued its high-speed run and didn't stop to help any survivors on the PT-109.

Unfortunately, the impact ignited the fuel that was on-board the PT-109. The flames erupted from both sides of the stricken hull while the Japanese warship barreled on.

PT boats were equipped with Packard engines that had been modified from aviation use. They were fueled by Avgas and were completely different from the diesel engines that powered most other Navy vessels. The gasoline engines gave them considerable horsepower – and thus speed, an advantage over similar diesel engines, but the Avgas was much more volatile than diesel fuel. It was the Avgas that burst into flame!

The conflagration of flame engulfed both parts of the PT-109.

But luckily, because the Japanese warship kept up its high speed, it had an enormous wake. As soon as the wake hit the remnants of the PT-109, it pushed each part out of the pool of fire. The remains of PT-109 were still perilously close to the flames from the Avgas, but didn't seem to be in any immediate danger. The walls of flames on the waters burned all around them, but seemed to be dying out quickly. Within twenty minutes after the collision, the flames finally died out and the seas were calm and dark.

Jack proceeded to conduct a quick check of his crew to determine who had survived and which ones needed help. There had been three other officers on board: Ensign Ross, Lt. Sharkey and Ensign Thom, plus ten sailors. He began to shout out their names. Quickly Ross and Thom answered, as did eight of the sailors. Two other sailors were missing, as was Peter Sharkey.

Kennedy jumped into the water and helped all the survivors to return to the remains of the aft of the PT-109. Because of the currents, it took a long time to get all the survivors back to the wreck.

As Jack was boosting the last of the survivors onto the floating wreck, Peter Sharkey suddenly swam next to him.

Jack said, "Hey, are you okay?"

Peter responded, "I'm not real sure. I think I was out for a while, but I'm pretty sure nothing's broken. I've just got some pains. How about you, Jack?"

Jack responded, "Yeah, well, I had a bad back before this night, and I guess it won't be getting any better. It hurts like hell right now. And I'm bleeding from some small cuts, but I don't think anything's broken. In any case, I won't let anything stop me."

They were all huddled on top of the remains of the aft section of the PT-109 waiting for dawn on August 2nd, as Kennedy assessed the situation. Unfortunately, one sailor was badly burned and another was suffering from minor burns while two members of his crew had probably perished in the collision. When dawn broke, there were no friendly forces anywhere nearby to rescue them.

Even worse, Jack was quite sure that what was left of the PT-109 was about to sink in the next few hours.

He made the decision to abandon it and to head for one of the tiny islands nearby. There were several to choose from, but he decided one of the smaller ones would be less likely to be occupied by the Japanese and they should head there. The last thing any of them wanted was to be captured by the Japanese after this ordeal.

They were an unlikely looking group of swimmers as they hit the water to head for the small island. The badly burned sailor was strapped to a float and Jack took him personally in tow to set out for the island. Another sailor had minor burns and was not a good swimmer anyway, so Peter towed him. Ensigns Thom and Ross followed with the other men. Some of them were good swimmers, but others were either non-swimmers or not good swimmers. They were tied to another float they had rigged from planks which had been part of the 37-millimeter gun turret on the PT-109. They all worked together to tow, push or otherwise get each other to the island.

All of the members of the group had long since shed their shoes, which only slowed them down in the water. Besides being shoeless, the entire group had very few clothes left. Kennedy was dressed only in his skivvies. Sharkey was in his military swimsuit and still had his Ka-Bar knife strapped to his waist. The other men had only their trousers or shorts and maybe a few shirts among them.

They had very little in the way of weaponry. Besides the Ka-Bar knife that Sharkey had, they counted six 45-caliber automatics, one 38-caliber revolver, and a few other knives. They had lost their first-aid kit, so there was nothing that they could do to tend even their minor wounds.

They all made the island intact and were glad to be able to rest on the beach. Unfortunately, it was a very small island; but fortunately it wasn't occupied by the Japanese. They scurried inland, hoping that they wouldn't be detected by any Japanese patrols. Over the next two days, Lt. Sharkey and Lt. Kennedy, as well as Ensigns Ross and Thom, all swam out to attempt to intercept PT boats. Unfortunately, none of them detected any U.S. presence.

Because their only food supply on the small island had been several coconuts, which had long ago been consumed for their milk and meat, Kennedy decided that they needed to move to a different island.

He decided to head for a small islet west of Cross Island, which was closer to the main waterway and which probably had more coconut palms. It was large enough to have more coconuts, but not so large that it was likely to have Japanese troops.

Kennedy decided to leave at noon on August 4th. He came to this conclusion because he knew that most of the enemy patrols occurred either near dawn or dusk. Going right in the middle of the day would probably be something they wouldn't expect. Additionally, leaving at noon would allow them to land at the new island just before dusk, so they might be able to take refuge in the dark should the island be occupied by the Japanese.

They used essentially the same arrangements that they'd used before to get to this island. Once again, Kennedy, Sharkey, Thom and Ross, as the strongest swimmers, took the lead in pushing and/or pulling everyone else. Some of the weaker swimmers at least held up their own, realizing that they couldn't rely totally on the others.

Jack and Peter were swimming near the front of the makeshift flotilla and were talking about their destination. Jack sought some reassurance about his decision. Jack said, "Peter, what do you think about this island that we're heading toward? Any chances there are Japs there?"

Peter responded, "Jeez, I hope not, Jack, but the ONI didn't share anything with me about all these little islands around here. We do know there are Japs on all the major islands."

Jack responded, "Yeah, who the hell knows? Let's just keep swimming ahead and hope for the best."

Peter agreed and said, "You're right, Jack. Luckily, I don't think it's more than a couple of miles to the island and the current is not that bad right now."

Only a moment later Jack said, "Jesus Christ, what the hell is that?"

He was looking behind them about 100 yards.

Peter's head swiveled around and he saw what Jack was worried about. It looked like five-to-seven sharks' fins. A whole group of sharks had suddenly tracked the group, maybe because of some of their blood in the water.

Peter said to Jack, "I think it would be good if we could speed this up a little bit and get to land pretty soon."

Jack asked, "Shit, Peter, what the hell are we going to do? With all these sharks around, I'm afraid we don't have much time before they attack. And we're towing all these guys, so we can't go much faster. There are no other islands closer than where we are headed, so I don't think we have any other option than to just keep going."

Peter said, "You're right. We've got to keep going. . . and maybe pray."

Then Jack yelled back at everyone, "Move it faster folks. Double time. We have sharks behind us now. Come on. Move it!"

The others looked around and saw the dorsal fins from the sharks starting to approach them and immediately started to kick faster. Jack and Peter had already started to pick up their efforts, but Jack suddenly felt a touch from a shark that had decided to approach him. "Shit," he said out loud.

Peter said, "What?"

Jack responded, "Well, one of those bastards just came by my leg and nudged me."

Peter then said, "Well, maybe they're just fooling with us so that they can attack all at once. Let's just keep going and see what happens."

But as Peter looked around, he saw that not only were there shark fins behind them, but there were several on both sides of them. It appeared that the sharks were readying for a massive attack.

They had several virtually helpless sailors in the water and neither Jack nor Peter knew how to rescue them from the imminent shark attack. Although they kept swimming toward the new island, the sharks were coming closer and closer.

Then one of them scraped Peter's leg. Peter knew he had to do something or they were all going to be attacked and killed. Peter said, "Jack, okay, buddy, you've got to start pulling all of these people because I'm not going there with you."

Jack said, "What are you talking about? You can't leave. You can't abandon us. We need your help," as he took the tow rope that Peter handed him.

"Well, Jack, these bastards are going to kill us if we just keep doing what we're doing. So it's time to do something different. This is probably pretty stupid, but it's all I can think of."

Jack said, "But you can't do anything different. What…"

He was cut off as Peter swam away. He could see that Peter had reached down into his sheath and extracted the Ka-Bar knife and was holding it in his mouth. Jack saw him swim right toward the middle of the sharks!

Just before he got there, Peter switched from a fast-forward swim stoke into a butterfly stroke, which was the noisiest and splashiest type of swim stroke. He rattled the water as his arms windmilled forward. He made an enormous amount of noise and splash which obviously attracted the attention of the sharks. He mimicked a wounded and distressed seal; so the sharks diverted their attention from the other swimmers to him. They were looking for the easiest and best opportunity possible for a meal!

Jack kept pushing toward the new island, but he couldn't help but look back to where Peter was now trapped in the middle of the sharks. He saw Peter flapping his arms and kicking his legs in the butterfly stroke. Then suddenly he saw nothing, absolutely nothing of Peter. He was sure that a shark had attacked Peter and dragged him underwater.

Jack really didn't want to turn his head around again, but subconsciously he was compelled to look. He looked back and the surface of the water was a maelstrom of fins and tails. He knew that the sharks were in a blood frenzy, and he knew Peter was dying in the middle of that mess.

But he also knew he needed to concentrate on saving the other people that depended upon him. So that is exactly what he did. He didn't have time for sorrow.

They kept swimming toward the new island, but Jack sometimes looked back where Peter had gone. He was astonished to see that the sea was still a violent mix of blood, dorsal fins and shark tails.

"*Jesus Christ,*" Jack thought. "*Peter diverted all those frigging sharks from us, but he's gone.*" Jack redoubled his swimming effort.

Jack thought again to himself, "*Peter sacrificed himself to save us and I can't let his death be in vain. I've got to get everyone through this.*" They were all still swimming as quickly as possible because they had all seen the shark attack.

When they finally reached the new island, Jack was pleased that everyone else had survived without any shark wounds and that the sharks were nowhere to be seen. In his mind he was sickened because he knew that the reason the sharks had gone elsewhere was that they had killed his friend, Peter Sharkey. "*Crap,*" Jack thought, "*Just crap.*"

Jack led his crew onto the small islet and got them to hide in the heavy brush. Luckily, this larger island was not occupied by the Japanese and had many more coconuts for them to eat. Jack couldn't eat much because he was nauseated every time he thought back to the death of Peter Sharkey. Without a doubt, Peter had saved all their lives by deflecting the shark attack; but Jack still became nauseated when he thought of the violent death that Peter had suffered in the midst of that swarm of sharks.

Jack knew he had to concentrate on his primary task, however, which was the survival of his crew. The next day, he and Ross swam out together to explore some of the other nearby islands. On one, they found a small Japanese box with 30 odd packs of crackers and candy. There was also a native lean-to there and a canoe with a barrel of fresh water nearby. They decided to take the canoe to head back to the rest of the crew on what turned out to be Nauru Island. Just as they were readying the canoe to leave, two natives were sighted offshore, but they fled rather than coming to the shore when Kennedy and Ross tried to signal to them.

That night Jack took the canoe into the passage, hoping to find a passing PT boat, but was unsuccessful. When he got back to the crew on Nauru Island, he found that the two natives they had seen yesterday had returned and were sitting there with the rest of the group.

Jack retrieved a green coconut from one of the trees and scratched a message into it. That message read, "Eleven alive. Native knows Posit & Reef Nauru Island Kennedy."

Jack handed the coconut to one of the natives and said, "Rendova, Rendova," indicating that he wanted the coconut to be taken to the PT base on Rendova.

The natives left with the coconut and everyone was smiling, but no intelligible words had been exchanged between anyone, since neither knew the other's language. They were all hopeful once the natives left, because they seemed to be friendly; but one never knew. That night the entire crew was extra vigilant, just to be sure that the natives hadn't sold the coconut with the message to the Japanese.

Their fears were dissipated the next morning when the natives returned with food and supplies. They also had a letter from the Coastwatcher commander of the New Zealand camp, Lieutenant Arthur Reginald Evans. The message indicated that the American commander, Kennedy, should return with the natives. Kennedy immediately complied. He was taken offshore to meet PT-157, which returned with him to the island and finally rescued all of the survivors of his crew.

The Coastwatchers were a group of Australian military personnel that had been positioned on numerous outlying Pacific islands to observe and report on the movement of Japanese troops and vessels in their observation area. Their contribution had already been invaluable to the American victory at Guadalcanal. Some of them lived in primitive conditions with the resident islanders on their posts and they performed with great effectiveness. They also developed a great rapport and trust with the indigenous natives, so the natives decided to return to the Americans on Nauru because they trusted the Coastwatchers.

On the evening of August 8th Kennedy's crew arrived back at Rendova, where the injured survivors finally received medical treatment. Kennedy and the others were greeted like royalty, since their compatriots on Rendova thought they had all been killed when the PT-109 was sunk.

The base commander at Rendova was Captain Willard Field. The captain faced a chronic shortage of qualified crewmen and officers to man his PT boats, so he arranged for the best possible treatment for Kennedy and his crew so that they might rest and rehabilitate and be ready to be returned to service quickly. The captain had no doubt that Kennedy was a capable commander and should be given a new vessel as soon as possible. He soon learned, however, that this would not be possible.

* * * * * * * * * *

General Douglas MacArthur had transferred his headquarters operation to Brisbane, Australia after he had been forced to evacuate the Philippines by the Japanese invasion. General MacArthur was one of the most competent leaders in the American forces. He possessed a phenomenal memory and an encyclopedic knowledge of people, events and geography. His most unique gift was his mental ability to assemble all these facts together so that he knew which people were at what location doing exactly what at most any point in time – both friend and foe!

He was also a very politically astute general. He had not been promoted to Supreme Allied Commander South West Pacific Area without knowing how to garner support among the politicians back in Washington, DC. He had a distinct leaning for the Republican Party, since they seemed to be more supportive of the military than the Democrats. But maybe that was just because President Franklin Delano Roosevelt, a Democrat, sometimes had to deny General MacArthur's requests for additional troops or resources.

General MacArthur reviewed all the military dispatches of the entire Pacific area each and every day. Although right now he shared command of the Pacific Theater of Operations with Admiral Chester W. Nimitz (with each controlling half of the area), he wanted to become Supreme Commander of the entire Pacific. Therefore, he looked for any event in the Pacific that would promote his achievements, as well as looking for any events in Admiral Nimitz's region that might diminish Nimitz's influence.

When General MacArthur saw the dispatch reporting the rescue of the crew of the PT-109, he noted that the commander of the vessel had been Lt. John F. Kennedy, whom he knew to be the son of a prominent Democratic politician in Massachusetts. MacArthur had been looking for a chance to court-martial a Navy officer for dereliction of duty to promote better discipline among the naval forces, which he thought were less disciplined than his Army troops. He thought this might be an opportunity to achieve his objective and also discredit the Democrats.

General MacArthur summoned his aide into the room and directed that a dispatch be sent to Rendova. Although MacArthur had no direct command responsibility over that base, any dispatch from MacArthur's headquarters would be taken very seriously.

When Captain Field received the dispatch, he didn't quite know what to make of it. It wasn't an order, but it wasn't something to be ignored either. It had come from MacArthur's headquarters in Brisbane, but was not signed by MacArthur; rather it was signed by an Army Colonel whom he did not recognize. The wire said, "It is suggested that Lieutenant (JG) John F. Kennedy be confined to residence pending investigation into the sinking of PT-109. It would not be advisable to reassign Lieutenant Kennedy to a new vessel before the conclusion of such investigation. More to follow."

Captain Field had already tried to take the best care of Kennedy and his crew. He knew that they needed time to recover from the ordeal that they had been through, but he was deeply troubled by the dispatch he had just received.

Although he feared the wrath of MacArthur, since there were recurring rumors that MacArthur would soon be given command of the entire Pacific region, Captain Field sent off a dispatch of his own. Although the normal military protocol called for Captain Field to respond slowly up the chain of command, he was concerned that MacArthur was planning to court-martial Lieutenant Kennedy. Captain Field, in a bureaucratic effort as courageous as any he had ever made in the field, sent a dispatch directly to Admiral Nimitz.

When Admiral Nimitz saw the dispatch that his aide brought to him, he placed a call to the head of the ONI. He was quite certain that he remembered that the PT-109 was on an ONI mission when it was sunk by the Japanese warship.

Admiral Nimitz thereby confirmed what he already knew. PT-109 was on an intelligence-gathering mission on orders from the ONI when it was sunk by the Japanese warship. The vessel's captain, Lieutenant Kennedy, was following orders exactly as he should have and in no way was guilty of dereliction as MacArthur might be implying.

For months Admiral Nimitz had been engaged in this parody of minor conflicts with General MacArthur. He and MacArthur had a decent professional relationship, with each of them respecting the other's areas of control. But he knew that MacArthur's goal was to be the Supreme Commander of the entire Pacific. Nimitz knew that he didn't have the word "Supreme" in his own title, but he also knew that he was completely in charge in his own region.

He resented MacArthur's efforts to try to overreach his command, and he particularly resented the fact that it appeared that MacArthur wanted to court-martial Kennedy to make an example of the deficiencies in Nimitz's area and embarrass the Navy and the Democrats. Nimitz was apolitical and had no desire for political office after the war, but he had a keen understanding of the political arena and knew that Kennedy's father was a very influential Democrat back in Washington. He was sure this fact had influenced MacArthur's actions.

Admiral Nimitz called Admiral William F. "Bull" Halsey, the commander of the South Pacific area. Following their discussion, they decided that it would be best if they could preempt any effort by MacArthur to court-martial Kennedy by awarding him a medal. It certainly wouldn't sit well with the American public if a war hero with a newly minted medal were suggested for court-martial by someone (like MacArthur) not directly responsible for his actions.

After the conversation with Admiral Nimitz, Admiral Halsey summoned his aide into his office. Admiral Halsey said, "I need you to draft a citation for the Navy and Marine Corps Medal for Lieutenant (JG) John F. Kennedy immediately. Get all of the relevant information from his file as quickly as you can. Lieutenant Kennedy was the commander of the PT-109, which was sunk by a collision with a Japanese warship. He exhibited extraordinary heroism by leading the survivors through treacherous waters to some safe islands until they could finally be rescued through his efforts and by natives and Australian Coast Watchers. I need you to draft the award citation immediately and bring it to me for signature.

"Then I want you to personally deliver it to Rendova. I want it there as soon as possible, so I want you to take Dumbo."

His aide said, "Dumbo, sir? I thought you needed him tomorrow."

"No, no," the Admiral said, "This is much more important. I need you to get to Rendova ASAP." Then the Admiral added as an afterthought, "Take that Lieutenant with you too."

His aide didn't need any more instructions. He knew which Lieutenant the Admiral was referring to and he was confident that he could be airborne with him and the citation within an hour.

* * * * * * * * * *

Jack Kennedy had been lying in his bungalow at Rendova for weeks now. He was growing stir-crazy from the inactivity. Although his back had long bothered him and was quite a bit worse after the injuries he had sustained during the sinking of PT-109, he wanted desperately to return to active duty.

But the base commander had continued to waffle on that issue and repeatedly told Jack that he just needed to rest. Jack had become quite worried that there was something more below the surface that was denying him a new assignment. He wasn't quite sure what it was, but it worried him more and more each and every day. On the few days when the base commander did come by to check on Jack's well-being, he was very evasive, which just worried Jack even more.

* * * * * * * * * *

"Rendova Station, Rendova Station. This is Navy One, Zero, Zero, Two, on final to land immediately."

The radio operator at Rendova was puzzled by the whole thing since they didn't have an airstrip at Rendova. He responded, "Navy 1002, be advised there is no airstrip on Rendova. We are a Navy base, not Air Force. Divert to Henderson Field on Guadalcanal. Repeat, divert."

The pilot responded, "I'm aware of that. We will be landing offshore. Please be sure that there are no vessels in our landing zone outside of the harbor."

The Rendova operator had never had a transmission like this, so he quickly ran for the radio officer on shift. The officer came back with him and got on the radio and said, "Navy 1002, please advise your intentions."

Navy 1002 responded, "We are on a five-mile final approach to land outside your harbor. Please advise everyone that we are Navy and not hostile. Also, we expect you to get all traffic out of our way."

The officer said, "Navy 1002, I don't have any instructions regarding your landing."

The pilot responded, "You'll receive your orders when we land. This is Admiral Halsey's personal aircraft and we are here on his direct orders. I'm bringing the orders with me. We'll be down very soon. Please make sure there's nobody in our way."

Five minutes later, those closest to the head of the harbor saw an enormous aircraft landing. Although they didn't know the designation at the time, it was a Catalina PBY. This one was the first assigned to the South Pacific theater and had been assigned to Admiral Halsey. As his personal aircraft, it had clearance to go anywhere it wished within the American forces area. After landing, it taxied through the water toward the docks, and then shut down its engines. The pilot requested assistance to moor the aircraft and transport his passengers to shore.

This was such an unusual occurrence that the radio officer had long ago alerted the base commander, Captain Field. Everyone on the shore was in awe of the size of this flying boat. No one had ever seen anything like it before.

A Catalina PBY has two engines and is as big as an Air Force bomber, but it can float! It is about 65 feet long with a wingspan of over 100 feet. It is the largest amphibious plane ever commercially developed. That is why the Admiral and his staff had conferred on it the nickname "Dumbo," based on the flying elephant of Disney cartoon fame.

The base commander ordered the launch of two small boats. One was directed to tie the aircraft to an existing mooring. The other was directed toward its passenger door so that it could allow the passengers to deplane and come ashore.

The admiral's aide and his associate did not wait until the aircraft was fully moored. They just jumped aboard the launch and headed to shore.

Captain Field was awaiting them as the launch arrived at the dock.

After they had made the proper salutations, Captain Field asked, "What the hell is that airplane? I've never seen anything so big that could both fly and float."

The admiral's aide responded, "That's a Catalina PBY and they're sure pretty."

"Not just pretty, but pretty enormous," Captain Field asked, "So how come you're here and how can I help you?"

The admiral's aide said, "Well, there's some worry about Lieutenant Kennedy after what happened with the PT-109."

"Yeah," Captain Field said. "I'm afraid that Kennedy's going to be skewered for just doing what he was told to do. He's a good skipper. And he protected his crew."

The admiral's aide said, "We know that because of your report. Admiral Nimitz wants you to know that he appreciates your informing him directly about this situation. He agrees with your judgment that this situation demands a speedy resolution. I'm here to help out. Can we meet with Lieutenant Kennedy?"

"Of course," Captain Field said, enormously relieved that he wasn't in trouble for circumventing the chain of command and going directly to the top. He was proud to hear that the Admiral agreed with his judgment.

Captain Field said, "He's in his residence right now, I think. I was told by MacArthur's office not to let him go too far."

"Yeah, we know," the admiral's aide said. "But we Navy always need to protect our own, eh?"

"Yes, sir," Captain Field said. "Just jump in this jeep and we'll be there in a couple of minutes."

Soon thereafter, they arrived at the tent city that comprised all of the residences of both the officers and enlisted men on Rendova. The officers had wooden floors in their tents and some better accommodations than the enlisted men, but basically nothing was very palatial.

Captain Field pushed aside the tent flap and walked into Kennedy's tent. Jack Kennedy had been lying on a bunk resting his back. He jumped up when he saw the base commander.

Jack saluted and said, "Welcome to my humble abode. How are you, sir?"

Captain Field responded, "I'm very well, Jack. There are some folks here that I brought to see you."

Jack said, "Folks? I was hoping you brought me a new boat. I'm sort of dying here of boredom. I really want to get back into the fight."

Captain Field said, "Yeah, I know, but maybe this will resolve that problem."

Jack looked beyond him and saw the admiral's aide. The admiral's aide wore insignia to indicate he was the aide of an admiral and a Navy Captain.

The aide said to Jack, "Are you Lieutenant John F. Kennedy?" in a very official voice.

Jack stood up even more rigid, saluted and said, "Yes, Sir. Lieutenant John Fitzgerald Kennedy at your service."

The admiral's aide said to him, "Well, I'm here to recognize your role in saving the lives of several of your crew and performing a great service to your country when you were obeying all your orders with the PT-109."

The aide continued, "We are in possession of information that you fulfilled all of your orders, which included the secret extraction of an ONI operative who had been assigned to gather information regarding the Japanese positions on several nearby islands. It's apparent that because of this fulfillment of your duties, your vessel was in the line of harm and was sunk. Your performance afterwards to protect and preserve the lives of the survivors of your crew was worthy of the medal for which you are now being recommended. Before I give you the official citation, I thought you might like to meet the ONI operative you were assigned to extract."

The man behind the admiral's aide then moved into view.

Jack was astonished when Peter Sharkey moved toward him. Jack thought he was looking at a ghost, or that he was hallucinating because of the tropical heat. Jack almost fell back onto his bunk from the shock!

Peter moved forward and clasped Jack's hand in a vigorous handshake. Then Peter and Jack embraced each other, which they did quickly and then pulled apart; both kind of embarrassed because men didn't usually embrace each other, especially naval officers.

"Holy Mother of God," Jack said to Peter. "I thought you were dead."

"Yeah," Peter responded, "I was pretty worried about that myself. I've never been in the middle of a bunch of hungry sharks before. But it wasn't as bad as I feared. Hey, I'm still here."

The admiral's aide said, "Lieutenant Kennedy, Admiral Halsey has decided to recommend you for the Navy and Marine Corps Medal. This is being given to you because of meritorious service in protecting and saving the lives of your crew after the horrible sinking of your vessel, the PT-109. I'm going to give you this citation now and then I'm going to step out for a few minutes, so that you might visit with Lt. Sharkey. Please keep it brief because Lt. Sharkey needs to join me on my return trip back to Admiral Halsey's headquarters."

The admiral's aide read verbatim from the text of a wire that he held in his hand:

To Admiral C. W. Nimitz
From Admiral W. F. Halsey
C.C. Flag Officers Pacific Theater, Pentagon Distribution
Subject: Navy and Marine Corps Medal
Lieutenant, Junior Grade, John Fitzgerald Kennedy, United States Navy is recommended for the Navy and Marine Corps Medal for heroism in the rescue of three men following the ramming and sinking of his motor torpedo boat while attempting a torpedo attack on a Japanese destroyer in the Solomon Islands area on the night of August 1-2, 1943. Lieutenant Kennedy, in command of the boat, directed the rescue of the crew and personally rescued three men, one of whom was seriously injured. During the following six days, he succeeded in getting his crew ashore; and after swimming many hours, attempting to secure aid and food, finally effected the rescue of the men. His courage, endurance and excellent leadership contributed to the saving of several lives and was in keeping with the highest traditions of the United States Naval Service.

With that the aide stuck out his hand to congratulate Jack, and Jack immediately shook it. He accepted the citation with his left hand and quite frankly didn't know how else to respond, so he just remained silent. The aide turned around and headed for the door, and left Jack looking at Peter.

Jack said, "Jesus, Mary, and Joseph, I thought you were dead."

Peter said, "Yeah, I came close. I have never been so scared in all my life."

"So what happened?" Jack asked, "How the hell did you get out of there? I saw the wild frenzy the sharks were in. I thought they were ripping you to shreds."

"Well," Peter said, "I had my Ka-bar in my mouth and after doing the butterfly stroke to attract their attention and get them away from you guys, I just held my breath when they got close and dropped down. On the way down, I caught one of those shark bastards with my knife right in the belly, and I saw him start to gush blood and guts. So it attracted all the other sharks. I think I cut a couple more as they went by, and then I just held my breath and went down further. I don't know how long I was down, but I remember thinking the longer the better. When I finally surfaced, I was pretty much away from the frenzy while the sharks were feeding on each other. I hoped that you'd escaped toward the island and were onshore by then, but I couldn't tell. I tried to head back in your direction, but the current pushed me way out in the channel. Luckily, just before morning, I was able to find a passing PT boat heading back to headquarters. So I jumped on board, told them you guys were still alive somewhere, but I didn't know where. And then they sent me back to deliver the information that I had been sent to find when you dropped me off."

"Jesus," Jack said, "What the hell were you doing that you couldn't tell me about?"

"Hey, sorry, Jack," Peter said. "I still can't tell you about it. But I believe it was important."

"Okay," Jack said. "I knew you weren't there just to go for a swim. Thanks for everything. I don't know what the hell has been going on here, but the captain's been silent and no one has given me any info."

Peter said, "Jack, I don't really know what's going on either. I'm not that high up enough to know; but I think, or at least the rumor is that MacArthur wanted to court-martial you to make an example of the ineptness of the Navy. And in response Nimitz decided to get you a medal as soon as possible. I'm not saying you don't deserve it, buddy, but I think that most officers don't get their medal citation personally delivered by an Admiral's aide in a Catalina PBY in a war zone."

Jack thought about that for a moment and then said, "Yeah Peter, I think you got that right. I don't know what's going on either, but I sure hope now I finally get a new boat. Lying here on this cot is just hell for my back and even worse for my mind."

Then the door opened and one of the aircraft crewmen signaled to Peter that it was time to leave. He and Jack shook hands and gave a brief hug to each other. They vowed to keep in touch after the war.

Within ten minutes Peter was back on the launch headed for the PBY, which soon departed for Admiral Halsey's headquarters. Everyone watching the PBY's lift-off marveled that such a huge "boat" could actually take off and fly.

Jack lay back in his cot and thought that things had finally been clarified for him. Even in the midst of war, there were still divisions over politics and even Army versus Navy. He had heard that MacArthur might want to run for political office after the war as a Republican, so this was possibly a way to advance his political base. Jack learned he needed to look for a political purpose behind everything. Since he and his family were staunch Democrats, he had to consider the possibility that MacArthur wanted to attack him for a political purpose. It was an important lesson for him, one which he remembered for the rest of his life.

Back in Brisbane, General MacArthur was furious when he read the dispatch from Admiral Halsey announcing that he had recommended Lieutenant Kennedy for the Navy and Marine Corps Medal, and that the citation had already been delivered to him at Rendova.

That effectively ended MacArthur's plans to court-martial Kennedy since there was no way that the American public would tolerate the court-martial of an American hero who had already been recommended for a prestigious honor like the Navy and Marine Corps Medal.

He made a mental note to exact revenge when he was made Supreme Commander of the entire Pacific. When that happened, the commander at Rendova, Captain Field, would see his career demolished.

MacArthur was absolutely sure that he would get appointed Supreme Commander, but in fact, that never happened.

Plus if Lieutenant Kennedy ever screwed up again, MacArthur was determined to nail him to the wall even if he didn't yet have direct responsibility over that area of the Pacific. If there were a second mistake by Kennedy, MacArthur would take it as high up as necessary.

But for now, MacArthur realized that his plans had been thwarted by Admirals Nimitz and Halsey, and he decided to let this issue pass and move on.

* * * * * * * * * *

Unbeknownst to either Peter or Jack, on August 27th the U.S. 172nd Infantry landed on Arundel Island. That was the island Peter had been sent to recon, but he couldn't tell Jack that. Because the American forces had attacked from an unexpected direction that was undefended by the Japanese, the Americans enjoyed a huge element of surprise and crushed the Japanese defenders. Apparently, somehow the Americans had discovered a deep-water channel for their invasion craft in the midst of a swampy area on the south side of the island that the Japanese didn't know existed. Since a visual examination of the surface waters from the shore led one to believe it was all swampy shoals, only a swimmer actually in the water could have determined the true depths. The Japanese knew invasion craft couldn't move through swamps. But – surprise!

Only Peter would ever know how that channel was discovered.

On September 5th, the 27th Infantry arrived to reinforce the 172nd. By September 21st, Japanese General Sasaki withdrew all his remaining forces from Arundel in defeat, and even abandoned the neighboring island of Gizo, which had presented a more menacing threat to naval traffic in the area. Without Arundel, he knew he couldn't defend Gizo. The Japanese suffered 345 killed and about 500 wounded – a massive defeat, while the Americans had only minor losses. Such was the result of the element of surprise.

* * * * * * * * * *

In early October, Jack was appointed commander of a new vessel, PT-59, shortly after he'd received the citation from Admiral Halsey. So, apparently, his time in Purgatory was over!

Several weeks later, he received a mailed envelope that bore no return address. Inside, there was no letter, just part of a page torn from the *New York Times,* which was dated September 23rd. It read:

"Americans Destroy Last of Enemy on Arundel." It went on to detail the complete destruction of the Japanese garrison at Arundel. It was a massive victory for the Americans!

Jack knew this had to be from Peter, and realized that Peter's information must have been instrumental in such a successful attack on Arundel. Peter most likely found an undefended approach to the island that allowed the American forces to surprise and overwhelm the Japanese forces.

He finally felt that his former crewmembers' deaths had not been in vain. So he would be able to sleep better, no longer troubled that their deaths might have been for naught. And, he had to admit to himself, he felt a certain amount of pride in his contribution to the mission.

CHAPTER FOUR

Unfortunately, Jack's back continued to get worse, which led to his discharge from the Navy in 1945, just before the Japanese unconditional surrender. In addition to the Navy and Marine Corps Medal, he had earned a Purple Heart, the American Defense Service Medal, the American Campaign Medal, the Asian-Pacific Campaign Medal and the World War II Victory Medal.

Although Jack Kennedy and Peter Sharkey had vowed to keep in touch during their last meeting at Rendova, both the war and time interfered with that. Jack Kennedy was a prolific writer, however, and always sent Peter a letter, not just a card, at Christmastime. Peter had a fleet post office address, which meant that the Navy could always locate him and forward his mail.

Peter's responses were concise and perfunctory. Peter was an engineer and not much of a writer. However, he did respond to Jack Kennedy's letters for a few years.

Jack had lots of success to report in these annual letters. In 1946 he was elected to Congress from a Democratic district in Boston. Peter was able to report that he likewise had been successful in his career goals – he had been promoted to Lieutenant Commander.

But when Jack wrote to Peter at Christmastime in 1950, his letter was returned as undeliverable by the fleet post office. Jack's initial thought was that Peter had left the Navy and started a civilian career somewhere, but he was also somewhat concerned that there was no forwarding address available.

As a member of Congress, Kennedy had some clout with the military. He sent a letter to inquire about the whereabouts of Lieutenant Commander Sharkey.

He received a very circumspect response that provided only more questions, rather than any answers. He learned that Lieutenant Commander Sharkey was still listed as an active naval officer, but his current whereabouts were either unknown or could not be disclosed.

The Korean War had broken out the previous June, and Jack was worried that Peter was involved in that conflict and maybe had been captured or went missing in action. The letter only reinforced his concern.

Over the next two years Jack continued to send Christmas letters to Peter, but they were always returned with the same message. Jack didn't know whether his friend Peter was alive, or dead or imprisoned somewhere in Korea. Although he tried to get more information from the Navy, they were unable or unwilling to provide him with anything more than the information he already had.

Although he worried about Peter whenever he thought about him, Jack continued to concentrate on his political career. In 1952, John Fitzgerald Kennedy was elected to the Senate of the United States. This was an enormous achievement and signaled to the Democratic Party that they had a real winner on their hands. Although Jack was still young and inexperienced in the Senate, many high-level Democratic politicians started to think that he might be an eventual Presidential candidate. He had charisma, charm and he was a genuine war hero.

Jack Kennedy's personal life continued to improve just as his political career was improving. Even his health was cooperating since his back pain usually was tolerable. Although he still occasionally experienced bouts of excruciating back pain, most of the time he was able to live with it without any obvious difficulties.

The young, handsome, wealthy and successful bachelor Senator generated many rumors about his romantic escapades. His name was linked to various beautiful women, but the speculation ceased when Jack announced his engagement to the lovely Jacqueline Lee Bouvier. Jacqueline was the daughter of a wealthy family that moved in the same high-society circles as the Kennedy family. She and her family were of French extraction and were of the Catholic faith. This was perfect for Jack Kennedy, since he was Irish and also of the Catholic faith.

Their wedding was scheduled for September 12, 1953 in St. Mary's Church in Newport, Rhode Island.

Jack had strong ties to Newport because of his previous naval career. Plus, Newport is only about 60 miles from Boston and 60 miles from the Kennedy family compound on Cape Cod, so it was a perfect location from the Kennedy perspective. Jacqueline's family owned an enormous estate in Newport and had risen up in the highest social circles there for decades. It was perfect from her family's perspective also.

The wedding invitations for Jack and Jacqueline's wedding were sent to almost 600 people. It was not that they had that many relatives or friends, but Jack was a United States Senator and Jacqueline was in the high-society circle in Newport, and all their colleagues and associates expected an invitation.

St. Mary's was an old traditional Catholic church with the traditional floor plan. The pews were on both sides and the main aisle ran from the front doors to the altar. Although it was a huge church by local standards, there was no way it could contain all of the visitors that wanted to attend these nuptials.

On September 12th, the ceremony in the church was attended by a large crowd of politicians and celebrities, with almost 800 guests trying to fit into the church. People packed into the seats and also lined the side aisles, with many standing throughout the ceremony. It was the premiere event of the Newport social season.

The reception would later be held at Hammersmith Farm, which Jacqueline's family had owned for decades. Hammersmith Farm was an enormous estate right on the ocean in Newport, where she had grown up during the summers. As a young girl, she had frolicked in a seaside playhouse that was almost as large as a l ocal residence.

When Jacqueline entered the church, she was radiant in a wedding dress of ivory tissue silk with a portrait neckline, a fitted bodice and which had a bouffant skirt that was embellished with more than 50 yards of flounces. She was given away in marriage by her stepfather, Hugh D. Auchincloss. She had a rose-point lace veil, which was first worn by her grandmother Lee, and it was draped from a tiara of lace and orange blossoms. Jacqueline also wore a choker of pearls and a diamond bracelet that was a gift from Jack. The bride's bouquet was a white and pink blend of orchids and gardenias.

Senator Kennedy wore an elegant tuxedo. The wedding ceremony was performed by Archbishop Cushing, a long-time friend of the Kennedy family. He was also a Cardinal of the Catholic Church. On Church matters, he reigned supreme over the entire New England area.

Before the mass began, a special blessing from Pope Pius XII was read. At the end of the service, the crowd displayed their approval with applause as the newly married couple shared a wedding kiss.

As Jack and Jackie were exiting the church, they were smiling and searching the pews for their friends and relatives. Jack spent most of his time viewing the right side, since that is the groom's side, while Jackie was devoting her attention to the left side.

Jack was shocked just before he reached the last of the pews. There in the middle of the pew stood a handsome naval officer that Jack immediately recognized. It was Peter Sharkey!

Peter was in a full dress uniform and was giving Jack a sort of half salute/half hand wave with his raised right hand. Jack responded with a wink to let Peter know he had seen him.

Jack and Jackie had a limousine waiting outside to whisk them to Hammersmith Farm. As they were exiting the church, they were swamped by well-wishers.

Before he boarded the limo, Jack summoned one of his aides and instructed him that there was a navy officer in the church that Jack wanted to personally invite to the reception. Jack told the aide the officer had been sitting in the last pew and sent him back into the church just before the crowd filed out.

Although there were many men in uniform in the church, the aide was quite sure which one Senator Kennedy had been referring to. Most people were still backed up in the church because of the slow movement to the exit. The aide pushed counter to the crowd and approached the young naval officer. He asked, "Are you Lieutenant Commander Peter Sharkey?"

To which Peter responded, "Yes, that's me."

The aide said, "Senator Kennedy has told me that he would be most pleased if you could join him at the reception at Hammersmith Farm. Senator Kennedy said that he regrets that he was unable to send you a personal invitation, but that you have been quite difficult to find lately."

Peter laughed and told the aide, "Of course I'll be there. Please tell Senator Kennedy that I appreciate the invitation. Also tell him that he still owes me for a bet that we made years ago – and that it has now grown to a substantial sum. I came to collect the money."

The aide wasn't sure whether he was kidding or not, but thought he was. He smiled and said, "Senator Kennedy also asked that you seek him out once you arrive at the reception because he would like to meet with you privately. He hopes that will be possible."

Peter smiled and told the aide, "Of course. Tell the Senator that I'm looking forward to speaking with him."

The mansion at Hammersmith Farm sits on the crest of a hill overlooking Narragansett Bay and the Atlantic Ocean. The view across the bay toward the ocean is absolutely spectacular. The mansion is surrounded by acres of rolling lawn and fields, but the lawn was now overcrowded by vehicles delivering attendees to the reception.

Although the mansion was enormous, the crowd made it seem small. When Peter arrived, he had to push past several press people outside just to gain entrance. But once he got inside, he was relieved to find that the mansion was not nearly as crowded as he feared.

When Peter spotted Senator Kennedy in the midst of a group of well-wishers, he moved to the back of the small crowd to wait, and was pleased when Jack noticed him.

Jack excused himself from the other people and moved to Peter. They shook hands and gave each other a brief hug. Jack said, "Come on, Peter. Let's go upstairs where we can talk for a couple of minutes without interruption."

Peter didn't have time to respond before Jack turned and headed to the stairs.

Once in a private room Jack said, "Mother of God, Peter, that's the second time I thought you were dead. Where the hell have you been?"

Peter responded, "Well, as you know, the Korean conflict was pretty brutal and I've spent most of the last couple of years out there."

Jack first noticed that Peter had been promoted to full Commander. He was about to congratulate Peter on the promotion, when he realized that the ribbon on the top of Peter's chest was navy blue, then white, then navy blue again. Jack recognized this to be the Navy Cross. Jack knew this was the highest honor bestowed by the Department of the Navy, second only to the "Medal of Honor" for valor. It was a medal awarded only for combat and only for demonstrating extraordinary heroism.

Jack exclaimed, "The Navy Cross? Wow, I guess you were busy in Korea."

Peter smiled, somewhat demurely and said, "Yeah, I was only doing my job, but some folks thought that the job was kind of difficult that day."

"What day," Jack asked. "Where were you? What were you doing? Tell me the story."

Peter said, "Well, you know, most of the things I do, I can't talk about, even to a Senator, but I would just tell you that Inchon is not somewhere that I'd recommend you might want to go for a swimming vacation. And the offshore islands suck even more. My official citation is so vague, you might have thought I was in Miami Beach that day."

"Okay," Jack responded, "But someday I'll get you to tell me the whole story about the Navy Cross."

Jack then asked, "But how come you don't have the Navy and Marine Corps Medal like I do?"

Peter responded, "Well, Jack, as you know, I officially wasn't there on the PT-109, so there was no way that anyone would give me a medal for something that happened somewhere that I wasn't."

Jack responded, "But I have one, thanks to you. I wouldn't have one without you. You should have one also."

Peter answered, "Don't flatter me, buddy. You earned your medal on your own. I had absolutely nothing to do with Admirals Nimitz and Halsey granting you your medal. It was way above my level."

Jack said, "I didn't mean that you had any influence on the Brass in getting me my medal. What I meant was that if you hadn't saved my life – all of our lives – by stopping the shark attack, I wouldn't have been around to get that medal."

Peter just smiled and didn't know what to say, feeling somewhat embarrassed.

Jack continued, "Well, even if the Navy won't give you the Navy and Marine Corp Medal, I still know you deserve it. Now that you're back, we need to keep in touch, and more than just once a year.

"I was so impressed when I saw the Navy Cross that I almost forgot to congratulate you on your promotion to Commander. I am so glad that the Navy appreciates your abilities. So, congratulations on your promotion, which I am sure is more than well-deserved and probably overdue.

"I've got to get back downstairs now to continue greeting my guests, but thank you for coming today and thank you for your friendship. We definitely need to keep in touch."

Peter was kind of embarrassed by all the compliments, so all he could do was nod his agreement as he and Jack shook hands and Peter headed for the door.

Just before Peter reached the doorway, Jack called out to him, "Hey, you bastard, don't you want your dollar?"

Peter turned and saw Jack smiling and waving a dollar bill. Jack said, "There was no provision for interest in our bet. So this is all you get."

Peter was laughing as he returned to Jack and snatched the bill from Jack's hand. Peter quipped, "I never thought I'd have to follow you from Rhode Island to the South Pacific and then back to Rhode Island to collect this, but it's better late than never!"

Then they hugged each other briefly and headed out the door and downstairs. Peter kept that dollar bill for the rest of his life.

* * * * * * * * * *

It was almost two months later when Commander Peter Sharkey received a bulky envelope in the mail. The return address showed that it was from the office of Senator John Fitzgerald Kennedy. Peter opened the envelope and saw that it contained both a letter and a small object.

The object turned out to be a Navy and Marine Corp Medal. He opened the letter, which was on the official stationery of Senator John Fitzgerald Kennedy.

It read:

By the authority which has NOT been vested in me, I hereby confer upon Peter J. Sharkey the Navy and Marine Corp Medal for Extraordinary Heroism in saving the lives of the survivors of naval vessel PT-109. His courage, endurance and excellent leadership contributed to the saving of several lives and was in keeping with the highest traditions of the United States Naval Service.

Under that, Jack wrote by hand:

Peter,

I know you can't wear this since the Navy didn't give it to you, but I also know you deserve it, so here is mine. Don't worry. I had one of my aides get a replacement for me by just calling the Pentagon and telling them that I couldn't locate mine. So, now we both have one.

Thanks again for your bravery against those sharks.

Best always,
Jack

CHAPTER FIVE

THE KENNEDY PRESIDENCY

January 20, 1961, was a clear and cold, but not frigid day in Washington, DC. It would be memorable because it was the Inauguration Day of President John Fitzgerald Kennedy.

About a week after the election results had been certified and Jack Kennedy was acknowledged to be the newly elected President of the United States, Peter had received orders to report to a new position in the ONI at the Pentagon. His orders authorized him to obtain housing there immediately, but he was not required to report until February 1, 1961. Peter was pleased to receive these orders, but was not particularly surprised to get them. He knew that the new President-Elect had probably arranged for them and had certainly arranged for the invitation to the inauguration which he had received by mail.

The inauguration ceremony was being held outdoors so it could accommodate the crowd that probably topped 40,000 or 50,000 people.

Although Peter Sharkey had received an invitation to the inauguration, the invitation didn't confer on him any specific rights of seniority or placement; so he just stood in the enormous crowd and waited for the ceremony to start.

It was quite cold, and most of the men and virtually all of the women in the crowd wore overcoats. Many of the men in the crowd wore hats and he saw that some of the dignitaries beginning to assemble on the stage wore hats also; some of them top hats, which he hadn't seen in a very long time.

Peter had worn his dress uniform without an overcoat. He had gotten a hotel room nearby since that was authorized by the orders he had received. But he left his overcoat there since he thought that on this occasion, he wanted to display his Navy uniform. Although he was quite cold, he didn't really regret his decision not to wear an overcoat. He was proud to be in his uniform as the ceremony began.

When President-Elect John Fitzgerald Kennedy came to the front of the stage, he was just wearing a suit with a standard jacket. He wore no hat, nor any topcoat, despite the cold weather. When he started to speak his Oath of Office several moments later, his warm breath could be detected by the steam clouds from his mouth.

"I, John Fitzgerald Kennedy, do solemnly swear that I will faithfully execute the Office of President of the United States of America; and will to the best of my ability, preserve, protect and defend the Constitution of the United States, so help me God."

John Fitzgerald Kennedy became the 35th President of the United States of America!

President Kennedy's inaugural address started just after lunchtime on January 20th. Although it was cold, most people didn't seem to mind or be affected by the weather. They were all enthralled by the new President.

Kennedy began, "We are the heirs of the first American Revolution." But soon after, he said, "My fellow Americans, Ask not what your country can do for you. Ask what you can do for your country."

The crowd applauded enthusiastically. President Kennedy's election and his speech provided optimism and gave hope to the American public about greater days ahead. His presidency would soon be referred to by the media as the Age of Camelot, referring to the illustrious reign of King Arthur in England.

* * * * * * * * * *

Peter also had an invitation to one of the Inaugural Balls scheduled for that night. There were several balls scheduled, and this particular one was intended mostly for military types, which was just fine with Peter. He didn't want to be in a crowd of politicians.

He brought along a woman that he just recently began dating. She was a tall, statuesque and athletic blonde, but they had not yet developed any personal relationship. Peter's date, whose name was Wendy, was a lawyer and younger than he. She worked for a law firm that was a major player in lobbying Congress.

They had dated only once before, a dinner, but he didn't consider that a great success. They had met at the gym pool that they both attended, and had a physical attraction. But after their first date, Peter doubted she would accept another date with him, because she did not want to be a military wife. She wanted to be a lobbyist, and probably wanted a lawyer lobbyist for a husband.

But for their second date, Peter offered her the opportunity to go to one of the Inaugural Balls. She jumped at the chance, since it would be great water-cooler talk – and provide bragging rights over some of the other young attorneys that did not get invited to any of the Inaugural Balls.

There was no denying it – she was just astonishingly beautiful. And she turned many heads when they entered the ballroom.

They mingled in the crowd at the Ball awaiting the entrance of President Kennedy and his wife, Jackie. When Jack and Jackie Kennedy walked into the ballroom, at first everyone was silent, and then everyone broke into applause as the band played *Hail to the Chief.* Jack and Jackie moved into the crowd and mingled.

Jack wore a white bow tie, a white vest and carried a white hankie in his vest pocket. He wore a dark suit that contrasted well with his accessories. Jackie was radiant, all in white. She wore white gloves and a cape with a high collar. She had a small clutch, also in white. Her bouffant hair was flowing free, but was pulled back enough to display her magnificent earrings.

All in all, the Presidential couple looked regal-worthy to reign at the Court of Camelot.

When Jack saw Peter, he waved at him to come forward. Peter's date, Wendy, had left for the buffet table, so he headed for Jack.

Jackie had left Jack to do her own socializing, so Jack was alone when Peter met up with him. Peter said, "Jesus, Jack that is the best frigging speech I've ever heard. I almost wanted to cry myself."

Jack said, "Yeah, I'm pretty proud of it. But what about that gorgeous blonde that you have with you? Are you pooning her?"

Peter said, "I'm not getting anywhere with her. She's a lawyer and she doesn't think much about the military, but she loves this political stuff and wants to be a lobbyist. I don't think I'll ever see her again after tonight."

Jack said, "Well, if she loves politicians, maybe I can help. Just bring her around. Jackie and I will be here about, I don't know, maybe another twenty minutes. Then we have to leave for another Ball. So you'll have to come back quickly."

"Okay," Peter said.

A few minutes later President Kennedy was out on the dance floor, continuing to meet the crowd, when Peter brought his date over to meet Jack. Jackie was still elsewhere talking to other folks.

Peter introduced Wendy to the President in a formal manner. Then, also formally, he introduced the President to Wendy.

Jack reached out and shook Wendy's hand and said, "So nice to meet you. Any friend of Peter's is a friend of mine."

Then Jack lowered his head in a very conspiratorial manner and whispered in her ear, "Did Peter tell you that he saved my life during the war?"

Wendy's eyes went wide and her face popped up at Jack. "No," she said, "Really?"

Jack, still in a whisper, said "Neither of us can talk about this because it's top secret, but it's the truth."

Wendy said, "I don't know what to say."

"Well," Jack continued, "During World War II, Peter was on a secret mission for the Navy, and I was in command of the boat we were on. But then, things got really nasty and Peter risked his life to save mine. I know Peter has a Medal for his heroism, since I personally awarded it to him. But it's so secret that he can't even wear it in public. That's absolutely all I can say. I've already said too much. And you must never divulge what I said to you. I know I can trust you. That's just between us."

To herself, she thought, "*Wow.*"

Then she exclaimed, "Of course, Mr. President, you can trust that I would never divulge anything you told me in confidence."

Jack continued, "I just wanted you to know that Peter is very important to me."

And then she was quiet, but she did grab Peter's arm tightly and start to rub his shoulder affectionately.

Jack winked at Peter and said, "Peter, I'll talk to you soon. Jackie and I have to leave now for some other Balls."

As he departed, Jack said, "Nice meeting you Wendy, and I hope we'll see more of you at the White House." Then he gave Peter another wink and left.

Wendy was overwhelmed by the President's comments. She said to Peter, "I'm kind of worn out by the crowd here, and I think we should go back to my apartment so I can get more comfortable."

Peter said, "Of course. Are you getting tired?"

Wendy said, "I'm not at all tired, and I hope you're not going to be tired either. I want this to be a long, long night. It's already memorable to me, but I want to be sure it's memorable for you too. Can we go now?"

Peter was smiling in anticipation of what Wendy had promised. He tried to prevent his voice from quivering in anticipation as he responded, "I'm ready. Let's go."

And then Peter thought to himself, "*THANK YOU, JACK!*"

* * * * * * * * * *

Immediately after his inauguration, Jack Kennedy assumed the responsibilities of President of the United States. For the next week he had non-stop meetings with the heads of all of the various agencies that now reported to him.

When the Director of the Central Intelligence Agency met with him, President Kennedy learned for the first time about the extensive preparations that had been made for a clandestine invasion of Cuba. This was ostensibly to be an invasion by Cuban exiles trying to retake their homeland and rescue it from the government of Fidel Castro.

President Kennedy had more questions than the CIA was able to answer, but this entire operation was proceeding under its own momentum like an unstoppable juggernaut that had been approved by the prior administration. Since President Kennedy was never one to back down from a fight, he decided to support the effort even though he had not been able to participate in, nor amend, the plans.

But President Kennedy did request that the CIA provide him with more details about the invasion plans.

At the next meeting with the CIA, President Kennedy had Commander Sharkey in attendance. It was not that President Kennedy thought that Peter Sharkey was an expert on invasions; he just wanted someone there that he trusted, so that he could discuss it with him afterwards.

At the meeting, President Kennedy learned more details about the planned invasion. It was to begin on the night of April 15th. He learned the Cuban exiles had been given eight Douglas B-26B Invader Bombers, which they planned to use to attack three major Cuban airfields. These B-26s had been prepared by the CIA and had been painted with the markings of the Cuban air force.

This would be followed by the invasion force that would land at the Bay of Pigs. The invasion force would be led by two CIA vessels, each containing a CIA operations officer and an underwater demolition team of five frogmen. Behind them would be the main invasion force of exiled troops that would be on four transport ships. The transport ships would also include tanks and other vehicles.

The United States aircraft carrier USS Essex was to patrol offshore and to be ready to launch massive airstrikes to support the invasion force. But the CIA was sure that this would not be necessary since they were convinced that, as soon as the exiles landed on Cuban soil, they would be greeted joyously by the Cuban people and would face almost no opposition. This proved to be disastrously wrong.

After the meeting, President Kennedy asked, "Well, Peter, what do you think about these plans? Are they going to succeed?"

Peter said, "I don't know, Jack. It seems to me like this whole thing depends on the reaction of the Cuban people to succeed. I saw some of the news reports after Castro's victory over Batista and the Cuban people seemed very much behind him. I also think that they're launching this invasion with very few aircraft, ships and troops. Obviously, I could be wrong, but this just doesn't seem like it's destined for success."

President Kennedy said, "Peter, that's exactly what I was thinking. I think these CIA folks have just gotten so carried away with their plans that they're basing their predictions on dreams. But it's so far along, I just don't think I can call it off. On the other hand, I don't want to risk any more American lives than those that the CIA is already putting at risk. I want you to be on the USS Essex while the invasion is beginning. I don't want to commit any aircraft from the carrier if things are already going badly."

Peter responded, "Of course, Jack. Just get my orders issued and I'll have plenty of time to go down to Florida and spend some time with the commanding officer of the Essex."

President Kennedy repeated, "This whole thing just doesn't seem right to me and I don't want to risk any of the airmen on the Essex in a situation that has no hope."

Peter said, "Jack, I understand and I'll let you know about everything that's happening."

President Kennedy said, "I'll get you a top security clearance so that anything you radio back to me will not be shared with anyone else. Also, I think you'll get more cooperation as a Captain, rather than a Commander. Congratulations on your promotion, Captain Sharkey, which you more than deserve. The paperwork has been in process for a couple of weeks, but I made a call today to speed everything up. I've got your new insignia here and it would be my pleasure to pin them on you."

Peter was surprised by this unexpected promotion, but just said, "I really appreciate the promotion, Jack. You know I'm a career Navy guy, so it's nice to know that I'm moving up in the ranks."

Jack responded, "You'll be an Admiral someday and I'm sure you'll be one of the best in the Fleet. And I want you to know that you were already on the promotion list, so I didn't influence that. I just sped things up. You worked for this promotion and you deserve it. Plus you have the Navy Cross, which obviously impresses the Promotions Board. In fact, it impresses everyone, including me."

Peter was too embarrassed by the compliments to say much, so he just replied, "I'm ready to get to work now, Jack. I'll talk to you soon."

They shook hands and shared a quick hug. President Kennedy said, "Godspeed, Peter. Talk to you soon."

* * * * * * * * * *

The Bay of Pigs Invasion started right on schedule on April 15, 1961, but that was the only thing that went as planned. The bombers controlled by the Cuban exiles attacked their targets, but although they scored several hits that destroyed Cuban aircraft, they were not able to really weaken the Cuban air force. Not that the Cubans really needed air support, since they had overwhelming land forces.

Invasion day on April 17, 1961 saw all of the invading forces able to at least land on Cuban soil, but that was about the only success that they ever achieved. Despite some small advances away from their beachhead, the expected support from the Cuban populous never occurred, and the response from the Cuban land forces was disastrous to the invaders.

On board the USS Essex, Captain Sharkey learned that 12 A4-2 Sky Hawks had been loaded aboard. These planes were from the attack squadron VA-34, which was known as the Blue Blasters. These planes were armed with 20-millimeter cannons and were to be used to support the invasion. During the voyage from Jacksonville, Florida toward Cuba, all of their identifying markings had been crudely obscured with flat gray paint. The planes began flying mysterious missions day and night and some of them may have been sent into Cuban airspace.

Captain Sharkey had been privy to all of the actions on the beach in Cuba and had learned that things were not going well. He used his security clearance to demand a radio connection to the Office of the President.

When Peter was finally connected to President Kennedy, he said, "Jack, this is just a disaster. These Cuban exiles have no will to fight and the Cuban populous supports Castro, not the exiles. Despite what you may be hearing from the CIA, this is just going to be a rout of the invaders."

President Kennedy responded, "Thanks, Peter. I knew I could rely on you for the truth. I don't want to risk any of the airmen on the Essex in this futile gesture. I'm going to issue an order immediately to make sure that the aircraft on the Essex are not used in this venture. I'm going to take care of that right now, Peter. I'll see you when you get back. Thanks again."

Peter said, "Bye, Jack," but the connection was already broken.

* * * * * * * * * *

Accordingly, the naval aviation part of the mission was aborted by President Kennedy at the last moment, and the entire crew of the Essex was sworn to secrecy.

President Kennedy was disenchanted and angered by the failure of the CIA, and later declared to some of his staff in private that he wanted to "splinter the CIA in a thousand pieces and scatter it to the winds."

Kennedy later commented to his friend, Ben Bradlee, who was a journalist, "The first advice I'm going to give my successor is to watch the generals and to avoid feeling that, because they were military men, their opinions on military matters were worth a damn."

This was great advice, but unfortunately, neither President Kennedy nor his successor President Johnson followed it when it came to the developing conflict in Vietnam.

There was a secretive group within the CIA, however, that blamed the failure of the Cuban invasion on Kennedy's weakness in not committing the air power of the U.S.S. Essex as they expected. They decided to develop plans to eliminate the President with Extreme Prejudice!

CHAPTER SIX

MARILYN MONROE

Peter Lawford was a handsome English actor who immigrated into the United States during the Second World War. Lawford, at age 14, had severely injured his right arm and was exempt from serving in the military. Since many of the major American actors such as Clark Gable and James Stewart were away at war, Lawford quickly rose to be one of the major romantic leads in films that were being produced by MGM.

He appeared with Frank Sinatra for the first time in a musical called "It Happened in Brooklyn," which was produced in 1947. After that, Lawford and Sinatra became close friends.

In fact, Lawford became one of a group of close celebrity friends that came to be known as the "Rat Pack." The members included Peter Lawford, Frank Sinatra, Dean Martin, Sammy Davis, Jr., and Joey Bishop. They were notorious for being a hard-partying group with high profile friends and associates.

In 1954, the handsome British actor married Patricia Kennedy, the sister of then-Senator John F. Kennedy.

Peter and Patricia Lawford had a house on the beach in Santa Monica, California. In October, 1961, they hosted a beach party and barbeque and invited many of their celebrity friends and family.

They invited President Kennedy and his wife Jackie, but really didn't expect either of them to show up. But President Kennedy called to let Peter know that he was planning to attend the gala.

The President's wife Jackie, however, had other responsibilities. She had borne a daughter to them in 1957. The daughter's name was Caroline Bouvier Kennedy and she was now only about four years old. Jackie had also borne a son, John Fitzgerald Kennedy, Jr. in 1960. The baby was born just about two weeks after President Kennedy had beaten his opponent, Richard Nixon, in the Presidential Election.

Jackie had decided to limit her travels to only those events that were most important for Jack's political future. She was a great mother who took her responsibilities very seriously. She did not want to leave her children in the care of nannies or sitters or even relatives, without a good reason. So a trip to a beach house barbeque did not meet Jackie's strict criteria. Therefore, she stayed home while President Kennedy attended alone.

There were a number of celebrities in attendance at the Lawford party, including Marilyn Monroe. When President Kennedy got there, the party was in full swing and he tried to make a quiet entrance. But naturally, that is not really possible for the President of the United States, who always arrives with a Secret Service detail to protect him, even though the Secret Service tries to be as unobtrusive and "invisible" as possible to minimize any intrusion at an event.

Once Jack arrived, several party attendees rushed over to speak to the President. President Kennedy met with each of them briefly and was very polite as always.

But he had spotted a gorgeous woman that he knew had to be Marilyn Monroe. He didn't want to rush through his conversations with the other attendees, but he really did want to meet Marilyn Monroe.

When he finally had the chance, Jack approached the gorgeous blonde woman and said, "Excuse me, but I wanted to say hello. I'm Jack Kennedy and you must be Marilyn Monroe?"

Marilyn turned around and batted her eyes flirtatiously as she said, "That's right. I'm Marilyn, and are you the Jack Kennedy that might just happen to be the President of the United States?" She asked the question so flirtatiously that Jack was caught a little bit off-guard.

Being a politician, however, he was used to making speedy recoveries. Jack said, "Well, that's my job right now, but four years from now I could be unemployed after the next election."

Marilyn laughed at his response and said, "I can't believe that Americans would be so stupid as to not re-elect a great-looking guy like you."

Jack responded, "Well, that's very nice of you to say, Miss Monroe, but I…"

At that Marilyn Monroe cut him off and said, "Please, Mr. President, call me Marilyn."

To which Jack responded, "Well, of course. I'd love to call you Marilyn, but only if you'll agree to call me Jack. Mr. President sounds way too formal."

They both smiled enticingly at each other. Now that they had begun this friendly banter, they spent most of the rest of the afternoon talking to each other. Although they were sometimes interrupted by other visitors approaching either one of them, they always gravitated back to each other.

At the end of the party, Marilyn and Jack gave each other a warm hug and suggested that they should keep in touch. Both of them expressed the wish that they might meet again.

They did meet again, but it was quite a bit later than either of them had thought. They spoke occasionally on the telephone during the period before their next meeting. They met again on March 24, 1962 at Bing Crosby's estate in Palm Springs, California. Although Bing Crosby was not an official member of the "Rat Pack," he was a noted celebrity who was friends with all of the members of the "Rat Pack," as well as numerous other Hollywood stars. It was at Bing Crosby's estate that President Kennedy and Marilyn Monroe began their affair. They were able to slip away from the party crowd at Crosby's estate and to find some privacy at a hotel not far away.

After that, the affair started to heat up with more frequent telephone calls between Marilyn and Jack. They were able to arrange another secret meeting during April, 1962.

Then on May 19, 1962 a gala celebration of President John F. Kennedy's 45th birthday was scheduled at Madison Square Garden. This party included numerous celebrities, various high-level campaign contributors, and a huge crowd that filled the entire arena. The media later reported that the attendees totaled over 17,000.

President Kennedy arrived with his Secret Service entourage and greeted many of the attendees as he made his way to his assigned seat. Once again, his wife Jackie did not attend since she preferred to be taking care of her children.

Peter Lawford was the Master of Ceremonies for the event, which also featured several other celebrities. The entertainers included Jack Benny, Maria Callas, Ella Fitzgerald, Jimmy Durante, Peggy Lee – and Marilyn Monroe.

With what he estimated to be about 20-to-30 minutes before Marilyn was scheduled to appear, President Kennedy left his assigned seat to head to the men's room – or maybe somewhere else.

Marilyn had just completed her makeup and was almost ready to head to the stage when she heard a knock on her dressing room door. She said, "Come in."

She was surprised and pleased when Jack Kennedy entered. Marilyn exclaimed, "I didn't think you'd be here now. Everybody's watching you out there, and I'm supposed to be onstage in about 20 minutes."

Jack said, "I know, but I just couldn't be this close to you and only see you onstage."

Marilyn asked coyly, "And why would that be?"

Jack said, "Well, you know why. I just hoped to get at least a kiss from you before the night is over."

Then Jack continued, "God, Marilyn, is that a dress or just your skin with decorations on it?"

Marilyn responded, "Do you like it, baby? I asked them to make it really close-fitting."

Jack said, "Close-fitting? It couldn't be any tighter than if it wasn't there."

Marilyn said, "I know, there's no room under the dress for any underwear, so I'm quite naked under this dress, just for you."

Hearing that Jack moved quickly to embrace her. He gave her a deep kiss while his arms encircled her and confirmed that, in fact, she was quite naked under the dress.

Jack had not planned on anything more than a brief, intimate moment with Marilyn, since thousands of people were waiting in the Garden for her performance. But after feeling her warm body next to his, he couldn't resist running his hand up to caress her breast.

As she had said, Marilyn was not wearing a brassiere, and her breasts were soft and warm and supple within the flimsy fabric of the gown. Her nipple immediately grew hard from Jack's caress.

Marilyn moaned from the caress and used one hand to pull his head and his mouth even tighter to hers as they shared an erotic kiss.

Marilyn was breathing heavily as she used her other hand to grab Jack's buttocks and pull his body close to hers. In truth, Marilyn had been having erotic daydreams about Jack as she had been preparing for this performance. The thought of going in front of thousands of people wearing only a skin-tight dress and no underwear was just so hypersexual that she was more than ready when Jack showed up at her dressing room.

Jack was becoming incredibly excited by the fact that Marilyn was naked inside this dress. He used one hand to reach down to caress her between the thighs and she immediately started to tremble.

Jack knew that he should get back to his seat in the audience, but he just couldn't pull himself away from Marilyn. She pulled her mouth free of Jack's and said, "Now, Jack. Do me now."

That was all the encouragement Jack needed. He yanked the dress up, intending to pull it up to her waist, but the dress was designed for her to step into it, and was way too tight to fit up over her ample thighs.

That didn't stop Jack. He just tugged even harder and succeeded in getting the dress up to Marilyn's waist, but the cost was that Jack had ripped the back seam of the dress. Both Marilyn and Jack heard the seam tear as the dress gave up its confinement and allowed Jack access to Marilyn's womanhood.

There is something primal and erotic about a man tearing the clothes off a woman when neither of them can wait to consummate their union. It just further inflamed their passion.

Marilyn fell back onto one of the dressing-room tables, while Jack quickly dropped his trousers and thrust deeply into her. Marilyn emitted a quick scream at the thrill while Jack immediately began a vigorous, rhythmic movement. It took only a few minutes until Marilyn and Jack joined together in a momentous climax.

Marilyn was left quivering, while Jack's knees almost gave out. Luckily, his bad back had not failed him and he was still able to remain standing after this incredible encounter.

They remained locked together in a sexual embrace for another moment or so until they both remembered that thousands of people were awaiting Jack's return and Marilyn's performance.

Jack gave Marilyn a sweet kiss as he withdrew and started to pull up his trousers.

Marilyn noted something as Jack began to get dressed. She said, "Jack, honey, didn't you wear a safety?" (This was a common term for the latex condoms that were used by men during the 1950's and 1960's).

Jack said, "Jesus, Marilyn, I never expected anything to happen tonight. I thought that we didn't have time, and so I was only coming down to say hello. Not that I'm not incredibly happy about what just happened, but I didn't plan it. Or prepare for it with some safeties."

Marilyn was quietly worried, but she sought to reassure Jack by saying, "Okay, Baby, don't worry about it. I'm sure everything will be fine and I know a few tricks to take care of it that I'll do later. Now you better get going and get back to your seat."

Jack said, "Okay, you're right. I'm leaving now." And then he leaned over and kissed Marilyn again warmly on the lips as he headed out of the dressing room.

Marilyn was sure that if she just took a warm bath and did a thorough cleansing of her private areas, she'd be able to prevent any pregnancy problems. This had always worked for her in the past, and she knew it must work since she had never gotten pregnant.

In fact, right now she was more worried about her biggest problem which was the torn gown. She rushed to the door, now that the President was gone, and yelled to summon her assistant.

Once the assistant showed up and saw the problem, she immediately left to find a needle and thread to sew Marilyn back into the gown.

Peter Lawford, as the emcee, was at a loss to understand why Marilyn was so late in arriving on stage. He knew she was in the theater. He made a play on the actress's lateness by giving her several introductions throughout the night. But until the last one, she didn't appear. When she finally came onto the stage very late, Peter Lawford introduced her as "the late Marilyn Monroe."

Marilyn was gorgeous as she took the stage, and the dress was stupendous. It was made of a sheer and flesh-colored marquisette fabric with over 2,000 rhinestones sewn onto it. The dress was so tight-fitting that, under the stage spotlights, the fabric seemed to disappear leaving only the glitter of the rhinestones brilliant on Marilyn's skin.

One of the famous politicians in attendance, Adlai Stevenson, was later to describe the dress as composed only of "skin and beads." But what wasn't obvious to the audience was that it was also composed of loops and loops of thread that Marilyn's assistant had used to sew her into it and repair the back seam.

The highlight of Marilyn's performance was when she sang "Happy Birthday" to President Kennedy. Her voice was unusually husky and sultry because of the intense encounter she just had with the President.

Marilyn sang the traditional "Happy Birthday To You," lyrics, but inserted "Mr. President" as Kennedy's name. She sang, in a cooing, sexy and erotic voice:

"Happy birthday to you,

Happy birthday to you,

Happy birthday, Mr. President,

Happy birthday to you."

When Marilyn concluded her performance, she slowly exited the stage, being careful not to rip the seam of the dress again.

Afterwards Jack came on stage and joked about the song. He said, "I can now retire from politics after having had 'Happy Birthday' sung to me in such a sweet, wholesome way."

He was obviously joking about the sexy delivery of the song by Marilyn in her racy dress. Both Marilyn and Jack left New York after that birthday party with great memories of their tryst. But Marilyn also left with something else that she didn't yet suspect.

* * * * * * * * *

After that sensational sexual encounter with Jack at Madison Square Garden, Marilyn became even more enamored of the President. He made her feel more alive than she had felt in years, and she approached their affair somewhat like a schoolgirl. It was not that she was naïve, but she ignored some important facts. Like the fact that the President was married with children.

Marilyn was somewhat embarrassed when she realized that she had not gotten a birthday gift for Jack. She smiled, however, as she thought, *"Well, I guess he got his birthday gift in my dressing room."*

But Marilyn decided to get him a real gift also. She purchased a watch, an expensive watch, and had it engraved with "Jack, with love as always, from Marilyn." And below that she had the date inscribed, "May 29, 1962." She arranged for it to be delivered to Jack at the White House.

One of his aides opened the package and saw that it included both the watch and a handwritten poem that was titled, "A Heartfelt Plea On Your Birthday." Although the aide wasn't sure whether he should read the poem or not, he did anyway. It ended with, "Let me love or let me die." The aide brought it to President Kennedy privately. After Jack had a chance to both read the poem and look at the watch, he handed them back to the aide. The aide was somewhat puzzled and said, "Mr. President, what do you want me to do with this?"

The President responded, "Get rid of it. I can't risk my wife seeing it."

The aide knew he was dismissed, but it was so sudden, he hadn't asked for any specific instructions as to how to "get rid of it." So the aide tore up the poem, but kept the watch. He didn't see any reason to destroy such a valuable watch and since the President didn't want it, he figured he might as well keep it himself.

Jack and Marilyn continued to have frequent, although not daily, telephone calls. Finally during the second week of July, Jack and Marilyn met once again at Peter Lawford's house. By now, Marilyn had missed her period and was quite sure that she was pregnant. She had also noticed that her breasts, already ample, seemed to be getting even larger, and she thought that she might be developing a very slight bulge in her abdomen.

Marilyn wanted to tell Jack about her suspected pregnancy, but she didn't quite know how to do it. Jack was talking about all his political plans and how he was already planning his re-election campaign. Marilyn knew that any public disclosure of her pregnancy would destroy both her career and Jack's.

So Marilyn kept her secret inside and acted as if nothing was wrong. After lunch, Marilyn and Jack spent the entire afternoon in bed. Possibly because of her condition and her changing hormones, Marilyn had developed a voracious sexual appetite. Jack proved to be not only willing, but also much more than able to fulfill all of her needs.

When they parted at the end of the day, they both pledged to get together again soon. But they both had busy schedules, so they would have to wait to see how things developed before they could schedule another meeting.

But once Marilyn was left alone, she privately began to dread her next meeting with Jack. She knew that if her suspicions were correct and she was pregnant, by the next time they got together that fact would be apparent to Jack. She didn't know how he would react. In fact, she didn't know how she herself was ready to react to this fact.

Although she had always wanted children, this unplanned, unexpected pregnancy was causing her extreme duress. She didn't know if she could handle the public embarrassment and she certainly didn't want to destroy Jack's career – or his marriage. She just didn't know what she should do.

CHAPTER SEVEN

THE MONROE CONSIPIRACY

It was before dawn on the morning of Sunday, July 29, 1962 when Frank Sinatra was awakened in the Executive Suite by a telephone call from the switchboard operator. He was the listed owner of the property, the Cal-Neva Lodge and Casino. Cal-Neva was a resort and casino straddling the border between California and Nevada on the shores of Lake Tahoe. Although Sinatra was listed on all the official documents including the gambling license for the casino as the owner, the government suspected that he was actually just a front man for Chicago mobster Sam Giancana.

Giancana, because of his background, could never have gotten a gambling license for this facility. But Sinatra, with his clean background and celebrity status, easily won the license when he bought the place. It was widely known that Sinatra and Giancana were close friends and there was an open secret that during the 1940s, Giancana had helped Sinatra expand his career.

The story was that Sinatra was under contract to bandleader Tommy Dorsey. Sinatra's career seemed to be just on the verge of skyrocketing, but if he had to be subjugated to the terms of the contract to Dorsey, that would be the end of his success. It was widely rumored that Giancana had accosted Dorsey, held a gun to his head, produced a release from the contract and said, "You put your signature on this or I'll put your brains all over it."

In any case, whether the story was true or not, Dorsey released Sinatra from his contract and Sinatra's career had skyrocketed upward ever since.

Sinatra answered the phone and said, "What the hell? It's early."

The hotel operator answered, "The house physician is on the line and would like to speak to you."

"Okay," Sinatra said, "Put him through." A moment later after a couple of clicks, he heard the doctor come on the line.

"Mr. Sinatra, I'm sorry to bother you, sir, but one of our guests at the resort attempted suicide tonight."

Sinatra knew that would be very bad publicity for any resort, and no one would ever stay in a hotel room if they'd learned that someone had died there in the past. So he was about to tell the doctor to remove the stiff in a way that looked like the patient was wearing an oxygen mask and had just suffered a heart attack. Resort visitors didn't care if somebody had been transported to a hospital and died there; they just didn't want to sleep in a room where someone had died.

But the doctor continued, "The guest took a large quantity of depressants along with alcohol, but I was able to pump her stomach and remove most of the pills. Some were still intact and had not dissolved, which probably saved her life."

Sinatra said, "So if everything's okay, why did you bother calling me this late?"

The doctor responded, "Mr. Sinatra, this guest is one of your personal friends."

Sinatra thought for a moment and said, "Oh. Which one?"

The doctor responded, "Miss Monroe, sir. And she's made some comments that I think you should hear."

"Holy shit," Frank Sinatra thought. *"Marilyn tried to kill herself here and there's something that the doc wants me to know. None of this could be good."*

Sinatra said to the doc, "Meet me in the lobby right now and we'll go outside to discuss this."

Sinatra pulled on a pair of trousers and a shirt and ran downstairs as quickly as possible. He never even stopped to tie the laces on his shoes.

The physician reported that Marilyn had attempted suicide, but now regretted her actions and vowed to never again attempt suicide. She was most remorseful for having tried to kill the baby that was developing inside her. She wanted some way out of this terrible situation, but didn't know what to do.

After the doctor had told him everything he had learned, Sinatra promised him a bonus for his wisdom and his silence, and then headed up to Marilyn's room.

By then, Marilyn had recovered somewhat from the drug overdose and was able to respond to the questions Sinatra posed to her.

Marilyn told him that she was disgusted with her previous life; although she had attained great fame she didn't want to live the Hollywood life anymore. But she had decided that trying to kill herself was stupid, weak and absolutely unfair to her unborn baby. She realized that she only wanted to be a great mother to her new baby.

Sinatra listened as she poured out her soul to him about why she had made this attempt to kill herself. She was so desperate and so helpless that Sinatra's heart went out to her. He knew he would help her regardless of what was needed.

Sinatra called his friend Giancana. Between them, they developed a plan that they thought would resolve Marilyn's situation. Sinatra discussed it with her and she agreed and asked him to proceed with it.

Sinatra spoke to Giancana again and they agreed that this would be pretty easy to arrange. Giancana could arrange all of the local actions, but neither of them knew how to arrange Marilyn's exit from California. They decided to proceed anyway and await any further developments.

Sinatra next called Peter Lawford, his friend in the "The Rat Pack." Lawford was also the brother-in-law of the Kennedys.

After learning all he could from Sinatra, Lawford called his brother-in-law, Robert Kennedy. Lawford had called him because Bobby was the most accessible of all the Kennedy confidants, and he was also the one that everyone recognized to be the most intelligent. In fact, Jack Kennedy, in private, had frequently mentioned how much he trusted his brother's intelligence and analytical skills.

When Bobby Kennedy got the call from Peter Lawford, he had a hard time coming to grips with the enormity of the situation. Lawford told him Marilyn Monroe had attempted suicide, and the reason she had done it was because she was pregnant and the father was his brother, Jack Kennedy. Bobby asked Peter Lawford for all the details.

Lawford explained, "Marilyn said that she was fed up with her Hollywood life. She was ashamed about being treated as nothing more than a sexual object, and that she couldn't subject herself to the shame and embarrassment of her pregnancy. Furthermore, she knew that if it were divulged, it would be the end of Jack's career – and probably his marriage. She just didn't want that to happen, so she thought suicide was the only way out."

There were several more telephone conversations back and forth between Bobby Kennedy, Peter Lawford and Frank Sinatra that day.

Finally, they all agreed upon a plan so that Marilyn could achieve her objectives. And, cover up for the President!

* * * * * * * * * *

It was almost midnight on Sunday, July 29, 1962 when President Kennedy heard his private phone ringing. The President was awake and reading reports in his office in his rocking chair. Sometimes the pain in his back was so severe that he couldn't sleep, so he would move to the office and read in the rocking chair. For whatever reason, the rocking motion seemed to reduce the pain.

He got up from the rocking chair slowly, and then moved to the desk to answer his private phone. He picked it up and just said, "Hello."

Although it was a secure line, he never knew if the White House switchboard might have inadvertently sent him the wrong call. But this call was definitely for him. It was his brother, Robert F. Kennedy, the Attorney General of the United States and Jack's closest confidant and most trusted advisor. Bobby, as he always did, said, "Jack, it's Bobby."

Although Bobby was quite confident that Jack would recognize his voice, they had been both schooled well in the social graces and had always been told to identify themselves at the beginning of telephone calls.

Jack said, "Hi, Bobby. I guess this must be important if you're up so late."

Bobby responded, "Jack, this is VERY important, but I want you to know that we have already developed a plan to resolve the situation."

Jack chuckled and said, "That's what I love about you, Bobby. You always come to me with an answer before you've presented me with a question."

Bobby said, "Well, brother, this is a bad situation and I hope that we can make this all work."

Jack was suddenly concerned by the tone of his brother's voice. Jack queried, "Okay, Bobby, it sounds like you've got bad news. What is it?"

Bobby said, "I've spent several hours talking with Peter Lawford. He's had several discussions with Frank Sinatra, who's out at the Cal-Neva Ranch and they have developed a plan to address this problem."

Jack knew about the resort that Bobby was referencing, since he had been there. It was a favorite destination of Hollywood celebrities and several less desirable types from the criminal underworld.

In fact, Jack felt a sudden trepidation since he quickly remembered that Marilyn Monroe was scheduled to visit there that weekend.

Jack asked Bobby, "Okay, I guess I'm ready for the news. What has Peter been talking to Frank about?"

"Marilyn was there this weekend," Bobby said. "And last night she attempted suicide."

"What?" Jack interjected. "Is she okay? What's going on? Why did she do that?"

Bobby said, "Calm down, Jack. I told you, I think we've got everything under control. I'm going to give you as much information as I can. Right now she seems to be doing fine. Peter told me that Frank's doctor pumped her stomach and removed all the pills and gave her a shot of something to revive her."

Jack said, "Are you sure she's going to be okay? I mean, that sounds pretty serious."

Bobby reassured him, "Peter said she's been awake and conscious all afternoon and talking to Frank to plan an alternative to her suicide."

"What do you mean?" Jack said. "An alternative? Why doesn't she just go back to Hollywood and resume her career?"

Bobby said, "Well, here's where it gets complex, Jack. It's not so simple. She can't just go back to Hollywood and resume her career as if nothing was going on, because quite soon she is going to be showing. She is pregnant."

Jack's mouth suddenly went dry and he almost croaked when he asked, "Bobby, is it me?"

Bobby responded, "She told Frank that she had not been with any other men in a long time and the baby is yours."

"Jesus, Mary and Joseph," Jack said. "I had no idea."

Bobby then said, "Well, that's one of the reasons that Marilyn decided to commit suicide. First of all, she couldn't bear the shame when it became publically known that she was about to have a child out of wedlock. But also she told Frank that she couldn't destroy your career and your marriage once the truth came out. The only alternative she saw was to kill herself."

Jack said, "Oh, my god, Bobby. She is so sweet and so caring. I never intended for anything like this to happen to her."

Bobby said, "Well, on the good side Marilyn is alive and recovering. Plus she has come up with a new plan of her own. She and Frank spent the afternoon talking about options. Marilyn is deeply ashamed about the suicide attempt since that would end up killing her baby. She said that she's always wanted children and that was the most important thing in her life in the past, and she wanted it to be the most important thing again. She doesn't have any further interest in her Hollywood life, but just wants to live a simple life where she can take care of her baby.

"She and Frank have come up with a plan to explain her disappearance. Obviously, she's such a great star she can't just walk out without the media tracking her down.

"So she and Frank developed a plan to stage a fake suicide. As you know, Frank's partner in the Cal-Neva resort is Sam Giancana. Giancana apparently has some connections that might be helpful in this plan."

Bobby continued, "Jack, you know Giancana is Mafia. If you and I get involved in this, we need to distance ourselves from Giancana as much as possible."

Jack responded, "Of course, Bobby. But it sounds to me like we're pretty desperate; at least I'm pretty desperate right now. Tell me the rest."

Bobby continued, "Marilyn and Frank worked out a plan for a fake suicide. She said Giancana would provide a dead body-double from one of the unfortunate nameless drug fatalities that occur every day in either Los Angeles or Las Vegas. There are plenty of blonde drug-addicted prostitutes and hookers that pass away each day in those cities, and Giancana knows that he could easily get one of his associates to deliver a body that resembled Marilyn's to her residence in L.A."

"Marilyn is sure that her long-term housekeeper will be able to keep her part in the plot. The housekeeper has always known how to keep a secret and Marilyn has promised her sufficient funds so that she will never need to work again. A lifetime annuity if you will.

"Also, Giancana apparently has people on the take in the LAPD and the coroner's office. Once the body arrives at Marilyn's residence, it will be identified as Marilyn and rushed through the process."

Jack questioned Bobby further. "Well, okay, even assuming that they can do the switch and the contact in the coroner's office is able to pull this off, where's Marilyn going to go and how the hell could she even get out of town without being recognized?"

Bobby said, "As soon as they have a body available, Marilyn will cut and dye her hair. She'll buy some plain new clothes for the trip. She said that she needs to leave the country because she would never feel safe from the media as long as she still lives here."

Bobby continued, "So I've contacted our cousin, Michael Brady, in Ireland. As you know, our family has been subsidizing our relatives over there for years and it's about time that they've repaid the favor."

Jack said, "Ireland? Well, that sounds like a good idea; at least we can trust our relatives to keep quiet about this. But how the hell is she going to get over there without being detected?"

Bobby said, "Well, Marilyn has told Frank and Peter that she thinks that she can arrange to get there on her own and that she can do it undetected. But she will need entry documents, like a new passport and things that we'll need to get for her."

Jack said, "Bobby, I don't see where I have any choice in this. What you've worked out sounds good to me, but how do we get her the documents, and what about someone going with Marilyn from L.A. to Ireland?"

Bobby said, "Well, we haven't worked that out yet. But you're right; she'll need somebody with her along the way, particularly when she gets to Ireland."

Jack said, "Okay, I'm calling Peter Sharkey right now. I don't know where he is, but I want him to come here so I can explain the whole situation to him. He's the only one that I trust to do something like this and I'm sure that he won't disappoint me."

Bobby said, "I think we're going to be able to fix this. I'll let you know as soon as I hear anything more. And let me know after you've gotten in touch with Peter Sharkey."

Jack said, "Thanks, Bobby. I really appreciate everything you do for me."

CHAPTER EIGHT

Sam Giancana had lived his entire life outside the law. He was born in Little Italy in Chicago from Sicilian immigrant parents. His early upbringing led him directly into a life with the Mafia.

He gained a lot of notoriety from the Mob during the late 1930s because of his knack for making money on the street and being an excellent "wheel man" with a get-away car. He also developed a reputation as a vicious killer. Then in 1942, he gained extra prestige when the story circulated how he had pressured bandleader Tommy Dorsey into letting upcoming singer Frank Sinatra out of his contract early.

Giancana was one of the attendees at the infamous 1957 Appalachian meeting of the Mafia in upstate New York at the estate of Joseph Barbara. The FBI had staked out the estate. The FBI photographed the vehicles of all the attendees as they arrived. Then the Feds raided the meeting. The Mafioso Capos tried to flee, but all were arrested on one charge or another. Because of this debacle, the Mob would never again attempt to hold a high-level meeting. All communications in the future would be by telephone only.

Although he was ostensibly the head of the Chicago Mob, Giancana's influence extended as far west as the Pacific Ocean. His chief on the West Coast was a hoodlum named Johnny Roselli. Roselli emigrated from Italy to Massachusetts with his family in 1911. His birth name was Filippo Sacco, but in 1922 he committed a murder in the Boston area and fled to the Chicago area, where he changed his name to John Roselli. There he became a trusted associate of both Al Capone and Frank Nitti.

Giancana called Roselli to tell him he had a problem in L.A. and needed a body to resolve it. Giancana said, "I need a female stiff. She needs to be of average build, about 5'6" or so, say 35 years old, and a blonde, although we can fix that if her hair isn't too dark. There's got to be no evidence of violence on the body. This has to be a drug overdose. I don't want you to arrange any premature deaths. Don't kill no one. I just want you to find me some broad that died from an overdose.

"I don't want no meat wagon or ambulance showing up to call attention to this. You've got to send somebody in a station wagon to pick up the stiff and deliver her to L.A. You need to call me and tell me as soon as you've got the body and then I'll tell you what to do with it."

Johnny Roselli was puzzled by this strange request from his boss, but he knew better than to either question it or deny it. Instead Roselli said, "Of course, Sam. I'll take care of it. I'll alert all my people right now in both L.A. and Vegas, and as soon as we find a stiff that meets what you want, I'll call you immediately."

Sam said, "Thanks, Johnny. Don't waste no time. Find the stiff as quickly as you can. But like I said, don't kill no one."

Johnny responded, "You got it, Boss. I'll take care of it ASAP."

* * * * * * * * * *

Jean Peters was a Hollywood star in the 1950's. She starred in the film, "Niagara," which also featured Marilyn Monroe. She and Marilyn became close friends during the filming of that movie.

In 1957, she married Howard Hughes. Howard Hughes was at various times in his life an engineer, an industrialist, a movie producer, a playboy and an aviator; but he was well on his way to becoming a recluse. He was now one of the wealthiest people in the world. As part of his empire, Hughes had purchased Trans World Airlines (TWA).

When the phone rang in Jean Peters' residence, she moved slowly to answer it. Jean Peters never rushed about anything anymore, since she was quite well-off financially. She no longer needed to hope for a call from an agent offering a part for her as an actress. She'd had a successful career, but now she just wanted to lay back and enjoy her success. And her retirement!

Jean Peters picked up the phone and answered with a simple, "Hello?"

"Jeanie," she heard, "it's Marilyn."

"Hey, sweetie," Jean said. "I haven't heard from you in a long time, but I hope everything's okay. I did see that thing for the President's birthday and you looked marvelous, so sensual, so. . ."

Jean stopped talking because she heard Marilyn sobbing at the other end of the line.

"Hey, honey, I'm sorry. Did I say something wrong?"

"No, Jeanie, nothing that you said or did. I'm just going through a really bad time now."

Jean said, "Marilyn, what's the problem? What's wrong?"

Marilyn responded, "Jeanie, can you keep a secret?"

"Ha," Jean laughed and said, "My life with Howard is full of secrets. I have so many secrets that I can't even remember them all – much less talk to anybody about them. If you have a secret that you want to share with me, I'll just file it away in the security vault in my mind with all the other secrets."

Marilyn said, "I need help and I hope that you will help me."

Jean Peters said, "Okay, Marilyn. I don't know what you're talking about, but if I can help, you know I will."

Marilyn said, "But it's real important that, if I tell you my secret, you won't divulge it to anybody else."

Jean said, "Of course, sweetie. As I told you, I know so many secrets, but I've never divulged any of them."

Marilyn said, "Actually, I always admired that about you. Even though information about Howard is so in demand by the media, you never divulged any of his secrets. Many others might have done otherwise."

Jean Peters said, "Yeah, well, Howard is a good person and I love him in spite of all of the devils that he struggles with.

"But what does that have to do with you calling me?" Jean Peters asked.

"Well," Marilyn said, "I'm in deep trouble."

"Trouble?" Jean responded.

"Trouble so bad that I tried to kill myself last weekend," Marilyn answered.

"What?" Jean Peters said. "Why would you ever do that or think that? You're young, you're beautiful, you're a celebrity and you've got a great future in the film industry. I don't understand."

Marilyn said, "This is something so personal that I just want to ask you one more time if you'll be able to keep this secret."

Jean said, "Of course, sweetie. Geez, I never talk about Howard's things. I wouldn't talk about yours either. What the hell is going on?"

Marilyn said, "I tried to kill myself because I'm pregnant. I just couldn't bear to think about the shame and embarrassment that I would suffer from all of the media once they found out the truth."

Jean Peters tried to provide an upbeat approach to the situation by saying, "Marilyn, don't worry about it. All you need to do now is just marry the father and lie about the date of insemination. Come on, you're not the first one this has happened to, so forget that suicide stuff, okay?"

Marilyn said, "Well, the suicide stuff is behind me, but I can't marry the father of the child because he's already married. Not only that, he has a career that would be destroyed if I ever revealed that he had fathered my child."

Jean Peters almost dropped the phone when she understood what Marilyn had just said. She had seen the birthday party of President Jack Kennedy at Madison Square Garden and remembered Marilyn just sobbing when she had mentioned it to her. She immediately connected all the dots.

"Holy shit," Jean Peters said. "The father of your baby is the President?"

Marilyn said, "Yes. I haven't been with anybody else, and there's no doubt who the baby's father is. I love Jack and I can't destroy his career. I just didn't know what to do. That's why I took all those pills."

Jean said, "Oh, God, Marilyn, I don't know what to tell you. Except I'll do anything I can to help if I can."

"Thanks, Jeanie," Marilyn said, "Because there is something that I hope you'll be able to do for me. I just want to disappear. The only thing I want to do in this world is be the best mother that I can to my baby. I need to get out of the United States."

Jean said, "Oh, so that's what you want – me to talk to Howard about getting you on a TWA flight?"

"No, it's not that simple," Marilyn said. "What I'm asking you to do is to have a TWA plane fly me across the Atlantic without any identification."

Jean Peters said, "Why so much drama?"

Marilyn responded, "If I just got on a plane and left the U.S., the media would follow me forever. They'd finally figure out where I was and they would learn about my child. Then they would be relentless in identifying the baby's father. I just can't deal with that. The best thing for me is to just disappear.

"I told Frank Sinatra about my situation, since I was at his Cal-Neva resort when I tried to kill myself. He is helping me to arrange a fake suicide, so I can disappear. He has friends that he says can find a dead blonde drug addict and deliver her body to my house. He also says that his friends can fix everything with the cops, so there will be no questions. I know it sounds kind of gruesome, but Frank says that there are many such girls that die early because of their addictions. Most of them are either unidentified or have been using an adopted name, since many of them are involved in prostitution. So they die as unknowns. At least this one won't be buried as an unknown in a pauper's grave. She will have a great resting spot in my space at the Westwood Memorial Park.

"Could you ask Howard if he would send a plane to Los Angeles to pick me up and fly me to Europe? I have plenty of money to pay for the flight."

Jean said, "I'm sure Howard will do this. He'll do anything for me. He never denies anything I request. And what the heck, it's only a training flight for his planes and they have to do that anyway. And he doesn't need your money. Howard has so much money that he'll never be able to figure out how to spend it all before he dies. So where are WE going?"

Marilyn responded and said, "I need to go to Dublin, but I think by your comment you thought you'd be helpful and go along. Actually, I appreciate that so much, but I just can't risk any notoriety and you're still a Hollywood Star. The media still follows your movements. You're alive and I need to be dead! This has to be done in complete secrecy. So thanks for the offer, but I just need to go alone.

"Actually, there will be someone along with me. He's a friend of Jack's and has made all the arrangements for me once I get to Ireland. So please call me back and let me know if Howard's willing to do this for me."

Jean Peters said, "Marilyn, honey, I'm telling you now that Howard will do this. Now I only have to tell him where and when. Didn't I tell you Howard never refuses me? Never, ever. That's one of the reasons I love him and would never betray him. So how soon will you know when you're ready to go?"

Marilyn said, "We're just waiting to hear from Frank's people. How much notice do you need?"

Jean Peters said, "I think about 12 hours for the plane to get there and fuel up, and then file its plans and head out."

"Okay," Marilyn said. "I'll get back to you just as soon as possible."

Jean Peters said, "Goodnight, sweetie. Thanks for calling me to help you with this. I always thought you were nicer than any of the other actresses I met in Hollywood. I'm happy that you consider me a friend and I'm really pleased that I can help out with this. I only wish Howard's problems could be solved so easily."

* * * * * * * * * *

Peter Sharkey arrived at Marilyn Monroe's residence on Tuesday, July 31, 1962. The housekeeper ushered Peter into the central living area where Marilyn quickly joined him.

Peter was overwhelmed by Marilyn's beauty, not that he was easily awed by stars or beautiful women, and in fact, he really didn't care about Hollywood celebrities. But Marilyn's beauty and grace were breathtaking. And she wasn't even wearing makeup!

He introduced himself, "I'm Peter Sharkey, and Jack Kennedy sent me here to be of whatever help I might be."

Marilyn smiled and said, "I'm going to need a lot of help and I'm glad that you're here."

Peter asked, "Can you please tell me about the plans that you've made so far? I've really only learned about plans in Ireland and what will happen after we land there. I don't know much about the plans here in America."

Marilyn said, "Well, some friends of mine have arranged to substitute some poor, deceased drug addict from Las Vegas or Los Angeles to replace me here. My housekeeper is in on the whole thing and I have trusted her forever. I've also given her enough money to provide her with a secure future for the rest of her life. Right now we're just waiting to hear from my friends about the timing on the substitute."

Peter couldn't help thinking to himself, "*Well, I guess if you're in movies all the time and they substitute doubles for you, you wouldn't be averse to using body-doubles in real life also.*"

Peter asked Marilyn about her personal matters. He worried that if she were going to develop a new life somewhere else, probably in Ireland, then she would need some financial support. They spent the next several hours going through Marilyn's bank accounts and investments. He needn't have worried. Marilyn was extremely wealthy from her movie studio contracts.

Peter decided that he would arrange for the transfer of 80 percent of her assets to secret new accounts in Switzerland. That way she would have access to the money in the future, and the ONI would assure that the transfers could not be traced. He decided it would be too suspicious if he transferred it all and Marilyn appeared to die penniless.

Peter didn't know how to arrange these transfers, but as a ranking officer in the ONI, he had access to financial experts. Although they usually spent their time trying to trace such transfers to track bad guys, they would also know how to make these transfers and he knew that their secrecy could be relied upon.

Marilyn told him that she had contacted her friend, Jean Peters, who was married to Howard Hughes, one of the most secretive individuals in the world and the owner of Trans World Airlines. She had asked Jean to see if Howard would provide a plane to fly her to Ireland, and had been assured he would.

Peter was introduced to Marilyn's housekeeper, a loyal employee of many years, whose involvement was essential to the success of their plan. While Marilyn had promised her a secretive lifetime annuity in order to gain her cooperation, that wasn't really necessary, Peter thought, since the housekeeper obviously had a close personal bond to Marilyn and would protect her even without the money. But the money guaranteed her silence and cooperation.

Peter and Marilyn worked on completing the details of the plan. Peter's contacts at ONI arranged for the transfer of a substantial percentage of Marilyn's wealth to a new account in Switzerland. He had instructed his ONI operatives to make sure that all records of the transfer were completely obliterated. He also arranged for new personal documents for Marilyn, including a worn Irish passport that indicated that the newly invented Jean Brady had ventured out from her home country of Ireland to the United States several times – probably to visit relatives in the USA.

It was late in the afternoon on Tuesday when the telephone rang and Marilyn answered it.

"Hi, sweetie. It's Jean Peters. I talked to Howard and he is willing, in fact more than willing to help you. He loves all this conspiratorial shit, and the more secretive things are, the more he likes them. Plus he told me that several of his pilots are due for training flights and that it would be absolutely no problem for him to send a plane to pick you up as soon as you need it. He can even fix the customs people at the Dublin airport so you can enter the country undetected. TWA owns customs inspectors at airports around the world. He also said that if you need anything else, just let him know. I told you Howard never denies my requests."

Marilyn responded, "Oh, God, Jeannie. You don't know how much this means to me. I am just so tired of this place and all the glitz and glamour and hate and hypocrisy. I just need to get out before I do something crazy again."

Jean Peters said, "Sweetie, are you sure I can't come with you? I've never visited Ireland."

Marilyn said, "Yeah, thanks again for the offer, but we're trying to keep this as secret as possible, so the less people the better. What do I need to do next?"

Jean said, "Well, you just need to let me know exactly when and where you want the plane. Keep in mind that it may take several hours for the plane to get there from wherever it's going to be coming from."

Marilyn said, "Okay, I should know pretty soon and I'll give you as much advance notice as possible."

Jean Peters responded and said, "Marilyn, I truly respect your decision about this and I'm sure that you'll make one of the world's best mothers. I decided several years ago that I couldn't tolerate the falseness of Hollywood anymore and dropped out. I'm glad that you now realize the same thing and I wish you the best in starting a normal, healthy life in Ireland."

Marilyn said, "Thank you, Jeannie. And I will call you just as soon as I know when we need the plane. And Jeannie, maybe someday you can come visit me and the baby. I don't think I'll have to be in Ireland forever, just until people forget about Marilyn Monroe and I can get on with a normal life."

With that, Jean Peters said, "Thanks for the invite, sweetie. Maybe someday I'll show up at your door." Then they hung up.

Marilyn turned to Peter and said, "Well, Howard's agreed to provide a TWA plane to get us to Ireland. I just need to give them as much advance notice as possible so that they can get the aircraft here when we want it."

Peter was incredulous that Marilyn could just summon up a transcontinental aircraft to be at her beck and call. But this whole scenario seemed quite unbelievable to him anyway. After all, he was just a Navy officer that grew up normally in Rhode Island. His life was nothing like normal right now!

Bobby Kennedy had been in direct contact with his cousin Michael Brady in Ireland, who was more than happy to help. All he knew was that Bobby wanted to send a pregnant woman over there. She was unmarried and didn't want to be shamed by her situation if she delivered the baby in the U.S. Brady suggested that the manor house he owned in the southeast part of Ireland would be safe, since it was in a rural locale and was located in the midst of other properties owned by other Kennedy relatives. Bobby thought that would be fine since he didn't think there would be any danger to the woman once she arrived in Ireland.

Very late in the day on Friday, August 3, 1962, Peter Lawford got a call from Frank Sinatra telling him that they had found a suitable body-double. He thought it was a drug-addicted hooker from Las Vegas, but Frank didn't want to push Giancana for any details. He thought the less he knew, the better, and Marilyn had already agreed that the less she knew, the better.

Peter Lawford immediately called Peter Sharkey with the news. Lawford said, "It's time for you two to move out. The wagon will be there tomorrow night and you need to be long gone by then. From what I've heard from Frankie, everything is arranged perfectly. You shouldn't have anything to worry about except getting out of there as quickly as you can."

Peter Sharkey said, "Okay, I'll tell Marilyn to call for the aircraft. We'll be out of here tomorrow and we'll be at the airport awaiting the plane after dark. It might take several hours for the plane to arrive, but we'll just sit it out at the airport. Is there anything else we should know?"

Peter Lawford responded, "I think everything is done, and if it's not, God help us all. Good luck to you."

In preparation for the clandestine escape, Marilyn had cut her hair short and dyed it light brown. She also wore a scarf and sunglasses when she and Peter left her residence and headed to the airport. Peter was driving a Navy car that he had requisitioned upon his arrival in L.A. earlier that week. He couldn't risk them going to the airport in a taxicab, which might have led to some type of uncomfortable recollections by the cab driver later. So he and Marilyn packed her few precious possessions into the car and bid farewell to the housekeeper. Marilyn could not take much with her since that might expose the charade.

The housekeeper was quite calm about the whole thing and stated that she was prepared to support Marilyn regardless of what the authorities might ask after the body was discovered. The compensation that Marilyn had promised her would provide her with a lifetime of financial security, so she was not about to say anything that might jeopardize that promise.

While Peter and Marilyn were heading to the airport, an unmarked van was heading to Marilyn's residence. In the back was an unfortunate young blonde woman who had died from an overdose caused by her addiction to heroin.

On Sunday morning the housekeeper called a number that she had been given, to report that her boss, Marilyn Monroe, was apparently dead in her bed from a drug overdose. The deception had begun.

The fix was also in with Giancana's contacts in the L.A. Police Department and the coroner's office. The coroner's van arrived almost simultaneously with the first police unit, which included a Detective Lieutenant, who quickly took control of the entire situation. Since there was no suspicion of a violent crime, the other LAPD officers maintained a quiet patrol outside the residence.

When the coroner's representative later emerged with "Marilyn's" body, it was respectfully covered in a coroner's body bag. None of the LAPD officers would have dared to suggest that they needed to see the body to identify it. It was just not their place, nor their responsibility.

So, on Wednesday, August 8th, "Marilyn Monroe" was buried with a dignified, but subdued by Hollywood standards, ceremony at the Corridor of Memories at Westwood Memorial Park in L.A.

Her death was shrouded in some suspicion, but no one was able to provide any concrete facts or evidence to question what had happened. To the media, indeed to the world, Marilyn Monroe either had tragically died accidentally or had committed suicide by overdosing on barbiturates and alcohol.

* * * * * * * * * *

Peter and Marilyn arrived at the L.A. airport, but did not go to the main terminal entrance. They had been given instructions to enter through a distant service entrance used by General Aviation (small private planes) and go to a service hangar to await the arrival of the airplane. It was quite dark in this section of the airport and Peter was somewhat uneasy since he didn't have his service pistol with him. They had been waiting several hours when a lighted pick-up truck showed up on the taxiway nearby.   The pick-up truck proceeded slowly toward them, and it was being followed by an enormous TWA jetliner. The pick-up truck guided the plane directly to the hangar where Peter and Marilyn were waiting.

Peter had previously arranged for the Navy to pick up his staff car the next day. They would send some enlisted sailors to retrieve the staff car and no one would be the wiser.

Peter drove the staff car up to the TWA plane, which opened an access door. This wasn't as if they were embarking commercial passengers, so there were no mobile steps being delivered to help them enter the plane. Instead Peter drove the car right up to the airplane and, after throwing Marilyn's few possessions and his duffel bag up to whoever was at the door to the aircraft – possibly the pilot or copilot, they both jumped onto the hood of the staff car and were pulled into the plane. Since this was supposedly a training flight, there were no stewardesses or other personnel on board. Just the pilot and copilot. The pilot was easily able to taxi back toward the runway with one wing passing safely above the staff car, which was left with its motor off and the key in the ignition.

Both the pilot and copilot had been given instructions from Howard Hughes that a transcontinental flight was planned, and then a transatlantic flight to Dublin.

The pilot moved the airplane closer to a lighted refueling area and requested fuel from the airport supplier. It took almost an hour to complete the refueling operation, so it was almost dawn when they finally departed L.A. on a flight plan for Bangor, Maine.

They listed this as a training flight for the TWA crew, and several hours later they arrived safely in Maine.

During the trip Peter spoke to both the pilot and copilot, while Marilyn kept to herself in the back of the plane and avoided interacting with the pilots. Secrecy and anonymity seemed the best plan for her.

Peter learned that both the pilot and copilot were Mormons, and that Howard Hughes had personally selected them for this flight. They said they thought that Hughes was a convert to Mormonism and that he trusted Mormon practitioners to keep secrets and do what they were told. They both told him that they could be trusted to never say anything about this flight, since that was what they had pledged to Hughes. Peter was reassured by this, since both of them seemed like clean-cut straightforward individuals. He'd never met a Mormon before, but he immediately trusted them – although he really didn't have any choice.

After refueling in Maine, the aircraft's initial flight plan was to head for New York City. Once airborne, the pilot canceled the flight plan.

He didn't reopen a new flight plan until the aircraft was out over the Atlantic Ocean and heading for Dublin, Ireland. The air traffic controllers that received his revised flight plan thought nothing of it, since airlines were always redirecting their aircraft to places where they were needed, not necessarily where they had been previously scheduled.

When the aircraft landed safely in Dublin, hours later, they taxied to a service building. Because of the length of the flights and the time-zone changes, it was now after dark on the next day. This service building was neither as big nor as well-lit as the facility they had left in Los Angeles, but the darkness suited their desire for secrecy.

When they taxied to the building, there were two rather nondescript sedans waiting for them, with four men standing outside the cars.

Once the aircraft had stopped, the copilot opened the access door. Then he threw down Marilyn's possessions and Peter's duffel, which were caught by one of the men on the ground. Once again they had no consumer steps, so Marilyn was first lowered out the door into the arms of two men on the ground. Moments later Peter descended likewise. As soon as they were off the plane, the crew closed the door and the pilot taxied the aircraft toward the refueling area for the return flight to the United States.

On the ground, one of the men walked up to Peter and introduced himself.

"Hi," he said, "You must be Peter Sharkey. My name is Michael Brady and I'm a cousin of Jack and Bobby, although maybe a bit distant cousin. Bobby told me about this whole situation and you can be sure that I will keep it as secret as possible. Also, the papers that I suggested you procure for her should list her as Jean Brady. I hope you were able to arrange that. That's my family name and I thought that might make it easier if any of the government authorities come out to our house with any questions. Our house is in a very rural area, however, and all of the local constables are IRA sympathizers and never question anything that we do."

Peter shook Michael Brady's hand and said, "I am Peter Sharkey and I'm pleased to meet you. This is Jean Brady, who is just back to Ireland after a visit to the United States."

After this introduction, Michael turned to Marilyn and said, "Jean Brady, it's my pleasure to welcome you back to Ireland, and let me assure you that your stay here will be safe and enjoyable."

Marilyn smiled and went along with the deception. She said, "Hi, Cousin Michael. It's been such a very long time since we've seen each other. But now that I'm back in Ireland, I feel better already."

She was an accomplished actress, and had already mastered an Irish accent. So much so, her "cousin" Michael Brady was startled. It was obvious that she would have no problems posing as an Irish woman, albeit an unusually attractive one.

And Marilyn really did feel better already. She'd escaped Hollywood undetected and both Peter Sharkey and Michael Brady seemed helpful, protective and friendly. Plus, Peter was very handsome in a very masculine way and reminded her somewhat of Jack Kennedy.

CHAPTER NINE

The island that comprises the Republic of Ireland, an independent nation, and Northern Ireland, one of the four countries of the United Kingdom, was a tinderbox of intrigue and violence. Both sides had official government positions to promote, and each had paramilitary terrorist groups supporting its positions. All these groups had spies monitoring the Dublin airport, since anything happening at the airport could affect their interests.

Ireland had long been a thorn in the side of Britain. Ireland is a large island to the west of Great Britain, also an island nation. They are separated by the Irish Sea. The history between Ireland and England is one of contentious warfare. During the 1500's, there were over 60 years of intermittent warfare. This led to England claiming dominance after 1603.

But the Irish never accepted this dominance, and the battles continued. Finally, a war of independence in the early twentieth century led to a formal truce, which created the Irish Free State. This Irish Free State became increasingly dominant over the Irish island, but the six northern provinces, which were predominantly populated by British immigrants who were members of the English Anglican Church, fought to maintain their independence. This led to the partitioning of the island between Northern Ireland and the Republic of Ireland. After the partition, the parliament of Northern Ireland voted that they would become a part of the United Kingdom which led to the continuing conflict.

When World War II broke out between Britain and Germany, the Republic of Ireland issued a Declaration of Neutrality. The motivation was that if Germany won the war, Northern Ireland might no longer be part of the United Kingdom and would finally be forced to rejoin Ireland itself.

In fact, this position on the part of the Ireland government led to fears on the English side, and hopes of opportunity on the German side. As a result, both Britain and Germany developed plans for the invasion of Ireland.

Britain's plans were only readied in case the Germans actually invaded Ireland. Because if that happened, the Germans would be perilously close to the western shores of Britain.

The British war authorities thought that the probability of a German invasion of Ireland was very low, but during the fall of 1940, Hitler had been threatening the invasion of England itself. While this was an unlikely eventuality, the British war planners needed to consider the fact that Ireland might be an easier target. Hitler had been incredibly successful in his Continental European and North African conquests, so the British knew not to take his threats lightly.

The reality, however, was that Germany really only possessed a land and air force. Their Navy, the Kriegsmarine, was largely ineffectual except for the submarine division, the feared U-Bootes. In fact, Germany's surface warships had been so ineffectual that they had not been able to prevent the evacuation of almost four million British and French soldiers from the shores of Dunkirk between May 27th and June 4th of 1940, when they were driven to the sea by the German Army. The British were even able to send pleasure boats and working fishing boats, not just war craft, to evacuate their soldiers without any threat from the German Navy. The German Air Force was able to sink some of these craft, but the German Navy never arrived. In fact, even the vaunted German battleship "Bismarck," which was touted by the Germans as the most formidable battle cruiser ever launched, was sunk by the Royal Navy during her first sortie into the Atlantic in 1941.

In truth, the Royal Navy enjoyed such enormous superiority over the German Navy that their dominance of the seas was almost complete. Except, of course, for those dangerous German submarines.

So given the reality that the potential German invasion of Ireland would probably never happen, the British Army never invaded Ireland. The Declaration of Neutrality, however, did serve to sour the relationship between Britain and Ireland.

By the early 1960s, the sectarian violence between Northern Ireland and the Republic of Ireland had begun to escalate into the violent clashes that later came to be known as "The Troubles," which was a secretive conflict that involved bombings and terrorist acts by both sides.

The Dublin airport was Ground Zero for the clandestine combatants in this conflict. They all maintained spies and informers at the airport and monitored everything that happened there.

The Irish government intelligence section was called the G-2, and it had a cadre of informants working at the airport. Although it was a government agency, some of its individual members were IRA sympathizers. Their sentiments were allied with the Irish Republican Army, a paramilitary group with violent leanings. The IRA also had some resident spies at the airport.

The government of Northern Ireland had its own spies monitoring the airport. Northern Ireland, as part of the United Kingdom, relied on the famed British Intelligence Service MI-5 for its intelligence, so there were also several MI-5 informants that worked the Dublin airport.

And then there were the spies from the Ulster Defense League, a paramilitary terrorist group opposing the IRA in Northern Ireland. They shared information with the British MI-5, but they still held their own interests.

It was impossible for any of these informants not to notice the arrival of an unscheduled TWA airliner that pulled up to a deserted service building and discharged two passengers. This was such an unusual event that all of these organizations moved quickly to try to monitor just what the hell was going on.

And the fact that two individuals had deplaned and departed the airport without having to go through Customs just compounded the mystery.

* * * * * * * * * *

The ancestral homeland of the Kennedy family was in Wexford County. Wexford County was about 100 miles south of Dublin on the southeast coast of Ireland.

During the late 1840s, Wexford County suffered some of the most devastating effects of what came to be known as the Irish Potato Famine. A virulent disease affected the entire potato crop, which devastated the Irish who depended upon potatoes for their major sustenance. All of President Kennedy's eight great grand-parents emigrated from Ireland to Boston during this terrible famine.

But by 1963, the horrible history of the potato famine was long behind them. Wexford County recovered and was now a thriving part of Ireland.

Michael Brady was the current owner of a manor house that had been in the family for generations. The manor house sat on a high knoll that provided a good view of the surrounding area. The fields surrounding the manor house had once again been converted to the cultivation of potatoes. The income from the potato farm provided Brady with a nice income, which was supplemented by a stipend he received from his cousins in America.

It was almost dawn when Peter and Marilyn arrived at the manor house after about a three-hour drive with Michael Brady and his friends. They were ushered in and found the manor house to be clean and utilitarian. Brady had prepared for their arrival and had fresh bread, ham and beer waiting for them. The men ate, but Jean only had some of the bread and ham and declined the beer since she wasn't sure if that would be good for her unborn baby. She did get water to complete her meal.

Afterwards, Brady showed Jean to her room and asked if she needed anything further, but she said she was fine.

After Jean was settled in her bedroom, Peter sat down with Michael Brady to discuss the situation. Michael said, "All I really know is that Bobby Kennedy called me and said that one of his American relatives was pregnant and unmarried and needed to get out of there. He asked me to find a safe place for her until she could deliver her baby."

Peter responded, "Well, that's all we're asking right now. But I think it would also be good if we could install some radio equipment here so you could keep Bobby and Jack informed about how she is doing. It also might be useful so you could tell Jack about what is happening here regarding the problems between Ireland and Northern Ireland."

Michael was more than willing to agree to this. He said, "Of course. When do you want to bring this radio equipment here and what do I need to do to prepare for it?"

Peter said, "I'll let you know, but it'll probably happen soon."

* * * * * * * * * *

Peter Sharkey returned to Ireland in September, 1962, accompanied by two ONI technical specialists who brought along some very sophisticated radio equipment. The radio equipment was absolutely state-of-the-art and would allow almost instantaneous transmissions between Ireland and the United States. It utilized a repeater station on the island of Winter Harbor in Canada. The repeater and amplifier station that was located there was maintained by the United States Navy, and would instantaneously retransmit such communications to Washington, DC.

When Peter and his associates arrived outside the manor house, Michael Brady came outside to greet them. Peter made the requisite introductions all around and then asked, "Where is Jean?"

Michael Brady responded, "Well, she's having some morning sickness. Don't you know, it's pretty common amongst new mothers-to-be, but I think she'll be out to greet you pretty soon."

Peter was relieved and said, "Okay, Michael. We need to set up this radio equipment. Our plan is to string the antennas through the trees to disguise them and prevent anyone from knowing that this radio station is here."

Michael said, "Of course, of course. Do you need us to help you in any way, like climbing the trees?"

Peter said, "I'm not sure, but if these technicians need some help, I'll let you know."

About two hours later, the ONI technicians had made great progress in stringing the antenna through the trees. It turned out that they did need a ladder that Brady provided. They put the radio equipment in the house and checked its operation by sending a message to their headquarters in Washington, DC and receiving an affirmative message back.

Several moments later Jean emerged from her bedroom. She wasn't wearing makeup, but looked beautiful as always since her beauty was natural and didn't depend upon makeup.

Once in the living room, she searched for Peter and upon spying him, she approached and said, "I'm so sorry that I wasn't here to greet you earlier, but I haven't been feeling well lately. I've heard that this is what happens during pregnancy, but I never thought that I'd be pregnant or that this might happen to me. So please forgive me for not being out here earlier."

Peter was touched and said, "Don't worry about it. It's not a problem. I've set up a radio station so that you and Jack can keep in touch. I'm sorry that you're not feeling well."

Jean smiled weakly and said, "Thanks for your understanding, Peter. I wish I felt better so that we could visit more. But unfortunately I truly don't feel very well right now. I'm quite nauseous and I think I should lay down now."

Peter said, "Are you okay? Can I help you get back to the room?"

Jean replied, "No, no, please just keep doing what you're doing. I'll be okay. I thought I'd be over this by now, but the nausea sometimes comes back."

CHAPTER TEN

CUBAN MISSILE CRISIS

Although the Cuban troops had repulsed the invaders during the Bay of Pigs debacle, the Cuban government was afraid that the United States would eventually launch another attack against them. At the same time, Soviet Premier Nikita Khrushchev was concerned about the growing nuclear missile gap between his country and the USA. Although they boasted otherwise, the Soviets had only a handful of fully functional, Inter-Continental Ballistic Missiles. On the other hand, the United States had over 200 ICBMs and was quickly building more.

The Soviets, however, had almost a thousand intermediate-range missiles.

Khrushchev knew that if he could position some of these intermediate-range missiles in Cuba, along with their nuclear munitions, he might be able to narrow the missile gap and equalize the potential battlefield with the United States.

Since the Soviets were providing major economic support to Cuba, Castro immediately agreed when Khrushchev suggested positioning nuclear missiles on Cuban soil. But they agreed to do it as secretly as possible to prevent the Americans from detecting their actions before the missiles were operational.

When he proposed his plans to the Soviet Politburo, technically the Politburo of the Central Committee of the Communist Party of the Soviet Union, of which he was the Chairman, Khrushchev asserted, "I know for certain that Kennedy doesn't have a strong background, nor generally speaking does he have the courage to stand up to a serious challenge." Khrushchev considered Kennedy to be "too young, too intellectual, and not prepared well for decision-making in crisis situations." He convinced the Politburo that Kennedy was both too intelligent and too weak to oppose them. The Politburo agreed to Khrushchev's plans.

They would soon learn, however, how wrong their assessment of President Kennedy was. Obviously, they either didn't know about, or didn't appreciate, the depth of his bravery during World War II. He had risked his own life on the front lines in defense of his nation, and he was more than ready to defend her again. They had seriously underestimated his courage and determination.

In secret, the Soviets began to construct nine different missile sites in Cuba. Six were for Soviet R-12 Dvina intermediate-range missiles and the other three were planned for more modern R-14 Usovaya intermediate-range ballistic missiles. The R-12 was the first Soviet operational intermediate-range ballistic missile that could be deployed with a nuclear warhead. It was also the first missile the Soviets had ever mass-produced.

The first consignment of R-12 missiles arrived in secrecy on the night of September 8th. This was followed by the arrival of a second consignment on September 16th.

On October 14, 1962, a U-2 flight piloted by Major Richard Heyser captured images of a ballistic missile construction site at San Cristobal in western Cuba. The U-2 was a high-altitude spy plane that the Americans deployed for clandestine reconnaissance of enemy territories.

The CIA reviewed the evidence from the U-2 flight on October 15th, and the next morning showed President Kennedy the photos and informed him that the CIA was absolutely certain they had discovered a Soviet missile site.

Over the next several days, President Kennedy met with members of the National Security Council and the Joint Chiefs of Staff to develop a plan of action. The Joint Chiefs of Staff unanimously agreed that a full-scale attack and invasion was the only solution. They knew that neither the Soviets nor the Cubans could stop the U.S. from conquering Cuba. Kennedy was skeptical, however, because he thought the Soviets might respond by attacking West Berlin, which was located 100 miles within the Soviet zone in East Germany.

Instead of an all-out invasion, Kennedy considered the possibility of targeted air attacks against all the known missile sites. Another option was to use the U.S. Navy to block any missiles from arriving in Cuba and to prevent any support staff from arriving on the island.

The Joint Chiefs of Staff were instructed to prepare for a possible invasion of Cuba, while the President continued to evaluate all options. Accordingly, the Army sent the First Armored Division to Georgia, and five other Army divisions were alerted for potential action. The Air Force sent many of its Strategic Air Command (SAC) B-47 Stratojet medium bombers to both military and civilian airports closer to Cuba. SAC also sent aloft many of its B-52 Stratofortress heavy bombers.

On October 20th, the President raised the military readiness status to Defcon 2, the second highest state. Defcon 2 instructed the military to be ready for war, and to prepare for immediate offensive and defensive action if needed. By October 22nd, President Kennedy had decided to impose a naval blockade around Cuba. Although a naval blockade was technically an act of war, the President thought that this would provide a serious response to the actions by the Cubans and the Soviets, without provoking an armed response by the Soviets. The President was also a former Navy officer, so innately he favored a naval response rather than an Army or Air Force response.

By 3:00 p.m. that day, President Kennedy ordered all his plans into action. He also instructed the State Department to inform the Soviets, the Cubans and all of America's allies about the actions that the U.S. was about to take.

Peter Sharkey had been summoned to President Kennedy's office on October 22nd. It was about 4:30 in the afternoon when the secretary showed Captain Sharkey into the office of President Kennedy. President Kennedy remained seated at his desk as he looked up and smiled at Peter Sharkey. The President said, "Hey,

Peter, don't be offended, but I can't get up out of this friggin' chair easily. My back is killing me. I've been sitting here for days signing orders and having meetings."

Peter said, "No problem, Jack. But you wanted to see me?"

Jack responded, "Yeah, but how about you walk over here first so we can shake hands? At least you can still walk."

Peter smiled and said, "Of course," as he walked to Jack. They shook hands and Jack gestured to Peter to take a seat on the chair in front of his desk.

Then Jack said, "Peter, we have detected Soviet nuclear weapons and missiles in Cuba. In the next few hours I'm going on national television to announce a naval quarantine of the island."

Peter interjected, "A quarantine? Isn't that an act of war?"

Jack continued, "I was presented with several options, including a full-scale invasion, selective aerial bombing or a naval quarantine. The military was pressuring me for a full-scale invasion. But I knew that a total invasion would provoke an extreme response from the Soviets. I thought about just using selective Air Force attacks, but that would still have led to numerous Soviet and Cuban deaths. I decided on a naval quarantine because that seemed to be the most prudent alternative. We would not be killing anyone unless the quarantine was violated. I don't think the Soviets realized how deeply we were worried about this situation and how much they had provoked us. I don't think they care at all about Cuba, and I think if we give them a chance for a way out, they'll take it."

Peter thought for a moment and responded, "That sounds like a very rational plan to me. How can I help?"

Jack said, "Well, because we needed to act quickly, I've ordered the Navy to proceed to implement the quarantine. What they've done is to designate the heavy cruiser USS Newport News as the flagship for now, until other naval assets can join the flotilla. The carrier USS Independence is steaming as quickly as possible to join the quarantine. Once there, they'll take a lead position in enforcing the quarantine. I want you on board the Independence as soon as you can get there. I think it's almost off the coast of Puerto Rico already, so if you catch a flight to Puerto Rico you should be able to board the Independence within the next 24 hours."

Peter responded, "Of course, Jack. But what do you want me to do once I'm on board?"

Jack said, "Peter, I just want you to keep your eyes and ears open. I want you to assess our team's readiness and to keep me apprised of the truthfulness of the reports that I'm getting from the Navy brass. And just like with the Bay of Pigs thing, I want you to contact me as quickly as possible if you come across any information you think I should know about immediately. Other than that, just use your own judgment."

Peter stood up knowing he had been dismissed. He said, "I'm on my way, Mr. President" and saluted quickly, rather than bending down to shake Jack's hand again.

Peter was almost to the door when he turned around and paused for a moment. He looked back at Jack without speaking. Jack looked up from his desk questioningly. He asked, "Peter is there anything else?"

Peter said, "Jack, what if there's a nuclear attack on the Capitol? Do they have some plans for you and the rest of the government?"

Jack smiled knowing that his friend was concerned about his well-being. He replied, "Don't worry about me, Peter. We've got a lot of safe places that we can head toward. I hope it'll never get to that, because if it ever does, my safety should be the last thing anybody in the U.S. worries about."

Peter just nodded and headed out the door, reassured somewhat about Jack's safety. Within two hours he was on his way toward the USS Independence.

At 7:00 p.m. that evening, President Kennedy delivered a nationwide-televised address to announce to the American public the discovery of Soviet Missiles in Cuba. He said, "It shall be the policy of this nation to regard any nuclear missile launched from Cuba against any nation in the Western Hemisphere as an attack by the Soviet Union on the United States, requiring a full retaliatory response upon the Soviet Union."

The President continued, "To halt this offensive build-up, a strict quarantine of all offensive military equipment under shipment to Cuba is being initiated. All ships of any kind bound for Cuba, from whatever nation or port, if found to contain cargos of offensive weapons, will be turned back. This quarantine will be expanded, if needed, to other types of cargo and carriers. We are not at this time, however, denying the necessities of life as the Soviets attempted to do in their Berlin blockage of 1948."

On the evening of October 24th, Soviet Premier Khrushchev sent a telegram to President Kennedy which stated that the Soviet Union viewed the blockade as "an act of aggression" and that their ships would be instructed to ignore it.

Upon receipt of this telegram, President Kennedy informed the Joint Chiefs of Staff about its content. The American military had already reached Def-con 2, and so they were ready for any threat.

All the Air Force's B-52 bombers were dispersed to various locations and made ready to take off, fully equipped and armed with nuclear weapons. They were told to be prepared for take-off on 15 minutes' notice. One-fourth of SAC's 1500 bombers were on airborne alert and constantly patrolling, while well over 100 ICBM missiles stood armed and ready for launch. American submarines had their missiles armed and ready to go immediately. Many of them had been ordered to move closer to the Soviet Union to guarantee a more immediate response and better accuracy.

By the morning of October 26th, the President had grown frustrated with the lack of any positive response. U-2 flights had disclosed that the Soviets were continuing to build their missile sites in Cuba. He told the Joint Chiefs of Staff that he now believed that only an invasion would remove the missiles from Cuba. He ordered them to prepare for such an eventuality.

He decided to give the matter a bit more time, however, to continue the diplomatic and military pressure and also to allow the U.S. military forces to complete their preparations. He knew from his experience during World War II that it took time to move tens of thousands of men, and thousands of vehicles and artillery pieces, from one place to another.

He ordered low-level surveillance flights over Cuba to be increased to once every two hours, and he issued orders that those flights could open fire as necessary to defend themselves. He also ordered a crash program for the Cuban exiles in Florida to develop a plan for a new civil government in Cuba if an invasion occurred.

Fidel Castro was incensed by the blockade. He was both embarrassed and infuriated because of his inability to take any direct action against the United States. He had ordered all his antiaircraft weapon emplacements to fire on any U.S. aircraft, but thus far they had been ineffective in stopping the aerial surveillance of Cuba.

He dictated a letter to Khrushchev that called for a preemptive strike on the U.S. Castro believed that at least four of the Soviet missile sites were now operationally effective, and he desperately wanted them to be used to attack the United States. He knew that such a preemptive attack would cause massive retribution against his island and his people, but his Latino macho was in control, as was his communist fanaticism.

While Khrushchev could care less whether the island of Cuba was incinerated and obliterated from the earth, however, he did care about the safety of his cities in Mother Russia. He knew that he was hopelessly outgunned by the United States in terms of deliverable long-range nuclear weapons. Khrushchev disregarded Castro's letter, treating it as insignificant in the conflict between the United States and his country.

Instead, he dictated a letter of his own. But it was not a reply to Castro. It was addressed to President Kennedy!

At 6:00 p.m. EDT on October 26th, the State Department received a message that appeared to be written by Khrushchev personally. It was a long letter that took several minutes to arrive by wire, and it took the translators additional time to translate and transcribe.

The letter said in part, "Mr. President, we and you ought not now to pull on the ends of the rope in which you have tied the knot of war, because the more the two of us pull, the tighter that knot will be tied. And a moment may come when that knot will be tied so tight that even he who tied it will not have the strength to untie it, and then it will be necessary to cut the knot, and what that would mean is not for me to explain to you, because you yourself understand perfectly of what terrible forces our countries dispose.

"Consequently, if there is no intention to tighten that knot and thereby to doom the world to the catastrophe of thermonuclear war, then let us not only relax the forces pulling on the ends of the rope, let us take measures to untie that knot. We are ready for this."

The letter continued, "I propose: We, for our part, will declare that our ships bound for Cuba are not carrying any armaments. You will declare that the United States will not invade Cuba with its troops and will not support any other forces which might intend to invade Cuba. Then the necessity of the presence of our military specialists in Cuba will disappear."

President Kennedy didn't know what to make of this letter from Khrushchev, or even whether it was authentic. He spent the next several hours discussing it with his advisors. He continued America's military readiness, but felt that the Soviets were offering a deal.

By the morning of October 27th, however, the situation in the field had grown dim. The conflict had reached a stalemate, at least as far as the public and the military knew. No one in the President's private circle knew what to make of the alleged letter from Khrushchev, or even if it had really been sent by the Premier. Maybe it was just a ploy to gain the Soviets time to launch a pre-emptive attack.

Accordingly, on that day the U.S. informed its NATO allies that "the United States, within a very short time, may find it in its interest and that of its fellow nations in the Western Hemisphere to take whatever military action may be necessary."

On that same day a U.S. U-2 spy plane was detected on an over-flight that was surveying the far eastern coast of the Soviet Union. The Soviets scrambled MiG fighters from their Wrangle Island base. In response the Americans sent aloft F-102 fighters from their base. The American fighters were armed with tactical nuclear air-to-air missiles. Each missile was designed to destroy not just a single enemy fighter, but all enemy fighters within a five-to-ten mile radius of the nuclear explosion. Luckily, neither side discharged its weapons.

In the Caribbean, another crisis was developing. The American destroyer, USS Beale, detected a Soviet submarine, later determined to be the B-59 that penetrated the quarantine line. After being detected and tracked, the Beale contained the submarine by dropping signaling depth charges on the B-59. Signaling depth charges are only about the size of a small hand grenade and are not meant to damage or destroy a target. They are just designed to let the target know that they are susceptible to further attack.

The Commander of the Beale reported to the flotilla commander on the USS Independence, who had been following all the developments. Captain Sharkey was asleep in his cabin after having spent most of the last 24 hours awake and in the control room on the USS Independence. He got a loud awakening when the Admiral's aide banged on his door. The aide told Captain Sharkey that the Admiral had requested his immediate presence in the control room. Peter had fallen asleep in his uniform, so he only needed to comb his hair back into place before he accompanied the aide up to the control room.

As soon as he learned about the Soviet submarine, the Admiral in charge of the flotilla immediately alerted all the other Navy ships about the presence of the Soviet submarine. But the Admiral was unsure about what actions to take next.

On board the Soviet submarine, they knew that they had been detected by the Americans and they were now running out of air. They only had two options. The first was to surface and suffer whatever consequences that might mean. The other was to use the nuclear-tipped torpedo they had on board. They had already been authorized to use this weapon if they suffered an attack from the Americans which "holed" them, meaning the enemy attack resulted in a hole in their hull which could sink them. The three ranking Soviet officers on the submarine argued amongst themselves about their next action.

Meanwhile, the commanders of the destroyers surrounding the Soviet submarine wanted authorization to switch from signal depth charges to real depth charges.

They were sure that the Soviet submarine was on an attack mission and they pressured the Admiral to authorize them to destroy it before it could attack.

On board the USS Independence, the Admiral was reviewing these requests from the destroyer captains to unleash their weapons, but he was unsure about whether such drastic action was yet justified. Captain Sharkey had been by his side for the last couple of days and, although he didn't know exactly what the captain's relationship to the President was, he did know that Captain Sharkey's presence on his vessel was because of a direct order from the White House.

Once Captain Sharkey entered the command center and had been briefed by the Admiral, the Admiral asked, "Well, Peter, what's your take on this situation? Should I just order the destruction of the sub or should I take the risk and wait to see if they attack us? Rumor has it that you are close to the President, so I'd like your input."

Peter responded, "Sir, I really don't know what to tell you, but the President did not send me down here to convey any secret orders to you. He just wanted me to keep my eyes and ears open."

Then the Admiral asked, "Peter, when you speak to the President, do you usually address him as Mr. President, or Jack?"

Peter responded, "The President and I served together in the South Pacific and so I call him Jack. But that doesn't mean I have any secret orders."

The Admiral said, "I understand, Peter, and I didn't want to put you on the spot. I just wanted to get a feel for how well you know the President and to see if you might be able to provide me with some insight into how the President might want me to respond to this situation. We don't have any time to contact him, so I need to make a decision now."

Peter said, "In that case, Sir, I'd be happy to share my thoughts. The President did tell me just before he sent me here that there were some high-level members of the Joint Chiefs of Staff that were pressing him for an all-out invasion of Cuba, much like the destroyer captains are pushing you now. But the President took the quarantine route rather than a full-scale invasion to minimize the possibility of worldwide thermonuclear war. I don't know which decision I'd make if I were you, but I think if the President were making this decision he would decide on patience. In fact, I am sure of it."

The Admiral responded, "Thanks, Peter, I just needed some reinforcement for my decision. I'm not giving those destroyer captains the order to fire on the sub. If the President could be patient with the entire Soviet Union, I can be patient with just one submarine."

On board the Soviet submarine under water, the situation was getting critical because they were almost out of air. The captain ordered the arming of the nuclear torpedo. He wasn't ready to fire it, but he wanted to keep all his options open. The officers finally agreed that firing the nuclear torpedo would be suicide and would have terrible worldwide consequences. But they were afraid of how their superiors back in the USSR would react if they surfaced and had to surrender their vessel. That, however, was the decision they eventually made.

Moments later, the conning tower of the Soviet submarine broke the surface and the Captain of the USS Beale breathed a sigh of relief. That information was immediately communicated to the Admiral on board the USS Independence. Captain Sharkey heard the news as well, and felt that a crisis had just been averted. The next time Peter met with the President, he would be sure to tell him how the Admiral on board the Independence had acted with great prudence and restraint.

Since the Soviet submarine had surfaced of its own volition and not displayed any aggressive actions, it was allowed to proceed away from the island of Cuba on the surface without being attacked or boarded by the Americans. It was allowed to simply steam away with its sovereignty intact. Rather than being reprimanded when the sub arrived back at its home base, the Captain and crew were all decorated for their bravery in facing the entire American fleet and escaping from the American trap. The Soviets always put their own "spin" on the facts.

While Kennedy and his advisors were still considering Khrushchev's message, on the morning of October 27th Khrushchev sent another, more detailed message. He stated, "You are disturbed over Cuba because it is only 99 miles by sea from the coast of the United States. But you have placed destructive missile weapons in Turkey, literally next to us. I therefore make this proposal: We are willing to remove from Cuba the means which you regard as offensive. Your representatives will make a declaration to the effect that the United States will remove its analogous means from Turkey, and after that, persons entrusted by the United Nations Security Council could inspect on the spot the fulfillment of the pledges made."

On the evening of October 27th, the President sent his emissaries to meet with Khrushchev's emissaries. After this meeting, President Kennedy drafted a response letter that basically agreed to the terms of the settlement that Khrushchev had proposed. The U.S. already considered the nuclear weapons that they had positioned in Turkey to be obsolete, so their removal was not particularly important.

At 9:00 a.m. Eastern Daylight Time on October 28th. Radio Moscow broadcast a message from Khrushchev. During the broadcast Khrushchev stated, "The Soviet government, in addition to previously issued instructions on the cessation of further work at the building sites for the weapons, has issued a new order on the dismantling of the weapons which the Americans describe as offensive, and their crating and return to the Soviet Union."

Kennedy immediately responded, issuing a public statement calling this, "an important and constructive contribution to peace."

The U.S. continued its quarantine, but in the following days, aerial reconnaissance proved that the Soviets were keeping their word and removing the missile systems. Between November 5th and November 9th, all the Soviet missiles had been loaded onto eight Soviet ships and had departed Cuba back to the USSR. The President ordered the military to stand down from Defcon 2. The crisis had passed.

After the withdrawal of all the Soviet missiles, the U.S. government declared the end of the quarantine on November 20, 1962. Although it took a bit longer, all of the U.S. missiles were disassembled and removed from Turkey by April 24, 1963.

President Kennedy had stood up to the Soviets and won the Cuban Missile Crisis. He had proven that he was not the weak leader that the Soviets had imagined.

But both the Soviets and the Cubans hated him for his success. Many in both the Soviet and Cuban governments sought revenge against the United States generally, and President Kennedy personally.

Although it had not been ordered to do so by Premier Khrushchev, the First Chief Directorate of the Soviet Committee for State Security, the feared KGB, immediately began secret plans to assassinate the American leader. The mission of the First Chief Directorate was foreign espionage. There were other Directorates, with missions ranging from suppressing internal dissent to providing security for government officials, but the First Directorate was the most dangerous of them all. Although the KGB theoretically worked for the Premier, in fact, it was almost a shadow government unto itself that frequently acted independently of the political leadership.

In Cuba, the Secret Police in the Ministry of the Interior was under the direction of Che Guevara, one of Fidel Castro's chief lieutenants. He had participated in its formation in 1959 and had arranged for its members to be trained by the Stasi, the dreaded East German Secret Police. They believed they had previously thwarted several attempts by the American CIA to kill Fidel Castro, and so they already had been working on plans to assassinate the American President. But now, with this embarrassment of Cuba by the Americans, Che ordered the Secret Police to develop a plan quickly – and execute it!

CHAPTER ELEVEN

In early December, 1962, the Office of the President announced that President John F. Kennedy would visit Europe in June of 1963. He would visit Germany, Ireland, England and The Vatican.

The West German government had long been proposing a visit by a high United States official to West Berlin to show solidarity between the U.S. and West Germany with the isolated West Berliners.

The President of Ireland was ecstatic to learn that President Kennedy would be visiting his country. As the first U.S. president of Irish heritage, the visit would be a great boost to Irish morale.

In England, the nation welcomed his visit as a reaffirmation of the long-standing bonds between their two countries.

And in the Vatican, Pope Pius XII was elated to hear about the planned visit by the President. He had great affection for the Kennedy family since they had been so cordial and welcoming when he had first met them in the 1930's, when he was just a Cardinal visiting the U.S.

But when the news reached MI-5, the response was just the opposite. The section responsible for controlling any insurgency in Northern Ireland and protecting it from any attacks became very concerned. They viewed the visit by the American President as another step toward some type of action to force the reunification of Northern Ireland to the rest of Ireland, all to the detriment of Great Britain.

That group at MI-5 began to develop plans to prevent this eventual assault on Northern Ireland. They were already convinced that the secret radio station they had discovered in Ireland was providing key information to the Americans. But they knew that although they could destroy the radio station at any time, the Americans could just immediately replace it with another radio station. It became apparent to the head of that section of MI-5 that the only way to completely stop the plot was to eliminate all the plotters, including the President of the United States.

Peter went back to Ireland in the middle of December, 1962, ostensibly to check on the performance of the radio station there. But this visit was more than just an official inspection.

Peter arrived in Dublin and spent a day shopping for baby gifts suitable for a newborn infant. He bought a baby bassinet, a stroller, a crib and various baby toys. He also bought a great quantity of diapers and other baby accessories.

Peter loaded all these things into the back of the Embassy car he requisitioned, and drove to the manor house. He did not announce his arrival in advance. He thought it would be nice to surprise Jean with some Christmas gifts for her new baby.

When Peter arrived at the manor house, Michael Brady was there to meet him. Michael asked, "Any news of what's going on with my cousin Jack?"

Peter responded, "Well, he's fine as far as I know. And I've heard that he's planning on visiting Ireland in the spring or maybe early summer."

When he heard that, Michael Brady's eyes brightened and he said, "That would be so nice. And do you think that he'll be visiting us out here?"

Peter said, "I'm sure he will and I know he appreciates all of your efforts on his behalf."

Then Peter asked Michael if he could help him unload all the things in the car.

They were both in the process of unloading the vehicle when Jean came running out of the house. She said, "Peter, Peter! How come you didn't tell me that you were coming?"

Peter responded, "Well, I wasn't sure that I'd be able to get here before Christmas, but here I am."

Jean smiled warmly and said, "It's so nice to see you again."

Peter responded, "It's always nice to see you, too. And I brought some things here for Christmas."

Jean stated, "But it's not Christmas yet."

Peter said, "I know that. But I have to go back to Washington before it's actually Christmas Day. How about I just bring in some of this stuff and we pretend that tonight is Christmas Eve?"

Jean's eyes lit up as she said, "Peter, what a nice idea! I've always loved Christmas. Can I help you bring some of this stuff in?"

Peter said, "No, no, let us do it. I don't think you should be doing any lifting in your condition."

Jean smiled and said, "I'm only pregnant, not disabled." With that, she grabbed one of the larger packages and carried it into the house.

After all the items that Peter had brought to the manor house were unloaded and delivered to the living room, Jean opened each one individually in the Christmas tradition.

Peter apologized for not being able to wrap them appropriately, but he was immediately forgiven by Jean.

Michael Brady and his three associates lived at the house along with Jean. They joined her in the living room while she opened the presents. All in all it was a very enjoyable night for everyone, and Brady and his friends, as well as Peter, celebrated it with a bit of Irish whiskey. Jean would have loved to have had a taste herself, but she was afraid that the alcohol might have an adverse effect on her baby. Plus she was already borderline nauseous and pretty sure the alcohol would push her over the edge.

The next morning, Peter, who had been sleeping on the sofa, was startled as he was awakened by a touch on his lips. At first he thought that he had been dreaming about a butterfly alighting on his lips. But then he realized it was not a dream.

Once awake, he found himself staring directly into Jean's eyes. The touch he had felt was her light kiss upon his lips.

As soon as Jean saw that he was awake, she said, "Merry Christmas, Peter. That's all I can offer you right now since I can't shop for gifts over here, but I want you to know how much I appreciate the presents for the baby. Not to mention all the help you have given us."

Peter responded, "Merry Christmas, Jean. And that's the nicest Christmas gift I could have imagined."

Jean smiled as she got off the sofa and headed to the kitchen to make coffee and tea for everyone.

* * * * * * * * * *

The surveillance of the manor house that MI-5 had been conducting was starting to produce some positive evidence. They knew that the Americans had installed a very sophisticated radio system in the house and had tried to hide the antennas in the trees. There would be absolutely no reason for the Americans to do this unless they were secretly planning to support the Republic of Ireland in a takeover of Northern Ireland. Colonel Conners was the head of a department within MI-5 that was unofficially referred to as the "Irish Section." The Colonel became convinced that this radio set-up confirmed his fears about the Americans supporting the Irish and their bid to take over Northern Ireland, which of course was British territory. He knew he could not let that happen. He began to make some preliminary plans to prevent that takeover from succeeding.

Through his contacts, he had already been able to determine that the visitors to the manor house included an American Office of Naval Intelligence operative named Captain Peter Sharkey. Captain Sharkey usually traveled using his own documents, so it had not been difficult to identify him. The Colonel also learned that the men who installed the radio and antennas were also members of the same Intelligence unit. His informants told him that Michael Brady was an Irish Republican Army sympathizer, so to Colonel Conners, that confirmed his suspicions. The Americans had decided to establish a clandestine radio station here to coordinate their future actions and those of the IRA to help the Irish Republic seize Northern Ireland!

Peter Sharkey scheduled another visit to Ireland to check on the "radio station" in February, 1963. He knew that Jean was scheduled to deliver her baby sometime during the month. He knew he couldn't stay there for the entire month, but he did want to be there to support her during this time. Before he left the United States, President Kennedy called Peter into his office to tell him that a secret trust fund had been set up in Switzerland for the baby, and Peter had been made the sole trustee. Jack wanted Peter to tell Marilyn that the baby would never have to worry about financial problems. Peter was going to tell Jack that Marilyn already had substantial financial resources, but Jack was so proud of his trust fund idea that Peter decided to remain quiet about Marilyn's money.

When Peter arrived at the manor house that evening, all the lights were on and there was an unusual vehicle parked at an odd angle in the driveway. The vehicle was a pick-up truck, but it had an attachment in the back that had various compartments opening out on both sides.

Peter rushed in, only to be restrained by Michael Brady. Michael said, "Hey, Peter. I'm so glad you're here. Jean's just gone into labor and we expect a delivery any moment now." Peter was surprised that he'd timed his visit so well, but he was pleased that the baby would be born soon.

Peter, Michael and the others all waited in the living room while the midwife was in with Jean. They couldn't risk bringing Jean to a hospital in Dublin because there would have been too many questions asked. So they procured the services of a local midwife. It was her truck in the driveway. Apparently all the compartments in the back of the truck contained everything that might be needed during a baby's birth.

Michael Brady was confident about the midwife's abilities since she had delivered him over thirty years earlier. Unless a serious medical problem develops, a midwife is usually able to handle the delivery of a normal baby.

Twenty minutes later, the midwife came out into the parlor and said, "Well, it's a boy and the mother is fine."

Peter, Michael and the others stood up and clapped.

The midwife said, "Now that the birthing is over, Jean is able to have visitors, but try to keep things short since she is very tired and needs to get some rest."

Both Michael and Peter immediately asked in unison, "Can we go in now?"

"Certainly," the midwife said, "go on in to meet the new Mother and her son."

When they go into the master bedroom, both Michael and Peter circled the bed but didn't say anything. Jean was lying there in a flannel nightshirt with her eyes closed. She had the new baby tucked between her breasts.

They just stood there quietly for a few moments since they were not sure whether Jean was asleep or not. But then her eyes opened and she saw both Peter and Michael. She exclaimed, "Peter, I didn't know you were going to be here. I can't thank both of you guys enough. I can't believe that I'm finally a mother. This is just so marvelous for me to have my own baby. I can't believe how insignificant my former life was even though I once thought it was so important. I know that the only important thing in my life now is my baby, my baby," she repeated, sounding like she didn't yet believe it.

And then Jean shut her eyes from exhaustion.

Neither Michael nor Peter had gotten to talk to her. They thought they were going to do that, but she fell asleep right in front of their eyes as she was talking to them.

So they slipped silently out of the bedroom and went back into the parlor where they broke out the best Irish whiskey and everyone toasted Jean's new baby. Even the elderly midwife awarded herself a libation for a job well done.

* * * * * * * * * *

Meanwhile back in the United States, a slender, weasel-like man was walking slowly down the street heading back to his rooming house when he saw a large well-tanned man approaching him.

As they got closer, the large man said in Russian, "Dobryj dyen, Alek."

This was a common Russian greeting and meant "Good afternoon, Alek."

Although he spoke Russian, Alek was immediately defensive as he responded in English, "Who the hell are you?"

Alek was always worried about being entrapped in the U.S. by the FBI because of the years he had spent in the Soviet Union.

The stranger then asked in Spanish, "Habla usted Español?"

Alek was puzzled, but he guessed at the meaning of the question. He said, "What? No, I don't speak Spanish. Who are you and what do you want?"

The stranger responded in Russian and said, "Since you don't speak Spanish, we can talk in Russian. Or we can speak in English if you prefer."

Alek said, "Of course I prefer English. I'm an American citizen. I did spend some time in Russia, but I am glad to be back here in my own country. I love America and I'm a good citizen. Where the hell did you come from anyway?"

The stranger smiled and said, "Of course, then, we'll talk English."

The stranger had a weird accent to his English that seemed to reflect both a Spanish and Russian influence. Alek said again, "I asked who you are and now I'd like to know why you are here."

The stranger responded, "Before I answer, are you in fact Alek J. Hidell, who was formerly in the United States Marine Corps and who spent some time in Russia?"

This was a name he had used frequently, both in Russia and after returning to the United States. Since he didn't think this would give away any knowledge that the FBI didn't already know, Alek acknowledged, "Okay, so you know who I am. Now who the hell are you?"

The stranger responded, "I'm a friend and I've come to work with you on a mission of great importance. America has no respect for any other nations and has an arrogant attitude. It has endangered the existence of the entire planet by threatening nuclear war over some trivial missiles in my country – Cuba."

Alek now inspected the stranger in some detail since he didn't completely buy the Cuba comment. The stranger was a formidable looking man over six-feet tall with massive shoulders. He had thinning brown hair and a very thick neck. His hands looked big enough to encircle a cantaloupe. His face was weathered like brown leather from sun exposure, but he didn't look Cuban. He looked Russian.

Alek decided to embrace the charade about Cuba, but didn't believe it for an instant. He asked again, "So why are you here? And who the hell are you?"

The stranger said in Spanish, "Yo soy El Coronel." Then he repeated in English, "Just call me the Colonel, since names are not necessary for our mission. I will call you Alek, since that is the name you have chosen for yourself and is a name fitting for a warrior in this battle between nations. The French call it a Nom de Guerre, and I think Alek is perfect for you. A small country like my Cuba needs to rely on big heroes to protect her. And I am here to ask for help from a great warrior like you."

Alek knew he was being flattered, and he savored the compliments as he asked, "So what do you want from me?"

"I'll get to that," El Coronel replied, "But first let me tell you about the inducements that I have been authorized to offer you. Of course, upon the completion of this mission, you'll first go to Havana where you will receive a Hero's Parade. Several weeks of honorary ceremonies will be held. Cuban women will be most thankful for your bravery.

"Later we can transport you to Russia if you want. There you will be regaled as a great protector of Cuba – a close Russian ally. The Russians will also grant you a generous lifetime pension and give you an apartment in Moscow, as well as a Dacha on the Black Sea. At that time you'll be able to summon your wife if you wish, although by then you'll also have so many Russian women who would desire you, that you might not be interested in your wife anymore."

Alek had spent a couple of years in the Soviet Union previously, and had been disappointed by his time there. He thought he would receive a hero's welcome back then, but all they offered was a meager existence. Alek realized that at that time, however, he had nothing to really offer the Soviets. Then he was only a grunt Marine.

But he had heard stories about very, very generous rewards to Americans who had provided State secrets or did a substantial favor for the Russian government. He was also well aware of the power of the Soviet government to both punish its enemies and reward its friends. He decided to work with El Coronel.

Alek knew that El Coronel wasn't any more Cuban than he himself was. The bastard was obviously a Russian, but he would play along with the deception because he knew that Cuba was totally supported by the Soviets, and that it was the Soviets, not the Cubans, that could provide monetary incentives for his cooperation.

The next afternoon, March 9, 1963, El Coronel picked up Alek after he left work for the day. El Coronel was driving a late-model car, which impressed Alek, since he did not have a driver's license and could not yet drive. He was sure he'd have a nice car in the Soviet Union once he'd done what El Coronel wanted.

As they discussed, there was an enemy of Cuba living in Dallas. His name was Major General Edwin A. Walker, who had resigned from the United States Army in 1961. Since that time he had led an active campaign against Cuba and was trying to become a major political figure.

Alek agreed with El Coronel's assessment that General Walker presented a serious threat to Cuba and should be eliminated, so they headed to General Walker's residence to reconnoiter his house. Alek brought along a camera to photograph the scene.

After they arrived at General Walker's residence, El Coronel and Alek stealthily walked around the entire house, keeping behind the bushes along the perimeter of the lawn. Alek used his camera to shoot several photographs of both the front and the rear of the house.

El Coronel parked his car out in the street in front of the house and admonished Alek not to include the car when he tried to take a photo of the front of the house. Alek assured El Coronel that his photo did not include the automobile, but Alek was secretly not so sure of that.

Anyway, after Alek drew a map of the property to accompany his photos, they headed back to Alek's rooming house. During the trip, El Coronel instructed Alek as to the weapon that he needed to order. El Coronel told him that he needed to buy a model 91/38 Carcano rifle. El Coronel assured Alek that this was an ideal assassination weapon which will prove successful in the attack on General Walker, and maybe some even-more-important later assassinations. El Coronel described his prior knowledge about such a rifle and praised its rapid bolt action which allows rapid repetitive fire, even though it's a manually operated rifle and not a full automatic one. Since fully automatic weapons were not available by mail order, this would be the next best thing.

Just before El Coronel dropped Alek off back at his rooming house, he gave him $200 in cash. He could easily have given Alek more, but he didn't want to raise his expectations too high at this point. This amount would be more than enough to purchase the rifle and also provide Alek with some extra spending money.

The next day Alek did as he was instructed and ordered the designated rifle from a mail order house.

He also ordered a pistol from a different mail order house. Although El Coronel hadn't told him to order a pistol, Alek thought it might be helpful during this venture. In any case, he loved weapons and since it was El Coronel's money, he thought this was just an additional gift that he should buy for himself. He received both weapons before the end of the month.

On April 10, 1963, Alek took one bus and then transferred to another bus to reach the home of General Walker. He was carrying the rifle wrapped in paper, since it was much too long to conceal any other way. After Alek left the second bus, he walked several blocks to General Walker's residence.

Alek waited until darkness so that he would have his best advantage. The lights would be on in Walker's residence and he could escape more easily in the darkness after the assassination was over.

At about 9:00 p.m., General Walker was seated at his desk in his office with the windows open. The lights were on in the office, so he was a very visible target.

Alek maneuvered silently in the bushes until he found a perfect shooting spot. He carefully lined up his target and then, after holding his breath to steady his aim, he pulled the trigger. The bullet missed General Walker's head as it crashed into the wall behind him. General Walker immediately dropped to the floor.

Alek cursed to himself when he saw that the General was not hit. He knew the police would be arriving soon, so he grabbed the rifle and ran from the scene.

As he was fleeing, he found an ideal place to stash the rifle where it would be hidden and he could retrieve it later. He didn't want to be caught with the rifle in his possession, but he didn't want to lose it either. After stashing the rifle, Alek ran back to the main street where he caught a bus to head home.

When the news of the attack on General Walker hit the American media, there were all sorts of conspiracy theories advanced. General Walker had a great many enemies.

But when the news reached El Coronel, he decided that although he could trust Alek for his commitment to the project, he couldn't trust his marksmanship to complete any projects.

El Coronel lost faith in Alek Hidell and so he stopped contacting him.

* * * * * * * * * *

Alek was disappointed when he didn't hear anything further from El Coronel. He knew that he botched the attack on General Walker and he was afraid that he'd never hear from El Coronel again.

Alek's economic situation deteriorated further during the summer of 1963. He got, and then lost, a couple of jobs.

Alek became desperate. He traveled to Mexico City and visited the Cuban embassy on September 27th. He requested a visa to leave the United States and go to Cuba, but the embassy officials were not cooperative.

Then he visited the Soviet embassy. He found them uncooperative also. Apparently the operation that he had been involved in was so secretive that none of the embassy officials knew anything about it.

Alek was disappointed by his lack of success. But when he arrived back in Dallas he discovered that someone had delivered a note from El Coronel. It contained a telephone number for him to call. After following the instructions he received, Alek got to speak to El Coronel, who knew about his desperate visit to Mexico City. El Coronel warned him not to do anything like that again since that would only blow his cover as an agent.

Alek was instructed to apply for a job at the Texas School Book Depository. El Coronel told him that it was imperative that he get this job and that he should not haggle about wages or anything else. He just needed to get the job and start to report to work faithfully.

Alek didn't know exactly why he was given these instructions, but he did exactly as he was ordered. He really needed a job.

* * * * * * * * * *

Eamon de Valera was born in Ireland in October, 1882 and had spent all of his life involved in Ireland's struggle for independence from Britain, and later for Irish reunification with the northern counties.

De Valera had been active during the 1916 "Easter Rising" which pitted Irish rebels against the British. His forces were forced to surrender and he was imprisoned. He had been sentenced to death, but his sentence later was commuted to life in prison.

As the political situation changed, de Valera was ultimately released from prison. But he had espoused violent actions in the past, and many of his British captors opposed his release, fearing that he would promote violence again.

But he was released, and they were proven correct. He still espoused violence.

He was a leader during the Irish War of Independence, which began in 1919. This was a guerrilla war mounted by the Irish Republican Army (IRA). This conflict ended in December, 1921 with the Anglo-Irish Treaty. This treaty ended British rule in most of Ireland, but not all of it. It established the Irish Free State. But it allowed six northern counties that were predominantly Protestant, and whose population consisted mostly of English immigrants, to remain aligned with Britain.

De Valera was against this treaty and was a leading participant in the ensuing Irish Civil War of 1922-1923. The war ended indecisively, which basically maintained the status quo between the Irish Free State and Northern Ireland.

But by 1932, his rebellious history notwithstanding, Eamon de Valera had entered mainstream politics. In March of 1932 he was elected President of the nation of Ireland, which had now outgrown its moniker as the Irish Free State.

It was de Valera who was in charge of the government on the eve of World War II. It was de Valera who promoted neutrality, hoping that this would lead to the reunification of Ireland. Many in the country advocated Irish participation in the war on the Allied side, but others saw England's difficulty as Ireland's opportunity for reunification, and were thus pro-German.

He was successful in getting Ireland to officially declare its neutrality in the conflict. He gained many new government powers such as censorship of the press, control of the economy and internment of suspected adversaries.

De Valera was under extreme pressure from the British during the war to support Britain, but he resisted until the end. In fact, de Valera sent a personal note of condolences to the German Minister in Dublin on the death of Adolph Hitler in 1945. This further damaged Ireland's relations with Britain and substantially worsened them with the United States. It wasn't so much that de Valera supported Germany, but he just desired complete independence of Ireland from England and wanted to reunify the entire island.

This goal of reuniting all of Ireland had remained out of his grasp throughout his entire lifetime. Now in 1962, he was 80 years old and desperate to take some action to make this happen. It would be the crowning achievement of his lifetime if he could do it, or his biggest failure if he couldn't. He spent hours each day plotting some way to make it happen.

When President John F. Kennedy, an Irishman and a Catholic, announced that he was planning to visit Ireland in June of 1963, de Valera began to firm up his plans. He held a great many meetings in his office to discuss the reunification of Ireland, and how he was sure President Kennedy would assist him in this momentous effort.

What he didn't know was that his office had long been bugged by MI-5!

Chapter Twelve

EUROPEAN VISIT

On June 23, 1963, President Kennedy departed for his tour of several European countries. He was scheduled to visit Germany, Ireland, England and the Vatican. Of course, Jack planned to meet with Marilyn and have his first meeting with his child while he was in Ireland. Maybe even get a little sex with Marilyn. Toward that end, he sent Peter back to Ireland once again to prepare everything.

He first arrived in West Berlin, where he made a brief visit to the Brandenburg Gate and looked into East Berlin at Checkpoint Charlie. Checkpoint Charlie was the main point for the trading of spies and captives between East Germany and West Germany. Following that, Jack addressed an enormous crowd of at least 150,000 people.

At the end of World War II in 1945, the victorious Allied powers reached the Potsdam Agreement on the fate of post-war Europe. This called for dividing the defeated Germany into four occupation zones, one each for the British, French, Americans and Soviets.

Additionally, the German capital of Berlin was likewise divided into four areas.

Unfortunately, Berlin was located 100 miles inside the Soviet zone. This did not initially appear to be a problem since relations between the Soviets and the other Allies were mutually supportive and cordial immediately after the war.

But later, those relations soured as the democratic Allies suspected the Soviets of trying to expand their communist empire.

These problems developed into outright hostility when the Soviets, in 1948, imposed a blockade on Berlin and thus effectively withdrew from the group of Allies. Since the agreement at the end of World War II did not require them to allow unfettered rail or road access to Berlin, they decided to block all traffic into the city.

In response, the remaining Allies launched the Berlin Airlift. This became an enormous parade of cargo aircraft delivering vital supplies to Berlin on a daily basis. In fact, so many aircraft landed at the three main Berlin airports that one was landing almost every minute of every day. This heroic effort by the French, British and Americans thwarted the blockade from the Soviets.

While this enormous parade of aircraft provided all of the necessities that the West Berliners needed, it also provided something more – it provided hope!

Now, as the enormous crowd of almost 150,000 people gathered to await the speech by President John F. Kennedy, many of them remembered the debt they owed to the Americans for supporting the Berlin Airlift, which had prevented the Soviets from controlling the city.

Jack delivered a marvelous speech before the enormous crowd. He spoke about how well the West Berliners endured despite the hardships caused by the Soviet restrictions on their freedom. He also pointed out that the western democracies have never had to install a wall to prevent their peoples from escaping. Quite unlike the Berlin Wall that the East Germans and the Soviets erected to prevent East Berliners from leaving. President Kennedy ended his speech by saying, "Ich bin ein Berliner," which means, "I am a Berliner."

The crowd exploded with thunderous applause. As Jack exited the stage, the applause never abated, even as he left for the airport to depart for Ireland.

Upon his arrival in Ireland, President Kennedy was greeted by the President of Ireland, Eamon De Valera. Afterwards, the President went to the residence of the American Ambassador, Matthew McCloaky, where he was scheduled to sleep each night.

Thursday, June 27, 1963 proved to be a great day for President Kennedy. Early that morning he had a brief meeting with the Prime Minister of Ireland, and then departed by helicopter to O'Kennedy Park in New Ross, Ireland. The park was named for a distant ancestor of President Kennedy.

At noon he departed New Ross and traveled to Dunganstown, Ireland. Dunganstown was the ancestral homestead of the Kennedy's. A reception was held there at the home of Mrs. Mary Ryan, the President's second cousin. He was greeted by many distant relatives, most of whom he did not know and had never met. But Michael Brady was there and he got to spend a few moments talking to him.

Michael had been instrumental in providing a safe sanctuary for Marilyn Monroe and her new baby. Kennedy had met him only once before and really didn't know him, but he was grateful for his assistance. He was pleased Michael had chosen to help him, and to repay the decades of support from the successful American Kennedys to the more impoverished Irish Kennedy family.

All the President's great grandparents had immigrated into Boston, Massachusetts during the Potato Famine of the late 1840s, which had devastated Ireland. Through hard work and dedication, both of President Kennedy's grandfathers had become successful Boston politicians by the end of the century. His paternal grandfather, Patrick J. Kennedy, started out as a tavern owner, but later became a banker and a representative in the Massachusetts legislature. His maternal grandfather, John F. Fitzgerald (aka Honey Fitz), became a colorful politician who served in both the Massachusetts State Senate and the U.S. House of Representatives. He served three terms as the Mayor of Boston.

Although his ancestors worked hard to obtain their personal success, they never forgot their Irish heritage. They were avid supporters of the Fenian Movement, which was an American-based group that pursued the reunification of Ireland. Although none of them were ever active Fenian members, they did provide financial support to the movement, as did a great many other enthusiastic Irish-Americans.

The American Kennedys always continued to send financial support back to the family members that had stayed behind in Ireland. That was just the way families did things back then, and as the American Kennedys had become more and more financially successful, they sent more and more support back to their family members in the Old Country.

So it was not unexpected that the relatives at the reception in the home of Mrs. Ryan would be overwhelmingly enthusiastic about meeting President Kennedy. After all, most of their families had been receiving at least some small stipend from the American Kennedys for generations. But the President knew immediately that the reception he received was warm and heartfelt and based on family ties, not any past monetary rewards. From there, he moved on to several other official receptions.

By the end of the day, President Kennedy had more than enough of the official ceremonies and was anxious to return back to the Ambassador's residence. It was not just that he was tired from all the ceremonies, but he knew that he was about to have a clandestine meeting with Marilyn, and meet their baby son for the first time.

* * * * * * * * * *

Just before dawn on Friday, June 28, 1963, Peter arrived in a borrowed U.S. Embassy car to pick up Jean and the baby. He had delivered them both the prior night for a clandestine meeting with Jack. Since the Ambassador's house was well back from the street and there were both U.S. Secret Service Agents and Irish police patrolling the perimeter, he hadn't had any difficulty bringing Jean to meet the President undetected by outsiders.

Jean had a shawl over her head and kept the baby close to her breast as she hurried into the backseat of the car where Peter was awaiting her. As soon as she had closed the door, Peter drove away quickly.

Peter said to Jean, "I think we're doing fine. I didn't see any cameras around, so I don't think anyone detected you or the baby."

Jean asked, "Do you still think that they might be trying to find me or figure out what happened?"

Peter responded, "No, I really don't think so. But we can never be too careful."

Jean said, "That's good, because I just feel so peaceful and happy here in Ireland and I really hope nothing will happen to force me to move."

Peter said, "I don't think you have anything to worry about, at least not right now. And the longer time goes on, I think there will be even less to worry about."

Then Peter asked, somewhat hesitantly, "So how did your meeting with Jack go?"

Jean said, "It was marvelous. Jack was so thrilled to see the baby for the first time. Even though neither of us had planned for this, he seems to be so pleased about the baby, just as I am. All in all, it was a great night."

Peter questioned, "All in all? So you and Jack had an enjoyable time together besides just sharing the baby?"

Jean looked at Peter with a slight smile on her face after hearing that and asked, "Peter Sharkey, are you asking if I slept with Jack again? And why would that be? Are you jealous?"

She had adopted an Irish accent that seemed so authentic that Peter could have sworn she was born here – if he didn't know otherwise.

Peter felt his cheeks flush with heat as he turned away from Jean and said, "No, no, of course not. I was just wondering how things were going."

Jean said, "Peter, are you blushing?"

Peter had sometimes been embarrassed by blushing when he was in high school, but he thought he was well past all that now. It always seemed to happen when he was talking to a pretty girl that he hoped to impress. He couldn't believe this bane of his teenage years had returned, but he felt a hot flushing in his cheeks that he had not felt in many years. He knew he must be blushing, but he still denied it and said, "No, no, of course not. It's just – ahh – just hot in the car." He was stammering.

Jean said, "Of course, you are blushing, dear Peter. I'm very flattered. It's nice to know that you care about me. And just for your information, Jack and I did not sleep together last night. That part of my life is over. I made a mistake dallying around with a married man once before, but that will never happen again. The rest of my life is going to center around my child and living a normal life."

Peter said, "I'm sorry. I really wasn't trying to question you about your personal life. I just was…"

Jean cut him off. "Don't give me any of that blarney, Peter Sharkey." (Both of them knew "blarney" was an Irish term for an outrageous lie.) I know men, and I understand about the questions they ask. Just for your information, the baby spent the night on the bed next to Jack. I slept on the sofa. Later I almost regretted not climbing into the bed next to the baby, just so he could be between his two parents, but in retrospect I guess that wouldn't have been a good idea. Jack might have thought it to be an invitation to something more. But it was so nice to see Jack and his infant son sleeping together in the bed when I awoke to get the baby and come out to meet you."

Peter said again, "I really am sorry. I didn't mean to… to… to intrude…"

Jean cut him off again. "Peter Sharkey, stop stammering and blushing. Just listen to me. I am so grateful to you for all you've done for me. I like you too. I'm not ready for a new relationship right now but maybe someday after this mess is done, you and I can get to know each other better. I'd like that. What do you think?"

Peter was surprised by her comments and he could only nod his head. He was virtually speechless. He couldn't trust himself to speak. And he knew his cheeks were now an even more vivid shade of red!

Jean leaned over and gave him a cooling kiss on his blisteringly hot cheeks.

* * * * * * * * * *

During the daytime of Friday, June 28, 1963, President Kennedy had a whirlwind of visits to historic Irish sites. He was whisked from place to place and received an enormous friendly and enthusiastic reception everywhere.

At 8:00 p.m. that evening he returned to the de Valera residence for a final dinner in Ireland before his scheduled departure the next day. Upon his arrival, President de Valera personally welcomed him at the doorway.

President de Valera said, "It's so nice to be able to see you again. Please come in and meet my other guests."

President Kennedy responded, "Of course. Thank you, sir, for your hospitality."

De Valera grasped the President's hand in a handshake and then continued to hold it as he guided him into the house. De Valera personally introduced Kennedy to all of the assembled guests. This was a small gathering and it seemed that the guests this evening had been selected by President de Valera because of their dedication to the reunification of Ireland.

Once President Kennedy had been introduced to all the guests, President de Valera suggested that they head to his office for a private discussion.

Once inside the office, President de Valera said, "I know that your family has long supported the reunification of Ireland. Some of your ancestors were generous supporters of the Fenian Movement, and most of your current relatives are supporters of either the IRA or Sinn Fein, so I know that I can trust you to also support our reunification."

Neither man knew that President de Valera's office had been bugged by MI-5 for years. Their conversation was now being recorded by MI-5.

President Kennedy wanted to be as supportive as possible, so he responded, "Yes, I think that it only makes sense for all of Ireland to be reunified, as long as it can be done in a peaceful manner."

De Valera answered, "Well, that's exactly how I feel, but I think it might take some rather forceful actions to make this happen. I've drafted some plans that I hope you'll be able to support.

"As you know, our army has been providing soldiers to the United Nations' action in the Congo. We've had over 5,000 men serve there and they have been very well trained by the UN while there. Unfortunately, we've also lost some soldiers to enemy action, but our men always performed with great bravery.

"As the conflict in the Congo winds down, we expect that these soldiers will all be back in Ireland along with much of the military equipment they have been using. We've been told that they'll keep all of their rifles and other weaponry. We've also been told that they'll be given the armored personnel carriers they've been using there. This would be so that they could continue to train on the use of these weapons, in case they might need to be deployed to support the United Nations again."

Jack said, "I know, Eamon. I've heard that the Irish soldiers have performed admirably during their deployment in the Congo. But I don't understand exactly what this has to do with reunification."

Eamon responded, "Just this, I believe that with these troops, we can mount a police action to protect Irish Catholics in Londonderry and other Ulster areas from attack by Northern Ireland terrorists. This would be a surprise intrusion into Northern Ireland, but would be announced very publicly afterward as an action just to protect innocent civilians.

"Our troops would quickly surround the small garrisons of British troops in Northern Ireland and would contain them to their bases. With the element of surprise, no one would fire any shots. Then with our troops firmly in control of the major cities, England would have no choice but to negotiate an end to the partitioning of Ireland."

President Kennedy was caught completely off-guard by this crazy proposal, so he said, "Well, I'm not sure that would work and you might have underestimated the response of the British. Plus why would these Irish-Catholic citizens in Northern Ireland suddenly need protection?"

President de Valera stated, "Well, of course we'd secretly stage some type of problem. Maybe a bombing or something that we could blame on the Northern Irish terrorists. Anything, just so it would be violent enough to justify our intervention."

President Kennedy was aghast at this suggestion to bomb innocent Irish Catholics in Northern Ireland just to set up a pretext for the armed invasion, but he knew that these were probably just the ramblings of an elderly leader who had reached nearly the end of his lifetime. So instead of responding negatively, President Kennedy decided to just act diplomatically. He said, "But how would you react if the British decide to respond by sending more troops?"

De Valera responded, "Well, of course, that's where the United States comes in. I know that you've got aircraft carriers in the Mediterranean and may even have one now off the coast of Scotland. I think if you were to position one of those carriers just off the coast of Northern Ireland, the British would get the point that the United States supports our action and thus would not try to send any troops into Ireland. It would be just like the quarantine you imposed on Cuba, except this one would require a much smaller force since Northern Ireland has only about 200 miles of coastline, which is less than one-tenth the coastline of Cuba."

President Kennedy was about to respond to these preposterous comments when there was a knock on the door. De Valera said, "Enter, please."

When the door opened, they were informed that dinner was being served and all of the guests were already seated. Since it would be disrespectful to keep the guests waiting, both de Valera and Kennedy retreated to the dining room.

There they were seated next to each other and they quietly continued their discussions about de Valera's plans. President Kennedy told him that he could not support any actions like what de Valera had proposed, and in no case would he ever be able to order a United States aircraft carrier to impose a quarantine, or in any other way support an armed intervention into Northern Ireland. President Kennedy told de Valera that the only way to reunify Ireland was peacefully, by the ballot box – not by any forceful means.

De Valera was disappointed by the President's response, but he didn't completely abandon his plan. He thought he might still accomplish his objectives without the support of the Americans or the American aircraft carrier.

But he'd have to wait until another time to think more about his plans. For tonight, all they needed to do was just enjoy the visit from the American President and promote the strong relationship between the Irish and the Americans. De

Valera thought he could eventually convince Kennedy to support his plans to reunite Ireland.

MI-5 had only been able to listen in on the conversations in President de Valera's office. Those conversations seemed to indicate that the United States would be supporting an armed invasion of Northern Ireland by experienced Irish troops after their return from the Congo. MI-5 did not have the dining room bugged, so they never heard Kennedy's negative response regarding the planned intrusion into Northern Ireland.

So from what MI-5 had heard, everything reinforced their belief that Northern Ireland would soon be under assault from Ireland, and that the assault would be supported by the Americans under the direction of their Irish President, John F. Kennedy. It might even involve an American Naval quarantine of Northern Ireland!

Before President Kennedy departed Ireland, he gave a speech to thank everyone for the warm reception he received during his visit to Ireland. He concluded his speech by saying that he hoped to return to Ireland the following year.

The citizens of the Republic of Ireland viewed this as a cherished promise, while the members of MI-5 viewed this as a threat. Possibly, Kennedy was planning to come back as a victorious leader who had helped the Republic of Ireland conquer Northern Ireland.

On Sunday, June 30, 1963, President Kennedy arrived in England to meet with Harold Macmillan, the Prime Minister. Together, they visited several prominent historical sites in London and met privately to discuss routine matters like trade and mutual defense.

On Monday morning, July 1, 1963, President Kennedy departed England and arrived in Italy. He was greeted at the airport by Antonio Segni, the President of Italy. The Presidents spent the rest of the day touring historical sites, and had several private meetings with the Italian Ministers and prominent politicians.

The highlight of President Kennedy's visit to Italy occurred on July 2, 1963, when he was privileged to visit Pope Paul VI at the Vatican. Pope Paul had just received his Coronation on June 21st of that year, and so this was the first visit that the Pope had agreed to with a major national leader since he had assumed the leadership of the Catholic Church.

Pope Paul knew that his predecessor, Pope Pius XII, was very fond of the Kennedy family and had spent some very memorable moments with them during his visit to New York before World War II when then-Cardinal Pacelli had not yet ascended to the Papacy. Pope Paul was very much looking forward to this meeting with the President.

When President Kennedy was ushered into the meeting room at the Vatican, he approached Pope Paul in a very warm and friendly fashion. He did not kneel or bow to the Pope, since that would be politically unpopular back in America. Instead, President Kennedy extended his hand in friendship and respect. The Pope took his hand and returned the handshake.

They lingered for several moments in the meeting room, so that the photographers could take all the photos they wanted of this momentous occasion. Then the Pope summoned President Kennedy to follow him into a private meeting room.

Once there, President Kennedy said to the Pope, "Your Holiness, thank you so much for granting me this audience."

The Pope responded, "Nonsense, Mr. President. Your election has done more to publicize the Catholic Church than any other event in the last several years. I am truly happy that you were able to make this trip to the Vatican."

President Kennedy responded, "Your comments are way too complimentary, Your Holiness. But I do appreciate them more than you know."

Now that the pleasantries were over, the Pope switched immediately to a subject that had already caused him much pain. He asked President Kennedy, "What do you think Fidel Castro is plotting next?"

President Kennedy was prepared for this question since he knew that Castro was a mutual enemy. President Kennedy responded, "We think he intends to spread his Communist revolution throughout South America, as well as extending it into Africa. Communism, although a flawed doctrine that doesn't appeal to the more prosperous countries of the world, still seems to be a desirable goal in the impoverished nations. So we think Castro is preparing to export his Cuban Revolution to the poorest nations in both South America and Africa."

The Pope was aghast at this revelation from President Kennedy. He exclaimed, "But how could that be? Cuba is but a small country."

Kennedy explained, "Yes, it may be a small country, but the Cubans are a population that possess enormous enthusiasm for the Communist system, since they have been freed from decades under various corrupt military dictators. Castro seems to have no difficulty recruiting volunteers to serve in the forces he intends to send to promote revolutions in other nations."

The Pope said to President Kennedy, "Castro has done horrible damage to the Catholic Church in Cuba. As I'm sure you're aware, he has confiscated Church property as well as beaten and imprisoned Catholic priests and nuns. He has even executed some of our people. He is obviously trying to eradicate the Church in Cuba and replace it with a cult of his personal idolatry."

Kennedy responded, "Yes, Your Holiness. I'm well aware of the damage he has perpetrated on the Church in his country. The United States seeks to restrict his influence from expanding beyond his island nation, and will take every opportunity presented to us to oppose Castro."

The Pope answered, "I am glad that you feel like that. I was sure even before your visit that you were a good Catholic and would oppose the type of oppressive actions Castro has perpetrated. I am encouraged to learn that the United States will be an ally with us to oppose Castro."

President Kennedy responded, "I think all men of free will would understand the danger that Castro represents, but I am afraid that in the impoverished nations that he expects to enlist in his crusade, there may be some uneducated people that won't see the deception he also presents. They just want to escape from the poverty in which they suffer."

The Pope said, "Unfortunately, I agree with you totally. I pray every day that Castro will not succeed in his evil adventures and I promise you that we will do all we can to oppose him. Now, Mr. President, is there anything that I might offer you personally?"

To that President Kennedy replied, "Your Holiness, would it be too much to ask you to hear my Confession?"

The Pope responded, "Of course not, my son. The salvation of souls and the forgiveness of sin is the thing that I consider to be of the utmost importance both for the Church and for me personally."

President Kennedy decided to preface his Confession with a comment. He said, "Your Holiness, before I begin, I want you to know that there are several sins that I've committed that I have kept secret during my Confessions to my local priests. I know that in itself is a sin since I subsequently took Communion, but given my position, I just didn't feel comfortable being fully honest with my local priests. I have been honest in my prayers to God. I am sure that I can trust you with everything I tell you, but I did want to let you know about my secrets."

Pope Paul responded, "My son, as long as you now confess to me all of your sins, I am sure that Almighty God will absolve you of each of them. Don't dwell on what happened in the past, just repent and resolve to do better in the future."

President Kennedy was obviously relieved and said, "Thank you, Your Eminence. Can we begin?"

Pope Paul responded, "Of course, my son. Please come over to this small chapel area in my office so we'll both be more comfortable."

When President Kennedy left the Pope's office five minutes later, he felt a great relief. There were several things that had weighed upon his soul and troubled him, even some that prevented a sound sleep. He now felt a great renewal and was looking forward to his return to the United States.

BOOK THREE

AFTER THE ASSASSINATION

Chapter Thirteen

IMMEDIATE AFTERMATH

After he had fired his second and final shot, Carlos had quickly broken down his rifle and stuffed the parts back into the toolbox. Then he walked slowly away from the street. He did not think anyone had seen him since the crowd was watching the Presidential Motorcade. He even doubled back once, going toward the main street, to ensure that it did not seem like he was fleeing the scene. In any case, no one approached him as he left the grassy knoll and walked back to the side street to rejoin Eduardo.

Once Carlos was back in their vehicle, Eduardo proceeded to exit Dallas at a very leisurely pace. They followed the plan and drove north across Texas to Tulsa, Oklahoma. Along the way, they completely disassembled the Dragunov rifle and disposed of its parts in varying ways along the route. Some pieces were tossed into lakes and others were buried. They were very thorough professionals and were sure the rifle would never be found.

Once they reached Tulsa, they removed the registration plates from the truck and left it in a poor section of town with the keys in the ignition. They hoped that someone would take the abandoned vehicle and drive it away. In any case, there was no way they could ever be traced to the vehicle.

They then proceeded to the airport where they purchased tickets to Ottawa, Canada, using new and different documents from the ones they had used when they entered Mexico. From Canada, they would head home.

* * * * * * * * * *

Meanwhile, after fleeing from the Texas School Book Depository Building, Alek, whose real name was Lee Harvey Oswald, walked to the bus stop and caught a bus back to his rooming house. Once there, he immediately went to his room and retrieved his pistol. Then he headed back into the street.

But Oswald was not quite sure exactly where the hell he was going now. He had been quite calm during the shooting and his earlier encounter with the Dallas policeman in the warehouse, but at those times he was confident that he had an escape plan provided by El Coronel. But now that plan was gone, just like El Coronel himself.

Oswald was sure that by now the police had found the rifle on the sixth floor of the Texas Book Depository and had probably connected him to it. His mind was racked with confusion and anxiety as he walked almost aimlessly down a nearby street.

He did not know it, but essentially the entire Dallas Police Force had just been called in to duty. There was not a cop in Dallas who would rest until the assassin was found. But this increase in force had just begun, and so at this moment only the regularly deployed officers were on the street. Unfortunately for Oswald, he was about to meet one of those officers.

When he saw a Dallas police cruiser pass by, traveling in the opposite direction, Oswald was sure that it was searching for him. He decided that he needed to do something to protect himself, but he wasn't sure what to do. He started to turn away, but suddenly stopped when he realized that would be suspicious to the cop.

Patrolman J.D. Tippit had joined the Dallas Police Department in July, 1952. Officer Tippit was manning Police Cruiser Number Ten and had just heard a radio transmission that broadcast a description of the suspect in the shooting of the President as being, "a white male, approximately 30 years of age, slender build, height 5 foot 10 inches, weight 165 pounds."

Officer Tippit decided to stop the man, both because he met the description and because he was eying the police cruiser very suspiciously. The man approached the cruiser and exchanged words with Tippit through the driver side window. Dissatisfied with the man's answers, Officer Tippit instructed him to move to the front of the vehicle. Officer Tippit got out of his vehicle and started to approach the man. But just as he got close, Oswald pulled out his revolver and fired several shots at point blank range, four of which hit Officer Tippit, killing him instantly.

Oswald fled on foot and decided to hide in a movie house named the Texas Theater. Unfortunately for Oswald, many people saw him either shooting Officer Tippit or fleeing the scene.

One of the witnesses watched as Oswald entered the Texas Theater. This witness notified the theater manager who contacted the Dallas Police.

Once inside the theater, Oswald shifted from one seat to another, and then to another. It was not that he thought any one was better than another, but he was just so nervous that he didn't know what else to do. He literally could not just sit still.

Almost two dozen policemen, sheriffs and detectives in almost as many patrol cars arrived at the Texas Theater shortly thereafter. These law enforcement officers surrounded the theater and covered all of the entrances and exits. Several of them entered the theater and confronted Oswald.

He resisted arrest and tried to draw his pistol, but they were able to overpower him before he could shoot. He was only able to punch a single officer before he was completely subdued. Once he had been completely restrained by the officers and was being led away, Oswald said, "Well, it's all over now."

Oswald was booked into the Dallas jail where he was initially charged with the murder of Officer J.D. Tippit. Several hours later, Oswald was also charged with the murder of President Kennedy. He would stay in the Dallas jail until he could eventually be moved to a more secure facility to await trial.

* * * * * * * * * *

The staff at Parkland Hospital had been alerted by the police regarding President Kennedy's shooting. By the time the limousine pulled into the emergency department parking area, there was already a large group of doctors, nurses, assistants and security officers awaiting its arrival.

The President was immediately removed from the back seat of the limousine and placed onto a gurney so that he could be rushed into the emergency room area. The staff, seeing how badly he had been wounded, decided not to stop in that area but to proceed right into one of the operating rooms at the hospital.

During this whole process, they tried to detect any vital signs and stabilize his condition before the surgery that they hoped to perform. But it was immediately apparent to all of the doctors who examined him that there was nothing they could do.

The President had no pulse, no blood pressure, and his eyes were fixed and dilated. It would also have been obvious to even a layperson who examined him that some of the President's brain and skull had been destroyed. There was absolutely nothing the medical staff could do to revive, resuscitate or in any way save the President.

At 1:00 p.m. Central Standard Time, after the two Roman Catholic priests that had been summoned to administer Last Rights to President Kennedy had completed their work, the doctors officially pronounced President Kennedy dead. But of course he had been killed instantaneously by the bullet that tore through his brain, and thus had actually been dead on arrival at the hospital.

Meanwhile, Governor Connally, who had also been severely wounded, was taken to emergency surgery. He underwent two operations that day, which ultimately saved his life.

The Vice President of the United States, Lyndon Johnson, had been in the motorcade in a limousine following President Kennedy's car. He arrived at Parkland Hospital almost immediately after the President's limousine.

As soon as Lyndon Johnson entered the hospital, he was escorted to a private waiting room. First Lady Jacqueline Kennedy was already in that waiting room with numerous aides and Secret Service agents. Lyndon Johnson moved to console her, while he noted with distress that her dress was splattered with many bloodstains.

They were together when one of the priests emerged from the surgery area to deliver the horrible news that the President was dead. They both broke down in tears, as did virtually everyone in the room.

The Secret Service immediately warned Johnson that this might be an international conspiracy, and that there might be plans to wipe out all of the American political hierarchy. Following their suggestion, Johnson ordered that no announcement of the President's death be made until after he had left the hospital and departed from Dallas.

With that, Lyndon Johnson departed with his party back to Air Force One. He arrived at the airplane just about the time that the official announcements about President Kennedy's death were released.

Of course, Air Force One continued to wait on the tarmac for the arrival of both Mrs. Kennedy, and President Kennedy's body, before it would depart.

At 1:38 p.m. Central Standard Time, Walter Cronkite, the CBS News anchor, was the first to break the news to the nation. Cronkite stated, "Ladies and Gentleman, I have just learned that President Kennedy died at 1:00 p.m. Central Standard Time in Dallas, Texas."

Cronkite cleared his throat as he adjusted to the shock of the news. Then he continued, "Vice President Johnson has left the hospital in Dallas, but we do not know to where he has proceeded. Presumably he will be taking the Oath of Office shortly and become the 36th President of the United States."

As soon as this news had been broadcast nationally in the U.S., it was forwarded throughout the world via various methods.

There was a minor crisis at Parkland Hospital that involved a ten-to-fifteen-minute confrontation between cursing, weapons-brandishing Secret Service agents and hospital doctors. The guys with the guns won the argument and President Kennedy's body was removed from the hospital and driven to Air Force One. Although the removal of the President's body from Texas without a release from a Texas judge might be illegal, there was absolutely no way that any of the Secret Service agents were going to leave Texas without the body of their boss. And no stethoscope-wielding doctor could really oppose and deny a Secret Service agent holding an automatic weapon.

Once Mrs. Kennedy and President Kennedy's body were aboard Air Force One, the aircraft immediately departed to return to Washington DC. On board the plane, Lyndon Johnson was sworn in as the 36th President of the United States.

Immediately afterwards, worried about the possibility of an international conspiracy, the new President ordered all of the military and all of the United States security forces to their second highest possible state – Defcon 2. Defcon 1, the highest state of readiness, had never been invoked, but Defcon 2 had been invoked once before during the Cuban Missile Crisis.

The U.S. Military immediately alerted their allies about the issuance of the Defcon 2 order. The British military attaché in Washington notified his superiors at Number 10 Downing Street, who immediately raised British readiness to their highest state. All the NATO members were notified that the United States was once again on a war footing.

But no further attacks materialized, and so two days later, President Johnson issued the order to stand down from Defcon 2.

Once the assassination of President Kennedy had been officially confirmed, the wire services in America, indeed throughout the world, were overwhelmed with traffic. In the U.S., every news organization was trying to discover the most recent developments. The U.S. television channels began their marathon coverage, which would keep them all on the air around the clock for the first time. This non-stop coverage would continue for the next four days until the official funeral had been completed.

All of the embassies and special interest sections in Washington were continuously bombarding their native countries with updates. For those countries without a direct relationship to the United States, like Cuba, they were getting their news from their allies and associates.

* * * * * * * * * *

When the news hit the governments of those nations traditionally friendly to the United States, their leaders immediately issued statements of condolence and sorrow. Many of them, realizing that they had lost a great friend, went even further.

Both Ireland and Israel declared days of mourning. In Ireland, President de Valera's dreams to reunify Ireland during his lifetime died right along with President Kennedy. Many of America's friends throughout the world declared that their flags would be held at half-mast out of respect for the slain president.

In some quarters, however, the news evoked much different responses.

Chapter Fourteen

WORLDWIDE REACTIONS

In Havana, Raúl Castro rushed into his brother Fidel's suite in the presidential palace after only a perfunctory rap at the door. No other person in Cuba would have ever thought to take such liberties, to rudely barge in on Fidel Castro, but of course they were brothers and confidants.

"Kennedy's dead," Raúl blurted as he rushed into the room.

Raúl continued, "Fidel, President Kennedy has been assassinated!"

Fidel looked up from his papers with that ever-present cigar in his mouth and said, "What? When?"

Raúl said, "It happened in Dallas today where the President was scheduled to make an appearance. He was shot in his car as it proceeded down the street."

Raúl continued, "I think congratulations are in order, Fidel, because it seems that you finally got him before he got you."

Fidel looked at his brother intently and said, "Raúl, please close the door."

Raúl was kind of puzzled by Fidel's reserved reaction to the news of the death of his most mortal enemy, but he did as Fidel requested. He turned and closed the massive door to Fidel's room in the presidential palace.

Once the door was closed, Fidel said, "Raúl, I knew nothing about this. I certainly have wished him dead many times, but I have never planned anything specific, although it's pretty well known that his government has been trying to assassinate me. Where did you get this information?"

Raúl stated, "It came in a wire from our embassy in Venezuela, but I think it was based on a news report from the United States."

Fidel then asked him, very seriously, "Raúl, did you have anything to do with this assassination?"

Raúl responded, quite puzzled, "Not me. Fidel, if I had anything to do with it, you'd know about it. I was sure that you'd arranged this, and I know that sometimes you do things on your own and don't need my advice."

Fidel said, "Well, it seems to me that everyone is going to immediately blame me for this assassination, as you just did. Raúl, I had nothing to do with it. But I'm sure that the entire world will blame me for it."

Raul responded, "But, Fidel, it's good news nonetheless. He's gone. Kennedy's gone."

Fidel said, "Yes, Raúl, that's a good thing, but I wish I knew who killed him and why."

"Who do you think?" Raúl asked. "The American President had many, many enemies."

"I don't know," Fidel responded. "But if there are any Cubans involved, I need to know that – and know it quickly."

"Cubans?" Raúl questioned. "But if you had nothing to do with it and I had nothing to do with it, then there's no one else in Cuba capable of plotting such an attack."

This was precisely what worried Fidel. He knew it wasn't him, and now he was sure it was not Raúl. Fidel knew that there was only one person in Cuba outside of him or his brother who was capable of conducting such an assassination. This person was one of his closest lieutenants, and the one whom he admired most and also trusted the least.

This person was Che Guevara. Che had a cadre of personal followers who reported only to him. They were loyal to Fidel only as long as Che told them to be loyal. If Che told them to oppose Fidel, they would do exactly what he said.

The assassination of the American President, if it were blamed on Fidel Castro, would serve Che's ultimate ambition to be the leader of Cuba. Indeed, Che wanted to be the leader of the entire world, once he had transformed it by violent revolution into a Communist world. Che lived for violence and revolution.

Once the Americans were convinced that Fidel had assassinated their president, they would be relentless in seeking retribution. They would either use overt air strikes against him or covert assassination attempts far in excess of the small attempts that had already been made against his life. Once Fidel was dead, the Cuban population would rally behind Guevara to support him in his continued resistance against the Norte Americanos. It was possible that Che could have orchestrated this assassination without Fidel's knowledge.

"Unfortunately," Fidel said, "There is one other in Cuba who is fully capable of arranging this attack. You know it could be Che Guevara."

Raúl thought for a moment and then said, "Yes, Fidel, of course Che could arrange it. He has many ideologues, who respond only to him and support you only because he does. I have never trusted him. And he might have arranged this thing because his ideology reigns supreme in his mind."

"Of course it does," Fidel said. "His ambition is great and I have no doubt that he aspires to rule Cuba one day. In fact, I think he aspires to rule all of South America some day. This might be a maneuver on his part both to remove Kennedy, an enemy of our country, and to get the Norte Americanos to remove me, so he could take over my position.

"Just think about it, Raúl. If the Americans believe I arranged the assassination of their president, they will never rest until they avenge him. In particular I worry about his brother, Robert Kennedy. A very powerful man. And as you know, my brother, the bond between brothers is deep and the loss of one would compel the other to exact revenge."

Raúl responded, "Well, Fidel, obviously it needs to be investigated. I'll do my best to find out if there's any connection between Che and the assassin in the United States."

Raúl continued, "It seems to me that if the assassin was sent by Che, if he is captured, he has been instructed to resist questioning for several days and then blame the whole incident on you. A quick confession by the assassin would seem false, but a long-term withholding of information wouldn't serve their purposes either. I think that the assassin is programmed to implicate you within a week of capture. So it would be in your best interest if the assassin were to be eliminated as soon as possible after his capture."

Fidel said to Raúl, "You're right, my brother. I agree with everything you've said. Please begin to plan to eliminate the assassin. And as you've suggested, do it quickly."

Fidel continued, "Work on it and get back to me. In the meantime, I think both of us need to be very careful and to keep a low profile. I'm not so sure, but I'm concerned that Che may have arranged a little 'American vengeance' on his own that would eliminate you and me, and that he could blame the move on the Americans. I think it's now time for both of us to be very, very careful.

"And I think we need to assess Che's position here in Cuba and figure out a way to gently remove him from the political scene, whether he's involved in this or not. I worry about the power that he is gathering amongst the masses because of his charisma. It was at his insistence that I sent several military trainers to Algiers earlier this year to instruct some fighters from the People's Movement for the Liberation of Angola. He wants us to provide more direct aid to the Angola rebels, so maybe I should agree to that if Che agrees to go to Angola to lead them. It would get him out of here in an honorable way.

"So, be very careful, my brother, and get back to me as quickly as you can with any developments."

With that Raúl left the room and Fidel was left engrossed in his thoughts.

* * * * * * * * * *

Because of the difference in time zones, it was already 8:30 p.m. when news of the assassination reached the Vatican. The Pope had just finished his evening

Vespers and returned to his chambers when his aide brought him a radio dispatch with the information. Rather than exhibiting any anger or outward sign of distress, the Pope merely said, "I'll be in my personal chapel. Please keep me informed the minute you have any more news about what happened."

The Pope headed back to his personal chapel because he knew that he needed to pray directly to God for some guidance on this matter. In truth, he hadn't demonstrated any emotions in front of his aide because he was in shock from the awful news.

The Pope had personally met President Kennedy only several months prior when Kennedy visited Europe. They had spent about 45 minutes together in private, and he had learned that Jack Kennedy was a devout Catholic. At the end of their meeting, he had heard Jack's confession and provided him with absolution. That provided the Pope with some solace, at least knowing Jack's soul was cleansed.

Much of their meeting had been spent discussing Cuba and Fidel Castro, the Anti-Christ leader there. Jack had confronted Castro over the Soviet Missiles stationed in Cuba and did not back down, even from a direct confrontation with the Soviet Union. A nuclear war was a definite possibility, but Jack Kennedy had won the showdown by remaining strong.

The Pope had lamented to Kennedy about the treatment Castro had levied upon the Catholic priests and Church properties in Cuba. Castro had confiscated churches and schools, and had imprisoned and beaten Catholic priests and nuns. His communist beliefs cast religion as an enemy, and Castro was attacking the Catholic Church whenever he could.

Once he got to his private chapel, the Pope was overwhelmed with grief about the assassination of President Kennedy. He cried in front of the altar and asked God why such a good man had to die? Kennedy was not only a good Catholic, but also a righteous human being. It all seemed so senseless.

The Pope also thought about who had ordered his killing. It was obvious to him that Fidel Castro, the Anti-Christ, in his effort to destroy the Catholic Church and all of its followers wherever it existed, was responsible for the killing. But, as the leader of God's Church on Earth, he needed to pray to God to find out if this was in fact the truth. After asking God for direction and enlightenment, the Pope suddenly felt a great peace befall him. He was sure this was a sign from God that confirmed what he already knew.

After his prayers, Pope Paul VI reflected on his memories about the Kennedy family and its relationship to the Church.

He and his predecessor, Eugenio Pacelli, (who became Pope Pius XII) had met and spoken often when Pacelli was just a Cardinal, and Giovanni Montini (who was now Pope Paul VI) was just an up-and-coming priest. During one of their conversations, Cardinal Pacelli had described to Giovanni the wonderful meeting he had had with the Kennedy family while in New York. He had been there to attend a luncheon just after the election of President Franklin D. Roosevelt. After the luncheon, he had been invited to the Kennedy family residence in Bronxville. Cardinal Pacelli told Giovanni that he felt like a member of the family, since his welcome had been so warm and intimate.

Pope Paul VI had always felt that he and Pope Pius XII had also been like family, since the previous Pope had always mentored him as a father would. He reasoned that if Kennedy was welcomed into the Pacelli family, he was also welcomed into the Montini family. Castro had not only attacked a good Catholic and a leader of the Free World, but he had also attacked a member of the Montini family!

Pope Paul VI prayed to God for guidance because he was unsure whether the plan he was contemplating was the right one or not. He knew it had been centuries since the Vatican had possessed its own armies and had pursued the Crusades. But since then, the overt power of the Vatican had waned as the Church had given up its materialistic army to concentrate on its spiritual mission.

But that didn't mean that the Vatican was impotent or unable to take some type of direct action. In fact, Pope Paul VI had secretly wished that the Church had been able to do more on its own to prevent some of the atrocities of World War II. He didn't want to sit idly by in this time of a great threat to the Church and its members.

The Pope didn't know how long he'd remained in the chapel, since he had been entranced in prayer, when there came a sharp rap on the door. It was his aide who came to deliver some additional news.

"Your Holiness," the aide said, "I have some additional news from America. It appears that U.S. law enforcement people have arrested the assassin of President Kennedy. His name is Oswald and he has connections to both the Soviet Union and Cuba."

This further confirmed the Pope's belief that Castro was behind this effort to destroy the Church. Castro had been blatant in his attacks on the Catholic Church in Cuba. Now he was blatant in his attacks on America. The Pope was now completely convinced that Castro had killed President Kennedy – not personally, but that he had arranged for his assassination.

The Pope knew he had to take some action to prevent further attacks upon the Church by Castro. It seemed to him that the appropriate action would be to terminate the assassin that had attacked President Kennedy. He felt that this attack should be conducted in a very public place, so that Fidel Castro would get the message that he was not safe anywhere in the world, if he continued on his path of evil destruction. The Pope believed in the Biblical doctrine of "an eye for an eye," that the punishment should equal the crime. Oswald needed to die for his crime!

He knew that that the great peace he had experienced following his prayers was the confirmation from God that he had been awaiting. The pontiff knew that it was time to act.

He needed to speak to Capitano Antonio.

The pontiff said to his aide, "Please summon Capitano Antonio and ask him to come here as quickly as possible. Tell him to be prepared for an immediate departure for a trip that might last two or three days. Also, contact our air service and tell them to immediately ready an aircraft. Tell them that the flight will be about 300 miles and will be over the Mediterranean, so they will know which aircraft to prepare."

"Yes, Your Holiness," the aide said as he bowed his head in acknowledgement and headed out the door.

Pope Paul VI thought again about the godless anti-Christ Fidel Castro, who ruled Cuba. He decided, *"Castro belongs in Hell! And the vile assassin he recruited will be there before him."*

CHAPTER FIFTEEN

OSWALD ASSASSINATION

Dawn was slowly casting out the dark shadows of the night in this verdant valley in Sicily, when the guard in the elevated tower near the villa spotted what appeared to be a human silhouette standing in the middle of one of the meadows, not more than 500 meters from the villa.

Since the entire valley was equipped with sensors to detect any intruders before they could get anywhere nearly that close to the villa, the guard was astonished to see this shape. The shape appeared to be a man who was just standing there immobile. As dawn broke, the shape clearly became a man.

The villa, indeed the entire valley, was owned by Salvatore Greco. He was supposedly a semi-retired landowner who had made his money in the export business dealing with the local citrus industry.

In reality Salvatore Greco was the First Secretary of the Sicilian Mafia Commission. He was the "Primus Inter Pares" – the first among equals. But this title was misleading and only used to assuage the egos of the other Mafia Dons in Sicily. In truth, he controlled all of the Mafia activities – in Sicily, Italy and around the world.

In Sicily he held direct control, and no major executions or operations were undertaken without his approval. In the rest of Italy, as well as in the rest of the world, he had Capos who had their own organizations, but who ultimately reported to him. His role in most of these organizations was relatively passive. But they knew if they did something he disapproved, their mistake could be fatal. He provided some support, either financially or with outside executioners. But mostly the Capos ran their own organizations and just looked to Greco for approval on major new endeavors or to settle disputes with other Capos. For this, they were all more than willing to pay him a small tribute to preserve the peace and advance their own success. So he collected a small percentage of the gain from all these illegal operations. Although it was a small percentage, it actually was a very, very large financial base.

Even in America, Greco still commanded respect and was acknowledged as the overall leader of the Mafia.

Greco lived in relative obscurity here in this remote valley in Sicily. But he was in contact by telephone or radio transmission with his Capos as needed.

Greco, with his exalted position, had many, many enemies – even some within his own organization. So he had purchased this villa and removed the citrus trees that had once surrounded the house. This provided a clear "fire zone" throughout the valley, and denied hiding places from potential attackers or assassins. He positioned sensors near the entrance to the valley, which should detect the presence of any intruders. The valley was essentially a box canyon, so the high hills and the wilderness on three sides of the valley provided a natural protection from intruders.

But Greco had also installed sensors on the tops of those hills to prevent the possibility of any assassin with a high-powered rifle from going undetected before he could shoot down at the villa.

Thus it was astonishing to the guard to see a human standing so close to the villa, who had not been detected by the electronic sensors. He immediately alerted the two patrol guards who were on standby just outside the villa. They jumped into a World War II vintage jeep and sped toward the intruder.

They stopped about three meters from the intruder and leveled their weapons at him. One guard was carrying a Lupara, a uniquely Sicilian type of sawed-off, break-open shotgun. The other guard, who had been driving, retrieved a World War II vintage rifle and was aiming that at the intruder.

The driver of the jeep shouted out, "Don't move," although the intruder was already standing quite motionless.

The driver yelled again, "Raise your hands. We're coming closer."

The intruder raised both his arms so that his hands were slightly above his head. Both the driver and the other guard dismounted from the jeep and approached the intruder warily. When they got quite close, the driver said, "Who are you and how the hell did you get into this valley?"

As they surrounded him with their weapons drawn, the intruder said, "My name is Antonio and I am here to speak to Signore Greco."

The driver laughed derisively and said, "Well, I guess you don't have an appointment or you might have come in the front driveway like all others. How the hell did you get this close to the villa without being detected?"

Antonio didn't respond to his question, but repeated, "It is very important that I speak to Signore Greco. Would you be so kind as to transport me to him so that I can do that? Time is of the essence."

The driver responded, "I don't know who the hell you are, but you're going to regret that you ever snuck in here."

The driver addressed his assistant and said, "Frisk him and let's get him in the jeep."

The assistant proceeded to frisk Antonio and reported back to the driver, "He doesn't have anything on him. No identification. No wallet. No money. Nothing, except the crucifix hanging from his neck."

The driver was particularly puzzled by this, but shouted at Antonio, "Get in the jeep. Get in the back seat. You'll be next to me. If you try anything, you'll be killed immediately."

Antonio willingly complied since he knew that he would be transported to the villa and would be closer to Signore Greco.

The guard entered the back with Antonio. The driver in the front picked up a two-way radio and informed the guard captain back at the villa that they were heading in with the intruder.

When the jeep pulled up in front of the villa, the guard captain and another guard were waiting for them. The guard captain was wearing a .45 automatic in a belt holster but did not appear to have any other weapon. The guard next to him was carrying a machine gun, a Thompson automatic that had probably been purchased on the black market after the war.

They pushed Antonio out of the jeep and prodded him toward the guard captain. Although Antonio was a very large man, at least 6', 2" tall and about 280 pounds, he did not resist the guards at all. In fact, he was so submissive that the guards failed to realize just how lethal he could be.

The guard captain repeated the previous questions, "Who the hell are you and how did you get in here?"

Antonio responded again, "My name is Antonio and I am here to speak to Signore Greco."

The guard captain said, "Well, Signore Greco does not speak to intruders, nor to penniless vagrants who show up in the middle of his fields. I want to know how the hell you got this close to the villa without being detected."

The guard captain turned to one of the guards and said, "Bring him into the 'conference room.'"

One guard led the way, with Antonio being pushed and prodded along behind him by the other two guards. The guard captain was right behind them, following and watching the whole process.

The "conference room" turned out to be a Spartan room with only one table and three chairs. It was obviously an interrogation room. Antonio noted that there were no decorations on the wall except for one fairly large mirror that hung on a side wall.

Once they reached the room and closed the door, the guard captain shouted at Antonio, "Sit in that chair and tell us who the hell you really are!" Antonio was facing four men, arranged in a Roman Phalanx against him.

Rather than sitting down, Antonio instead said, "I'm not here to sit. I'm here to talk to Signore Greco. Would you be so kind as to tell him that I'm here and would like an audience with him?"

With that the guard captain laughed again and said, "You might be a ballsy bastard, but you don't give orders around here. Now sit in that chair like I told you."

With that, the guard holding the vintage rifle prodded it toward Antonio to force him to sit.

Rather than sitting, Antonio grabbed the rifle by its barrel with his right hand and jerked it forward, pulling the guard off balance. He had extraordinary strength, and with just his right hand he pulled the guard airborne off his feet. As the guard flew forward toward Antonio, he hit the guard in the temple with his left hand. The guard dropped like a rag doll.

The other guards started to react, but they were no match for Antonio.

Although he was holding the rifle by the barrel end rather than the butt end, he had more strength in one arm than most men had in both arms combined. His entire life had been spent exercising to build his strength and stamina, learning the ancient martial arts secrets of his Order that dated back before the Crusades, and leading a Monastic life of self-denial and prayer.

He swung the rifle up immediately and crashed the butt directly into the face of the guard holding the Lupara. Antonio sensed, quite correctly, that the Lupara was his most dangerous worry in these close quarters.

As the guard who had been holding the Lupara crumpled to the ground, Antonio next used the rifle like a reverse bayonet. Although he was holding the rifle only by the barrel, he had full control of the weapon. After he had used it to crush the second guard, he thrust it toward the third guard who had been holding the machine gun. He caught him right in the throat with the butt of the rifle. That guard made a strange gurgling sound as he too crumpled to the ground.

That left only the guard captain, who had been at the back of the Phalanx formation and who was now struggling furiously to get his automatic pistol out of his holster, which had a military flap on the top. Antonio flipped the rifle around, so that he now had the butt stock in his hands with the barrel pointing toward the guard captain. Antonio was much faster than the captain.

Antonio said, "You will stop and you will drop that gun to the floor. I don't want to hurt you, but if you don't comply, I will have to kill you."

The guard captain was astonished by how quickly this intruder had overcome all his guards, who were trained and experienced men. The guard captain knew that he needed to put his gun on the floor immediately or he would join them, either unconscious or dead.

Although the guard captain had dropped his gun to the floor and was standing compliantly there awaiting further instructions from Antonio, Antonio raised the gun toward the captain and appeared about to shoot him.

Instead, at the last minute, Antonio swung the gun to the right and shot the wall mirror near its uppermost left corner. The glass immediately shattered into thousands of shards that sprayed mostly into the cavity behind the mirror. This turned out to be a darkened room with several individuals standing there observing them, behind the remnants of what Antonio had correctly perceived to be a one-way observation mirror.

Antonio yelled, "I need to speak to Signore Greco and I need to speak to him now! I didn't shoot at any of you observers back there, but I easily could have lowered my aim and killed you all. I don't want to kill any of you, but I am on a mission and I will not be deterred from talking to Signore Greco. One of you needs to fetch him immediately and bring him here."

There was a moment of silence and then Antonio heard one of the observers say, "I am Salvatore Greco and I would ask you to please be merciful with my men. I don't know who you are, but I will talk to you. However, you have to know that if I don't like what I hear, you will never leave this place alive. If you were sent here as an assassin, your death will be very unpleasant."

Antonio responded, "If I had been sent here to assassinate you, Signore, you would already be dead. My mission is to enlist your assistance, not to cause you any harm."

Salvatore Greco was greatly puzzled and somewhat terrified by these events, since no one had ever penetrated his headquarters before. He told the other men in the observation room with him to holster their weapons. He said to Antonio, "I am coming out into the room now and I don't have a weapon. Please hold your fire and don't harm my men, so that we may talk."

Antonio said, "As I told you, I am not interested in harming you. I am here to enlist your help."

Soon after the conference room door opened and Greco and two of his guards came into the room. Neither of them was holding weapons in his hands, although both of the guards had side arms attached to their belts. The guards entered first, forming a "human shield" for their boss who entered right behind them.

He said, "I am Salvatore Greco and you said you wanted to talk to me. So talk. First, who the hell are you?"

Antonio said, "My name is Antonio and I have been sent here on a mission from the Vatican to seek your help."

Greco said, "From the Vatican? What are you talking about?"

Antonio said, "The information I have is to be shared only with you. I'll be happy to drop this rifle now and to accompany you somewhere where we can talk privately."

"Before we go anywhere," Greco said, "You need to tell me not just where you came from, but who the hell sent you here and why."

Antonio said, "I was sent by the Representative of God Almighty here on Earth, and I can only tell you why once we are in a private place without any other observers."

Greco would have dismissed the intruder as a religious lunatic except for the fact that he had just noticed that Antonio was wearing a heavy gold ring. This ring was obviously valuable and bore the image of two knights on a single donkey. Greco knew that he had seen that image before, maybe in history books in school; and suddenly he realized with a start that it was the insignia of the Knights Templar. This was a Catholic military organization that had fought with distinction during the Crusades, and that everyone thought had disappeared hundreds of years ago.

Greco asked, "I just noticed your ring and it bears an unusual image. Where did you get that ring?"

Antonio said, "Signore Greco, I am anxious to speak to you and explain all these things, but I cannot do it with others around. If we could just proceed to a private area, I can answer all your questions."

Well, Greco thought to himself, as long as this guy drops the rifle, I should be relatively safe in my office. Plus, I have two revolvers in the desk, just in case this Antonio tries something unpleasant.

"Okay," Greco said. "Just drop the weapon and I give you my word my men will not attack you. If you follow me, we will go into my office where we can talk further."

Antonio trusted Greco at his word and dropped the rifle. It really didn't matter much anyway; Antonio was just as lethal without a gun as with one. Even the crucifix around his neck could be turned into a deadly weapon if Antonio needed it.

Greco headed for the door and Antonio followed him. Once they were in Greco's private office with the door closed, Greco said, "Okay, you wanted to talk. Here you are. Talk. What the hell is going on? First of all, who the hell are you and where did you get that ring?"

Antonio responded, "My name is Antonio, as I said. And I was honored to be given this ring as a sign of my devotion to the Church, to His Holiness the Pope, and to God himself."

Greco said, "Is that really a Knights Templar ring? I thought all the Templars were dead."

Antonio said, "I'm surprised you recognized the ring. While it's true that the Knights Templar are no longer the large public organization we once were, we still exist to serve the wishes of the Pope and to protect the Church. And above all, to serve God. I am honored to be the current Grand Master of the Knights Templar."

"But," Greco said, "What the hell does that have to do with me? Don't you know, or hadn't you heard that I'm not exactly a religious man?"

Antonio said, "While it may be true that your path is not the same as some others, His Holiness knows that you were born a Catholic, and he is sure that someday you would like to join your deceased forbearers and loved ones in the love and mercy of our Lord, Jesus Christ."

Greco replied, "I'm afraid that I've done many things that will prevent that from ever happening. I did things I thought were necessary at the time, but as I've aged, I've realized that I lost my soul in the process. So, what's done is done. But you did say that you came here to enlist my help."

Antonio said, "His Holiness sent me here because he is concerned about things in this world that threaten the very existence of the Church. The Church has been under siege in Cuba by the new dictator, Fidel Castro. Castro is surely aligned with the Anti-Christ, might even be the Anti-Christ himself, and has been attacking all of the Church's people and facilities in Cuba. His Holiness is convinced that Castro is the one who arranged for the assassination of President John F. Kennedy. The American President was both a staunch Catholic and a supporter of the Church."

Greco said, "Yeah, I saw the news. It's a shame that they killed him that way right in front of his young wife. That would never happen in Sicily. Sometimes in my business, people have to die, but we have our principles and never want to cause that to happen in front of the family."

Antonio continued, "His Holiness wants to eliminate the assassin to both avenge the killing and to make an example to Fidel Castro, so he will realize that he himself could be at risk if he continues his pattern of attacks against the Church."

Salvatore Greco was born and raised in Sicily. He had spent his whole life exposed to the concept of Vendetta – the revenge killing of someone who has killed one of your own. He understood why the Pope would wish this done. Greco asked, "Is that what you want? I mean, is that what His Holiness wants? He wants me to terminate the assassin?"

"That is correct," Antonio said, "And he wants it done in a very public and obvious way, so there could be no question that the assassin did not die a natural death. This is to be an example to Castro, and the more public the better. Also, His Holiness would prefer it if you could find a non-believer or at least a non-Catholic to handle the chore. While this is certainly a religious mission, His Holiness would rather that this be handled by someone else."

Greco said, suddenly suspicious, "But why would His Holiness think that I might be able to arrange such a thing? I am just a simple Sicilian farmer."

Antonio said, "Signore, the Church knows more about your operation than you could ever imagine. Your capos, your lieutenants and your soldiers all worry about their immortal souls and confess their deeds to our priests regularly. Although we have vast and detailed information about your operation, we have never used it against you or them. So please don't try to be coy with me. Just tell me that you understand what we want done and that you will agree to help us."

Salvatore Greco, shocked that the Church knew so much about his operations, said, "Okay, I'll help. I do know some people in the USA that could do this."

Antonio said, "I'm sure you do, Signore. And His Holiness would like this to be done very, very soon. I should add that in response to your help, His Holiness wants you to know that he personally will pray for the absolution of your immortal soul."

Although Greco was a hardened Mafioso, he was still a human being. He had been raised Catholic and grew up in a strict Catholic family. Sometimes, he did worry about the eternal damnation to which he thought he was destined.

Antonio continued, "I will relay your decision to help His Holiness. Now, I suggest that you make a full confession and ask for God's forgiveness."

"What?" Greco said surprised. "A full confession? Here… now?"

Antonio said, "Don't be puzzled. I am a priest as well as a warrior. I serve God in every way that I can. I think that it would be wise for you now to make a full confession, ask for God's forgiveness and receive Communion at Mass this Sunday. If that is too risky, I am sure that we can arrange for your local priest to come here to celebrate the Mass and administer the sacrament. His Holiness will also say a prayer for you personally, to ask God to forgive you of your sins, since you have agreed to help with this task."

With that, Antonio removed the crucifix from around his neck and held it in his hands as he began to pray in Latin.

Salvatore Greco, head of the worldwide Mafia, immediately dropped to his knees, like the compliant altar boy he once was. All his life he had been a Catholic, but because of his profession, it had been many long years since he had even attended church, much less made Confession. He bowed his head before Father Antonio, made the Sign of the Cross on his head and chest and said, "Bless me, Father, for I have sinned. It's been way too long since my last confession."

* * * * * * * * * *

On the morning of Saturday, November 23, 1963, Pope Paul VI made a speech referencing the tragic death of President John Fitzgerald Kennedy. It was just about the same time that Capitano Antonio was meeting with Salvatore Greco in Sicily.

Pope Paul said, "We're deeply shocked by the sad and tragic news of the killing of the President of the United States of America, John Fitzgerald Kennedy, and the serious wounding of Governor Connally; and we are profoundly saddened by so dastardly a crime, by the mourning which afflicts a great and civilized country and by the suffering which strikes at Mrs. Kennedy, the children and the family.

"With all our heart we deplore this unhappy event. We express the heartfelt wish that the death of this great statesman may not damage the cause of the American people, but rather reinforce its moral and civic sentiments and strengthen its feeling of nobility and concord; and we pray to God that the sacrifice of John Kennedy may favor the cause he promoted and help defend the peace and freedom of all the peoples of the world.

"He was the first Catholic President of the United States. We recall our pleasure in receiving his visit and in having discerned in him great wisdom and high resolution for the good of humanity. Tomorrow we shall offer the holy sacrifice of the Mass, that God may grant him eternal rest and comfort, console all of those who weep for him on his death and see that not hatred, but Christian love, will reign among all mankind."

Salvatore Greco controlled an enormous web of Mafia-related criminal enterprises throughout the world, although the American branch was growing so quickly that – while it was not yet the case – it might someday be able to challenge the leadership of its Italian homeland.

Greco was experiencing a great sense of relief, since he had just received absolution from all his previous sins from a priest that had been sent by the direct Representative of God on earth: His Holiness, the Pope in Rome. He had just sent the priest in a jeep back to the airport to meet the Vatican plane. He knew it was only 2:00 a.m. in New York when he called Carlo Gambino, but did not hesitate to wake him up. Gambino was known in the U.S. as the Capo di Tutti Capi (the boss of all bosses). While it might be true that Gambino was the boss of all bosses in the United States, he still reported to Greco in Sicily, the international head of the worldwide Mafia.

Gambino answered the phone and said in an irritated voice, "What?"

In response he heard, "Carlo, it's important and we need to talk right now."

Gambino immediately recognized the voice of Salvatore Greco and told him, "Of course, my Don," (which was a title of honor). "What do you want me to do?"

Greco said, "Carlo, I'm sorry I had to call you in the middle of the night, but this is something that can't wait until the morning."

Gambino responded, "Of course. I understand that. Sometimes in our positions we don't get much sleep. What can I do for you, my Don?"

Greco said, "I need you to arrange a hit on that assassin who just killed President Kennedy. I need you to do it now, and I want you to do it in as public a fashion as you can arrange."

Gambino responded, "What? I don't understand. We've been tormented by the Kennedys for years, with all their committees and investigations. I thought that his death was good for us. Why are we trying to avenge his death?"

Greco responded angrily, "I'm sorry, I guess you misunderstood. I didn't ask you for your analysis of this whole situation. I called you to tell you what you need to do. Now is that too much to ask?"

Gambino immediately knew that he'd been put back in his place, below Greco in the Organization, so he responded, "Of course not. It was just something I said. Forget it. Okay, fuhgeddaboudit. I didn't mean nothing by it."

Greco responded, "Its okay, Carlo. We just need to get this done and it's really important for me that it's done quickly. Capisce?"

"Yes, capisco, my Don." Gambino said. "But I think it might take some time to get it arranged."

Greco responded, "You don't have no time. It's going to happen now. Today, tomorrow, the next day – no later! You don't have a week to get this done, Carlo. You've got to get it done now. And I want you to get a guy that's an Unbeliever. I don't want no Italians. I want you to get somebody else. And I want you to have the gun in his hand and shooting that assassin in public so everyone can see that it was no accident."

Gambino responded, "Of course. I'll take care of it. Um, I heard you, but exactly how many days do I have before we have to kill him?"

Greco said, "Yesterday would be better. Three days max. But I'm hoping you won't take that long. If you can't get it done by then, I'll have to find someone else."

Gambino had never heard Don Greco so emotional about a hit, so he said, "I'll work on it immediately. I'm sure I can take care of this. Just give me a day to figure out how to do it and I'll give you the details."

"Okay," Greco said. "And let me tell you that if you're successful with this you'll get a substantial bonus. And let me also tell you that if you fail at this, you will have horribly disappointed me. This is one of the most important assignments I've ever given anyone, so failure is not possible. If you don't get this done as we've discussed, I'll find someone else who will do it – and that will be the guy that takes your place."

Gambino, surprised by the threat that Don Greco had just made, responded, "You can count on me, Don Greco. Please don't do anything rash. I'll call you tomorrow with my plan. I'll take care of everything."

Once his conversation with Greco concluded, Gambino was worried about the threat that Don Greco had just made and immediately got on the phone to speak to one of his Capos – this one in Dallas, Joseph Civello. Civello knew just the guy to carry out the plan: Jacob Rubenstein, a mob wannabe. This guy was Jewish and heavily in debt to the mob, and was likely to do anything Civello instructed him to do. Plus he was known to have an enormous ego and would probably respond to the explanation that he will be an American Hero because he will have killed the assassin of President Kennedy.

Civello met with Rubenstein at lunch and told him if he does this, his debt to the Mob will be completely paid off. He also stroked his ego with the American Hero gambit. Rubenstein immediately agreed, and Civello provided him with a Colt Cobra 38 handgun.

On the morning of Sunday, November 24th, the basement of the Dallas Police Headquarters was abuzz with activities. They had made elaborate plans to transfer Lee Harvey Oswald, the now-charged assassin of President John F. Kennedy, from the police department to the nearby county jail. They had even taken the extraordinary step of arranging for an armored car to transport Oswald, so as to protect him from any retribution by irate U.S. citizens.

But the Dallas Police erred by allowing a considerable number of reporters and media types into the basement corridors to await the transfer and report on its progress.

In addition to the reporters, the crowd also included a man without any reporter's credentials. But there had been no one screening the attendees, nor had any of them been frisked for weapons.

This man was Jacob Rubenstein, who had legally changed his name to Jack Ruby. He was of average height and was somewhat overweight. He had a receding dark hairline, but that was hidden by the jaunty fedora hat that he wore. He also wore a dark suit and thus looked as respectable as the actual members of the media crowded into the corridor.

No one in the police department ever expected any type of attack within the "high security" of the police department building, and certainly didn't expect anything to happen in front of so many television cameras.

But at 11:21 a.m. Central Standard Time, while the TV cameras were rolling and the authorities were moving Lee Harvey Oswald toward the armored car, Jack Ruby stepped out from the crowd and fired his 38-revolver into Oswald's abdomen at point blank range.

There were millions of television viewers who witnessed the attack and who were astonished by the brazenness of it. The television cameras went dark once the enormity of the situation became apparent. Jack Ruby was immediately overwhelmed and disarmed by Dallas Police officials. Lee Harvey Oswald crumpled to the floor in a pool of blood, fatally wounded after being shot in the abdomen.

Pandemonium reigned, as no one had ever expected such an outrageous attack right in the very heart of the Dallas Police Department headquarters. It couldn't have been any more public, since it occurred on television in view of the entire world!

The response to the televised killing of Lee Harvey Oswald varied greatly. In the U.S., Joseph Civello immediately called his boss, Carlo Gambino, who had himself just seen the video.

Civello said, "Carlo, I knew this guy could get the job done, but as you know, sometimes people chicken out. You told me you wanted this done in as public and visible a fashion as possible, and I think you'd have to agree that it doesn't get more visible than this."

Carlo Gambino responded, "I can't argue with you about that. The guy did everything we asked. Now you'll be sure to take care of him like you promised, right?"

Civello said, "Of course, of course. We don't want him ratting us out for not keeping our part of the deal."

"That's good," Gambino said. "And you're going to get a nice reward for your part in this."

"Thank you, Don Gambino," Civello said. "If there's anything else that you need, please call me right away."

Gambino next traveled to an associate's house to use his telephone. He never tried to call Salvatore Greco from his home phone. That was only used for incoming calls from Greco, and usually only so they could arrange for a conversation later on a different telephone.

It was early evening in Sicily, so he felt comfortable that he would not be imposing on Greco after hours.

When Salvatore Greco answered the phone, he had already seen the video. He immediately said to Gambino, "Congratulations, what a great job. Just perfect."

Gambino said, "Well, you did tell me that you wanted the assassin dead and you wanted it done in a public fashion. You know I always try to do exactly what you want of me."

Greco responded warmly, "I know that, Carlo. And I'm sorry I was a little bit forceful when I last spoke to you, but I wanted you to know how important this was to me. But now that you've done such a good job, I've noticed that the Swiss bank account that I set up for you seems to be rather meager lately. I have decided to rectify that situation and I think if you check on the balance in that account two or three days from now, you will be pleased."

Carlo Gambino knew that Greco had promised him a reward for good performance and had threatened him if he failed. The Mafia thrived because of its system of rewards and threats. But he was pleased to hear Greco confirm that he would get a substantial bonus.

"Thank you, Don Greco," Gambino said. "And as you know, I am always at your service."

Salvatore Greco then wished him a good night and broke the connection.

In Sicily, Salvatore Greco did not have the nerve to call the Vatican to ask to speak to the Pope. But he was sure that the Pope would soon see the video and realize that Greco had fulfilled the vow he made. Salvatore Greco now was sure that the Pope would pray for his soul, and felt a great relief that he now has a chance for the redemption of his soul.

* * * * * * * * * *

In Cuba, both Fidel and Raúl Castro had been meeting in Fidel's office when an aide rapped loudly on the door. Raúl turned and said, "Enter, please enter."

With that, the aide rushed in to report the killing of the assassin of President Kennedy. He stated that the video was on all of the U.S. television stations and offered to turn on the television set in the Presidential office so they could watch it. Raúl looked toward Fidel for agreement and then asked the aide to turn on the television set and tune into a Miami television station. Obviously, Castro was concerned about anything happening in the United States since it might affect Cuba, so he had a television receiver capable of getting all of the Miami stations.

Once the television set was on, the aide retreated from the office. Fidel said to Raúl, "Well, that was certainly quick work if you arranged this."

Raúl responded, "I wish I had, Fidel, but we were only in the planning stages of trying to figure out how we could get at the assassin. We were thinking that we might be able to kill him during the early days of his trial. We never thought we could get to him inside the headquarters of the Dallas Police Department. This brazen attack must have been a suicide mission by this Jack Ruby guy. He must have known he could not escape after shooting Oswald in the police headquarters. This is completely unexpected."

They both watched the video and then discussed the puzzling event between themselves. Fidel said, "It seems this Jack Ruby has mob connections and I think the mob figured that I arranged for the assassination of Kennedy. They hate me even more than Kennedy for shutting down their casino operations in Havana and cutting off that source of profits. I think they killed this Oswald guy thinking he was working for me. You and I need to be extra cautious for the next several months, since I think we'll be facing more attacks by both the mob and the U.S. government. I want you to triple the guards around our compound. Get started now and be very careful, Raúl, so we both survive the next several months."

* * * * * * * * * *

The Pope was informed about the video by his aides as soon as it was available. After watching the elimination of the vile assassin who had cut down President Kennedy, the Pope retired to his private chapel to pray. He asked the Lord for forgiveness for the shooter who had killed the assassin. He asked the Lord to reward him with a heavenly reward after his death even though he was not a Catholic, because he had been on a divine mission.

The Pope was always saddened whenever a human life was lost, no matter how vile that life might have been. But the Pope realized that sometimes people had to die for the greater good of humanity and the Church. In that respect, the Church was not unlike all the national governments on earth.

* * * * * * * * * *

Back in the United States, the shocking killing of Lee Harvey Oswald only deepened the mystery surrounding the assassination of the President. J. Edgar Hoover, the Director of the Federal Bureau of Investigation, was particularly perturbed by the shooting.

Hoover had immediately suspected the Cubans, the Soviets and the Mafia of the assassination of the President. They all had reasons to hate the President. The Cubans and the Soviets hated him for the embarrassment of the Cuban Missile Crisis and the botched Bay of Pigs invasion. The Mafia hated him for the investigations conducted by the administration and the President's brother – Bobby Kennedy, the Attorney General, which had forced them to curtail some of their operations, particularly with the labor unions.

Hoover had immediately been informed about Jack Ruby's ties to the Mafia, so that would seem to rule the mob out of the assassination. Why would they kill Oswald if he was their own guy? Or did it just mean that they felt they had to eliminate Oswald, since he might ultimately cave in and confess to the mob's involvement. Anything was possible.

He also knew that Oswald had a Cuban connection, having been a member of "The Fair Play for Cuba" organization. Was he sent by the Cubans to kill the President and then been killed by the mob to send a message to Castro? It was well known that the mob hated Castro since they had lost all their casinos and gambling revenues after the Cuban Revolution. But the mob also hated the Kennedys, both the President and his brother Bobby, the Attorney General. Why would they kill the killer of someone they hated? None of this made any sense to J. Edgar Hoover. The shooting of Oswald just complicated everything, since now he could never provide any information to law enforcement.

On November 26th, J. Edgar Hoover issued a formal request to the Dallas Police Department to provide the FBI with "everything they had on the case." Since the FBI was the preeminent authority in law enforcement at that time, the head of the Dallas Police Department ordered all his officers to immediately comply.

CHAPTER SIXTEEN

Peter Sharkey, like virtually everyone in the United States, fell into a virtual paralysis following the death of President Kennedy. The television networks went to continuous, 24-hour coverage for the first time ever. People were glued to their television sets.

Peter Sharkey waited until the day after all the public funeral activities had concluded. Then he contacted Attorney General Robert F. Kennedy, the brother of his late friend, President John F. Kennedy. Peter had spoken to the President's brother a few times, but he knew now they had to talk.

Despite his sorrow, Robert F. Kennedy returned to his office to resume the duties for which he was responsible. Although he'd endured an enormous personal tragedy, he still had to administer the enormous federal apparatus that was the Justice Department.

All his calls were being screened by his secretaries to assure that the ones that reached him were only the ones that needed his immediate attention. His office switchboard had been inundated with condolence calls for the past several days. But the call from Peter Sharkey was immediately put through to the Attorney General.

When the phone rang, Kennedy answered with a plain, "Hello. This is Robert Kennedy."

On the other end of the line, Peter Sharkey said, "This is Peter Sharkey, Mr. Kennedy and..."

He was cut off when the Attorney General exclaimed, "God, Peter, I need to talk to you and I was waiting for you to call me. I wasn't quite sure how best to get in contact with you, but I'm so glad that you've called me now. I need to know what you know about what the hell is going on here. My whole world has changed and just..."

With that Robert Kennedy's voice faded out a bit and Peter knew he was choking up about losing his brother.

Peter responded, "Well, Mr. Kennedy, there are some things going on in Ireland that you need to be aware of."

Attorney General Kennedy responded, "Please, Peter, just call me Bobby. I mean, I know that you and Jack were friends and it would make it easier if you just call me Bobby and I'll call you Peter. How's that?"

"Thank you, Bobby," Peter responded. "And here's the thing that I think you should know about. There was a big problem in Ireland just after Jack was assassinated."

Bobby responded, "I know that. I've gotten all the reports. I lost a cousin and it seems that we've both lost a woman and her child. Do you have any idea what the hell is going on over there? And do you think this is related to Jack's murder?"

Peter said, "I don't know, Bobby. I really can't tell. I also heard about the killings in Ireland. I doubt that this is just a coincidence. I think I need to go to Ireland to find out more about what happened over there, but I can't do that without some authorization here in the U.S. I also think that we need some support there. This investigation into both what happened to Jack and what happened in Ireland is going to need a lot of resources. I think we need to meet with President Lyndon Johnson and tell him the whole story and enlist his help. I certainly can't figure this whole thing out on my own."

Bobby Kennedy said, "Okay, I'll set up a meeting with you and me and President Johnson. I agree that we can tell him everything and not worry about any disclosures. My brother always said positive things about President Johnson, so despite some of the reports in the media lately that even accuse Lyndon of arranging the assassination, I know they were friends and that we can rely on President Johnson to keep our confidence."

Peter said, "Thanks, Bobby, but I also think that we need to include some American Navy brass to get this done. I'm nowhere near high enough to be able to use my position to get some cooperation in Britain or Ireland where I think it might be needed. My boss is Admiral Rufus Taylor, the Director of the Office of Naval Intelligence. Although on paper I report to him, he always knew that I basically reported just to Jack. He understood that was what the President wanted and he was comfortable with that. He's a good man and I'm sure we can trust him. Can you arrange to also get him to the meeting with President Johnson?"

Bobby said, "Of course, Peter. And I agree with your thoughts. We need as many friends involved in this investigation as we can possibly get. Without compromising secrecy, of course."

* * * * * * * * * *

When Peter Sharkey entered the anteroom to the President's office at the White House the next day, Admiral Taylor was already sitting there waiting.

The Admiral looked at him questioningly and said, "Peter, I didn't know you were coming here. Do you know what this is all about?"

Peter gave him a quick salute since they were both in uniform and said, "Yes, sir, I know exactly what this is all about, and you might be surprised by what you're going to hear."

The Admiral said disapprovingly, "I hate surprises. Why didn't you tell me all this before we got here?"

Peter responded, "I'm sorry, Admiral. But things are happening so fast that it was all I could do to even get Attorney General Kennedy to include you in this meeting."

At that Admiral Taylor's eyes widened and he said, "What? Attorney General Kennedy set up this meeting?"

Just at that moment the outer door to the room opened and in walked Attorney General Robert F. Kennedy. He walked right up to Peter Sharkey and not only shook his hand, but also gave him a hug – a rather long hug, after which both men seemed to dab their eyes to hide tears.

Admiral Taylor had always known that, although on paper Captain Sharkey reported to him, in fact Peter reported directly to the Commander-in-Chief, President John F. Kennedy. He also suspected that Peter was very close to the Kennedy family. Now that he had seen how the Attorney General had responded to seeing Peter Sharkey, Admiral Taylor immediately buried any thoughts about questioning Peter further as to his not informing him about this previously. In fact, why should he be upset since it was Peter who had insisted that the Admiral be at this meeting? Peter moved quickly to introduce Admiral Taylor to the Attorney General and vice versa.

Moments later the doors to the President's office were opened and the Attorney General, Admiral Taylor and Captain Sharkey were ushered inside. Once inside President Johnson moved to greet all of them. He was always a congenial host.

After welcoming them, President Johnson said, "Well, Bobby, you requested this meeting, so I guess it's up to you to tell me what this is all about."

Robert Kennedy said, "Thanks, Lyndon, for seeing us on such short notice, but there are many things that have happened that you don't know about and I think some of them might be related to the killing of my brother, Jack."

Lyndon Johnson's eyes widened somewhat when he heard that. Lyndon said, "Bobby, you know Jack and I always got along and if there's anything, I repeat, anything that I can do to find his killers, you just need to let me know."

Bobby Kennedy responded, "I know that, Lyndon. You've been a good friend. And now there are some new things you should be aware of that I hope you'll keep in complete confidence. All great leaders have some secrets and, Lyndon, I know you're proud of some of yours. But there are some that just should remain secret forever."

President Johnson smiled and nodded in agreement. Bobby Kennedy continued, "Well, I'll give the short version to you and Admiral Taylor. Before I start I want you to know that Captain Sharkey did everything he did at the request of my brother, so no matter what you think about the ethics or legality of this, he just did his duty as requested by his Commander-in-Chief, who coincidentally was also his good friend. If there is anyone to be blamed, I'll take the blame since I knew exactly what my brother was doing and participated in all these events."

President Johnson and Admiral Taylor looked at each other kind of puzzled, but they both nodded in agreement to proceed.

At that, Bobby Kennedy continued, "I have to say again that this conversation is absolutely top secret, but here's the story. My brother Jack had an affair with Marilyn Monroe. It was sometimes reported in the media or suggested, but no one knew whether that really happened. But it did. And Marilyn became pregnant with Jack's baby."

President Johnson, who had been almost impervious to many of the shocking things that he'd heard through the years, still stifled a gasp when he heard that. In fact, he was so shocked, he rocketed upright out of his chair.

President Johnson exclaimed, "Son of a bitch. I could have sworn something was going on between them. But I never knew for sure. They are better at keeping secrets than I am."

Having said that, he dropped back into his seat.

Robert Kennedy continued, "Marilyn Monroe did not commit suicide last year, but she did attempt to commit suicide the week before her reported death. She wanted to protect the President and not cause him embarrassment because of her pregnancy. Although she did try to kill herself, a doctor was able to revive her.

"She then decided that killing herself was absolutely wrong for her, and that she just wanted to escape Hollywood and raise her baby somewhere without all the celebrity. She arranged her own disappearance with some characters of shady background. I'd prefer not to go into that now. She also arranged her own escape from the U.S. with a secret airline flight to Ireland provided by Howard Hughes, the owner of TWA. When she arrived in Ireland she was provided with safe haven by a cousin of mine.

"But that safe haven in Ireland was attacked and destroyed just after Jack was killed. My cousin and some of his friends were killed, but we don't think they killed Marilyn or the baby. The local authorities are dismissing this as an IRA bomb factory that exploded, but we know that is not true. Now it's possible that attack might be just a coincidence, but we need to investigate whether or not the attack and the assassination are in some way connected."

Bobby Kennedy continued, "So, Lyndon, what I really want is for you to authorize an expanded investigation into the killing of my brother. Because of the international implications and the need for extreme secrecy, I want you to appoint Admiral Taylor as the head of this top-secret investigation. I hope you'll make all the other agencies report to him and answer to him in whatever they do."

President Johnson was astonished by everything he had heard, but he said, "Okay, Bobby. I'll do whatever you want. We've got to find out who these bastards are that shot Jack."

Then President Johnson stood and went over to Bobby Kennedy. He said, "I want you to know that I was honored when Jack picked me as his running mate. Despite media reports to the contrary during the primaries, Jack and I always enjoyed the friendliest of relationships. Your sorrow at his loss is my sorrow. I'd readily give up the Presidency tomorrow if it would bring him back."

Bobby Kennedy stood up and shook Lyndon's hand. He was moved by what Lyndon Johnson had just said and had tears forming in the corners of his eyes. He could only say, "Lyndon, thank you for everything."

Then President Johnson said to Admiral Taylor, "Rufus, I am appointing you to head the investigative team and determine exactly what happened to President Jack Kennedy. I'm going to get you all the support that you need – anything you need – so just call me if you meet any bureaucratic roadblocks. All of our Federal agencies, including the FBI, will report to you on this matter. You understand that? I said anything you need, anything at all."

Admiral Taylor had not expected any of this, especially being appointed to head the investigation into the assassination of President Kennedy. He was overwhelmed, but he nodded his head, "Yes, Mr. President. Thank you, sir. I'll let you know as quickly as possible about what kind of additional resources I'll need, but the O.N.I. will get started immediately."

As he left the President's office, he thought about what just happened and realized that the Attorney General had probably never even heard his name before Peter Sharkey mentioned it. His appointment was obviously because of Peter Sharkey. Peter didn't just get him invited to the meeting; he made the recommendation to get him the responsibility for the entire investigation. He vowed not to disappoint the President, the Attorney General or Peter Sharkey. He would provide Peter whatever support he needed for this investigation.

* * * * * * * * * *

The next day, J. Edgar Hoover arrived 15 minutes early for his 9:00 a.m. meeting with President Lyndon Johnson. Although J. Edgar had met Lyndon Johnson many times before, since they both had long careers in Washington, DC, this was the first time that J. Edgar had officially met with the new President. J. Edgar was not at all nervous about the meeting. He was used to dealing with various upper-level politicians, statesmen and even presidents. His long career as the head of the FBI was the result of his ability to deal with, and sometimes manipulate, those politicians. He knew that information equaled power, and he had long employed his organization to collect information on anyone that he thought might be of use to him in the future. Although his official mandate was to deal with entities and individuals that might be a threat to the United States and its internal order, J. Edgar interpreted this to mean that any individual or entity that might threaten him personally would also be a threat to the United States.

In his briefcase, J. Edgar had a portfolio that included a summary of almost 50 different extramarital affairs that the FBI could document had been committed by Lyndon Johnson. Besides the summary, he also had five individual folders with the details of each of those encounters. J. Edgar was sure that Lyndon Johnson would be most cooperative in retaining him as head of the FBI because J. Edgar would give him assurances that these files would never be released to the public as long as Hoover remained the curator of those files at the FBI. It was a tactic that J. Edgar had used successfully throughout his career.

Instead of making him wait, as some low level bureaucrats liked to do to assert their power, Lyndon himself opened the office door at five minutes before 9:00 a.m. to welcome J. Edgar. After the usual round of pleasantries, Lyndon instructed J. Edgar to seat himself directly in front of Lyndon's desk.

Lyndon began the discussion by stating, "Well, J. Edgar, I do appreciate your time this morning. I thought we should have this conversation to establish our future working relationship."

J. Edgar immediately responded, "Yes, Mr. President. I'm so glad that you invited me here, because I do want to have a good working relationship with you."

Lyndon Johnson said, "Well, J. Edgar, first of all, you don't need to call me Mr. President. I think Lyndon would be good since I'm hoping that we will be good friends and have a good working relationship in the future."

J. Edgar nodded vigorously and was waiting for an opportunity to present some of the items that he'd brought along.

Instead Lyndon Johnson said, "J. Edgar, there's a rumor in these parts that you might have threatened some of my predecessors or various other people with some private information that your organization may have gathered about them. I'm sure that's just a rumor, but I thought we should get that rumor discussed up front between us right away. You see, I do have some incidents in my past that might prove embarrassing to my wife, Lady Bird. My lovely Lady Bird loves me and I love her beyond all else. I don't want to cause her any embarrassment.

"Now let me just tell you that there are some things I might have done that some people might not approve of. On the other hand, my lovely wife and I have an understanding regarding these things. She understands that a man of power in positions like I've had is sometimes tempted by women who throw themselves at him. Despite his best efforts to repel those women, sometimes he succumbs to their charms.

"Lady Bird has been very tolerant of my weaknesses. I have confessed to her at least 50 times about my transgressions and she has always forgiven me. She knows that I love only her and the others don't matter to me. Although it might even be true that there are 50 others that I may not have even remembered, that the FBI might have come across during some unrelated investigations, and that maybe have become part of my file.

"It really doesn't matter to me if those transgressions would be made public, except that I might have to apologize again to my Lady Bird, and I do not like to cause her any distress. You do understand that, don't you, J. Edgar?"

J. Edgar sat there obviously confused. As best as he could tell, Lyndon Johnson had just confessed to him of approximately a hundred extramarital affairs and didn't seem to be bothered by it at all. All J. Edgar could do was say, "Yes, Mr. President, I understand," and nod – although he really didn't understand at all.

Johnson continued, "Also, J. Edgar, while these activities might not be very popular among the prim ladies of Boston, in my home state of Texas, I believe that my constituents understand that I am quite a swordsman and that, because of that, they respect me. The men look up to me and my achievements in that area. And the ladies, while they may chatter about it, secretly admire the fact of my masculinity. So while I would hope that you would not find anything in my file that might embarrass my dear Lady Bird, I don't think that there's anything in your files that might have any effect other than to enhance my reputation as a swordsman amongst my constituents in Texas. What do you think, J. Edgar? Do you understand what I'm saying?"

Again, J. Edgar could only nod because he didn't really understand, although he didn't like the way this whole conversation was going. He already knew that he didn't possess any power over Lyndon Johnson because of the files he had in his briefcase. But he wisely decided to never bring them up and to just keep the briefcase locked.

Lyndon continued, "Well, J. Edgar, there's also some rumors about your relationship with Clyde Tolson, an Associate Director at the FBI, with whom you are particularly friendly."

J. Edgar hadn't expected this attack regarding his relationship with Tolson, but he quickly said, "Lyndon, there's nothing to do about that. He is just a close friend and he is… he is… just…"

Lyndon stopped J. Edgar because he was starting to stammer.

"J. Edgar, I'm really not interested in any personal relationships that you might have. I think it's admirable that you have some close friends, both male and female, that you support them and that they enjoy your company and you enjoy theirs. So I don't think that it's of anybody's interest what one's personal activities are. Neither yours nor mine. I think you would agree with that also, wouldn't you, J. Edgar?"

Again, J. Edgar nodded, and was starting to wonder about where this conversation was going. He was afraid his job was in jeopardy.

Lyndon Johnson said, "J. Edgar, the people of the United States demand an answer to the assassination of President John F. Kennedy. He was, despite some false news reports to the contrary, a dear friend of mine. I personally want to know the truth about what happened to him, and I want to avenge or bring to justice the perpetrators. Now, I am telling you that I expect your complete cooperation. I want you to pledge to me that you will divulge absolutely everything that your organization has found out about this dastardly crime, and I want you to tell me that you will cooperate in absolutely everything that I instruct you to do.

"I know you have a certain pride in the FBI, and want to protect your organization and sometimes keep some information proprietary to them so that you usually have an edge, but I want you to know I will not tolerate that. My intention is to reappoint you to the Directorship of the FBI as long as you continue to do the things I ask of you. If you refuse in any way, or if I find out that you are withholding information from me, you will be terminated.

"I want you to know that I am not at all worried about any repercussions from that, and if I do terminate you, I will position it because I am disappointed in the way you were handling the investigation of the assassination of President John F. Kennedy – and I can assure you that the American public will support me in my decision. Now is that clear?"

J. Edgar, somewhat shaken by the bluntness of Lyndon Johnson's tone, stood up and said, "Yes, Mr. President. Please let me be of service to you. I have nothing but respect for the office of the President of the United States, and I did consider John F. Kennedy one of the best presidents that I have ever met. He was always gracious when I spoke to him. I pledge to you that I will do anything that you ask of me and that I will immediately divulge to you any new developments that any of the people in my organization develop. Please let me continue to serve you."

Lyndon stood and walked to Hoover, clasped his hand and said, "J. Edgar, I am pleased that we're going to work together on this, and I believe we will have a long and fruitful working relationship. Now, let me tell you some things that you may not know. Please sit down again."

Lyndon walked back to his desk chair and sat and looked at J. Edgar. "There are international ramifications to the assassination," he said, "of which you may not be aware. Therefore, I have appointed Admiral Rufus Taylor, Director of the Office of Naval Intelligence to be the lead investigator into the assassination of President John F. Kennedy."

J. Edgar Hoover looked at President Lyndon Johnson in astonishment and said, "The Navy, sir? The Navy? I don't understand."

Lyndon Johnson said, "Well, Admiral Taylor should be here in just a moment and will provide you with the answers to your questions. He's also bringing along Captain Peter Sharkey, who works for him and who was a personal friend of Jack Kennedy. Peter and Jack both served in the Navy together and had a close personal relationship for years. Peter has some information that has never been divulged in public that he will divulge to you here, and that I insist you keep secret. You'll also understand why I have assigned this investigation to the Office of Naval Intelligence since it has international ramifications.

J. Edgar was relieved that his period of interrogation and trepidation was over. He lived for the FBI and would have laid down his life for the agency if necessary. He would have been devastated if he had lost the directorship of the agency. In a way, he admired Lyndon for his ability to operate outside the system, but perform within the system. Sort of as he himself had been doing for years. He had just pledged his full cooperation to the President, and J. Edgar was a man of his word. He didn't know why the Navy was involved in the investigation, but J. Edgar knew that the more he could help the Navy in this endeavor, the more President Johnson would owe to him in the future. Moments later, Admiral Taylor and Captain Sharkey were ushered into the office. They divulged everything they knew, which left J. Edgar Hoover shaking his head in amazement. J. Edgar again pledged his complete cooperation, and he agreed to meet regularly with Admiral Taylor to share information and report new developments. They mutually decided that the FBI would handle the U.S. investigation and the O.N.I. would handle the international investigation. Accordingly, Admiral Taylor ordered Captain Sharkey back to Ireland to gather more facts regarding the attack there. He would be given as many O.N.I. investigators as he needed.

CHAPTER SEVENTEEN

IRELAND INVESTIGATION

Peter arrived back in Dublin after an overnight flight from the United States. Although he had slept on the long flight across the Atlantic, he had immediately taken a nap after he checked into his hotel room in Dublin. But now he was refreshed and showered as he left the hotel for some important appointments.

During his first two days in Ireland, Peter had very little success dealing with the local police in the county where the massacre had occurred. Everyone in that small, rural police force just wanted to take the easy route out of this situation. They were more than willing to believe what had happened at the manor house had been nothing more than an explosion that killed IRA terrorists who had been there assembling a bomb for nefarious purposes. They did accompany him, however, to the charred ruins that had once been the manor house. As far as Peter could see, there was almost nothing left of the residence.

The local constabulary had absolutely no interest in opening any deeper investigation. But in fact it was not that they were lazy or part of a cover-up, they were just no more than a small group of local cops who had no real investigation skills. They were pretty much limited to just chasing local hooligans and drunkards and dropping them in jail for a night or two. They had neither the will nor the ability to investigate an actual major crime. But the one encouraging thing Peter learned from speaking to them was that, although there were several badly burned bodies, none of them appeared to be a woman – and certainly they had not detected the corpse of a baby. They were not skilled investigators, but they could at least count bodies. Peter needed to learn what happened to Jean and the baby.

At the start of his third day, Peter headed to the curb to hail a taxi to take him to his appointment at the headquarters of the Dublin police force. He didn't know if the Dublin police would be any more cooperative than the local constables, but he wanted to be thorough. As Peter approached the curb to hail a cab, a smiling young Irishman moved toward him.

Peter looked up as the stranger said, "Excuse me, but might you have a match for a cigarette?"

Peter responded, "I'm sorry, I don't smoke. So I don't have any matches."

But as Peter was saying that, the stranger moved quite close in front of him and said, "Actually, Captain Sharkey, I know you don't smoke, and I'm not really looking for a match. What I do want you to do is not move abruptly because I have .45 automatic pointed at your abdomen beneath the newspapers in my hand. Now I know that you're a military type who might want to fight about this, but I need to advise you that I have two associates. They are both behind you, one at your left flank and one at your right flank. We have you in a triangle so that any of us can shoot you at any moment without worrying about the bullets passing through you and hitting any of us. Do you understand what I'm saying?"

Peter instinctively started to turn around but the stranger stopped him with a loud voice as he said, "Captain Sharkey, I told you not to move abruptly. Don't do anything that would force us to shoot you. That is not why we are here."

Peter calmed down for a moment and said, "Okay, so then why exactly are you here?"

The stranger said, "We need you to come with us, sir, because there are many things going on in Ireland that you don't know about. And my leader would like to talk to you about this."

Peter said, "And just who is your leader?"

The stranger said, "You're in no position to ask questions. Now, here's what we're going to do. You'll continue to smile at me and you will accompany me to our car just over there. My associates will be behind both of us, and please be certain that they are ready to kill you if you don't cooperate."

Peter nodded in agreement, and as they walked toward the car, he could hear the footsteps of two men behind them. He knew that the stranger was not bluffing about any of this.

The stranger pushed Peter into the backseat of the vehicle while one of his associates entered the backseat from the other side. Peter was sandwiched between both of them, and they both had their .45 automatics trained on him, but just out of reach. He knew that these were experienced gunmen and if he tried to overpower them, at least one of them would probably be able to shoot him.

The other associate climbed into the driver's seat and they sped off to a destination that Peter could never have imagined.

The stranger said to Peter, "Please don't be frightened, sir. We are not going to harm you in any way. Although I didn't know any of the true Irishmen that were killed in that manor house recently, I consider them my brothers since we all serve the same common cause."

Peter asked, "Well, if you're not going to harm me, can I just get out now?"

The stranger chuckled and said, "Now I know you're an Irishman because of your sense of humor. But I'm sure you're not that naïve. We didn't go to all this effort just to drive you around town for a few minutes. As long as you don't cause any trouble or try to resist, you'll be back at your hotel in time for your supper. But in the meantime, you have a very important meeting to attend."

"Meeting?" Peter asked. "With whom, and where, and why?"

The stranger responded, "You'll learn soon enough. So it'd be best if you just didn't bother talking anymore. Would you mind quieting down now so that we can all enjoy the ride?"

Peter knew that he just received the Irish equivalent of a command to shut up, so he did just what was requested.

The ride took almost two hours before the vehicle finally stopped at the end of what had obviously been a rough dirt and stone road, since the car had vibrated nastily for the last few miles. His captors had put a blindfold around Peter's eyes about a half-hour before their arrival to prevent him from recognizing where he was going. But that really wasn't necessary, since Peter wasn't familiar with the Irish landscape and wouldn't have known exactly where he was anyway.

Once they'd pulled Peter out of the car and ushered him into the meeting room, they took off his blindfold.

Peter looked quickly around and saw that he was in a very plain Irish living room, and in front of him was seated a pale, thin and very sickly gentleman. This gentleman was seated on a Spartan wooden chair to support him in an upright posture. Next to him were two tall, green oxygen tanks. From the tanks there was plastic tubing that dangled and hissed, but which the seated gentleman was not using. In fact, what he was doing was smoking a cigarette. From the pile in the ashtray in front of him, this was clearly not his first smoke of the day.

Peter also saw that he was surrounded by at least four armed Irishmen, the three that had brought him here plus one more new one. He abandoned any thought of trying to muscle his way to an escape. He was about to speak when the emaciated gentleman in the chair addressed him.

"I understand that your name is Captain Peter Sharkey. Is that correct?" the seated gentleman interrogated him.

"Yes, it is," Peter said. "And who might you be?"

Peter was surprised when the emaciated guy actually identified himself by saying, "My name is William Flynn. You may not have heard of me, but the Brits call me Billy the Butcher. In the Republic, they call me Billy the Defender. Unfortunately, my new nickname should now more likely be Billy the Breathless."

He laughed at his own joke with a racking chuckle that ended in a rasping cough. Although he was obviously having trouble breathing, Flynn continued to suck regularly on his cigarette. Peter responded, "Well, this is an unusual way for us to meet. Perhaps you'll tell me why you've abducted me."

Flynn smiled at that and said, "Abducted is such a nasty word. If we'd abducted you, it might have meant we were going to harm you. Instead, think of it as being invited to a meeting and we just didn't want you to say no."

Peter responded, "Okay, so I guess now you'll tell me why you invited me to this meeting."

Flynn said, "We have been monitoring your movements in and out of Ireland for some time. We know that you arrived here with someone else, probably a woman, in the middle of the night on a private, unscheduled TWA airliner that came from the United States. From there you proceeded to the manor house of Michael Brady, which has just been destroyed by the Brits. After that you returned several times, at least once with two other gentlemen who proceeded to set up a very sophisticated radio system and antenna at the manor house. We don't know exactly what type of radio equipment you installed within the house, but we suspect that it had intercontinental capabilities and was used to report information back to the authorities in America. Would you like to tell me more about why you've been here and what was going on?"

Peter declined and said, "Well, you obviously know when I've been here and what I was doing. I don't think there's anything more that I can offer. But you did say 'we have been monitoring.' Who is 'we'?"

Flynn replied, "My group is called the IRF – the Irish Reunification Force. We are a group of patriots who feel that the political approach espoused by the IRA is ineffective, and so we chose to take a different approach."

Peter understood his meaning, but asked anyway, "You mean a violent approach?"

Flynn avoided his question and instead queried Peter, "Are you a Catholic, son?"

Peter was caught off guard by the question, but said, "Well, I was born a Catholic, but I can't say that I'm a faithful attendee at church."

Flynn smiled at that and said, "Well, neither am I, but I'm glad to hear you're not one of those Protestant bastards."

Peter replied, "Well, I'm sure you've 'invited' me here to discuss something other than my religious practices."

Flynn said, "You're a feisty bastard. That doesn't surprise me since you're Irish. You've got armed guards all around you, but you still look me right in the face. I like that, and that's why I'm going to tell you more about what's going on here in Ireland. Please, sit."

Peter took a chair opposite Flynn and relaxed a bit, since it seemed apparent that they didn't invite him here to kill him. Flynn said, "First, let me express my sincere condolences to you on behalf of all my associates on the assassination of your President, John Kennedy. We all admired him and we were so proud and honored when he came to visit us last summer. I don't know whether any of the things that have happened here in Ireland have any relation to his killing in the U.S. In fact, I think not, because it seems pretty apparent that he was killed by either the Cubans or the Soviets, or maybe by both of them acting together. But I did want to give you some information about the massacre here."

Peter responded, "Thank you, Mr. Flynn. I would appreciate any information you could give me about anything that could relate to either of these matters. But just a moment ago, you said the manor house was destroyed by 'the Brits.' What did you mean by that?"

Flynn said, "Well, first of all, you need to know that the story about the manor house exploding because Michael Brady was constructing an IRA bomb is complete bullshit. While Michael was a true supporter of Irish reunification, and was sympathetic to the IRA, he was a member of Sinn Fein – the political wing of the IRA – and always favored a political rather than a military settlement. He never supported the methods promoted by the IRF, so there would never have been a bomb in his house.

"Also, my information is that there was both a woman and her child in residence at the house; I think she was the one that arrived with you on that TWA flight. She subsequently gave birth to a male child with the help of a midwife who also supports the Irish cause. Plus our informants reported the delivery of infant formula to the house, as well as baby food. I can't imagine Michael ever risking their safety by having bomb-making materials in the house."

Peter said, "I can't agree with you more, sir. I knew Michael, and regardless of what his political feelings were, he would never have risked the life of Jean and her baby." Peter intentionally mentioned Jean's name to let Flynn know that he trusted him with some information also.

Flynn continued, "My people tracked a small team of Brits that traveled down from Northern Ireland on the night in question. They are members of a very secretive group called the "Irish Section" that is part of the British Intelligence Service, MI-5. The leader of this group is Colonel Brian Conners and he's as soulless as any vermin that ever contaminated the Earth. The mission of this group is to disrupt, torture and kill Irish patriots that belong to the IRF, the IRA or any other group promoting reunification. Unfortunately, this small group of men, we are sure, attacked the manor house and massacred the inhabitants. Then they planted a bomb to destroy the evidence and blame everything on a mistake by the IRA."

Peter asked, "But why would they attack the house? If Michael Brady wasn't a violent terrorist, why would they do that?"

Flynn said, "Well, we don't know exactly, but these MI-5 villains often do things that are inexplicable to us. But from some information that we've gathered, it appears that they believed that the manor house was a secret radio station transmitting important data back to the United States regarding the efforts of the Republic of Ireland to achieve reunification. While we don't know exactly what happened during the attack, we do believe that the attackers took the woman, her child and all the radio equipment back with them when they left the scene."

Peter asked, "The woman and the child, are they okay? Do you know anything about that?"

Flynn said, "As far as we know, they were not killed in the explosion. The local constables did not report finding the bodies of a woman or a child in the ruins. I'm pretty sure that the attackers took the woman and the child, as well as the radio equipment, back into Northern Ireland to their headquarters."

Peter said, "So they're alive then, and at the headquarters of this group?"

Flynn said, "That's what I think, but I can't guarantee anything. Many of our supporters have been abducted to their headquarters, only never to be seen again."

Peter said, "Well, where is the headquarters of this group? Can you tell me something more?"

Flynn said, "It's in the far northeast of Northern Ireland on the ragged coast near the town of Carrickfergus. I could give you more info, but I think that's enough for this meeting. I am running out of breath."

Flynn continued, "As you can see, I'm not well and probably won't live very much longer. These damn fags have killed me, but I can't resist caressing their smoke. I want you to investigate and learn that what I've told you is the truth. Then when you have more confidence in what I've told you, maybe I'll be willing to share more. But you should know that if you inquire about me with the Brits, all you'll find is that they consider me a terrorist and want to kill me as badly as I want to kill them."

Flynn paused to cough repeatedly, and with a deep racking sound that culminated when he finally coughed some vile phlegm into his handkerchief.

Then he continued, "My men will give you a telephone number to call to get in touch with me. I want you to know that I will help in any way I can to avenge the deaths of Michael Brady and his friends in that manor house. And if you find that these British villains were somehow involved in the assassination of your President, please be assured that I'll do everything in my power to help you avenge him also. Now my men will take you back to your hotel. Please forgive me if I don't stand up to shake your hand and bid you goodbye, but even standing is too much of an effort for me now."

Peter was confused by everything he had just heard and seen. He was empathetic about the distress that Flynn was in because of his disease, but Flynn admitted he was considered a terrorist by the British. He also didn't know whether Flynn was telling him the truth, or whether this was just some type of story to advance his purposes. In any case, they returned Peter unharmed to his hotel.

Peter spent the next day having meetings with the Dublin Police and county officials. But unfortunately, they were as unproductive as his meetings with the local constables. They were all convinced that it was a case of Irish terrorists that had been killed when one of their own bombs exploded prematurely.

Finally, Peter headed back to Washington. Before he left, he used his Navy access code to place a secure telephone call to Admiral Taylor to request a meeting with him and Director Hoover. He told the Admiral about his abduction by William Flynn, and asked the Admiral to get as much information as possible about Flynn and his shadowy group, the IRF.

On the long flight back, he thought about his strange meeting with William Flynn, and decided that the man knew he was near death because of his medical problems and probably was speaking the truth. But even if this alleged vigilante group of MI-5 agents had attacked the Brady manor house, it didn't seem likely that they could have been involved in the killing of the President.

But it was still the best lead he had gotten regarding the whereabouts of Jean and the baby. Although he wasn't ready to admit it, even to himself, he had fallen hard for Jean. He wasn't sure if she felt the same way about him, but he thought she might. It didn't matter how she felt. He was determined to find her and the baby.

Chapter Eighteen

J. Edgar Hoover suggested that the meeting be held in his office since he had much information to share with Admiral Taylor and Captain Sharkey. Before the meeting Admiral Taylor picked Peter up in his car. That way they would have about a half-hour to talk privately before meeting Hoover.

Once they were in the Admiral's car, Peter reported his frustration at the lack of cooperation and the lack of information provided by the Irish authorities. Then they spent most of their time discussing Peter's abduction by William Flynn and the information that he had provided to Peter. Admiral Taylor had been able to confirm that the IRF was one of several violent splinter groups that had split off from the IRA as the IRA had seemingly adopted a more conciliatory approach to Northern Ireland.

Admiral Taylor agreed with Peter that it sounded somewhat like a death-bed confession from a doomed man, but it also could be just a misleading smoke screen that Flynn was providing to divert any investigation from what might have really happened. They knew there was a possibility that Flynn might be lying about the entire thing. Lying would be far from the most heinous thing he had ever done. They agreed, however, that they needed to investigate everything he had said.

When they arrived at the FBI building, they were quickly escorted into the Office of Director J. Edgar Hoover. J. Edgar welcomed them and said, "Thanks for coming by to meet so quickly after Captain Sharkey's arrival back from Ireland at eight o'clock last night."

Now neither Admiral Taylor nor Captain Sharkey had told J. Edgar the exact time that Peter arrived back from Ireland. But J. Edgar seemed to know virtually everything he wanted to know about whatever was going on in the United States, so they weren't surprised by his comment. Admiral Taylor responded, "Thank you for meeting with us on such short notice, but Peter has been able to discover some interesting information while he was over there."

J. Edgar said, "Well, we also have gotten some additional information regarding Lee Harvey Oswald. Please let me go first and I'll tell you what we've learned."

Admiral Taylor responded, "Certainly. That would be very helpful."

J. Edgar then gave them a brief summary of everything the FBI had discovered about Lee Harvey Oswald. Information such as the confirmation that Oswald owned the Carcano rifle and that he had purchased it under the alias Alek J. Hidell.

But then, J. Edgar proceeded to mention that the Dallas Police Department had done an inventory of all of Oswald's possessions that they found after he had been killed. The Dallas police force shared all this information with the FBI.

J. Edgar said, "There were three photos in his possession when he died, that were taken at the residence of General Edwin Walker. General Walker, since his resignation from the U.S. Army in 1961, had been conducting a virulent and vocal campaign against Cuba. It was suspected that General Walker planned to run for public office and would use his hatred of Cuba to appeal to the public. He had been the subject of an unsuccessful assassination attempt in April of 1963."

J. Edgar then stated, "We now believe that Oswald might also have been responsible for the attack on Walker."

J. Edgar had copies of the three photographs and showed them to Admiral Taylor and Captain Sharkey. The first two photos were of the back of the residence.

The third photo was the front of the residence and included an image of a vehicle parked in the forefront of the photo. Admiral Taylor asked J. Edgar whether they had traced the vehicle, since the license plate was clearly visible in the photo. J. Edgar responded, "Yes we did, but it's completely clean. The vehicle belongs to the British Consulate in Dallas."

As soon as they heard that, both Sharkey and Taylor looked at each other in amazement.

J. Edgar had spent his whole life in law enforcement and knew how to interrogate suspects and gauge their responses. He immediately knew that what he had said about the vehicle had triggered a sudden, high response from his visitors. So J. Edgar asked, "Well, that seems to have piqued your interest. What was it that got you so excited?"

Admiral Taylor responded, "J. Edgar, Peter has just had a very unusual experience during his trip to Ireland. He was abducted by a shadowy Irish group that claimed that the killings at the Brady manor house were carried out by a secretive group of British agents from MI-5. We were just preparing to tell you about all this when you asked to first talk about your new information. But I think now Peter should describe everything."

So Peter briefed J. Edgar on everything that had happened in Ireland. He provided even more detail than he and Admiral Taylor had discussed in the car.

Admiral Taylor asked if the FBI could find out who might have driven that car on that date to the residence of General Walker. J. Edgar responded that it probably wasn't Oswald since he didn't have a driver's license. He promised to get his men on it as quickly as possible. J. Edgar suggested that they meet again as soon as he had gotten the information.

It was the next day when Admiral Taylor and Captain Sharkey were again ushered into the office of J. Edgar Hoover. After the usual pleasantries, J. Edgar informed them, "Well we've been able to track down who was driving that sedan registered to the British Consulate that day. The vehicle is one of several maintained by the Consulate for use by visiting dignitaries.

"On that day, the vehicle was on loan to Jeffrey Duncan, the 'Trade Representative' of the British Foreign Trade Office for the Southern United States."

Admiral Taylor then questioned, "But why was he there and why was the car there?"

J. Edgar then smiled because he had a secret they didn't know. J. Edgar said, "Well, neither Jeffrey Duncan nor that department of the British Trade Office actually exists. The vehicle was assigned to someone who had presented completely fraudulent credentials when he visited Dallas.

"My men have very good contacts within the security forces at the British Consulate, and they have determined that the credentials this guy presented appeared to be absolutely authentic. They were perfect copies of authentic British documents, but were thoroughly fraudulent. They were so perfect that our contacts believe they had to have been produced by some department of the British government."

J. Edgar continued, "I think we need to investigate more about what William Flynn said. Maybe there are some British connections to not only what happened in Ireland, but also the attempted assassination of General Walker – and maybe even the assassination of the President. I think, with your concurrence of course, that we should meet with President Johnson to inform him of what we've discovered."

Both Admiral Taylor and Captain Sharkey were incredulous by what they just learned about the vehicle. It was owned by the British Consulate in Dallas and it had been driven into the vicinity of General Walker's home prior to an assassination attempt by someone sporting a fraudulent, but very authentic-looking, British ID. And Lee Harvey Oswald had to have been there at the same time, since he had the incriminating photograph in his possession at the time of his death. They both nodded their agreement with Hoover's suggestion about a meeting with President Johnson.

The President met with them the next day. Admiral Taylor briefed the President on all of the developments in the case, including Peter's abduction and the mysterious driver in charge of the car that was in the vicinity of General Walker's residence when Lee Harvey Oswald was there. Although there was some initial skepticism about the information provided by the Irish terrorist leader, William Flynn, who had abducted Peter, there did now seem to be some circumstantial evidence to support his claims.

"Oh, my god," President Johnson exclaimed, "What the hell is going on here?"

Admiral Taylor responded to the President and said, "We don't know, sir. We haven't been able to establish any further information, either here or in Ireland."

The President turned to J. Edgar Hoover and asked, "Can't your people find out more about this supposed department at MI-5? And can we get any more information about whoever it was that presented those fraudulent credentials at the consulate in Dallas?"

J. Edgar always liked to stay ahead of the questions with his answers. He also knew how to grandstand a bit.

J. Edgar said, "Actually, Mr. President, we've been working on that around the clock. Just before I got here I received some new information that I haven't yet been able to share with Admiral Taylor and Captain Sharkey, but I'm sure you'll indulge me because time is of the essence."

J. Edgar Hoover continued, "We have many friends and informants, including some at the British Consulate in Dallas and even some within MI-5 in Britain. We sometimes provide them with information, and they sometimes reciprocate with information. It's a friendly relationship amongst two allies.

"But I have to tell you that there is almost no information available about this supposed department at MI-5. MI-5 is secretive enough, but its existence is still known and acknowledged. We couldn't find any of our friends who would even acknowledge that this "Irish section" exists at MI-5. But a couple of them did say that they had heard rumors about such a group.

"And there is no current information about a possible Colonel Brian Conners. If he is the commander of this department, his existence is hidden as well.

"The records that we did find on someone named Brian Conners, however, showed that he served with distinction during World War II. He was in the SAS as an enlisted man and was briefly captured during the invasion of Sicily by the American forces, who suspected him of being an Italian spy. He may have even been shot and wounded by the Americans, but we can't be sure of that yet. His exemplary performance later in the War led to a "battlefield" promotion for him. He also participated in the Suez War, where he was again captured, this time by Egyptian troops or the Bedouin militia. His captivity ended once the Suez War was over, but he abruptly left the SAS soon thereafter.

"Interestingly, he never seems to have left the British payroll. Our contacts in the British Exchequer report that he is still drawing a very handsome salary. But our contacts could not determine for which department he works. One contact said this is the most unusual thing he has ever seen in his thirty years in government service.

"We also were able to obtain a photo of the Brian Conners that was in the SAS. Although we only got the photo image about an hour ago, we wired it to Dallas and one of our agents, who is very close with the contact at the British Consulate in Dallas, immediately ran over there to show it to him. Although the Consulate employee wasn't completely positive since this was a photo of a younger man, the Consulate contact did think that the photo bore a remarkable resemblance to the phony trade representative that had used the Consulate staff car."

J. Edgar paused theatrically and then said, "I think there might be a big problem in Britain that we need to investigate."

Since this was new information to everyone except J. Edgar, it took a few moments for it to sink in to the others. But then President Johnson said, "Well, it appears that there might be some bad actors in MI-5. I think it's time that we get some help, on the other side of the pond as the British say."

Admiral Taylor agreed as he said, "Those were our exact thoughts, Mr. President. We think it's time to discuss this situation with someone in the British government. As you know, the assassination of President Kennedy is so sensitive a topic with the American public that we need to keep this as secret as possible until we know the truth. So we would like to recommend that you discuss this directly with the British Prime Minister."

President Johnson said, "Of course, I agree with that completely. In fact, I'm going to get him on the phone right now."

President Lyndon Johnson was not only a man of words, but also a man of action. He didn't like to waste time and had no patience for anything.

Before President Johnson could reach for the phone, however, Admiral Taylor said, "Excuse me, Mr. President, but if you'll permit me, I'd like to give you some additional recommendations that we have."

Johnson hesitated and said, "Okay, what else do you recommend?"

Admiral Taylor responded, "Well, we need someone in Britain that I think we can trust. If MI-5 is somehow involved in this, we certainly can't trust them. There is a gentleman over there that I've met several times throughout the years named Admiral Caspar John. For the last four years he has been the British First Sea Lord. In that position he was the head of the entire Royal Navy. I've heard he just changed jobs and is now on their Security Commission, but I think that he can be trusted and that we need to have an upper-level contact in Britain as this investigation develops."

President Johnson stated, "Okay that sounds like a good plan to me. And I do agree that we need to have some high-level help over there because this may get messy."

President Johnson then picked up the phone and instructed his secretary to place a call to the British Prime Minister. The Prime Minister was now Sir Alec Douglas-Home. The last Prime Minister, Harold Macmillan, had left office in the middle of October, 1963.

It took several minutes for the President's secretary to arrange the secure transcontinental telephone call with the British Prime Minister. The secretary spoke to the Prime Minister's secretary, and finally about 10 minutes later, both men picked up their telephones.

President Johnson started the conversation with, "Hello, Alec. Thank you for taking my call on such short notice."

The Prime Minister responded, "Of course, Mr. President. You can call anytime."

President Johnson said, "Please, please, call me Lyndon. I don't want any formalities between us. Is that okay, Alec?"

To that Prime Minister Alec Douglas-Home responded, "Of course, Lyndon. We should be cordial with each other. Now, what can I do for you, since you called me?"

President Johnson stated, "Well, we have discovered some very disturbing information that may involve some lower-level members of your government. I don't know that it would be wise for us to discuss this situation on the phone, even though we have the most secure telephone lines available. It is extremely complex and will take a rather long time to explain. What I'd like to propose is that I send Admiral Rufus Taylor, the Director of our Office of Naval Intelligence, and his assistant, Navy Captain Peter Sharkey, to meet with you in person to discuss this whole situation. They can be there quickly since I'll give them top priority on military flights from here to Britain."

Prime Minister Douglas-Home was puzzled by the need for secrecy. But he responded anyway, "Of course, Mr. President... I'm sorry, of course, Lyndon. I'll be happy to meet with your representatives just as soon as they arrive in London."

President Johnson responded, "Thank you, Alec. I have one further request for you."

The Prime Minister asked, "Of course, what would that be?"

President Johnson responded, "Because of the nature of these discussions and the disclosures that my people are going to make, we think it would be prudent to have someone else at this meeting. Since I'm sending Admiral Taylor, he has suggested that he would like to have the former First Sea Lord, Sir Caspar John at the meeting. I just want to suggest this since there may be some need for action after the meeting."

The Prime Minister was puzzled, but he had always had a friendly relationship with Sir Caspar John, so he immediately agreed. In fact, Sir Casper John had just joined the Security Commission upon leaving the Navy, so he might be the ideal guy to have at a meeting that could affect their country's relationship with the

United States and that could greatly affect their security. Plus the Prime Minister assumed, based on the fact that the President was sending two American Navy men and had requested a British Navy man as the liaison, that the matter probably involved a Navy issue. He never suspected the problem was actually with MI-5.

President Johnson thanked the Prime Minister for his help and assured him that they would talk again soon. As soon as the President's telephone call concluded, President Johnson said, "Okay, gentlemen, let's get going and get this done."

* * * * * * * * * *

When Captain Sharkey and Admiral Taylor were shown into the office of Prime Minister Alec Douglas-Home at Number 10 Downing Street in London, Admiral Caspar John was already there. Admiral Taylor and Admiral John moved immediately to shake hands since they had met previously. Then there were introductions all around.

The Prime Minister asked, "So what exactly did you want to meet to discuss?"

Admiral Taylor responded, "Well, this is a long story, but I'll try to make it as brief as possible. As you all know, we have recently suffered the assassination of our President, John F. Kennedy. We believe that there might be a small group in your MI-5 Intelligence Service that may have had some involvement in this. We also think that they were involved in an attack in Ireland that happened almost simultaneously with the assassination. We are not accusing your government of anything, of course. If someone was involved, we hope these are just some low-level rogue elements in the intelligence service that may be carrying out their own agenda. We just want to know the truth. And we want to make sure that whatever happened doesn't affect the relations between your country and ours."

The Prime Minister was aghast at hearing this. He asked, "What do you mean? Why would some part of our government be involved in any of this? Our countries have had the closest of relations for over a hundred years."

Admiral Taylor said, "Well, we're here to tell you everything that we know so far, and we want to enlist your help to discover the things that we don't know."

Admiral Taylor asked, "Shall I continue?"

When the Prime Minister nodded affirmatively, Admiral Taylor gave him the full briefing on the investigation thus far. When he had concluded, Admiral Taylor said, "Thank you, Prime Minister, for listening to all this evidence. I'd like to ask Admiral John what he thinks."

Admiral John responded, "This is so unusual that I don't know how to respond just yet. But I promise you that our investigation will be conducted in absolute secrecy. Just give us some time to look into all of this and report back. I'd also like to suggest that we question Roger Hollis about his knowledge of this 'Irish Section.'"

Admiral John explained, "Hollis is the Director General of the Security Service and has overall command of MI-5. I recommend that we invite him to our next meeting."

Everyone nodded in agreement and the meeting adjourned.

At 1:00 p.m. the next day, the same group reconvened at Number Ten Downing Street. The Prime Minister had summoned Roger Hollis to the meeting. Despite the fact that it was a part of his organization that was the subject of the investigation, no one suspected Hollis of any complicity in the attacks. Everyone agreed he might have valuable information about just what might have occurred.

As soon as Roger Hollis arrived, he was introduced to the attendees, and then faced some very direct questions from the Prime Minister. The Prime Minister had just recently risen to his office and had not previously met Roger Hollis. So to start off, he asked, "You are the leader of MI-5, isn't that correct?"

"Of course," Roger Hollis responded, "Yes, I am."

Then the Prime Minister asked, "There is a group or a section within MI-5 that seems to be targeted toward preventing terrorism in Ireland. Is that correct?"

Hollis responded, "Yes, sir, that is correct, as far as I know."

The Prime Minister frowned as he said, "What do you mean, as far as you know?"

"Well," Hollis responded, "that group only presents me with an annual budget that I include with my overall budget. I never had any instructions to participate in anything else that they did."

The Prime Minister said, "What? Don't they report to you?"

"No, sir," Hollis responded.

"How can that be, since they are part of MI-5," the Prime Minister asked angrily. "If they don't report to you, then who the hell do they report to?"

Hollis was puzzled by the question, but he responded anyway, "Sir, they report directly to you!"

The Prime Minister's normally florid British face suddenly glowed red with anger as he shouted, "What the hell are you talking about? I've never even heard about the existence of this department in MI-5 until yesterday."

Hollis responded, "Well, sir, it was my understanding from my predecessor that this particular section always reported just to the Prime Minister. This arrangement, I understand, dates back to the Second World War when Prime Minister Churchill established this section to deal with potential problems in Ireland. It has always been rumored that they employ some extralegal tactics that might have been necessary during the war."

The Prime Minister questioned, "You mean there's a group in your organization that supposedly reports to me, and that decides for themselves how they respond to things in Ireland or anywhere else that they might choose? And you have no control over them?"

"Sir," Hollis replied, "I didn't set this system up; I only inherited it – just as you did. I thought your office was supervising them. Just like my predecessors, I only included their budget requests with my own to provide them with financial secrecy."

With that, the Prime Minister calmed down a bit and said, "Well, then, just who the hell are these people? You did say that they are part of your budget, did you not?"

Hollis responded, "Yes, sir. Once a year their commander, Colonel Brian Conners, brings me his budget proposal for the next year. It is almost always

15% above the previous budget, but he tells me that I have no right to review his budgets, nor question the amounts. He always says that if I have any problems with anything, I should discuss them with the Prime Minister. Well, of course you can understand why I would never contact the Prime Minister's office about something as mundane as a few pounds in the department budget of a small section of my agency."

The Prime Minister questioned, "Do you know any of the other members of his group?"

Hollis replied, "No, sir, I don't."

The Prime Minister asked, "Do you even know how many there are?"

Again, Hollis responded, "No, sir. I don't have that information either."

At that, the Prime Minister paused to collect his thoughts. He was astonished by everything he had been hearing. Behind him, the Americans were also puzzled and confused by this arrangement. Apparently, there was a small group in MI-5 that was able to operate without any upper-level control. But when they heard that the leader of this group was Colonel Brian Conners, they became convinced that what William Flynn had said was true.

The Prime Minister then asked, "So, you did at least have some involvement with this group during the budgeting process?"

"Yes, sir," Hollis responded. "But as I said, all I did was include it in my overall budget, and it was always approved. I never heard any problems about them overspending their budgetary amounts."

At that, the Prime Minister stood up and responded animatedly, "So at least these folks report to us to get their funding?"

Hollis said, "Well, I'm sure of that, sir, since someone has to be paying their bills."

The Prime Minister asked, "Please tell me which department of our Exchequer is responsible for administering your budget and expenses?"

Hollis said, "Our overall budget is included in the budgetary department that funds all of the departments of the Home Secretary. Because our expenditures include many top-secret projects, the exact budgetary amounts are screened and blocked from the public. But we do have individual accountants assigned to each of our specific departments. There would be one accountant assigned to this group, which by the way is officially called Section N, although I have heard it referred to informally by the accountants as the 'Irish Section.'"

The Prime Minister requested, "Can you please call over to the accounting department and find out exactly who this assigned accountant might be? Then request that the accountant come over here as quickly as possible."

"Of course," Hollis replied. "Is there anything else that I need to do right now?"

"No," the Prime Minister said. "Just do that as quickly as possible. We'll take a short break while you make that call."

Once Hollis left to find out who the accountant was and to request that he or she come immediately, the Prime Minister said to the others in the room, "I can't believe what I've just heard. It seems impossible to me that, somehow, a small group of rogue agents could be operating on their own without any proper upper-level control. It might be possible that this group was established during World War II so that it could circumvent the normal laws during that terrible time, but I can't understand how it could still exist now. I assure you that no one wants to find out everything about this more than I do."

About an hour later, the accountant arrived. They expected a short, fat, old and gray-haired stodgy gentleman. Instead, they were surprised to find that the accountant was a fairly attractive female who was likely in her early 30s. When she was summoned to this meeting by Roger Hollis, she had the foresight to bring along with her the ledgers regarding Section N of the MI-5 Intelligence Service.

Roger Hollis introduced her to the rest of the attendees. He said, "This is Miss. Abigail Crowley who has been in the Department of the Exchequer for the last eight years. She has brought along several ledgers relating to the section we have been discussing. I would like to ask Ms. Crowley if she could please describe to us exactly how expenses and disbursements are handled for this group."

Miss Crowley responded, "Certainly, sir. It's actually a very simple process, at least from an accounting perspective. When I receive either expense reports or summaries of expenses from the department, I check them for accuracy and further check to be sure each one of them has been approved by the section head, who in this case is Colonel Brian Conners. As long as the amounts are accurate and the expenditure has been approved, I issue appropriate debits and credits into the section's account. I must say that this section has been one of the most accurate that I've ever been associated with. They virtually never have any major discrepancies."

The Prime Minister further questioned, "But do you actually review the purposes for which these expenses have been incurred?"

Miss Crowley responded, "No, sir. That's not my job. I just make sure that everything is accurate and that they are not overcharging the Exchequer by exceeding their budget. If that had been the case, I would inform my supervisor, but that never happens."

The Prime Minister asked, "But you do have all of the records for the expenses that this group has incurred, is that correct?"

"Yes, Prime Minister. And if there's anything specific that you would like to know about, I'm sure I can find it in my ledgers right now."

Thinking back to the possibility that Colonel Conners had been in America in March of 1963 and had secretly met with Lee Harvey Oswald, the Prime Minister asked, "Do you have records of any travel expenses that the Colonel and any members of his staff might have made around early March of 1963? Specifically might there have been any airline tickets to America."

Miss Crowley thumbed through her ledgers until she found the specific page she sought. Then she said, "Yes, sir. Here it is. Colonel Conners apparently was on a British Airlines flight to Dallas in early March, the 6th, according to the ticket. He only stayed a couple of days, and then returned on the same British Airways ticket on March 10th."

When they heard this, everyone in the meeting felt that this was confir-mation that Conners had been involved with Lee Harvey Oswald and the attempt on the life of General Walker – and probably the assassination of President Kennedy.

The Prime Minister then asked, "Miss Crowley, can you also check the travel records for the Colonel during November, 1963? Did he ever go back to Dallas?"

After flipping through the ledgers once again, Miss Crowley reported, "Yes, it appears that Colonel Conners flew to Canada on November 16th, and then caught a connecting flight to Dallas, Texas. Then he returned via the same route on November 24th."

Everyone had been taking notes as Miss Crowley spoke, but they all dropped their jaws when they heard this. Here was the "smoking gun" they were looking for.

The Prime Minister suddenly developed an ashen complexion as he realized the enormity of what he just heard. Someone in his government had been in Dallas during the assassination of President Kennedy – and more than likely was involved in it.

Peter was incredulous as he heard these simple financial records that implicated the British in the assassination of Jack Kennedy. He thought, "*The Soviets and Cubans are our enemies and we thought they killed Jack, but the British are our friends and it appears they were the ones who actually killed him. The world has been turned upside down!*"

The Prime Minister then asked Miss Crowley, "Were there any other members of this section that were traveling during the same time period?"

Miss Crowley had the answers on the same page, since that was her travel account page. She said, "Oh, yes, sir. Here are some additional travel expenses. Two members of the group flew from here to Mexico City via Bermuda and Puerto Rico on November 12th. But here's the puzzling thing." Miss Crowley paused as she frowned and contemplated what she was reading.

The Prime Minister said, "Puzzling? Please continue, Miss Crowley."

Miss Crowley said, "Well, it appears that they did not return from Mexico City, but instead returned from Tulsa, Oklahoma on November 30th, although I have no records of how they traveled from Mexico City to Tulsa. But the group often drew large cash advances labeled as travel expenses, and the Colonel always approved them, even if they never provided supporting invoices. That would not be so unusual since many times people pay cash for trams and such, but in retrospect, these amounts were much higher than the norm."

The Prime Minister questioned her further and said, "So, Miss Crowley, do you also have payroll records for this section?"

She responded, "Oh, of course, sir. Let me just flip to that section. Would you like to know how much each of them makes?"

The Prime Minister first said, "Well, thank you, Miss Crowley. I would like to know that. But first, could you just tell me how many are on the payroll for this section?"

She looked down at her ledgers and then responded, "Well, there are ten in this section, including Colonel Conners. I would tell you that they all seem to make a tidy sum, much more, I believe, than most others in comparable positions in MI-5."

The Prime Minister asked her, "So you do have all their names, correct?"

She said, "Yes, sir. Of course."

The Prime Minister asked, "Do you have personnel files for them?"

"Oh, no," she responds. "Those records would be in the Personnel Department."

"But you do have their names, and you could provide me with that information. Is that right?"

"Of course," she said. "I can write them now for you, if you'd like, or before the meeting is over. Or I can send them to you in a letter if you prefer."

The Prime Minister said, "Please, Miss Crowley, if it wouldn't be too much trouble, list for me all of the members of this group before you leave."

Turning to Roger Hollis, the Prime Minister said, "Please contact the Personnel Department and have someone bring me those files immediately." Hollis stepped out of the meeting to make the call.

"Miss Crowley," the Prime Minister said, "Let me ask you another question. Are there any other large or unusual expenditures being incurred by this section?"

She responded, "Well, weaponry is rather a large part of their budget. Of course it's much smaller than payroll, but large nonetheless."

The Prime Minister said, "What exactly would be included in this account?"

Miss Crowley said, "Well, this group seems to incur a great number of charges for weapons that they procure from the arsenal group department."

The Prime Minister asked, "The arsenal group?"

To that Miss Crowley responded, "Oh, yes, sir. You know the group that buys all the weapons for MI-5 and stores them until they're issued to the individual sections. Once the weapons are issued to the individual sections, the department head has to provide a charge slip to the arsenal department to account for the weapons being transferred from one department to another. Likewise, if any department requires unusual modifications to weapons, those charges also need to be justified and accounted for."

The Prime Minister looked at Miss Crowley with some degree of appreciation as he asked, "So do you know what weapons and modified weapons this section has been issued during the last year? Is there anything you think might be unusual?"

She replied, "I don't think it's particularly unusual for a group such as MI-5, but I should mention that this section did procure a great many weapons with suppressors on them."

The Prime Minister asked further, "If Colonel Conners were to request a modified weapon with a suppressor, or even just a standard weapon, how would he normally go about doing it?"

"Well, I'm sure he would just contact the arsenal department and file a requisition order, with the chargeback number for the Colonel's department so the weapon could be charged to his group."

The Prime Minister said, "Thank you so much, Miss Crowley. I appreciate all the information you've given us, and I would further appreciate it if you would give us those names now, and also allow my secretary to make a copy of all of your ledgers."

She responded, "Of course, sir. I'll do that now and if you don't mind, I would like to just stay here while the ledgers are copied. I do not want to let anything out of my sight since accuracy is important, as you know, and these ledgers have been entrusted to me."

The Prime Minister said, "Of course, Miss Crowley. And thank you again."

But, although the Prime Minister had just thanked Miss Crowley and had dismissed her, Captain Sharkey interrupted. He said, "Excuse me, Prime Minister, but I have a question to ask of Miss Crowley, if you don't mind."

The Prime Minister agreed and said, "Certainly, Captain. Ask any questions you think might be necessary."

Although Peter wanted to find the assassins who killed his friend, President Kennedy, and also to find the murderers who had attacked the manor house in Ireland, his main priority now was to find Jean and the baby. Captain Sharkey asked Miss Crowley, "Do you know where this group is headquartered?"

She said, "Oh, I'm sure I do have that information, but I'm not sure that it's here with me since these are financial ledgers. However, let me take a look under the rent section."

After thumbing through the ledgers for a moment, Miss Crowley said, "Oh, yes. Here we have some information. Since it's a rather large monthly charge, I would assume that it's probably a very large headquarters building. I can check the utility accounts to see about the electrical charges, if you would like me to estimate how large the facility is." Miss Crowley was the consummate accountant.

Captain Sharkey said, "No, thank you, Miss Crowley. This is all very, very helpful to us. But if you could just tell us the location of that facility, I would greatly appreciate it."

Remembering Flynn's comments, he asked further, "Is it in Carrickfergus, Northern Ireland?"

Miss Crowley was puzzled by that question as she replied, "Well, I'm sorry, sir, but I don't have that information along with me since all I have are the financial ledgers. However, our regulations prohibit us from paying rent for any facility leased by any department unless we have an executed copy of the lease on file.

I'm sure that I have a copy of the lease available back in my office, but I did not bring that along."

Peter was astonished by the bureaucratic efficiency of the British. It seemed that the Colonel complied with all the financial requirements to keep his department well-funded, and was too arrogant to suspect that anyone would ever be able to track him through these records.

Peter addressed Miss Crowley, "I'm sure we would all appreciate knowing exactly where this group's headquarters are located. If you would be so kind as to retrieve the lease for us, I am sure we would all be grateful."

Miss Crowley responded agreeably, "Of course, if that's what the Prime Minister wants." She knew she didn't take orders from the Americans.

The Prime Minister said, "Yes, yes, Miss Crowley. Please get us that information as quickly as you can. And please do not discuss anything about our meeting with anyone. Your accuracy and precision is a tribute to you and your department, and I commend you for it." Miss Abigail Crowley's cheeks flashed a quick blush as she lowered her eyes demurely at the compliment from the Prime Minister.

Once Miss Crowley left, the Prime Minister addressed the other attendees. He said, "Well, this case is getting ever stranger, the more we learn. It appears that we have a rogue section of MI-5, with ten members, that operates on its own outside the law, but which is meticulous about complying with its budgetary requirements. I think we need to speak to the commander of the arsenal department to find out more about what weapons this group has requisitioned and when they requisitioned them. Mr. Hollis, please find out who that commander is immediately, and ask him to show up here as soon as possible."

While they were waiting for Miss Crowley to return with the lease records, Peter remembered a line he thought he had heard in a movie. It might have been about how the FBI had been able to finally topple the gangster, Al Capone, for tax fraud. It was, "Always follow the money!" How true that was proving now!

When Miss Crowley returned, the Prime Minister asked, "Do you have the lease?"

Miss Crowley responded, "Of course. There had to be a lease on file or we would never have approved the lease payments. You can't be too careful about anyone trying to steal a few quid from the Crown."

The Prime Minister had to admire her accountant's mentality, and he was certainly appreciative of all of her cooperation, so he asked, "Well, then, could you share with us the location of the headquarters?"

Miss Crowley responded, "Well, sir, it's a bit of a puzzling lease to me since it does not seem to have as much location information as we would normally find, say for a building in London. But maybe the terminology is just standard for properties in Northern Ireland. I'm not an expert in real estate. What it says is that the location is the former residence of the MacDonnell family in Carrickfergus, County Antrim, Northern Ireland. So, yes, the location is in Carrickfergus as Captain Sharkey asked earlier. I can't for the life of me understand how he could have known that. The lease doesn't have a street address or number, so it might be a farmhouse or something rural."

Following that disclosure, the Prime Minister thanked Miss Crowley again for her assistance and dismissed her after she provided a copy of the lease.

Roger Hollis then said, "The commander of the arsenal is here. His name is William Johnson, and he was a former Master Gunner from the British Army before he joined MI-5. I am sure he knows weapons exceptionally well, and will be able to provide us with some useful information."

When Master Gunner Johnson entered, he was obviously nervous. Politicians worried him. But when he saw the U.S. and British Navy uniforms, he relaxed somewhat. He was much more at ease with military men than politicians.

The Prime Minister noted his unease and tried to relieve it, "Thank you for coming to meet with us on such short notice, Master Gunner Johnson. I'm sure you have a lot of questions about why you've been summoned here. But please let me assure you that it has absolutely nothing to do with any poor performance on your part, or complaints about you from anyone. We are conducting an investigation of an entirely different department of the government, and we just require your complete and honest cooperation."

Johnson was relieved by this, since he hadn't any idea why he had been summoned here so hurriedly. Now that he knew it wasn't because of any complaints, he smiled and said, "Of course, Prime Minister. Please just tell me what I can do to help."

The Prime Minister said, "There is a group within MI-5 that I believe is called Section N. It seems that they have a fairly large annual budget and frequently procure firearms from your department. We would like to learn a little bit more about just how that works."

"Of course, Prime Minister," Johnson responded. "It's really quite simple. Any of the departments can submit a requisition to us. They specify the weapons that they want to procure. If it involves a custom weapon, they need to submit a complete specification sheet listing exactly the modifications that they desire. Once we review it and I approve it, either the weapon is issued or the custom work is scheduled. If the specifications are unrealistic, I deny the request and send it back to the originating department for rework.

"We manage the shooting range and the arsenal, but also have an exceptionally well-equipped machine shop that can perform virtually any type of gunsmithing. We even have a small group that can produce custom or experimental weapons, or ammunition that might be desired by the department."

So the Prime Minister questioned further, "You mean that as long as you have a workable requisition, you just provide what is requested?"

"Of course, sir. And we try to do it as quickly as possible," Johnson responded. "After all, we are a support group for the guys that are actually out there in the field. But you know, we always get a signed receipt whenever we deliver the requisitioned item so that we do not have any budget deficits or deficiencies."

The Prime Minister asked again, "So you have complete records for anything that might have been requisitioned by Section N?"

"Of course," Master Gunner Johnson responded. "If I had known that was what you were interested in, I would have brought those files along. The accountants require that we keep all the documents filed by section, and then by specific categories within those sections. I personally hate the bloody paperwork, but they have never found any financial problems in my department, so clearly, I take that responsibility very seriously."

"Is there someone in your department," the Prime Minister asked, "That could bring those records over here now so that we could ask you more specific questions about Section N?"

"Of course, Prime Minister. My secretary is actually the one that does the remarkable job of keeping all this paperwork in order. I will ask her to retrieve everything for Section N and bring it here now if you would like me to do that."

The Prime Minister responded, "Yes, please. Please do that and then you can wait outside until she arrives. As soon as she's here, let my secretary know so that you can come back in."

Johnson nodded affirmatively and was relieved to be out of the "hot seat," and able to head for the door.

Once Johnson had left the meeting, the Prime Minister asked the others, "Well, do you have any questions about what we should ask when Johnson's secretary returns?"

Admiral Taylor said, "I think we should ask to see all of the requisitions for the entire year of 1963 if the records are not too voluminous."

Shortly thereafter, Johnson's secretary showed up with the files. When Johnson and the secretary were shown back into the meeting room, the Prime Minister explained, "Thank you for bringing these records. We are looking into Section N of MI-5, and trying to find out more about the operations of that group. Master Gunner Johnson told us that you might have some of that information. We don't want to pressure you, since this is not an inquiry into any problems in your department. So please just relax and let me ask you a few questions."

The secretary was about 60 years old, and although she looked like a gray-haired grandmother, she appeared to have a great deal of poise. She said, "It is nice to meet you, Prime Minister. My name is Jennifer Hines, and I have spent my entire career with the department. If there's anything you need to find, I'm sure I'm the one to do it."

The Prime Minister asked her to describe the requisitions from Section N.

She responded, "We frequently get requests from that section for suppressed weapons. They seem to have a preponderance of Colt 25 automatics with suppressors, and a large number of cases of hollow-point ammunition for those weapons. I didn't get this far in my career in this department without knowing a fair amount about weapons and ammo. A suppressed Colt 25 with hollow points is a preferred close-range assassination weapon within the Intelligence Services."

The Prime Minister was somewhat surprised by her knowledge about weaponry, but that reassured him as he asked, "Could you tell us what other weapons Section N might have requisitioned during 1963, and particularly since you are knowledgeable about weapons, let us know about any that you think might be unusual."

Secretary Hines responded, "Well, they did also requisition a few other small sidearms, like 45 automatics, but they already had many of them, so I would not classify that as unusual. And they do have a substantial number of fully automatic rifles that they've requisitioned throughout the years. But there were at least two unusual requisitions, if you don't mind my saying so."

The Prime Minister responded, "No, no. Please, we want you to say so. Tell us what you think."

Secretary Hines responded, "Well, since Section N usually requisitions either sidearms, like pistols or revolvers, or fully automatic rifles, the two requisitions that I thought were unusual were for sniper-type rifles."

Jennifer Hines thought she heard a gasp from one of the attendees at the meeting, but she continued. She said, "Well, here I'll have to defer to Master Gunner Johnson so he can provide you with more details about those two weapons. He and I have already discussed this matter outside, and we are in full agreement that these were two unusual requests."

Johnson then continued, "The first request was for a British .303 No. 4 MK-1 Sniper Rifle. Of course, we have several of them available in our arsenal, but they wanted one with a suppressor. It was also equipped with a scope and would be expected to be effective out to at least 600 meters.

"The other requisition was much more unusual. The Colonel wanted a Dragunov rifle that would be modified to be more silent and more concealable than the standard issue. The Dragunov is the best sniper rifle that the Soviet Union has yet produced. It is very modern and we only have a few that we were able to obtain clandestinely. At his request, we took a standard rifle and removed the production stock and replaced it with a small metal frame that could be attached quickly. We shortened the barrel and affixed a suppressor. The suppressor was designed so that it could be attached or detached with only a quick, one-quarter turn. We also removed the standard high-power scope and replaced it with a much smaller low-power scope. Then, at the Colonel's request, we attached a small fire-proof sack to collect the shell casings, so that no evidence would be left for the shooter to retrieve if he had to deploy the weapon and escape quickly."

The Prime Minister questioned, "Didn't this seem like such an unusual request that you might have needed to notify your superiors? By the way, is it Roger Hollis that you report to?"

"Yes, sir. I do report to Mr. Hollis, and I might add that he's a fine leader. But no, I get unusual requests for weapons each and every day. These were unusual for Section N, but it's not my job to review them."

The Prime Minister said dismissively, "Well, thank you for that information, Mr. Johnson."

But then Master Gunner Johnson continued, "Excuse me, Prime Minister, there was one more very unusual part of this requisition that I haven't yet told you about. MI-5 has been researching new weaponry, as you might imagine, and my group has been involved in work on frangible bullets. These are bullets that are designed to self-destruct once they hit a target. Although our research is still in the initial stages, it has been most successful. We were gratified that the Colonel recognized the success of our research when he requisitioned frangible bullets to be used on the cartridges for the Dragunov sniper rifle."

The Prime Minister frowned as he asked, "You mean you developed frangible bullets that can't be detected after they've hit a target. How can that be?"

Johnson smiled as he said, "Yes, sir. That was our objective, and I think we've been able to achieve it. The bullets are molded from a graphite amalgam similar to the "lead" in a common wooden pencil. Once they hit the target, the force of the impact causes the bullet to disintegrate into particles of gray dust. We still have some technical difficulties to work out for the different calibers, but for the most part, this ammunition will soon be available to anyone in MI-5 that needs it."

The Prime Minister said, "Well, thank you, Master Gunner Johnson for all of your help and all of your information. Please let me instruct both of you that you are not to talk to anyone, particularly anyone in Section N, about any of this. Is that clear?"

They said, "Yes, sir. We understand," almost in unison, as they left the meeting room.

Roger Hollis then said, "I understand the head of the Personnel Department for MI-5 has arrived. His name is Richard Moore and he has brought along the personnel files for Section N."

When Richard Moore entered the room, they were surprised to see a gentleman who looked so old; it was surprising that he was still working. Although looks can sometimes be deceiving, this gentleman certainly seemed to be well beyond his eightieth year.

The Prime Minister said, "Welcome, Mr. Moore. Please tell us what your records show about Section N that is headed by Colonel Conners."

Mr. Moore proceeded slowly, but with a calm clear voice. He said, "I'll do the best I can to give you all the information that I have. I want you to know that I've been in the Personnel Department here for over 50 years and I thought I'd seen it all. I usually don't need to do a detailed review of the content of any individual personnel files unless there has been a complaint, and there has never been a complaint about this department before. But now that I've reviewed some of these files, I have to say that they are the most troubling I've ever seen."

The Prime Minister questioned him, "Troubling? Troubling in what way?"

Mr. Moore responded, "Well, sir, although Colonel Conners has an impeccable record dating back to his early days in the SAS in the Second World War, the rest of his department seems to have been plucked out of military prisons."

The Prime Minister was shocked as he asked, "Military prisons? How can that be?"

Mr. Moore responded, "Well, I don't know about that, sir. All I'm telling you is what I find in my records, and my records show that all of these men seem to have some convictions for violent actions in their past."

"Could you give us an example?" the Prime Minister asked.

Mr. Moore responded, "Well, first of all, let me tell you that besides Colonel Conners, his department includes two well-paid people at the level of lieutenant or above. Then his department also has an upper-level sergeant and six lesser sergeants. Everyone in the department is exceptionally well paid. All of them are at the very top of the pay grade for their level.

"As an example, one of his lieutenants, I'll use that term although MI-5 is not truly a military organization, was convicted of murdering seven Bedouin captives who had been detained by his unit during the Suez Canal affair. After his conviction, he was sentenced to thirty years imprisonment; but then after only serving two years, for some reason he was released into the custody of Colonel Conners and joined the Colonel's department."

The Prime Minister squinted his eyes at this alarming information and asked, "You said that all of the members of his department have backgrounds like this?"

Mr. Moore responds, "Oh yes, sir. In fact, many are much worse than this. Some of his sergeants served in Northern Ireland, had been convicted of blatant atrocities against Irish civilians and had been sentenced to lengthy terms, even life imprisonment."

The Prime Minister asked, "But do you know how Colonel Conners could have obtained their release from the prison system?"

Mr. Moore responded, "Well, I don't know for sure, sir, since I'm not in the Judiciary, but my guess is that he might have presented some type of official document or warrant to the prison wardens, who would then have released those men into his custody. As you know, MI-5 has a very important role protecting the security of Britain, and a prison warden would be hesitant to deny a warrant for release issued by a division of MI-5."

The Prime Minister then said, "Mr. Moore, thank you so much for this information. We will need copies of each of the personnel files you have brought. One of my secretaries can copy them now while you wait."

Once Mr. Moore left the room, the Prime Minster addressed Admiral John, Roger Hollis, Admiral Taylor and Captain Sharkey. He said, "Oh, my god, gentlemen, I can't believe what I'm hearing. Every time we get a new piece of information, it is worse than the last piece. This is just a disaster that has been building undetected for years.

"It appears that Colonel Conners has assembled a crew of violent men who do not respect the Rule of Law. It seems he has been using this group as his personal vigilante squad to not only pursue Irish civilians that he deems to be terrorists, but also attack the President of the United States.

"I think we need to develop a plan to eliminate Colonel Conners and his criminal group, and also to rescue the woman and her baby."

Then the Prime Minister turned to Admiral John and said, "Casper, this whole thing stinks more and more. Sniper rifles and secret bullets and Conners in Dallas when the President is assassinated. Oh my god, Casper. I can't believe this. We need to rectify this. How can we do it?"

Admiral John said, "Prime Minister, I can't agree with you more. In a court of law, this might be circumstantial evidence, but there is no innocent way that Conners should ever have been in Dallas in November, nor being there when General Walker was attacked. While we don't know for certain that the two members of his team were also in Dallas when the President was killed, we do know that they flew to Mexico City and returned from Tulsa. Dallas is right between those two cities, so we can assume that they traveled through Dallas. And everything else further convinces me that Conners is responsible for this tragedy."

Peter then interjected, "Tragedies, I would say, since his group also attacked Michael Brady's manor house in Ireland, killing several innocent victims and kidnapping a woman and a child."

Admiral John said, "Yes, yes, of course, Peter. I'm sorry. I did not mean to forget about them. Obviously there are several wrongs here that need to be righted. And we need to get the woman and the child back safely. We need to find out more about the location of the Section N headquarters."

Further investigation by the Prime Minister's staff, about the lease for the property in Northern Ireland that was being used by the "Irish Section" of MI-5, revealed it to be an old castle on the Northern Irish coast. That was why it had a nondescript address. Castles didn't need to have a mailing address.

The lease did have the exact location of the property in question. It was on the south shore of Belfast Lough. This area was the subject of numerous military actions throughout the last 1,000 years. The town of Carrickfergus had been besieged by the Scots, the Irish, the English and even the French, and was home to Carrickfergus Castle, an enormous castle originally constructed by the Normans during the twelfth century and later expanded by various kings and conquerors. The "MacDonnell residence" was a much smaller castle that had been constructed on the other side of Belfast Lough. It was still, however, a formidable fortress.

It had been constructed hundreds of years ago by a Scot whose raiding party had been successful in securing this plot of land. He had decided to stay and construct this castle. The land surrounding the castle was quite barren, so the original owners had to have made their living by marauding and raiding other settlements.

It was now owned by his descendants. They needed to contact the current owner to determine more about the structure. Luckily, the lease had been drafted by a law firm in London that represented the owner of the structure.

Upon learning this, Peter volunteered to contact the lawyers as soon as possible. He wanted to visit them that afternoon, and the Prime Minister agreed. The Prime

Minister issued a letter of introduction for Peter Sharkey before he contacted the law firm. Although it carried no legal weight, it did establish his credentials.

* * * * * * * * * *

As soon as Peter contacted the lawyers and showed them the letter from the Prime Minister, they agreed to cooperate with Peter's request and put him in touch with their client, Christopher MacDonnell, the owner of the MacDonnell castle.

It turned out that the owner lived in London and was quite willing to meet with Peter that same day. When Peter arrived at the penthouse apartment that MacDonnell occupied, he was impressed by the elegance of the furnishings.

He knew that he was in the residence of an extremely wealthy man.

But when Christopher MacDonnell appeared, he was perfectly down-to-earth and friendly. He asked, "So I understand that you're here to ask some questions about a property that I own in Carrickfergus."

Peter said, "Yes, sir, that's why I'm here. We have some questions about the current occupants and exactly what's going on there."

"Well," MacDonnell answered, "I really don't know much about that. I'm only the landlord. My family has owned that property for centuries, but it's a terrible real estate investment now. My father thought that maybe he could improve things after the war, so he brought in electricity and improved the plumbing, but it's a nasty spot that would never attract tourists, so I rented it to a British group that uses the property for astronomical observations. It's probably ideal for that since it's so far away from any city lights."

Peter said, "Well, I appreciate your help on this. But we are trying to figure out exactly what is going on there on your property. Do you or any of your associates have detailed plans of the property? You know, blueprints or such items?"

MacDonnell said, "Of course, of course. When my father installed the electric and the plumbing after the war, his architects drew up very detailed plans about everything. I don't have them here, but I'm sure I have them at my office, which is a just a block away. Would you like me to ask my secretary to bring them over?"

Peter was elated to hear this information and responded, "Yes, please, Mr. MacDonnell. That would be so helpful."

At that, MacDonnell called his secretary and instructed her to bring the blueprints over to his residence. Once MacDonnell's secretary arrived with the blueprints, Peter questioned MacDonnell about all the features of the structure. Peter was interested in finding the weakest point to assault the structure, but he was disappointed to learn that there was virtually no weak point anywhere.

It was a traditional castle constructed entirely of stone, with exceptionally thick walls. It didn't have a moat, but it did have high stone walls and observation turrets at all of its corners. The main entrance was equipped with an enormous wooden gate that could open wide to allow animals, vehicles and visitors to enter into the central courtyard. But that gate would be hard to breach in a frontal attack. Naturally, Peter couldn't share any of these thoughts with MacDonnell, who couldn't be expected to condone any damage to his property. It would be easier to pay reparations later, than to get advance approval.

The courtyard could easily be defended from invaders by the occupants on the parapets above. Surrounding the central courtyard were various residential spaces and offices. Although the structure was designed to repel attacks from warriors on horseback brandishing arrows and swords, it was still a formidable obstacle to attack by more modern forces.

The parapets and observation points were all simply protected with small outlets that could only allow a gun or some other weapon to be pointed outward. It was thus very unlikely that weapons directed from the outside would be able to hit anyone firing from inside the structure.

But upon further questioning, Peter learned more about what was done when the structure was modernized. MacDonnell had already mentioned that they had brought in electrical lines and installed modern plumbing. When they redid the plumbing, the rocky ground prevented any type of septic drainage system. So they had to install substantial holding tanks to allow the waste to biologically degrade, and then seep into the ground.

MacDonnell complained about the cost of these systems, but their installation was demanded by the local authorities before they would issue clearance for the structure to become a tourist hotel. MacDonnell continued to lament about how his father had misjudged the marketability of this area to the tourist trade. Millions wasted according to MacDonnell, so when the opportunity to rent to the British astronomers came along, MacDonnell jumped at it.

Since the effluent from the sanitary facilities was now treated and drained into the ground, an ancient cistern that had formerly been used to dispose of the waste from the structure was now unused, but still present on the property. The cistern connected directly to the sea through a drainage tunnel.

Peter reviewed the blueprints of the tunnel from the cistern to the sea and noted that it was about 300 meters from the sea entrance to the bottom of the cistern.

MacDonnell told him that during the modernization process, his family had installed a metal gate between the sea and the tunnel to the cistern. They didn't want any marine creatures living in there. It was less expensive to install the gate than to plug up the tunnel.

He also stated that they had discovered the remains of an ancient portcullis or grate deep within the tunnel from the sea to the cistern, but no attempt had been made to remove it. This information troubled Peter since it might be an impediment if he tried to enter the castle by this underwater channel. But since it was so old, Peter thought that most of it had probably rusted away.

Peter learned that the cistern was about 30 or 40 feet above sea level. The castle had been built along the roughest edge of the promontory, so it was atop the steepest part of the rocky cliff above the sea. The cistern also had a stone rim surrounding it that MacDonnell estimated at about three feet high. So Peter concluded that it was about 40, maybe 45 feet maximum, from the water level in the cistern (which would be at sea level) to the top of the rim of the cistern. This would change with the tides, but Peter still knew that no matter whether it was high tide or low tide, it was still way too high for a man to scale without some type of assistance.

Peter asked to borrow the blueprints for copying. Although MacDonnell was initially hesitant, Peter showed him the letter from the Prime Minister and MacDonnell reluctantly agreed. Peter brought the copies back to his room and studied them late into the night.

The next morning, the group reconvened in the Prime Minister's office. The Prime Minister stated, "We need to develop some detailed plans. I think time is of the essence if we are going to rescue the hostages."

Peter was the first to respond since he was pleased that the Prime Minister had started the planning discussion with the rescue of Jean and the baby. He said, "I want to lead the rescue party that goes into Northern Ireland to retrieve Jean and the baby. I have some thoughts about how we might do that, but it will require cooperation from Admiral John and some of his special operations folks.

"I think that the rescue at their headquarters will be much easier if we can get most of Colonel Conners' men out of there before I attempt to go in. I also have a suggestion on how we might do that.

"There is one man that seems to hate Colonel Conners more than anyone in the world. I'd like, with your concurrence, to contact William Flynn to see if he is willing to cooperate with us in this venture. I know that according to the MI-5 files, he is a terrorist, but I think that his help could be valuable."

Admiral Taylor was the first to question Captain Sharkey about his suggestion. He asked, "What do you have in mind that we would need to employ Flynn? Don't you think that's risky given his past record?"

Captain Sharkey responded, "I really don't know all of the history between Billy Flynn and Colonel Conners, but it's certainly filled with mutual hatred. I think in this case, we might consider the old adage that the enemy of my enemy is my friend."

Captain Sharkey then presented the details of what he was proposing.

When the meeting adjourned two hours later, they had agreed on a plan.

Peter headed to a telephone and called the number Flynn had given him. He was pretty sure he was about to make a bargain with the devil, but he truly didn't care as long as it would help him rescue Jean and the baby – and eliminate the villains that assassinated his friend, Jack Kennedy.

Admiral Taylor headed back to the American Embassy and called President Johnson on a secure line. Once he was connected to the White House, he heard President Johnson say, "Hell, man, I've been waiting to hear from you. What's going on over there?"

To which Admiral Taylor responded, "Well, Mr. President, you won't believe everything that I've learned. It will take almost an hour to fill you in on all of this stuff. Can I do that with you now or do we need to talk later?"

President Johnson said, "I've been waiting long enough. If you learned anything at all about who killed Jack Kennedy and how we can pay the bastards back, I'm ready now. In fact, I'm telling you I don't want to wait. Let me hear it."

Admiral Taylor responded, "Okay, Mr. President, but it's kind of lengthy, so sit down while I go through everything we learned."

It took about 40 minutes for Admiral Taylor to fully brief President Johnson on what he'd learned in England, and about the plan of action they had developed jointly with the Prime Minister.

President Johnson was astonished by what he heard, but as Admiral Taylor said, the facts spoke for themselves. Apparently there was a very bad rogue section of the British Intelligence Service MI-5 that had not only masterminded the assassination of President Kennedy, but had also actually been directly involved in pulling it off.

Admiral Taylor then told the President that the Prime Minister would like to speak to him as soon as possible to discuss these plans.

The President responded, "OK, I'll call the Prime Minister now. Thank you so much, Rufus, for everything." With that the President broke the connection.

Then he placed a transatlantic call to the Prime Minister. As always, it took several minutes.

When the encrypted line was finally opened and the Prime Minister was on the line, President Johnson said, "Alec, it seems that we have to take some serious actions to correct the problems that we have here."

To which the Prime Minister responded, "Lyndon, I am so embarrassed by all of this that you can't believe how bad I feel. Although this whole system was set up well before my administration, I accept full responsibility for all these wrongs and I pledge to you that I'll do everything that I can to correct them. Anything you ask of me, I'll be happy to provide."

The Prime Minister continued, "I think that we developed a good plan during my meeting with Admiral John, Admiral Taylor and Captain Sharkey. I have given Admiral John full authority to issue all the orders to put this plan into effect. I hope that you'll be able to support this plan and issue the appropriate orders also.

"Lyndon, I hate to tell you this, but if any of this information ever got out to the British public, it would certainly be the end of my administration."

President Johnson responded, "Well, I can understand that, because if the American public ever found out that some British agents killed Jack Kennedy, I don't think there's anything I could do to prevent a horrible quest for revenge, and as you know, I certainly don't want that. The American Congress incorporates all the emotions of the American public, and I'm sure they would vote to take drastic measures to punish your country for what these bastards did. We can't let that happen. You and I need to remain united to face the threat of the Soviet Union. The security, maybe even the existence, of our nations depends on this. I don't blame you for Jack's death, and I don't want the American public to blame you either. So I think you and I need to agree on a plan to clean up this mess – and not make it public!"

The Prime Minister was relieved. "Thanks, Lyndon. I just don't know exactly how this happened or how this group got to exist within our intelligence service for so long, but I'm personally involved in all of the investigations now. I need to tell you that everyone in that rogue group had a violent past, and they all spent time in prison. No one will shed a tear for them. I think the plan that has been developed is the best possible solution for all of this.

"It would certainly, I think, save my government from being toppled over this potential scandal."

President Johnson responded, "Well, we don't want that to happen. We don't want anything to happen that might jeopardize the close friendship and mutual defense pacts that my country and yours enjoy. I am also worried right now about the developing conflict in Vietnam that may require deployment of substantial United States resources. If I send troops, maybe many troops, to Vietnam, the United States will have to rely on you and your forces to oppose the Soviets in Europe."

The Prime Minister said, "Thanks, Lyndon. You know you can count on us. Britain will commit whatever forces we need to counter the Soviets in Europe, particularly if you need to send your troops to Vietnam. We will have your back, just like you always had our back. I'm so glad that we are of one mind on this."

President Johnson then ended the conversation with, "I'll give the necessary orders to my people. We'll do our part to make this work.

"And thank you again, Alec. It is nice talking to you and we'll have to get together soon. Maybe schedule a summit meeting. Goodbye for now."

After his conversation with the Prime Minister, President Johnson placed a call back to Admiral Taylor. It was very short, and simple.

President Johnson said, "You just tell me what needs to be done and I'll order the Secretary of the Navy to issue those orders. Now exactly what have you planned?"

The plan that Admiral Taylor detailed involved deception to draw most of Conners' group out of their headquarters, and thus offer better odds to rescue the woman and the baby. It also required the use of the British Special Boat Service, whose participation Admiral John had promised. On the American side, it required the use of some new top-secret weapons. And it also needed some aerial support.

Once Admiral Taylor had provided the President with all the details of the plan, President Johnson said, "Okay, I've written down all of your requests and I'm going to speak to the Secretary of the Navy immediately."

President Johnson then called the Secretary of the Navy and instructed him to report to his office early the next morning so they could discuss this mission. At the conclusion of their meeting the next day, the Secretary of the Navy immediately issued the appropriate orders. Admiral Taylor was to coordinate all the American actions with those of the British. Now they got down to some detailed planning.

BOOK FOUR

FINAL JUSTICE

Chapter Nineteen

Brian Conners enlisted in the British Army at sixteen years of age. Although he was underage at the time he enlisted, when this tall, muscular guy showed up volunteering to enlist, the recruitment officer immediately filled out the paperwork. Conners told the recruitment officer that his parents had been killed during the bombings in London. Unfortunately, all his records were destroyed in the bombing also.

In truth, the recruitment officer didn't care about the accuracy or honesty of any of those statements. He had a quota to fill and he was way behind since it was getting more and more difficult each day to find able-bodied men that were not already in uniform. Britain was involved in a war for its survival and no one was picky about the details when someone wanted to enlist. Particularly not this recruitment officer.

To meet his quota, the recruitment officer would have even filled out a personal affidavit verifying that this new guy was his nephew, or neighbor, or maybe even adopted son. In fact, the recruitment officer would not have cared if he had learned that Brian Conners was not the young recruit's real name. In reality, Conners had been born in Ireland and had been named Brian O'Connor, but he changed it as soon as he and his mother were able to leave Ireland and come to London.

Brian loathed his abusive Irish father, and because of that he despised all things Irish. In contrast, he adored his British mother and came to love all things British. Brian dropped the "O" from his last name to Anglicize it and changed "O'Connor," to "Conners." His older brother, Charlie, had similarly changed his name when he had previously enlisted in the British Army.

Brian Conners' brother, Charlie, had volunteered for the Special Air Service (SAS), and so that was what he also did as soon as he completed his basic training in the British Army. Brian trusted and idolized his older brother and wanted to follow in his footsteps.

Because Conners hated all things Irish, he immediately began to copy the accents of the Londoners he met. Within six months, any trace of an Irish accent had completely disappeared. He didn't want his accent to give away his Irish heritage. He proved to have a talent for linguistics and accents.

Conners was now a member of 2 Special Air Service, an elite unit he volunteered to join. Since he enlisted in the Army, Conners had volunteered for each and every dangerous assignment that had been offered to him. This was a new unit, and although all the team members were dedicated and fearless, this was their very first combat parachute raid.

Conners was on an aircraft and sat in the middle of the group of ten men on this team. For reasons unbeknownst to any of the men on board, their team had been code-named "Pink." They didn't think it was a name designed to inspire fear in the enemy should they ever learn the code name of the team.

His team, along with another team code-named "Brig," on a different transport aircraft, was heading for a drop zone in northern Sicily. It was nighttime on July 12, 1943, and the Allied invasion of Sicily had commenced about three days earlier. The mission of the two teams was to disrupt communications and transport of the enemy by landing behind their lines.

Conners and his teammates were all trying to check their weapons one last time, but the weather outside the aircraft was awful, and the plane vibrated and shook too violently for them to do that. They were entering a violent storm, but the plane lumbered forward anyway. Apparently, once again, the military hierarchy did not care about details like the weather and how that might affect these parachutists.

The team leader tried to stand in the front of the plane and review their objectives, but the violent buffeting of the aircraft prevented him from standing upright. After a few tries, he dropped back into his seat and yelled to the team that they should just follow him out the door.

Conners was looking forward to this action since it would be the first time he would be able to confront the Italian and German enemy. He had absolutely no fear, since he had survived the daily hell that was his childhood. Instead he was possessed by a simmering internal desire to kill the enemies of his beloved country – Britain.

He had no doubt that he could fulfill this mission, since he had already killed. Killing came very easy to him. His killing of his father over a year earlier had left him with no regrets, but rather brought him great relief. He had eliminated the monster that had caused great pain to his mother, his brother and himself.

He felt that he had been born in hell, and had spent his entire childhood in hell. He, his loving British mother and his older brother, Charlie, had been subjected to daily abuse and subjugation by the monster who was his father. His father, Liam O'Connor, was a drunken Irish lout who seemed to live only to terrorize his family.

Liam was a monster, both literally and figuratively. His once fair complexion suffered from the ravages of years of chronic alcoholism. He had developed red splotches on his cheeks and forehead. His nose was a bulbous, venous globe that floated in the center of his florid face. And he was missing several front teeth, either from neglect or from the bar fights in which he regularly engaged.

When his face was contorted in anger, a regular daily occurrence, he was truly hideous to behold.

His behavior was just as horrible as his appearance. He regularly fought with everyone that came in contact with him, from co-workers and supervisors on the waterfront sites where he occasionally found work, to strangers and barkeepers in the pubs he frequented. He had been ejected and banned from innumerable pubs, but he had always been able to find a new place that would take his money and serve him alcohol – until he would cause some type of disturbance and get banned from that one also.

Unfortunately, the way he treated his family was even more monstrous than how he treated outsiders. From his earliest remembrance, Conners spent each night with his mother and his brother, waiting in fear of the return of their father. Liam O'Connor was a day-laborer who worked along the docks in Dublin. He was paid his wages each day and immediately headed to the local pub to spend those wages. He was a violent drunk with a hair-trigger temper.

Dinner was always a torment where Liam would berate and slap their mother for any imagined infraction. The food was always horrible according to Liam, and he would abide no excuse that she didn't have enough money to buy anything better. Brian and Charlie were regularly slapped so hard that they fell off their chairs at the dinner table. Sometimes they were hit for eating too fast, and sometimes they were hit for eating too slow. They were hit for being too silent, and they were hit for talking too much. They knew they were going to get hit regardless of what they did, so dinner was a fearsome time for them all. Brian and Charlie always rushed to finish eating and avoid further torment.

It was what happened after dinner that was even more fearsome than the violence at dinner itself. The drunken Liam would banish the boys to their upstairs bedroom and would push, or even sometimes drag their mother into his bedroom. There he would subject her to her nightly marital rape. The children could tell that their mother was being subjected to violence each night because they could hear her screams, even outside the walls and the door of the bedroom. But as young children, there was nothing they could do to confront the ogre that was their father.

That changed on Charlie's 16th birthday. Their mother had purchased a small cupcake to celebrate the occasion. The sight of the birthday cupcake enraged his father at dinnertime, as he labeled it an extraordinary waste of their limited funds. Liam backhanded their mother so hard that she not only fell off the chair, but also hit her head against the hearth. It knocked her unconscious, and Brian and Charlie feared that she was dead.

Charlie, possibly feeling that at sixteen he was now a man, charged his father to try to defend his mother. He grabbed a metal frying pan from the stove as he ran toward his father. Liam was looking the other way at his wife on the floor as Charlie smashed the metal pan into the back of Liam's head.

Liam turned quickly around, completely unscathed by the attack. Possibly his extreme drunkenness prevented him from immediately feeling the pain, or maybe his skull was just so thick that it could not easily be injured.

Liam roared with anger and grabbed Charlie with one hand while he beat him relentlessly with the other. Brian was terrified by everything that was going on. He knew that he couldn't help his brother against his father, but he moved quickly to try to help his mother on the floor.

Liam continued to beat Charlie until he was bloody, senseless and unconscious. Liam then dragged him to the front door. He threw Charlie out into the street and screamed, "Don't ever come back here, ya little bastard, or I'll kill ya next time."

Liam then moved toward his wife and Brian. He grabbed Brian, yanked him away from his wife and tossed him like a rag doll across the room.

Liam screamed at him, "Get upstairs ya little bastard, or you'll get just what your brother got."

With that Liam threw some water from the kitchen table on his wife, and when she roused somewhat, he grabbed her and dragged her off to the bedroom.

As he was heading for the bedroom he glanced back at Brian and yelled, "Didn't ya hear me, ya little asshole. Get upstairs now or I'll kill ya."

That was all Brian needed to hear to make him scurry upstairs. He knew he couldn't help his mother right now, but he was pretty sure that his brother was the one who really needed his help.

Brian opened a second-floor window and climbed out and down to the back-yard. He moved around to the front and knelt next to his brother, who was lying in a crumpled heap just outside the front door.

He didn't have anything to wipe the blood from his brother's face, so he ripped off parts of his undershirt and used that to dab some of the blood away from his brother's eyes and mouth.

Brian said, "Charlie, Charlie, are you okay?"

His brother didn't immediately respond, but he did shiver somewhat in Brian's hands. Brian was reassured to know that his brother was, at least, still alive. Brian knew he couldn't bring Charlie back into the house because Liam would surely kill him.

There was a small factory near the river by their house that had been abandoned since the start of the war. It had been locked up by its owners, probably when they went off to join the Army. He carried his brother to the rear of the abandoned factory and broke a back window with a rock. He reached in, opened the window, and then crawled through. He groped his way around in the dark until he found his way back to the rear door. He unlocked it and brought his semi-conscious brother inside.

Although the electricity had been shut off, it didn't make much difference right now since the entire inside had some illumination from the moon and stars. Luckily, the water was still on and he was able to soak more of his undershirt and use it to cleanse his brother's face.

Although the factory had been closed for the past few years, the former occupants had left many of their belongings behind, probably assuming they would one day return from the war and resume operations at the factory.

Brian retrieved a teacup from an office desk and was able to use that to get water to his injured brother. Charlie regained consciousness only long enough to take a few sips of water, and then passed back out.

Brian then found some old jackets hanging in one of the office closets. Although the only place to sleep was on the hard wooden floor, he was able to spread the jackets over both him and his brother to help warm them through the night. Brian wasn't worried about being missed by his father since he knew the drunken bastard had no doubt passed out by now.

When they awoke the next morning, Charlie had recovered substantially. His cuts were all superficial and had stopped bleeding. Although his bruises were numerous and looked horrible, they didn't seem to be serious. Thankfully, he had no broken bones.

Charlie said to Brian, "Well, you know I've got to go now. I can't go back in that house or he'll kill me."

Brian said, "But what will you do and how will I get on without you? And what about Mum?"

Charlie answered, "You've got to be strong for her, but don't make the mistake that I did. Don't let that bastard know that you intend to attack him. He's big as an ox, but he's also as dumb as an ox. You need to use your brain as well as your strength when you decide to attack him. And you know you'll have to do that or he'll never leave our Mum alone."

Brian said, "Of course, I'll do that. Of course. Of course. Of…"

Brian kept repeating himself, clearly upset. But then he blurted out, "I swear I'll kill that bastard. He won't get away with what he did to you and Mum tonight."

Then Brian asked, "Where can you go?"

Charlie said, "I've had it with friggin' Ireland. I'm heading for England and I'm going to join the British Army as soon as I get there. I'll be changing my name to Conners, with an "e" at the end like the Brits spell it instead of an "o" like the Irish, and dropping the "O" in front, so if you need to contact me use that name. Once I'm in the military, I'll write to Mum and let her know how I'm doing. Also, I'll try to send some money as soon as I get on the Army payroll."

With that the brothers embraced, and Charlie, feeling somewhat recovered from the devastating attack by his father, headed down to the waterfront. Because they lived near a river that had considerable commercial shipping traffic from Dublin to London, Charlie was confident that he could work his way onto a ship to transport him to London.

Brian returned to the house since he was sure that by now his father had left for another workday. He entered and found his mother crying inconsolably on one of the few still-upright chairs in their parlor.

Brian hugged his mother and tried to dab away her tears with his fingers. He reassured her that Charlie was alive and had left for London. Hearing that, his mother stopped crying and opened her eyes to stare directly into his.

His mother said, "God help me, Brian, I don't know how I could have married that monster. When we were younger, he was dashing and strong and handsome in a very masculine way. Back then, he wasn't drunk every night. I swear to the Lord that if I'd ever known how things would turn out, I would have killed myself before subjecting you and your brother to this."

Brian could only respond by hugging his mother tightly, and vowing to himself that as soon as he possibly could, he would kill the monster that tormented them.

After Charlie's expulsion, their lives reverted back into the regular daily sequence of domestic terror for the next several months. They almost never spoke of Charlie's absence. In fact, Liam only once commented about it. It was about a week after he had thrown Charlie out the door.

Liam complained to his wife, "Now that that bugger Charlie is gone, ya should have more money to buy better food for us. He always ate too much, he did. And now that he's gone, there should be more for us. So why the hell is my plate still as small as before?"

Neither Brian nor his mother responded to this, but just sat in silence and agony as always.

Brian was still in school, but about a year after his brother had been thrown out, Brian took a new route home after school. He would be turning sixteen soon and he felt it was finally time for him to act like a man. While on this new route, he came upon a railroad crew that was installing a new rail spur from the river to some commercial buildings. The crew was clustered around an outdoor table enjoying their afternoon break.

As Brian passed them, that was when he saw it. It was exactly the type of weapon he'd been imagining to use. It was a large, blunt, heavy hammer on a short handle. It had the head of a sledgehammer like the ones the men slung on a three-foot handle, but this handle was only about a foot long. The head was very substantial and he knew that it was capable of doing the job for which he intended it – which was to crack his father's skull.

Because the workers were all engrossed in their break conversations and snacks, Brian had little difficulty snatching the hammer and heading rapidly home with it.

Brian knew his father's route home most nights now from his new, regular pub which had not yet barred him for his violent outbursts. Liam would walk along the road by the river for several blocks before turning inland toward their flat.

Brian picked a particularly dark and foggy night to lie in wait for his father. He hid down a narrow alleyway and held the prized hammer ready at his side.

He could not escape the feeling that this was his destiny, and that he would finally be able to free his mother from this horror and once again join his brother.

The shape of Liam was unmistakable as he lurched up the darkened street. He was also muttering some Irish song to entertain himself, so Brian recognized his voice as well.

As soon as Liam passed by the alleyway, Brian approached quietly from behind. In his drunken state, Liam neither heard nor detected the presence of the stalker behind him.

Brian swung the hammer with all his might and caught his father directly on the back of his skull. Unlike the frying pan that had bounced off Liam's skull when he was hit by Charlie, this heavy hammer brought him to the ground. Liam was out cold, but Brian noted that he was still breathing. The blow had not been fatal, as Brian had wished it might be.

Brian moved quickly and dragged the unconscious Liam across the road and down the steep bank to the river. He pushed Liam head-first into the water, but held his feet from the shore to make sure he didn't float away and recover.

Brian was careful not to rush this step because he knew that if Liam survived, both he and his mother would suffer all the more for it.

Although he didn't have a watch, Brian counted off the seconds in his mind until he was sure that his father's face had been underwater for almost ten minutes. At that point he couldn't detect any pulse in the legs anymore and he was convinced that the Monster was finally dead. But Brian held onto him, keeping his face underwater for ten more minutes, just to be sure. He worried that the Monster was negotiating with the Devil to return to life, promising to do even more evil to his family!

When he was finally sure Liam was dead, Brian pushed the corpse out into the river, where it silently sank. This time of year there was very little current in the water, and the corpse would probably lie there undisturbed for several days until it started to bloat and float to the surface.

Brian climbed back up the riverbank with the hammer still in his hand. He didn't want it to be found near the body, which might provoke some suspicion about the death. He jogged about a quarter of a mile down the road until he came upon a small dock jutting out into the river. He ran out onto the end of the dock and tossed the hammer as far out into the river as he possibly could. Without any weapon to be found near Liam's corpse, Brian was quite sure that the police would conclude that he had fallen in a drunken stupor, hit his head and dropped into the river where he drowned.

It was about four days later when the local constables visited his mother to inform her that, unfortunately, they had found the deceased body of her husband floating in the river.

When he came home from school, Brian acted surprised, but both he and his mother shared smiles of relief that the Monster was finally gone.

They immediately made plans to leave Dublin and go to London where his mother's sister lived. Just as soon as they arrived in London, Brian left his mother in his aunt's good keeping and headed to the recruitment office for the British Army.

* * * * * * * * * *

While Brian was still in the airplane, enjoying these thoughts of past vengeance against his primal enemy, his father, and looking forward to his first encounters with new enemies, the airplane rocked violently and shook him from his reverie.

It was time to jump.

One by one, the team members jumped through the exit door into the black abyss beyond the aircraft. Brian had made several training jumps in parachute school, but they had not prepared him for the maelstrom he was now entering. The violent winds seemed to swirl in all directions, and after he waited the appointed number of seconds to pull his rip-cord, the parachute just caused even more buffeting from the wind. He was sure that the wind sometimes blew him upward, defeating the pull of gravity trying to return him to earth. He lost all contact with the other team members and was flung hopelessly about by the wind. He had absolutely no idea where he was headed, and he had absolutely no control over determining his ultimate destination.

Unbeknownst to him, the violent storm would eventually claim the aircraft he had just left. The aircraft bearing his team "Pink" was lost, including all crew members and the team commander. Neither the aircraft nor their remains would ever be found.

When Conners finally hit the earth, it was actually not earth at all, but sea. He had dropped into the Mediterranean and the waters around him were churning insanely because of the violent storm. He struggled to rid himself of the parachute because it quickly filled with water and was dragging him down. As soon as he had gotten rid of the parachute, he tried to determine a direction toward land.

He could see vague lights in one direction off to his left and tried to swim toward those lights. The wind and waves all conspired against him, but the worst problem of all was that his boots and clothing were now waterlogged and weighing him down. He needed to get rid of the boots first because they had filled with water, and were like dual anchors entrapping his feet and drawing him down to a sunken death.

He finally was able to get rid of the combat boots, but knew he also had to get rid of the small pack he'd been carrying that contained most of his clothes. The larger pack with his supplies and his weapons had gone down with the parachute earlier.

He stripped to his skivvies and swam desperately toward the dim lights.

Conners was not a great swimmer, but he was an extraordinarily strong man. He would not give in to the waves, but kept kicking and clawing his way toward the shore. When he finally reached the beach after what seemed like an eternity, he was exhausted, cold and clad only in his underwear. He knew he was in enemy territory and dragged himself behind some brush on the beach in order to try to hide from any enemy patrols.

Conners fell asleep from exhaustion, for how long he did not know. It was still dark, however, when he was awakened by the sound of someone approaching along the beach.

Despite the wind and the rain, the enemy still had people patrolling the beach. He wasn't sure if this was a German soldier, an Italian soldier or a member of the local militia, but he feared being detected.

The man was carrying a flashlight to illuminate his path. When he got closer, the guard apparently saw the footprints and marks that Conners had left on the beach. The guard was alone, which was a good sign, but he was wearing a helmet of some type and had a rifle, as well as the flashlight.

Conners could tell that the guard was about to head in his direction by following the footprints. Conners moved as quietly as he could and made more footprints moving away from the area where he had been hiding. He then doubled back and hid behind a tree along the path he had just made. He found a stout chunk of fallen branch that was about two-feet long and which could serve as a suitable club.

The guard was concentrating on the footprints as he followed his flashlight beam off the beach and into the brush. He never heard anything as Conners stepped behind him and hit him in the neck with the club. Since the guard was wearing a helmet, Conners knew not to bother hitting him in the head, but aimed for that vulnerable point below the helmet and above his shoulders.

The guard dropped down, but was not knocked unconscious. Conners immediately leapt on him and proceeded to strangle him. Luckily for Conners, the guard had dropped the rifle when he had been hit and was not able to fire a shot.

Despite the guard's struggles, Conners' superior strength allowed him to suffocate the guard rather quickly.

He stripped the guard's clothes from the corpse and donned them himself. He took the Italian liras from the man's wallet, but did not take his identification. Then he dragged the man's body back across the beach and pushed it as far as he could out into the raging sea.

Conners did not know exactly, but had a general idea of where he might have landed. He decided to head toward Palermo, the capital of Sicily, which he knew was the ultimate target of the Allied forces. Because he didn't have a compass, he could only use dead reckoning, which would mostly come from determining the position of the sun during the next day.

Although he was cut off from all the other members of his team, Conners felt good because he had survived the jump and the storm, and now had both new clothes and a military rifle. He decided to proceed up the beach about a quarter of a mile and then find another hiding place to await the dawn. He was incredibly exhausted.

When he awoke just after dawn, Conners assessed his situation.

First of all, he was soaked to the skin. The violent winds and heavy rain of the previous night had stopped, but the small bush he had selected to hide under had provided absolutely no protection from the rain. Conners only knew that he was on a beach and that it was probably on the northern shore of Sicily. He knew that was his intended drop zone, but he had no idea how far off-course the storm had blown the plane. Nor any idea how far the winds had tossed him while in the parachute.

He knew he had to be somewhere on the north coast of Sicily, however, and knew that Palermo, the capital, had to be due west from his current position. While the objective of the Allies was to take the entire island, the capital city of Palermo was sure to be one of their first objectives, and so he headed there in the expectation that British troops would eventually arrive in the city. He had absolutely no idea how far away from Palermo he was, but decided that he had no other choice but to head in that direction. He had no compass, but was able to use the position of the sun to determine which direction was west.

He mentally reviewed his personal situation as well. Although he was soaked, the warm Mediterranean summer sun would soon dry his clothes. He was wearing the stolen Italian uniform he had removed from the corpse of the guard he killed the previous night. The shirt and the slacks fit relatively okay, but the boots were way too small.

He also had an Italian bayonet in the belt sheath he had obtained from the dead guard. He used the bayonet to cut away the toe sections of the boots so he could fit his feet into them.

Most important was the rifle he had obtained from the dead guard. He examined it carefully for any markings and saw that it was labeled a Carcano model 91/38. The rifle was bolt-action and magazine-fed. He ejected the magazine and was pleased to find that it contained a full complement of ammunition.

He was concerned because the rifle was just as wet as he was. He knew that a wet rifle would be prone to rust and corrosion. These problems could cause the rifle to malfunction, which might happen at a critical time.

He disassembled the rifle and laid each part on a nearby rock out in the sun to dry. He also removed all the cartridges from the magazine and similarly arrayed them on the rock.

Conners decided that patience was necessary if he was going to survive the trip to Palermo. He was quite sure that he'd need a functioning rifle somewhere along the journey. He knew it was better to hide here and allow both his uniform and the weapon to dry thoroughly before he set out.

Of course he also knew it would take days before the British forces would reach Palermo, so he was in no hurry to arrive there while the Germans and Italians were still in control. He was a man who knew how to bide his time and select the best moment to strike, so this waiting did not bother him.

It took several hours for his uniform and the weapon to dry, but once all was ready, he set out on his trek. Of course, just prior to leaving, he reassembled the rifle. He worked the bolt several times and was pleased that it was very free and easy to move, which would allow rapid firing. He had no idea about its accuracy since he had never seen such a rifle before, but he hoped he would never need to use it.

He decided to follow the shoreline as much as possible to reach Palermo, which he knew was a coastal city. He would try to stay along the border between the beach and the brush as much as possible. He developed a routine whereby he would dart into the underbrush for a couple of minutes to assess whether the beach ahead was clear. After he'd made that assessment, he would walk briskly along the beach or over the shoreline rocks for about a quarter-mile. Then he would dart back into the underbrush again.

Although he had initially set out during the day, Conners decided it would be safer for him to travel as much as possible under the cover of darkness. He had no way of seeing his path after dark, however, so that wouldn't be completely possible. Finally he decided to limit his travels to the early-morning hours just preceding and following dawn, as well as the times just before and after dusk. He knew it would slow his progress, but it seemed to be the safest option.

When nighttime came and it got too dark for him to see, he selected a suitable hiding place in the underbrush and slept for hours.

He awoke just before dawn and resumed his journey. Thus far he had not encountered any German or Italian guards along the beach. He found this unusual because he was sure that by now both the Germans and Italians were very aware of the Allied invasion. Possibly it meant that they had shifted all of their troops to the southern battlefields to try to stop the Allied advance.

By the end of the second day, he was still making slow progress toward Palermo. Unfortunately, he had absolutely no idea how far away it was, and he was absolutely ravenous since he hadn't eaten in two days.

He decided that he would have to risk a visit to one of the small fishing villages he had been passing in order to find some food, and more importantly, water. That night, about midnight, he found a suitable fishing village to enter and was able to move around undetected. He saw a small grocery shop with an apartment above it, neither of which had any lights on. He was about to try to force the entrance door open, but found to his surprise that it was unlocked. Apparently these villagers trusted each other.

He entered and did a little "midnight shopping." Although he didn't find any water, he did find wine and juice in bottles. He also found sausages and bread. He ate as much as he could right there in the store and then carried away enough to provision himself for at least the next three days. He hoped by then to reach Palermo, and hoped even more that by then the British forces would also be there.

It was now the morning of the third day since he had begun his journey, and Conners was suddenly startled by a shout in Italian.

Although he didn't speak Italian, he was quite certain he had been told to stop and identify himself. Although he was wearing an Italian uniform and carrying an Italian rifle, he did not have a helmet or any credentials to identify himself as an Italian soldier.

He searched for the source of the voice and saw an Italian soldier emerging from the brush about 50 yards ahead of him.

He walked slowly toward the Italian soldier so as not to alarm him by fleeing. But he didn't speak because, of course, he didn't speak Italian.

Then Conners noted with some concern two other figures emerging from the underbrush just behind the Italian soldier. They were also Italian soldiers and formed up behind him to protect the first soldier. They formed kind of a tiny phalanx as they walked toward Conners. They all had their rifles pointed in his direction.

He kept his rifle pointed toward the ground to appear passive. He knew that in an extended firefight at this distance he would be at a terrible disadvantage. His only chance was to get close enough to them to shoot quickly before they suspected an attack.

The lead Italian shouted something that Conners obviously could not understand. Conners responded by cupping his left hand behind his ear and then waving his hand in what he hoped was a universal gesture of "I can't hear you" or "What do you mean?"

This gesture seemed to relax the lead Italian somewhat, and so Conners and the Italians all proceeded toward each other.

When they were about 50 feet apart, Conners raised his rifle with his right hand, grabbed the stock with his left, and shot the lead Italian in the chest.

Rather than firing, the other two Italians were so surprised that they ducked toward the ground. That proved to be a fatal mistake. Conners worked the bolt on the rifle and immediately shot the soldier on the right. From the ground, the other soldier now recognized the danger and tried to rise and point his rifle at Conners.

But Conners worked the smooth-flowing action of the Carcano rifle again and was able to shoot the third soldier before he was able to return fire.

Conners examined the men he had just shot and he was quite sure that the leader was dead. There was no pulse in his neck and no discernible heartbeat.

The other two soldiers had fared better because he had not had as much time to aim for their vital parts. They were both down on the ground, but both still alive. Conners resolved that little problem by stepping back about four feet from the prone figures and pumping one bullet into each of their heads.

He didn't want to waste any ammunition, although he now could have collected the three rifles from the Italian soldiers. But he still had a long way to go and could not burden himself with any extra weight. Besides, he now liked how the Carcano rifle had performed and felt he had sufficient ammunition for any further encounters.

He pulled the bodies into the underbrush and set off again at a quickened pace. He hoped that their bodies wouldn't be discovered until he had put many miles between them and himself.

Conners' journey proceeded uneventfully for a few more days, until he was approaching Palermo. His provisions had long since been exhausted and he knew he would have to visit another village to find more food and drink.

That evening Conners attempted to enter a small village on the outskirts of Palermo. He had not gotten very far when suddenly he heard "Halt," in English.

Conners felt relieved since he believed he had finally reached the British lines.

The voice repeated again, "Halt and drop your rifle. Put your hands in the air." Conners took a moment before he decided what to do, since he was still wearing an Italian Army uniform.

His hesitation was a bad mistake. A single shot rang out and he felt a bullet penetrate his left upper arm. The rifle fell to the ground since he could no longer hold it with the wound in his arm.

From the alleyways surrounding this street, Conners saw at least five soldiers heading toward him with their rifles at the ready.

"Don't shoot him," he heard the lead soldier say, "Maybe we can learn from him where the other Italian soldiers are hiding."

Hearing that, none of the other soldiers shot again, but one of them ran quickly up to Conners, kicked his rifle away and knocked Conners to the ground. Once he hit the ground, the soldier kicked him again, in the face this time. That was enough to knock him unconscious and it would be several hours before he came to.

When he awoke, he had a battlefield bandage on the bullet wound in his arm. He was in the back of a field ambulance. The man sitting nearby was wearing an American military uniform, not a British. The American said, "Do you speak any English?" assuming that Conners was an Italian soldier.

Conners responded in perfect, London-accented, English, "I am a British soldier. I parachuted here several days ago, but a violent windstorm prevented me from rejoining my unit. I've been heading here to try to rejoin the Allied forces.'

His comment brought several chuckles from the other American soldiers in the back of the truck. So the head American soldier said, "That's great. You've decided to fly in here and drop down and conquer the island all by yourself. So I guess they gave you some ID to prove that's who you are, because I think you're a fucking Italian spy."

Conners heard that comment with some alarm and said, "I don't have any ID left because I lost everything when I parachuted into the ocean. I was…"

His comment was cut off in midsentence when one of the American soldiers smashed him with the butt stock of his rifle. Conners fell sideways and blood started to spurt again from the wound in his arm.

The American said, "We have absolutely no information about any parachute drops by any Allied forces in this theater. Therefore, you must have been here all along. I suggest that you tell me more about both the German and Italian troops that are in this area."

Conners said in desperation, "I told you, I'm a British soldier."

"Wrong answer," one of the Americans said as Conners got a clout in his head with the butt of another American rifle.

He awoke hours later in a dark cellar. He had no idea where he was because there was very little light. He could only assume from the smell that this was some kind of root cellar that the local peasants used to store their onions and garlic after harvest.

His arm was still bleeding and he felt very faint, both from the beatings and from the loss of blood. He suspected that the frigging Americans intended to just let him die down here in the darkness.

Maybe that would actually have been a better finish he thought, when the Americans dragged him out hours later and began to beat him during an inter-rogation. They seemed convinced that he was some kind of spy, and pummeled both his face and his wounded arm. He lost even more blood and when he was finally unconscious, they threw him back into the root cellar.

By the next day when he was pulled from the root cellar again, he was barely alive. He saw that they had placed another rudimentary field bandage on the wound, but it was not enough to stop the renewed bleeding from his arm and shoulder. His initial captors had now apparently moved on and he was in the custody of some type of prisoner acquisition unit.

They had an Italian interpreter that tried to communicate with him, but of course he didn't speak Italian. Luckily, they did have a medic along, who cleaned and re-bandaged his wounded arm.

He was brought into a police building the Americans had obviously requisitioned from the local populous. While being questioned by the American officer in charge of this inquisition, he was able to discern that the Americans were now in control of Palermo and all of its outskirts. These men were all part of General Patton's Army.

Although he was not beaten again, they still didn't believe his story and decided to transfer him to one of the permanent prisoner units.

He was held captive in one of the cells there for another week. During this time he wasn't beaten again, and did receive a minimal amount of food and water. He came to despise the Americans who had treated him so badly.

Eventually, upon the fall of Sicily to the Allied forces, he was brought out of his cell. He was led into an office area where there was a proper British officer.

Apparently the British officer had reviewed Conners' file and had verified that there had actually been an Operation Chestnut, which involved landing the two Special Air Service Parachute teams in northern Sicily. Because most of the team members, as well as its leader, Major Geoffrey Appleyard, had all died, it had been hard to verify Conners' identity. But now the Americans finally turned him over to the British officer so he could be repatriated to his own countrymen.

The British forces now controlled all of the eastern part of the island of Sicily, and Conners was treated well once he had been sent back to them. Eventually, his wounds from the American beatings and the American shot to his arm would heal, but his hatred of Americans for the way they had treated him would never heal!

He rejoined his unit, which went on to conduct parachute operations behind the German lines in France, as well as operations in Belgium, the Netherlands and eventually into Germany itself.

Conners was fearless during all of these operations, and took over control of his unit after a drop behind German lines in France when the unit commander did not survive the drop. He personally was able to reassemble the dispersed parachutists and reestablish them as a lethal fighting unit.

As a result of this successful operation, Conners received a field promotion to Lieutenant. He was now an officer in the British Army.

He continued to perform with amazing bravery throughout the rest of the war. The fact that Conners, on a personal basis, didn't fear death because he might actually welcome it was unknown to his superior officers. But that didn't have anything to do with how they rated his performance. They didn't know or care about his motivations, or even if he might be subconsciously suicidal; they just were impressed by his performance.

So even after the war ended Conners still remained an officer in the British Army. Although the end of the war had resulted in a substantial decrease in the number of men under arms, the upper echelon of military commanders realized that this would not be the last war Britain would ever have to fight. Therefore, they didn't want to lose their best warriors.

And Conners was obviously one of the best.

By 1956, Brian Conners' career in the Special Air Services continued to progress successfully, and he had been promoted to Captain. He availed himself of all the educational opportunities the British Army provided. Although he had never excelled as a student during his childhood because of the hell-on-earth he endured at home, once freed of that problem he proved to be an exceptional learner. He studied history and learned as much as he could about the conflicts between England and its enemies, especially Ireland. Plus he studied languages and proved to be a naturally talented polyglot. He became proficient in Russian, which he thought would be important since the USSR was likely to be Britain's next major enemy. If war broke out with the USSR, he theorized that he might be airdropped into Russian territory and that command of the Russian language might help him to escape alive. He also studied other languages because he found he had a skill for that. He already knew some Italian, but he learned Spanish, German and even Mandarin Chinese.

Captain Conners was now in command of an SAS team that was to participate in the invasion of the Suez Canal zone. During the briefing for his mission, he had been told this was part of joint English, French and American operations to seize the Suez Canal since the Egyptian president had decided to nationalize it, which might cut off access to this vital shipping lane from the Allies.

Captain Conners' team was part of the British advance attack group. The team was to seize the El Gamil Airfield from the Egyptians, so the Allies could use it to land even more forces to continue the attack.

On November 5, 1956, the British SAS parachuted into Egypt as scheduled. The French commandos followed soon thereafter.

To everyone's surprise, however, the Americans decided not to join the invasion!

* * * * * * * * * *

The Suez Canal was opened in 1869 after almost a decade of work financed by the French and Egyptian governments. The canal connected the Mediterranean Sea and the Indian Ocean. It provided a direct route between the two and eliminated the necessity for vessels to go around the entire continent of Africa. It proved vital for the transport of goods and services between colonial powers like Britain and their far-flung colonies like India.

Although the canal was owned and financed by the French and Egyptian governments, in 1875 the Egyptian ruler faced a financial crisis and was forced to sell his shares in the canal company to the British government. Thereafter the canal was jointly owned by both the British and French governments.

But in the early 1950s, the monarchy of King Farouk was overthrown by the military in a coup led by Gamal Abdul Nasser, who became President of Egypt. Nasser proceeded to capitalize upon the growing nationalist sentiment developing in his country by opposing the French and British ownership of the Suez Canal. Nasser further consolidated his power by severing his relationship with the western powers.

He recognized the Communist government of China and negotiated arms deals with Communist states. These actions led the United States and other western investors to withdraw their financial support from the Aswan Dam, which was a massive project to harness the power of the Nile River.

When this happened, Egypt turned further toward the Communist countries for support, and was able to get the USSR to step in to continue the construction of the Aswan Dam.

On July 26, 1956, Egyptian President Nasser seized control of the canal and declared its nationalization by Egypt.

The French and British were outraged by this action and immediately began to try to recover control of the Suez Canal. They launched actions on the diplomatic front, while they developed military plans should the diplomatic effort fail. They both sought to gain the support of their traditional ally, the United States.

They also enlisted the help of Israel, which had only become a nation several years earlier because of actions from Britain with the support of the United Nations. The newly-minted Jewish state quickly became a willing participant in the potential invasion.

By the end of October, 1956, all diplomatic efforts to resolve the conflict had failed, so according to plan, Israel began the invasion by sending its troops across the Sinai Peninsula. Immediately thereafter, both the British and French sent an ultimatum to President Nasser to reverse the nationalization of the Suez Canal.

Nasser responded by sinking all 40 ships that were present in the canal, thus closing it to all shipping.

This infuriated the French and the British and they initiated their military actions. They fully expected the Americans to provide them with support and reinforcements and to quickly move into the conflict.

Captain Conners had been told that his group would soon be reinforced by both French and American troops. He had no way of knowing that the Americans were not coming this time.

The landing was mostly successful, but both Captain Conners and several of his paratroopers had been blown off course.

Once Captain Conners landed, he proceeded to pull off his parachute as quickly as possible. He had his rifle strapped to his back and his pistol in his holster. His backpack contained his hand grenades. He was somewhat disoriented since he wasn't quite sure where he had landed. He headed for the low point around him to seek shelter and found a sand encrusted wadi, or dry streambed.

Once he had a few moments to clear his thoughts and recover from the hard parachute landing, Captain Conners headed south to rejoin his men and help in the assault on the airfield.

He had only gone about 30 paces down the wadi when he was startled to hear an angry voice yell at him in Egyptian from the rim of the wadi.

He didn't speak Egyptian, but he could tell that this was a hostile voice. He assumed it meant STOP. He was about to pull his weapons and turn to face the voice, when he heard another angry voice from the other rim of the wadi.

It repeated, "Stop" in Egyptian.

Conners now realized that he was completely surrounded by Egyptian forces. Although there were only two people that had yelled at him, they were on opposite sides of the wadi, and so he knew he was surrounded. When he looked up, there were at least 10 Egyptians on each side of the wadi above him. They all had rifles pointed at him and appeared ready to shoot if he made a wrong move.

He dropped his weapons and awaited his capture. Conners stood in the bottom of the wadi with his weapons at his feet and his hands in the air. He knew he had no chance of escape.

Moments later two of the Egyptians descended into the wadi and slowly approached him. He couldn't understand a word they were saying, but one of them had handcuffs displayed in front of him, and the other was indicating that they wanted him to drop his arms and hold his hands together in front of him so he could be cuffed.

Captain Conners had no choice but to comply. Once they had the handcuffs on him, his captors pushed, shoved and dragged him to the top of the wadi where he saw the rest of his captors for the first time.

They were a group of ragged and unkempt Bedouins, but they all had rifles. He didn't know whether to be relieved since their lack of military training might allow him a better chance of escaping, or to be more afraid since they probably had never heard about the Geneva Convention regarding the treatment of prisoners.

The men all had deeply tanned and wrinkled faces, even the young ones. Some of them wore kerchiefs around their heads, similar to what he had seen English grandmothers wear. All the others wore white headdresses that were cut just above their eyes in front, but which extended on the sides and back all the way down to the shoulders to protect their ears and neck from the sun. They also had some type of headband around the top to hold this all in place.

They wore Bedouin robes, but one of them who was obviously the leader, was wearing an Egyptian Army military tunic as well. Apparently this was some kind of local tribe that had been conscripted to join the Egyptian Army as a militia unit.

This group that had captured him consisted of an odd mixture of the past and the present. The leader was seated in a vintage World War II jeep that had probably been left behind by the British at the end of World War II. Behind that jeep was a trailer into which he was unceremoniously dumped. Several moments later, about four of the Bedouins climbed into the trailer to ride with him. Because it was a very small trailer, they laid their feet on him for the trip.

For his first several days in captivity by the Bedouins, Captain Conners was pretty much left alone since they could not understand each other because of the language barrier. During this time, he was only given a very minimal amount of food and just enough water to survive.

He was usually securely tied up and forced to spend the night under the trailer attached to the jeep.

He had still never seen any regular Egyptian Army officers or troops. He had no idea of the Bedouins' plan for him.

Then one night the camp erupted with glee. He didn't know what was going on, but the Bedouins were obviously having some kind of party as the noise level got higher and higher. The Bedouins started to shriek and shout and even fire their rifles into the air.

After the party had progressed for more than an hour, some of his captors came to Captain Conners and pulled him out of the trailer. The Bedouins had a small campfire going nearby, and their other jeep and trailer had been backed up with the trailer close to the fire. He could see that all the Bedouins were glassy-eyed and energized.

They pulled Captain Conners to the back of the other trailer and tied his hands to both sides of it. He was bent over, facing the trailer with his chin touching the back of it. Then they grabbed each of his legs, pulled them apart and tied him by the knees to the edges of the trailer. He was absolutely helpless and unable to move, and was spread-eagled at the back of the trailer.

Captain Conners was a keen student of British military history and had read all of the writings of Lieutenant Colonel T. R. Lawrence, who was commonly known as Lawrence of Arabia. He knew that during Lawrence's captivity by the Arabs he had suffered sexual abuse from them. In his writings, Lawrence of Arabia described how he had been both beaten and buggered by his Arab captors.

Captain Conners was afraid that he was about to suffer the same fate.

Moments later some of the Bedouins cut the shirt from his back and slit his trousers so they fell down below his knees. Captain Conners' worst fears were soon realized. He was abused just like Lawrence of Arabia.

When he was finally repatriated with his unit, he had suffered so much pain and humiliation that he vowed revenge against his Bedouin enemies, as well as the Americans and the Irish.

* * * * * * * * * *

In the United States, President Dwight Eisenhower had reached the conclusion that the era of Colonialism was over and that the paramount need in the U.S. was to procure Arab oil. Accordingly, he decided that he could not support the British and French invasion of the Suez Canal.

Not only did Eisenhower decide not to send American military forces into the fray, he also directed the government to apply financial pressure to both Great Britain and France to end the invasion. President Eisenhower recognized that money made the world go around, so he decided he could best end this invasion by choking off the British finances.

President Eisenhower ordered George Humphrey, the Secretary of the Treasury, to prepare to sell the U.S. government's holdings of Sterling Bonds. The government had held these bonds to aid post-war Britain's economy, and they were a partial payment of Britain's enormous World War II debt to the U.S. government.

If the United States carried out this threat, it would lead to a massive devaluation of the British Pound. Within weeks of such a move, Britain would be unable to afford to import all the food and energy supplies it needed to even just sustain the population.

When Britain's Chancellor of the Exchequer, Harold Macmillan learned of this threat, he promptly advised his Prime Minister, Anthony Eden, that the country could not sustain such a financial setback and urged him to settle these differences as quickly as possible.

Faced with these adverse actions from the United States, Britain – and later France when informed that the British were backing down – had no alternative but to seek a cease-fire in Egypt and ultimately negotiate a settlement that ceded the Suez Canal to the Egyptians.

The final agreement called for the full withdrawal of all British, French and Israeli forces from the Canal area by December 22, 1956. It ceded full sovereignty over the Canal to the Egyptians. It also called for the full repatriation of all prisoners of war, so Captain Conners was finally released back to the British.

* * * * * * * * * *

It had been the worst two months of the Captain's life with almost daily beatings and torments, not to mention the most humiliating treatment in his entire life. The only solace Captain Conners had during his period of captivity was that he knew his brother, Charlie, was not at risk during this conflict. Charlie had written Brian several months before the conflict began. He informed Brian that he had been offered a much better deal with a different branch of the British government. Charlie was getting a substantial pay increase and would not have to wear a uniform anymore. And he would be serving the British cause by opposing Irish terrorists. Brian was looking forward to learning more about this career change once they could finally get together again when the hostilities were over.

Once he was back to his unit, Conners discovered the full extent of the double-cross by the Americans. He had thought that he couldn't hate them any worse after what happened during the Second World War, but the pain and disgrace he suffered during his extended capture by the filthy Bedouin militia ramped his hatred up to a much higher level. The Americans had backstabbed Britain! And gotten him buggered.

* * * * * * * * * *

By the spring of 1957, Captain Conners' SAS regiment had been ordered back to its home base in Britain. Conners had written several times to his brother, Charlie, to check on his welfare and whereabouts. He had not received any response, which worried him greatly. Although Charlie had told him in his last letter that he had a much better job offer, Brian still had no idea what that was.

But then one day he came back to his room in the bachelor officers' quarters at the base to find a tall, stately-looking gentleman waiting for him outside the room in the hall. The stranger was dressed in civilian clothes, but had a distinctively military bearing.

As Captain Conners approached, the stranger said, "Pardon me, but are you Captain Conners?"

Captain Conners responded politely, "Yes, I am. Is there some way I could be of service to you?"

The stranger answered, "I am Colonel Thornton and I was hoping that you could give me a few moments of your time to speak in private."

Captain Conners was a little dubious since this alleged "Colonel" was not in uniform, but he invited him into the room anyway, "Of course, sir. Would you like to just come into my room for a few moments or would you like to go somewhere else?"

Colonel Thornton replied, "No, no, please, let's just go into your room. All I'd like is some private time with you."

With that Conners opened the door to the room and they both entered. Although his room was small, it included a private bathroom, a small kitchen area and a living area with a fold-out bed. There were also two comfortable chairs in the living area. Captain Conners asked the Colonel if he would like some tea, saying, "Please, Colonel, sit down and make yourself comfortable. Might I make you some tea?"

The Colonel responded, "No, thank you about the tea, but I will take a seat. And I think it would be wise if you could take a seat also, because I have some news that you will find most disturbing."

Conners looked at the Colonel and saw that his face had turned very solemn. He was suddenly very worried about his brother Charlie. He almost shook as he took a seat opposite Colonel Thornton and said, "What news do you have?"

Colonel Thornton said, "First, I'd like to introduce myself further. I am in charge of a top-secret department in the British Intelligence Service known as MI-5. My department is responsible for monitoring and responding to threats against Northern Ireland that might be attempted by any partisans seeking the reunification of Ireland by illegal or terrorist means. It was my honor to have had your brother Charlie working for me for the last year, during which he performed courageously and admirably. But now I have to inform you that, regrettably, he was killed while performing his duties to Britain."

Conners jerked upright from his chair and exclaimed, "No, that can't be! Charlie was always so strong. He just couldn't have been killed."

They were both silent for a few minutes while the magnitude of the disclosure was absorbed by Conners.

Conners squeezed his eyelids together so tightly that they actually started to hurt. He was trying mightily to suppress the tears that seemed ready to burst forth at any moment. He was sure that this Colonel Thornton was telling him the truth, since Charlie had never gone so long without responding to one of Brian's letters. But he refused to break down and cry like a baby in front of the Colonel. He would save his grief until later, when he was alone.

Conners caught his breath for a moment and then asked the Colonel, "Can you tell me what Charlie was doing for you, and how and why he was killed?"

Colonel Thornton responded, "I'm going to do that, but let me give you some background. First of all, I want you to know that I was the one that recruited your brother to serve in my department. So from that standpoint, I am somewhat responsible for his death. But he made the choice to join my unit without any coercion on my part and proved an enthusiastic and reliable member of my team.

"Your brother had served bravely in the SAS during World War II, and I have brought you some of his things that he had left with us before he went on his last mission. During the last war, Charlie received not only the Star of Africa Medal, but also a Bronze Oak Leaf because he had been mentioned in several Dispatches for his bravery." (A Dispatch was a British Citation for Bravery.)

The Colonel continued, "I am sure that Charlie would have wanted you to have both his medals and the certificates that accompanied them."

Brian responded, "Thank you for that, sir. Charlie never mentioned these medals to me, but then again, he was never one to brag about anything. Please continue, and tell me how and why did he die."

Colonel Thornton continued, "The existence of Northern Ireland is constantly under attack from Irish terrorists from the Republic of Ireland. In order to be better prepared to defend against these attacks, we always need more information about potential threats. That was why I recruited your brother. Because of his upbringing, he spoke with the proper Irish accent that would allow him to mingle freely in Northern Ireland. Both the Irish Republican Army and several more violent splinter groups have been killing and creating terror in Northern Ireland to attempt to influence the reunification of Ireland. These groups have tortured and killed far too many British and Northern Ireland soldiers and constables.

"Your brother was sent undercover to a reputed IRA hotspot in the city of Derry. He was successful in obtaining a job as a bartender in a pub that was known to be a gathering spot for IRA partisans. He had been working there for several months and had developed a reputation as a trusted IRA sympathizer. But all the while, he had been relaying valuable information about potential plots to us. He had also been successful in finding Irish terrorists and personally eliminating them – some with very extreme prejudice." (That meant they had suffered a very violent death.) "He always got valuable information from these terrorists before eliminating them.

"But then, his reports suddenly ceased. When we went back to examine his prior transmissions, he had reported one potentially troubling incident.

"He had a room above the pub in which he worked, and there was only one bathroom that was shared by all four roomers on the second floor. There was a bathtub in that single bathroom. Apparently Charlie had been taking his weekly bath when one of the other roomers unexpectedly entered to use the facility.

"When Charlie had been accepted into the Special Air Service, he had gotten an SAS insignia tattooed onto his right bicep. Charlie reported that the other roomer might have seen the tattoo when he unexpectedly entered the bathroom, but Charlie didn't seem particularly concerned about it, and we weren't either, until he disappeared.

"Unfortunately, I need to tell you that about two weeks after he stopped reporting to us, his body was found about two miles outside the town. Even more regrettably, I have to tell you that your brother was both tortured and mutilated. His death was not a pleasant one. He suffered several mutilations, including the removal of the skin on his bicep that contained his tattoo of the SAS insignia."

When Conners heard that, he could contain his tears no longer. He fell back into his chair and tears gushed from his eyes. He moaned, "Dear Charlie, dear Charlie, how could that happen to you? I should have been there. It's my fault. I should have been there."

Colonel Thornton interrupted him and said, "There is nothing that you or I, or anyone else, could have done to save him from the savagery they subjected him to. But we can exact revenge upon those bastards, treating them exactly the same way when we find them."

Conners said, "But how will you know who they are and where they are? Then even if you get them they'll just spend years in jail."

Colonel Thornton responded, "That's where you're wrong, Captain Conners. My unit does not operate according to those formal rules. Our mission is to respond to those dirty Irish terrorist bastards in just exactly the same way that they have been treating our people. We want to set an example, that anyone who treats our people so badly can expect to receive absolutely no mercy from us once they're captured. In my unit, retribution is quick and horrible. We believe in an eye for an eye and we don't let legalities get in our way."

Conners stared at the Colonel for a moment and then asked, "But how can you get away with this? It seems like a great idea, but isn't there some problem with the barristers?" (Barristers is a British term for lawyers.)

Colonel Thornton responded, "We operate as a special department of MI-5 that reports directly to the Prime Minister, and we have clearance from the government to do whatever is necessary. Sometimes it is necessary to circumvent traditional legal systems to deal with terrorist threats. We don't arrest our opponents and bring them to justice; we deliver justice on the spot. I am here to ask you to join my unit so that together we might find and take revenge upon your brother's killers. You would still retain all of your benefits from your military service and I can even offer you a substantial increase in pay grade."

Conners was overwhelmed by this offer, but he asked, "What about my men here at SAS. How could I explain to them that I'm leaving?"

Colonel Thornton said, "Don't worry about that. We'll tell them that you've been promoted to a new unit and that you will continue to serve Britain in a greater cause. So will you join us?"

Captain Conners said, "Of course, it would be an honor to join you. But do you have any idea who the bastards are that killed my brother?"

Colonel Thornton responded, "Our best information is that your brother was tortured and killed by an Irish terrorist named William Flynn. He has been nicknamed Billy the Butcher because he always mutilates his victims. He is the leader of an IRA splinter group known as the Irish Reunification Force, or the IRF. Flynn and his IRF members are among the most bloodthirsty and vicious of all the Irish terrorists. They are one of our main targets, but remain one of the most elusive. Finding Billy the Butcher and his associates will be one of your main priorities."

Colonel Thornton continued, "Just let me provide you with one more thought. And that is I am thinking of retiring in the next few years and you would be coming in as the most senior member of my unit. If you perform as well as I expect you will, given the dedication your brother showed, you would be in direct line to replace me. Although we are not exactly military, you would then get the title of Colonel and take command of the entire unit."

Conners said, "I already told you I was ready to join, but thank you for that potential opportunity, sir. What do we need to do next?"

Colonel Thornton said, "I've already prepared your separation orders from the SAS since I was sure that you would join us. Just pack your things and get ready to go."

When Colonel Thornton died under mysterious circumstances during a mission two years later, Captain Conners succeeded him as leader of the section. He became Colonel Conners and proceeded to redirect the group in even more violent ways. He retired or transferred some of the more conservative members of the group and replaced them with men with even more murderous inclinations.

CHAPTER TWENTY

THE CONCLUSION

Colonel Conners had personally come to Ireland to participate in either the killing or the capture of William Flynn, the bloody terrorist nicknamed Billy the Butcher who had tortured and killed Conners' brother, Charlie. His spies had long been reporting that Flynn was suffering from terminal lung cancer, and this past week they began to report that his death was imminent.

Colonel Conners received various reports from his spies that William Flynn was planning a final grand meeting with all his subordinates, both to select his replacement and to bid them all goodbye. Colonel Conners wanted to know who might be next in line to succeed William Flynn upon his death.

He pushed all of his sources to try to find out where Flynn was, so he could apprehend and kill him before he died. Colonel Conners wanted to learn the location of this upper-level meeting so he could destroy not only William Flynn, but also his subordinates.

Eventually, Conners learned the location of the "summit" meeting of all the IRF members. It was to be held in an isolated house in a rural farming area in the village of Skerries along the coast of the Republic of Ireland. Colonel Conners had absolutely no compunctions about attacking this meeting in the Republic of Ireland.

He sent two members of his team as an advance party to provide surveillance of the meeting. His team watched throughout the day as various members of the IRF arrived.

When Colonel Conners received confirmation from his men that the meeting was, in fact, being held, he arrived with four more members of his team and prepared to attack his enemies. Upon his arrival, he received a report from his team leader there. He learned that virtually all of his worst enemies were there in the house already. They had been delivered by cars that sped off once the passengers had entered the cottage. Apparently, the IRF was so sure of its secrecy that it hadn't required any emergency escape vehicles to remain nearby in case of attack.

Conners was observing the house himself through binoculars when he saw a truck bearing the logo of a local brewery pull up. This brewery truck stopped just before the back door, which was protected from the frequent rains by being located in a covered alcove set into the wall of the house. The driver dropped the truck's back-loading gate. Then he went inside the truck and started to roll a keg of beer off the gate and into the house. But he stopped moving the keg at the tailgate, so he could back the truck up even further into the alcove to make it easier to deliver the keg.

Colonel Conners thought this was just typical of drunken Irish louts. They were going to deal with the death of William Flynn by getting drunk.

It made Colonel Conners smile for a moment as he remembered a joke about the Irish. *What's the difference between an Irish funeral and an Irish wedding? Answer: There's one less Irish at the funeral.*

After the brewery truck pulled away from the house, Colonel Conners plotted his attack on the IRF. He believed that they were all now drinking heavily. He decided to wait for an hour or more to attack, so the IRF bastards could get thoroughly drunk and be easy targets.

* * * * * * * * * *

The American aircraft carrier, the USS Independence, was cruising in the eastern Mediterranean Sea when its Captain received encrypted orders for a Top Secret mission. The Independence was a Forrestal class aircraft carrier, which was conventionally powered (rather than nuclear) and which normally carried approximately 90 aircraft. It had recently been assigned to duty in the Mediterranean as part of the United States Sixth Fleet.

When the captain of the Independence read the orders he had received, he saw that they were marked "TOP SECRET, Your Eyes Only." The munitions that would be on board the flights as described in the orders were top secret and experimental. Plus the destination of the target was completely unexpected. But, the Captain never questioned an order.

Therefore he personally made the assignments of the pilots and weapons officers. He personally conducted the preflight briefing and verified that the experimental secret munitions had been successfully loaded on the aircraft. Since this was a top-secret operation, this was his personal standard operating procedure. The pilots had the proper security clearances and they had already been involved in several tests of the experimental munitions. They learned they were going in support of a ground attack team from the British Special Boat Service. And they were going to attack a target in a neutral country, Ireland. They were told that no matter what happened, they could neither land nor crash-land in Ireland, since that would cause an international incident. If they experienced any difficulties, they needed to ditch at sea.

The mission would involve two McDonnell Douglas F-4 Phantom II long-range supersonic jet fighter bombers. The Phantom was a large bomber that could carry over 18,000 pounds of weapons, but for this mission only one of them would carry a weapon. The other one would carry an ancillary device known as a laser designator that was necessary to direct the weapon. The mission would also test whether a ground-based laser designator would be better than the airborne one. One of the weaknesses of the new experimental munition was that the airborne laser designator was difficult to control. It was thought that a ground-based designator would be more stable and thus more accurate. But obviously it would not work in an airborne assault situation unless there were already ground forces available to operate the designator. So this mission would employ redundant targeting systems.

The mission would need aerial refueling since the target destination was a great distance from the Independence. But the pilots were well-experienced at aerial refueling, so they were not uncomfortable about the long-range flight.

The weapon system that the two F-4 B Phantoms were carrying was an experimental "guided" bomb that had been developed secretly in the United States by Texas Instruments. It was designated the BOLT-117, which stood for (BOmb, Laser Targeted-117). It was the world's first laser-guided bomb and would be officially commissioned into the United States Air Force in 1967. The Dash 117 in the designation referred to a standard US M-117 bomb. Basically the experimental munition used a standard bomb that had been outfitted with the laser guidance system developed by Texas Instruments. The M-117 had a nominal weight of 750 pounds and contained approximately 400 pounds of high-explosive. That amount was enough to level about a city block in almost any urban area. It would almost vaporize an isolated house in a rural area.

The military was still testing how to best utilize this new weapon. This mission, however, had clearance from the very highest authority, President Lyndon Johnson (although the pilots didn't know that), so the weapon was being deployed tonight before completing all its tests. But the preliminary tests had all been successful. The need for ultimate secrecy on this mission was paramount. No one wanted to risk an unguided bomb destroying the wrong target and leading to an international incident. All involved in the decision to deploy it agreed that it was the best choice.

The F-4 B Phantom had the pilot in the front and the weapons officer behind him, in a tandem position. The new munition was designed so that the weapons officer in the back could use the laser designator on the target while the pilot flew the plane, but the early tests utilized two aircraft, with the first flying the bombing pattern and the second utilizing its weapons officer to operate the laser designator. Even in this scenario, the laser designator was difficult to control and sometimes the guided munitions landed off-target, but they always hit where the misdirected laser had aimed them. Even then they were still much closer to the target than they would have been with no guidance whatsoever.

So in addition to the airborne designator on the second aircraft, the British Special Boat Service assault team to Ireland would deploy a ground-based laser designator. They would also deploy a small, portable VHF omnidirectional radio transmitter. This transmitter would send out a signal onto which the aircraft could home. Although it was short-range, only about 100 miles because of its battery power, that would be more than sufficient to guide the jets to the target.

The mission officers were instructed about their refueling points and where they were to circle and wait before the final target designation. For this mission, the lead aircraft carrying the bomb was designated Tango 1. The second aircraft which contained the airborne laser was designated Tango 2. Obviously, one of the mission commanders had a sense of humor about the names, which were a play on the saying, "It takes two to Tango," in reference to the need for both an aiming aircraft and an attack aircraft.

The aircraft departed the carrier without any difficulty and headed westbound, traveling across both northern Spain and southern France. Although no one had requested any official clearance to enter those countries' airspace, the mission officers knew that neither of those countries was likely to detect them, nor try to interdict them. After all, no one was threatening either country, so their air radar technicians would likely assume that any unidentified traffic was civilian aircraft anyway.

The aircraft entered the Bay of Biscay and proceeded north into the Celtic Sea. From there they headed northbound to await the designation of their target. Once on station, the aircraft switched radio frequencies to contact the ground team leader that had the land-based laser designator. This radio contact had been given the code name "Flashlight."

* * * * * * * * * *

After the sun had set around the meeting house, the music from inside became even louder. The voices, although indiscernible from the outside of the house, were also growing much louder and drunkenly raucous.

Colonel Conners had finally reached the end of his patience. He was anxious to confront his mortal enemy, Billy the Butcher.

Conners instructed his men to be careful when approaching the house, but not to be fearful because most of the Irish terrorists inside were probably already drunk and ready to pass out. They might be belligerent, but would not be well-coordinated.

He had his two point men kick in the front door and precede him with their automatic weapons. They were all surprised when they met absolutely no resistance. Although Colonel Conners thought this would be an easy invasion of the house, he was puzzled by the complete lack of any opposition. He expected at least a few drunken Irish louts to try to stop his men.

He proceeded into the main living room of the house where he found an emaciated, thin and almost skeleton-like figure sitting on the sofa. The figure was smoking a cigarette, while next to him were two very tall green oxygen tanks that were providing oxygen to the tubing and mask the man was wearing around his neck, rather than around his face. He had obviously decided that it was more important to smoke than to breathe.

Most of Colonel Conners' team followed him into the house and searched all the rooms. They left two men outside to cover their back.

His men could detect absolutely no one else in the house. Next to the man sitting on the sofa, there was a tape recorder repeatedly playing loud music and Irish voices. Colonel Conners was flummoxed. He didn't understand exactly what was going on, but suspected a trap. He went directly to the frail figure smoking a cigarette on the sofa and demanded, "Are you Billy Flynn, you bloody bastard?"

Flynn responded, "Well, that would be me as ever was. And why the hell are you here in my house?"

Colonel Conners was upset by the arrogance of this frail figure, but said, "I'm here to make you pay for all the horrible crimes you've committed throughout your life. You won't just die a natural death from your diseases, you lousy parasite. I think that your horrible health now will be fair retribution for all the terrible things you've done throughout your life."

William Flynn started to smile, but then hacked repeatedly since he couldn't take a breath. When he could finally breathe again, he inhaled again from the cigarette and then dropped it into the ashtray. He choked a bit on that drag and then coughed out the smoke as he responded to Colonel Conners, "I know I'm close to death now, and I will have to pay for my sins when I meet my maker. But so will you, Brian Conners. You are the one I hated most throughout the last few years. Your brother had absolutely no humanity in him and committed the worst things imaginable. But I was lucky enough to exact revenge against him. And whenever you attacked my men or other Irish patriots, I paid you back double each time. For each and every atrocity you and your men committed against my people, we fought back with two actions against yours."

Colonel Conners responded, "Well, you evil old Irish bastard, you won't be fighting back anymore. You're heading to our headquarters where you'll spill out all the secrets about your organization while enduring more pain than you ever imagined."

William Flynn said, "I don't have much of my life left, but before we leave, can I have another cigarette?"

Colonel Conners didn't much care about that since Flynn had been constantly smoking since they entered the house. He was very uneasy about the whole situation, but things were progressing so fast that he wasn't quite sure what to do about them. He needed a few minutes to collect his thoughts and determine a plan of action.

William Flynn opened his pocket cigarette case, which had an ornate leather cover. He extracted a single cigarette and lit it from the embers of the last cigarette he had been smoking. He was a life-long chain smoker and that was obviously what had put him in this condition.

Flynn took a long drag from his new cigarette and then pushed the cigarette case in front of Colonel Conners. When he got the proposal from Captain Sharkey to act as bait for this trap, Flynn knew he would not survive his part in the plot. But he also knew that he was a dead man walking and would rather die a quick death from a bullet instead of a slow, lingering death in a hospital bed. He readily agreed to Sharkey's proposal since he couldn't resist the chance to take Colonel Conners and several of his men along with him on his death trip. He knew this would probably provoke the Colonel to shoot him, but Flynn decided to torment the Colonel one last time as he offered the cigarette case to the Colonel and said, "Colonel, may I offer you a cigarette?"

Colonel Conners looked down at the cigarette case and saw that on top of the ornate case was a leather insert bearing the insignia of the Special Air Service. He immediately remembered that his brother's body was mutilated by the removal of the skin on his arm that had the tattoo of the insignia of the SAS. He was sure that the leather on this cigarette case must be the desecrated skin from his brother's body which had been tanned like some common cowhide to preserve it.

Colonel Conners became enraged and pulled his .45 automatic out of the holster. He emptied the entire clip into William Flynn. Conners hadn't initially intended to kill Flynn; he had meant to capture him and extract more information from him about the IRF. He was looking forward to the information-gathering process because it would've been particularly painful to Flynn. In fact, Flynn would not have survived the process. But Conners was in no way unhappy with what he had just done. He retrieved the cigarette case and clasped it to his chest. He felt sure that the covering on the box had once been the skin on his brother's bicep with the tattoo of the SAS insignia, and he treasured retrieving this sacred relic from Flynn.

But Colonel Conners now was sure that he had been led into a trap. He didn't know exactly what his former archenemy, the now-dead Billy Flynn, had planned, but Conners suspected that the IRF operatives that had snuck out of this cottage earlier on the brewery truck were probably surrounding the cottage even now. His suspicions were confirmed when he heard a gunshot in the distance and a bullet hit the building right near one of his operatives.

He immediately yelled an order for all of his men to get back into the house, so they could provide a collective defense against the assault he expected from the IRF terrorists.

Conners thought to himself as his men were rushing back into the house, "*How the hell could I have been deceived so easily by this old drunken Irish lout terrorist? I think my hatred for him clouded my judgment.*"

But things were looking up for Colonel Conners since all of his men made it successfully back into the house without any of them being killed, or even wounded.

He was sure that his men were much more than a match for the Irish terrorists outside the house. His men had automatic rifles and plenty of ammunition.

He gave further orders to his men to re-disperse inside the house in defensive positions until he could regroup them into a fighting force to escape from the house. Some of them immediately knocked the glass out of the windows and began to spray suppressive automatic-weapons fire out of the windows of the house. The Colonel was confident that he could not only get out of this trap successfully, but also kill several more Irish terrorists in the process. He had no way of knowing that, outside, he was facing not Irish terrorists, but members of the elite British Special Boat Service. As skilled as they were, however, there were not very many SBS team members outside.

The SBS members countered the fire from inside the house with accurate return-fire. They had automatic weapons, but had them on non-automatic operation so as not to alert the defenders in the house that they might not be just IRF terrorists. They continued to contain the inhabitants with selective fire and thus prevent their escape.

The SBS was entrusted with two important missions. This was the first of them: to land a small operative team on the Irish coast and proceed to the house where the IRF meeting was being conducted. The other was to send a small amphibious force to Belfast Lough. Both teams were on Rigid Inflatable Boats with high-horsepower outboard engines that had been extensively modified to silence them. They could proceed at very high speeds since they bounced over the sea, rather than plowing through it. But with all their engine modifications, such as submerged engine exhausts, they were very stealthy.

The teams were delivered to their different departure points by British frigates. The warships dropped off the teams and then lay offshore to await their return – and anyone else they brought back with them.

The first team, which consisted of six men, landed successfully and moved into position well outside the lines that Colonel Conners' men had established when they first surrounded the house. Conners' team had been looking inward, while the SBS team enveloped them from further out. They were the ones that fired the first shot toward the house to let the intruders know there were hostile forces opposing them outside the house. This led the Colonel to order his two outside guards back into the house – which was the plan.

While the Colonel's men were retreating back inside the house, two members of the Special Boat Service proceeded to a meadow on a small hill about 500 meters from the house. It was the highest ground nearby and offered a clear visual path to the cottage.

First they set up the portable Vertical Omni directional radio transmitter to guide the jets on their final approach to the target. Next they set up a tripod that had an electronic gadget on top. They had just now been trained how to use this "secret weapon." Because the weapon was so secret, they had not been told exactly how it would be able to destroy the target. Although the team leader clearly knew it was a target designator for aircraft that would deliver the bombs, that information did not get fully communicated to the men deploying the laser. They were only instructed how to aim it at the target. They were told to leave it shining on the roof of the target until the target was destroyed, and then to dismantle it and bring it back to the boat with them.

Once they had set up the tripod and turned on the laser designator, they pointed it toward the top of the house and watched as it produced a small, but very bright, dot of light on the roof.

The two men didn't know why an airplane would need a small light to help it see a target as big as a house. As they talked about it, it didn't make sense. They began to fantasize that maybe this "secret weapon" was really a "Ray-Gun," like the ones they had seen on the telly in cartoons, which might ignite the house and cause it to burst into flames, but they were disappointed because seemingly nothing was happening. They could only see a small point of light on the roof of the house. Even this was becoming more difficult to see because of the amount of gunfire coming from the house.

But unbeknownst to them, the two F-4B Phantom jets that had been circling the area to await the laser target designation were already setting up their bombing run.

"Flashlight, this is Tango 1, do you read me?" the pilot of Tango 1 asked.

"Affirmative, Tango 1," Flashlight responded. "The VOR is with me and my men – not, repeat, not at the target. The target is at a bearing of eight-seven degrees and approximately 500 meters distant from the transmitter. We have illuminated the designator."

With the information from Flashlight and the transmissions from the VOR radio, the pilots and weapons officers in the jets now knew the exact position of the target. The laser designator now would enable their smart munition to home in perfectly on the target.

Since there was a laser designator deployed on the ground, the second plane that had the laser designator on board was only there as a backup. The pilot of the second plane just provided defensive coverage for the bombing run and a training run for his weapons officer. Not that any defensive coverage was needed over Ireland, but it offered an excellent training opportunity to the pilot and his weapons officer.

The instrumentation in the attack aircraft showed a bright red "Laser Detected" light as the pilot began his bombing run toward the target. But before he could release the bomb, the light suddenly went out. Either the designator had failed or his aircraft detector had failed. He aborted the bombing run and circled in a right turn past the target. As he did so, he said on his radio, "Tango 2, this is Tango 1. Lights out on board."

Tango 2 responded, "Roger that. Is the problem in your detector?"

Tango 1 said, "I don't know yet, but we are starting a systems check."

His weapons officer in the back seat had immediately begun to check all his systems. The weapons officer in Tango 2 had done likewise, to determine if his system was ready to provide back-up if it was the ground-based laser that had failed.

Just then, both pilots heard the ground team send a radio report, "Tango 1, this is Flashlight. Bulb out, repeat, bulb out. Also, we are taking heavy fire from inside the house. We think they are massing for an escape from the house. We will attempt to contain them inside as long as possible. Do you have a back-up plan?"

The attack aircraft pilot repeated the question to Tango 2, "This is Tango 1. Tango 2, do we have a back-up plan?'

The pilot of Tango 2 responded, "You betcha. We have all systems go. We are completing a left 360 and will fire up the "candle" in approximately 90 seconds."

Since they were all on the same radio frequency, the pilot in Tango 1 then said, "OK Flashlight, guess you heard that. We have our own 'candle' and will be over the target with ETA in 120 seconds. Just hang on and we'll light things up for you."

This wasn't combat, so the pilots didn't need to take any evasive maneuvers. The Irish sky was actually quite clear over the target, unusual in an area that experienced frequent rain showers and heavy cloud cover.

Tango 2 made a smooth approach toward the target and its weapons officer used their laser to illuminate the target easily. The pilot of Tango 1 this time had a bright "Laser Detected" indicator on his instrument panel. It was such a clear night that he could see the target himself as he released the bomb.

* * * * * * * * * *

Colonel Conners was supremely confident that he could defeat the small opposing force of ill-trained Irish terrorists outside the house. He was further confident that his plan to mount a counter-attack and allow his men to escape the house was sure to succeed. He had just given his men the order to attack when the entire house blew up – and blew all of them into oblivion. And probably directly into hell, where they all belonged!

Just when the two SBS team members who had set up the laser designator had decided that the "secret weapon" was a dud and a failure because its light had gone out, the house was destroyed by an enormous blast and a fiery conflagration whose heat could be felt by them, even 500 meters away.

Maybe it wasn't a "Ray Gun," but the house was completely obliterated. They didn't understand how this little light had destroyed the cottage even after it went dark, but they respected its power as they stowed it away and made their escape from Ireland with the rest of their team, heading back to the coast to meet the frigate and return to England.

* * * * * * * * * *

The second SBS team had twelve members on two boats, plus an American they were delivering to an area close to the shore. The American was equipped with diving equipment.

The SBS team members were instructed to drop off the American diver and then proceed around the promontory and set up a defensive line across the exit road from the castle which sat on the top of the rocky outcrop.

Their mission was to prevent anyone from escaping from the castle after the attack by the American diver, if that was necessary. Their mission also included directions for them to mount a frontal assault on the castle if the American diver had not been successful by the deadline. They had explosives to blow open the heavy medieval doors into the castle if that was required, and they were instructed to do whatever else was necessary to seize the castle and secure the release of the hostages. Additionally, they were told that this was an absolutely "black" operation and that the Royal Navy was not desirous of obtaining any prisoners from the mission. They knew what that meant!

The SBS team delivered Peter as close to the shore as they could without being detected. He slipped overboard, cleared his mask and began breathing through his air tanks. He hoped he had everything he needed to be able to rescue Jean and the baby.

Once he dropped out of the boat, the rest of the SBS team proceeded to the shore to prevent anyone from escaping from the castle. They were on a 60-minute deadline for the diver to accomplish his mission, or else they would just blow the doors apart and invade the castle.

Once in the water, Peter immediately headed toward the entrance to the tunnel which led to the cistern. He had not only his underwater breathing apparatus, but also several unusual weapons.

Peter was wearing a wetsuit since the water in this area was exceptionally cold. He had a watch under the wetsuit on his left wrist and a compass on his right. He knew the plan called for him to be in the castle and complete his mission within 60 minutes, so the watch was important. Once Peter reached the opening to the tunnel, he discarded the compass and began to cut the gate open.

He knew there had been a gate installed at the mouth of the tunnel when the owners had modernized the structure, so he used an underwater thermite cutting torch to cut the lock on the gate. He had been trained to use such a torch during his training for an Underwater Demolition Team when he was in the Navy Seabees during World War II.

Once he burned the lock off the gate and swung it open, Peter discarded the thermite torch and swam up the underwater tunnel toward the cistern.

The first part of his journey turned out to be pretty easy since there was no current or obstacles in the tunnel, but then he reached the ancient portcullis that still had some rusted parts intruding into the tunnel. Although it was ancient, it hadn't yet rusted entirely away.

Peter proceeded carefully through the portcullis, but he was suddenly hung up when his air hose caught onto one of the razor-sharp rusted spines of the ancient gate. Peter pulled forward to get away from the obstruction, but all that did was serve to sever the hose, and now Peter couldn't get any air. But he knew that he had to get into the castle to rescue Jean and the baby within the time deadline, so he wouldn't turn back.

He inhaled as much air as possible from the remains of the hose before it filled up with seawater. Peter dumped the now useless air tanks and swam forward.

He was holding his breath, hoping that he could reach the cistern before his breath ran out. It was a long swim and Peter's lungs were soon straining from the exertion and the lack of oxygen.

He had a light attached to his forehead that he had been using to find his way up the tunnel, and he suddenly found that he was in front of a pile of skeletons. Normally a pile of bones would not scare him, but this sudden encounter with human remains almost made Peter gasp out his last breath.

It got even worse when Peter saw with alarm that one of the skeletons suddenly started to move toward him, seemingly ready to attack. Peter forced himself to close his eyes and mentally convince himself that this could not be happening. It was only a skeleton.

He was afraid that he had begun to hallucinate, which is one of the early signs of oxygen deprivation – and kind of an early warning sign of imminent drowning. Despite his sudden shock, Peter knew he had to open his eyes and get to the cistern before he drowned. He opened his eyes and looked down again at the skeletons.

Peter realized that the movement he had just observed was not one of the skeletons moving toward him, but was instead the movement of some crabs that were feeding on whatever remained of the flesh on one of those skeletons.

Peter hoped that none of those skeletons were the remains of Jean or the baby.

He couldn't have known, but the most recent body that had been thrown into the cistern was that of the radio operator from the Brady manor house. He had not survived the wound he'd received during the assault on the manor house, and when the Colonel's team had brought his body back here, they had just thrown it down into the cistern to join the remains of their many other victims.

Although he was shocked by what he had just seen, Peter knew that the surface water in the cistern must now be directly above the pile of bones. He raced upward. His lungs felt like they were bursting when he finally broke through the surface and gulped fresh air. Peter used to practice holding his breath when he was a kid diving for clams, and got pretty good at it. He had even employed this ability in the South Pacific during the war when he faced a shark attack. But he knew he'd just beaten his lifetime record.

Once Peter surfaced at the bottom of the cistern, he removed a sack he had been carrying on his shoulder. It contained an item that had been provided by the British. It was about 18 inches long and about four inches in diameter. The British military called it a mortar, but that might seem a little dramatic. In reality it was a tube with a pneumatic propellant that could shoot a grappling hook out of the tube.

The grappling hook was installed inside the pneumatic tube before Peter left the assault ship. To the grappling hook was attached a lightweight, though strong, nylon rope. The rope had knots every two feet so that Peter would have something to grasp as he climbed up the rope. Since both the rope and Peter's hands would be wet, the knots would provide gripping points so his hands wouldn't slip.

The grappling hook had retractable tines that would be compact until they deployed. Once the hook had pulled out the entire rope, the momentum would yank it to a stop and the tines would immediately deploy. Then Peter could pull them back so that they could latch on to the top of the cistern.

Peter treaded water as he held the pneumatic tube above his shoulder. There was hardly any recoil when he fired the device and sent the grappling hook upward. Because it was a pneumatic device, it made very little noise.

Peter really only had one chance at doing this successfully. If the grappling hook didn't lodge against something, but instead fell back into the cistern, there was virtually no way that he could toss it back manually. And he could never climb the smooth, slippery walls by hand.

Luckily the tines of the hook lodged against the outside wall of the cistern and Peter was able to begin to climb the rope up to the surface.

Once he reached the courtyard, Peter tossed the grappling hook back down the cistern. He didn't want any of the inhabitants to see it and realize they had an intruder in the castle. Furthermore, he knew he would not need it again. He needed to exit by the front gate with Jean and the baby – or he would exit in a body bag. There would be no retreating here.

The castle had been equipped by Colonel Conners with a very sophisticated exterior warning system that would have alerted the inhabitants if anyone approached the front of the castle. The inhabitants relied entirely on this sophisticated system, and were therefore not prepared for an intrusion in any other way.

Peter knew that the Colonel and most of his men had departed for the Republic of Ireland to attack Billy Flynn, but he wasn't sure how many remained behind.

While he didn't know it yet, there were only three members of the Colonel's team left in the castle to guard the hostages and provide communications with their deployed team members. One of the men maintained a vigil outside the hostages' room to make sure the woman didn't attempt an escape. The second man rotated with the first, each on 12-hour guard duty.

The third man was a more senior sergeant who took on all of the communications and quartermaster responsibilities. He had his own room next to the radio room, so he was on-call virtually 24 hours-a-day. He also maintained their inventory of weapons, which were located in a small nearby room. When he was not actively monitoring the communications equipment, his responsibilities included the cleaning and maintenance of all the weapons.

Although the man not on guard-duty usually would be resting or eating, this night the off-duty guard was strolling one of the parapets at the top of the castle while he smoked a cigarette. When Peter rolled over the top of the cistern and onto the grounds of the courtyard, the guard was luckily looking outward rather than into the courtyard. Peter was relieved that the guard didn't see him.

Peter decided his best move would be to eliminate the man on the parapet first, before he tried to go deeper into the rooms of the castle.

Because a gun would have been either useless, or at best unreliable after being underwater for so long, Peter had also brought along his Kabar knife and one other weapon. This weapon was top-secret and had been in testing by both the American ONI and the British SBS. It had been designed by Heckler & Koch and was designated the HK P11. It resembled a revolver with five large barrels. Each barrel contained a cartridge that held a steel dart about 10 centimeters long. Each dart contained a very small solid-fuel rocket. It was designed to be waterproof – and could even be used underwater. The rocket fuel was ignited by an electrical spark and was impervious to water.

This weapon also had the advantage that the rocket was almost silent when it discharged. It did make a sound, but the sound was more like a "whoosh," rather than the loud report from an ordinary gun.

Peter removed the weapon from the pack he had been carrying around his waist. He mounted the stairs carefully so that he didn't make any noise.

Once Peter reached the parapet level, he studied the smoking guard carefully. He thought it might be better to eliminate him with his knife. If he could do it, that would be perfectly silent rather than the slight noise that the HK P11 might make.

Peter was about to withdraw his Kabar knife when the guard turned abruptly in Peter's direction. Although Peter had been as quiet as possible when he ascended the stairs, he was still soaking wet. Apparently the water dripping off his wetsuit had alerted the guard.

Although the guard didn't have a flashlight to immediately spot Peter, the guard did pull his 45 automatic and aim it in Peter's general direction.

Seeing this, Peter fired the HK P11. He had only fired the weapon five times previously. Only a very limited amount of ammunition had been available for this mission. The mechanism containing the five cartridges had to be sent back to the factory after firing because it could not be refilled. So Peter had been given one set of five cartridges to fire in practice, and thus had only the current five cartridges for his assault into the castle.

Since Peter had practiced firing the first five cartridges during the daytime on an open practice rifle range, he was now startled by just how loud and how bright the cartridge was when the rocket was fired. In fact, it looked like some type of luminous firework as it tracked from the weapon into the body of the guard.

The man fell backwards after being hit by the rocket-propelled dart, clearly having suffered a lethal wound, but even while the man lay critically wounded, the propellant in the dart continued to burn and smoke.

Peter had never seen anything like it. It was like the rocket-propelled dart was continuing to try to penetrate deeper into the victim. Once the propellant was exhausted, the dart's flame went out. The guard was clearly dead.

Peter then did a reconnaissance of the entire castle. He detected the on-duty guard outside of one of the bedrooms. He hoped that the guard was there because Jean and the baby were inside the room. Peter didn't like to make assumptions, but there was no other reason he could think of that a guard would be needed outside a bedroom.

When Peter detected the room containing the radio equipment, he could hear someone talking, either on the telephone or the radio equipment. It seemed to Peter that this was the command and control headquarters for the operation, and that someone inside was trying to communicate with the Colonel.

Peter decided that it was more important to eliminate this individual and stop any communications with the Colonel, rather than to simply attack the guard outside Jean's room.

He knew that if he just attacked the guard, the radio operator could alert the Colonel, and the Colonel might have some way to cause pre-planted explosives to destroy the castle. He didn't have any information if that might be possible, but with the Colonel, anything was possible. Plus he had no information about the success of the bomb attack on the Colonel.

Peter couldn't take that chance so he knew he had to eliminate the radio operator first. But when he tried to open the door to the radio room, he found it was locked. Apparently the radio operator enjoyed some privileges here in the castle and didn't want to be bothered by anyone unless they were invited.

Peter didn't think he had any other option but to destroy the lock on the door with one of the Heckler & Koch rocket darts. He knew that the shattering of the door would alert both the radio operator and the guard, but he couldn't see any other alternative.

Peter stood back and fired the second cartridge. It hit the door just below the knob and right above the lock. The noise was much louder here in the confines of the hall than it had been outside on the parapet.

The dart shattered that section of the door, and it folded inward from the impact.

The radio operator was shocked by the sound of the door shattering. But he had an automatic rifle ready at his side and he grabbed it as he turned toward the door.

Peter, however, had already entered the room and was aiming the HK P11 at the radio operator.

The radio operator was in the process of raising the automatic rifle when Peter's third rocket dart caught him in the chest. Again, the effect was spectacular as the rocket-propelled dart continued to try to burrow deeper into the man's flesh. But unfortunately, the radio operator had his finger on the trigger of his automatic weapon and as he died, his finger tightened on the trigger. He sprayed bullets randomly against the walls and the ceiling of the radio room.

Luckily, none of them came close to Peter, but the sounds of gunfire echoed through the castle.

The guard outside Jean's room decided that he could not rush out to find the source of the gunfire since he needed to guard the hostages. So he opened the door and entered the bedroom where Jean and the baby were located.

Jean was terrified by the sounds of gunfire and by the sudden appearance of the guard in the room. He ordered her and the baby off the bed and toward the back corner of the room so he could watch them better as he stood in front of them to guard the entrance to the bedroom door.

After killing the radio operator, Peter ran toward the bedroom since he knew the guard had to have heard the sounds of gunfire. He proceeded as fast as he possibly could, but still didn't know if there were any other adversaries in the building, so he couldn't rush there as quickly as he might have liked. He didn't want to be killed by an unknown member of the Colonel's team who might be lying in wait.

When he reached the outside of the bedroom, he found no other members of the Colonel's team there to confront him. But now he knew that the guard was in the bedroom with Jean and the baby.

He had seen the spectacular effect that the rocket-propelled dart had on the door to the radio room, so he decided that he had to shatter this door as well. He thought that might so surprise the guard that he would be able to get a drop on him. In any case, he didn't think he had any other option and time was running out before the SBS team outside would blow up the front gate and charge into the castle.

The SBS team had been ordered to prevent any escape from the castle, so they were waiting outside, ready to keep any of the Colonel's men from escaping. But they also had the mission to enter the castle by the deadline if Peter had not been able to achieve his objective. Peter knew they would probably come in with guns blazing if there was still a gun battle going on in the castle when they made their entrance. Such an assault might endanger Jean and the baby.

Peter stepped back and to the side of the doorway and fired the HK P11 once again. It hit the door right near the lock and shattered that section of the door into splinters.

Although the guard was surprised when the door suddenly shattered, he was a trained military man and immediately sprayed the doorway with a full clip from his automatic rifle.

But that left him without ammunition when Peter rushed through the broken door. The guard didn't have enough time to reload his weapon, but he did have enough time to pull a knife from his belt and grab Jean.

Although Peter still had one cartridge left in the HK P11, he couldn't fire it since the guard was now behind Jean and holding a knife at her throat. Jean was holding the baby next to her bosom and was clearly terrified.

Peter ordered the guard, "Drop the knife now and I won't kill you."

The guard responded, "Drop that gun now and I won't kill her." To emphasize his point, the guard nicked Jean just below her chin. She screamed at the cut as blood dripped from her wound.

Peter shouted, "You bastard! You're going to die for that!"

But the guard responded, "She'll be dead before you can even get close to me. Now I'm going to cut her again if you don't drop that gun."

Peter didn't think that he had any other choice because the guard clearly was ready to cut Jean. He didn't want her to be hurt again. Peter said, "Okay, okay. I'm dropping the gun." And then Peter did just that.

Peter told the guard, "I am only the first one of an assault party that is outside the castle right now. There's absolutely no way for you to escape, so you need to just drop the knife now and let the woman go. If you do that, I promise you I won't pursue you. You can just make your escape anyway you can."

The guard said, "I have nowhere to go unless I have some protection. So the woman comes with me. I don't know who you have outside, but if they don't let me go, the woman and the baby will both die."

Peter was unsure how to respond to that threat and thought that maybe they were in a stalemate and he should just wait until the SBS team entered the castle. He worried that the hopelessness of the guard's position might motivate the guard to kill Jean and the baby.

They glared at each other, neither of them sure what to do next.

But that problem was solved when Jean, who had been holding the baby in her left arm, suddenly seemed to try to twist to the left out of the guard's hold. But that was not her true intention. Instead of trying to escape, she was just trying to gain some leverage as she spun back to the right and used her right arm to elbow the guard in the face with all her might. The guard obviously underestimated her once he had cut her. He thought that would frighten her, but all it really did was piss her off!

The guard was caught off balance by the blow and stumbled backward as he lost his grip on Jean.

She pulled away and ran toward the bathroom with the baby, leaving Peter to deal with the guard. Peter pulled the Kabar knife from its sheath and lunged toward the guard. Although the guard had been stunned by the unexpected blow, he was still able to slash Peter with his knife as Peter lunged forward. The guard's knife caught Peter in the side, but it was a slashing cut rather than a penetrating wound. It made a large wound in Peter's rib cage, but didn't seem to hit any vital organs.

The guard was not that lucky, however. Peter's momentum propelled him into the guard as he held the Kabar knife directly in front of him. Peter thrust the knife upward as soon as he reached the guard. The knife caught the guard just below his ribcage and then ripped upward into his chest, deep into his heart. Peter was well-trained in close-quarters combat and this was one of most lethal wounds that could be inflicted with a knife. His training taught him, if you can't get the throat, get the heart.

Although he was bleeding profusely from the wound in his side, Peter hoped he wasn't critically injured.

The guard, however, would never recover. His body lay in a pool of blood with the Kabar knife still imbedded in his chest.

Jean ran back into the room once she saw that the guard was down and Peter was wounded. She gave Peter an enormous kiss and said, "Peter, my god, you're always saving me. It's no wonder I love you."

When she said that, Peter was about to tell Jean that he loved her too but as he opened his mouth to speak, everything went black. He fell to the floor in a widening pool of blood.

When Peter fell, Jean screamed, "No, Peter, no. You can't die on me."

Then she fainted dead away. After all she'd been through, the sight of Peter bleeding his life away was just too much for her to bear. The baby cried as he fell to the floor with his mother, but there was no one to hear him.

* * * * * * * * * *

When Peter regained consciousness, he was lying on the bed and Jean was holding him on one side. She held the baby on her other side. The team leader of the SBS assault force was next to the bed on the opposite side from Jean. He said, "Captain Sharkey, Captain Sharkey, can you hear me?"

Peter opened his eyes and said, "Yes, yes, I guess I just passed out. My side hurts a lot, but I don't think it's that bad."

The SBS officer said, "That's correct, sir. I agree. I think it was just the sudden drop in blood pressure from your loss of blood that caused you to pass out. The wound seems to be superficial, but you did lose a lot of blood. We've applied some compression bandages to the wound and I gave you an injection of morphine that should make you feel better."

Peter looked up and saw Jean smiling at him, although she still had a worried look on her face. Peter asked the SBS leader, "Are they all gone? Are we still in danger here?"

The SBS team leader smiled and said, "There's no one dangerous left here, sir. Except for you, that is! If the Yanks ever give you up, I think you could have a future with the SBS. You did a remarkable job eliminating these villains, and both the woman and her baby are fine. Now we need to get out of here as quickly as possible. You are still bleeding some from the wound, and we need to get you back on board our boat and get you to hospital back in England."

Jean said, "Peter, I was so worried watching you bleed there. And when you passed out and fell, I thought you had died. I love you so much. I knew I didn't want to live without you, so I was afraid my life was over too."

Peter responded, "I love you too, and I was so worried about you when these bastards kidnapped you and the baby."

Jean said, "I don't know what's going to happen next, and I don't know where we're going, but I'm not going anywhere unless it's with you."

Peter smiled feebly as Jean leaned down and gave him another kiss. He was about to respond, when once again he blacked out.

EPILOGUE

President Lyndon Johnson requested a meeting with Admiral Taylor and FBI Director J. Edgar Hoover to discuss the aftermath of what had happened. They already knew that Captain Sharkey had rescued the hostages and eliminated the men that had held them captive. They also knew that the bombing of the house had killed all the other members of the rogue group from MI-5. Accordingly, they assembled in the Oval Office to discuss what was to happen next.

President Johnson was the last to arrive at the meeting, so Admiral Taylor and Director Hoover were already seated in his office when he entered the room. Johnson said, "Gents, I'm sorry I'm a little bit late, but I just spent the last hour on the telephone with the Prime Minister in London. He told me that once his people clean up the castle in Northern Ireland, they will transfer the lease to some British astrological society, in line with who the landlord originally thought were his tenants.

"He also assured me that all the financial records of the 'Irish Section' have been reassigned to other MI-5 accounts and the specific incriminating records have been destroyed. He is confident that the existence of the 'Irish Section' has been obliterated.

"Then I spoke to Bobby Kennedy. I wanted to discuss everything with him, both personally and professionally before we met. Bobby is still the Attorney General and I wanted to make sure he was comfortable with my plans. Everything went well, so please relax."

Both Hoover and Taylor stood up to greet him and shake his hand. Once they were all seated, President Johnson said, "I received a telephone call from Peter Sharkey from Hawaii. He and the woman and the child are heading to the South Pacific to begin a new life with some friends that Peter has there. Peter has asked me to help them disappear and I think that's the wisest course for all of us. He has resigned his commission in the Navy and relinquished any rights to a military pension. He assures me that he and the woman have more than enough resources to begin their new life together. I didn't know about this 'together' thing previously, but maybe they just grew closer amidst all this trouble. In any case, I have decided to grant them the anonymity they desire."

Lyndon continued, "Marilyn probably violated some California statutes when she faked her suicide, so maybe there's a law or two broken there. Particularly regarding the substitution of the anonymous dead body. Who knows where that came from and how the deception was carried out?

"And maybe Jack bent the law a little bit when he set up a radio station in Ireland to keep track of his personal affairs. But I don't think our national interest would be served if any of these things were to be exposed.

"I think that Jack and Marilyn had many friends, including the Attorney General who assisted them in this deception, and thus were all co-conspirators, not the least of them being Peter Sharkey. But I doubt we would have had this successful conclusion without him. I think that it is best for all concerned to just let Peter and Marilyn disappear.

"All in all, I think this was a clean end to a nasty business. The actual perpetrators of the assassination were all eliminated and the U.S. and British alliance has been preserved. Although the facts will never be publically presented to the American public, the greater good has been preserved at a time when we need the United Kingdom and our other allies to stand with us, united against the possibility of a cataclysmic confrontation with the Soviet Union. The threat of nuclear war with the Soviets is a very real danger and we need the British by our side if war breaks out. They have admitted their problem and have helped to solve it.

"We can not risk the possibility that the U.S. public would react against the British and demand the end of our mutual defense treaties and our support for the Brits, if they were to learn that some rogue British agents assassinated President Kennedy. Prime Minister Douglas-Home agreed with all of this, which is why he provided British military support to help resolve this situation. As I said, he has instructed his staff to remove all traces of the rogue MI-5 department known as the 'Irish Section.' Now, I think we need to do likewise to establish a clean end to this.

"Since I assured Peter that I would do all I could to shield him and Marilyn from any future problems, I am tasking both of you to eliminate all records of their existence. Admiral Taylor, you need to go back and delete all of Peter's Navy records as far back as World War II. J. Edgar, you need to do likewise for Peter, and also eliminate any of Marilyn's records that could conflict with her official suicide. I think you'll both agree that we should provide these folks their wish for anonymity."

Admiral Taylor said, "Mr. President, I'll put my staff on this immediately. Peter Sharkey will never show up as ever having been in the United States Navy."

J. Edgar said, "I agree, Mr. President. They deserve a peaceful future and, per your instructions, my organization will eliminate all records going back as far as we can regarding Peter Sharkey, maybe even as far back as his birth. And Marilyn Monroe will remain forever dead and buried."

Lyndon Johnson then said, "Thank you, gentlemen. I knew I could rely on you. Now since it's early in the day we don't have champagne to toast, but I do have coffee and donuts. So will you join me in a small celebratory toast to the successful conclusion of this operation?"

Both Admiral Taylor and J. Edgar Hoover moved to the small coffee table and poured themselves a small libation – coffee, not champagne. Then all three of them touched their coffee cups together and smiled. They knew that the killers of President Kennedy had been brought to the ultimate justice and they were pleased that the United States had emerged victorious from this horrible black period. They all knew that the American public would never be able to learn the details of what had happened, but they were still very pleased with the outcome. The United States needed Britain at its side to provide a united defense against the Soviets in the face of any potential nuclear conflict, and they were all sure that the actions they had taken would preserve the Anglo-American alliance.

So now on paper, all records of Peter Sharkey were deleted. It was as though he had never lived. But of course, in reality, he had lived a momentous life. All traces of his wife Jean's history had been removed also, except of course for her previous records as Marilyn Monroe. All Peter and his new wife, Jean, wanted was to disappear from the public and live their life in anonymity on the South Pacific Island where they had decided to settle. Peter had forged great friendships with Australian and New Zealand military officers during the Second World War and the Korean conflict, and one of them had suggested this island to Peter. Then the officer agreed to forget that he had ever known Peter before he emerged with his new identity.

They had substantial assets, and they knew they could live very comfortably on their island estate. Peter and Jean had new identities provided by the ONI, so they were confident that no one would ever discover their previous identities.

Jean's infant son arrived with her on the island, but over the next several years, he welcomed two new brothers who joined the family. Peter and Jean raised their sons and educated them on the island during their early years, but sent them to high school and college in Australia when that time came. One of them even went to graduate school in the United States.

They didn't want to be disturbed by outsiders – and they weren't. President Johnson had promised them protection and a new identity. He had kept his word!